Wet Bones

WOL-VRIEY

Novellas and Short Stories By Wol-vriey

Big Trouble in Little Ass

Forever Ago Sunshine

Wet Bones

WOL-VRIEY

Burning Bulb
PUBLISHING

Wet Bones
By **Wol-vriey**

Burning Bulb Publishing
P.O. Box 4721
Bridgeport, WV 26330-4721
United States of America
www.BurningBulbPublishing.com

Cover illustrated by Gary Lee Vincent, using photographs by Peter Heeling (skitterphoto.com Creative Commons License) and Pexels.com/Pixabay (Creative Commons License).
Author Photo: Lolade Akinsowon © 2014.

First Edition.

Paperback Edition ISBN: 978-1-948278-05-8

Printed in the United States of America

CHAPTER 1

Matt

Matt Seaver awoke in a large, damp, and smelly room. It was early evening. Beams of fading daylight came in through two open windows, one at each end of the room. Specks of dust danced like John Travolta in the light beams.

Matt heard a car start up somewhere nearby. He listened more closely. He corrected himself. No, the vehicle wasn't starting, it was being revved. The initial sound of it starting was likely what had roused him from unconsciousness.

He heard tires roll on gravel. The vehicle's sound receded from him.

Matt was lying on his back. He unwisely tried to sit up. That was when the pain hit him, a splitting headache as though the top of his head had been hacked off with a machete. Along with this, Matt now realized that his hands were tied behind his back and his feet bound around the ankles. Worst of all, there was a gag in his mouth. The gag smelt of motor oil.

I'm a captive. The realization hit Matt like a bullet to the brain. Along with it came a surge of intense fear. For a few minutes he fought to break free of his bonds. Finally, exhausted, he gave up. The cords binding him were tied too tightly, and also . . . too *expertly*. This latter understanding merely increased Matt's fear. It meant that this wasn't his captor's first rodeo. The man had done this before. To others. Maybe to many others.

Matt Seaver was a student of Broadcast Journalism at the New School of Radio and TV in Albany in New York State. He'd been hitchhiking, travelling west from Raynham, on his way back to school. The last ride he'd got had dropped him off at Fiskdale (the driver had turned down south to Holland), so Matt had stood by Route 20 with his thumb out. Finally a pickup truck had stopped for him. The pickup's driver had said he was on his way to Stockbridge and sure, he'd give Matt a ride, and to hop on in.

Stockbridge was right on the Massachusetts–New York border. Thankful, Matt had hopped in, only to get knocked unconscious a minute later. And now here he was.

And now here I am, he thought. The panic flooded him again. And the damn pain in his head! Oh God! The truck driver must have hit him with brass knucks. Matt recalled seeing a metal glitter in the truck's interior just before his lights got put out. The left side of his face felt swollen and he was having difficulty opening his left eye. But this wasn't the cause of his headache. It felt to Matt like he'd picked up another injury whilst being dragged around. Like maybe his head had bashed against a wall or doorway.

His head throbbed like it was going to explode on him.

He forced himself upright. The pain in his scalp was crippling, but now that he was awake he found it too uncomfortable lying on his back. Besides, he needed to know where he was.

So, with his head feeling like it would split in two, he sat up. To do this he had to first worm his way back against the nearest wall and use it for leverage. Somewhere during this maneuver he reopened the wound on his head. Blood spilled down through his hair and into his eyes. He blinked to clear them. Then he looked around.

The first thing he noticed was that while lying on his back he'd grossly mistaken the size of the room he was in. This place was more of a hall, a hall with high and unpainted stone walls. But then he realized that he was sitting on straw. Then he saw the crates piled against the far walls and the farming equipment (a rusty old tractor with flat and cracked-open tires, and the equally rusted corn head from a missing combine harvester), along with several dusty coils of chicken wire over on his right.

I'm in a barn! he thought feverishly.

He calmed down and studied his prison. The barn was about forty yards long and twenty-five yards wide. Except for the crates and farm equipment, it was empty. Matt was currently seated by one of the lengthwise walls, beside a door. The door looked unpainted. It was more likely though that its paint had all peeled off over the years. The entire structure gave Matt the impression of long disuse. Of abandonment. This impression was reinforced by the many holes in the roof where the shingles had fallen in. The roof itself was set over thick timbers, several of which sagged dangerously under the weight of age. Even the straw looked and smelt ancient.

Ten yards from the far end of the building lay a circle of raised stones. The circle was six yards across and six inches high. Its stones were green with moss. The liquid mirror of reflected light in the circle's center, and the mud around its base, gave Matt the impression that it was a well, maybe a little pond or spring that had been fenced in and at one time used for watering livestock in this abandoned place.

The barn had three doors: the one he was sitting beside (which, from the design of its handle seemed to open into an office or storeroom), and a massive double door at either end. All three doors were shut. The nearer double door, the one on his right, had a missing slat. Peering through it, he saw the start of a stone walkway.

Suddenly, Matt heard a noise behind him. The sound, completely unexpected in this desolate building, startled him. He jerked around from looking outside the barn. Body trembling, he stared back inside.

He sat stock-still. His pulse was racing, his heart beating hard. The noise hadn't been the sound of mice or rats. He was certain of that. It had, however, been a familiar noise. He was just too nervous to immediately place it.

Once Matt calmed a bit, he realized what the sound was. It was the sound of spilling water, of water slopping onto the ground.

Water? His eyes focused on the stone-ringed pool at the far end of the barn. Earlier, the pool had been placid, its surface calm and undisturbed. Now, however, the water was rippling. Bubbles were popping from it. Matt could also see spilling water, little rivulets of wetness still running down the pathways of mortar that connected the stones.

And (this bothered Matt the most), part of the rim of the pool facing him now glistened with something that wasn't water. A thick smearing of a clear jelly-like substance lay over the stones on the left side of the pool, as if . . . as if some creature inside it had lifted itself up out of the water and peeked at Matt while he was himself peeking out of the barn.

Matt knew for certain that the goop hadn't been there the last time he'd looked.

The hairs on the back of his neck stood up stiff.

There was also now a strange smell in the air, one that he couldn't place. It was close to the stink one got after crushing certain insects, that unpleasant smell that made you wish you'd just left the damn bug alone. The smell worried Matt as much as the jelly on the stone circle did.

The water surface settled again.

Matt decided it was time he got well away from here. Thankfully, he still had all his clothes on.

There was a knife in his rucksack, but he couldn't see the rucksack anywhere.

By pressing himself against the wall and pushing with his hands, Matt regained his feet. The effort of doing so, however, reopened the cut on his head and restarted his headache.

He stared at the blood on the wall. There was quite a lot of it.

He winced at the sight. *Ouch!—I need a doctor.* Besides which, his left eye was swollen almost fully shut now.

While waiting for his head to cease hurting, Matt watched the pool. Its surface was placid again. No bubbles, no danger. Maybe it had just been a fish. A fish that had gotten caught in the underground stream that fed the pool.

The iridescent jelly still shone on the stones though. Now *that* was a problem. A fish couldn't have done that, could it?

Well, whatever the case, Matt was in too much of a hurry to worry about it. He needed to escape and fast. The night was falling fast now. The barn had lights, but no one was going to turn them on. And would he even want them to?

Matt knew that the darker the barn got, the more perilous his escape attempt would prove. Already, he could hardly see out of his left eye.

Still, at the moment he figured his chances of getting away were good.

The vehicle he'd heard on waking must have been the pickup truck that had abducted him. He'd heard it leaving. That meant the driver likely wouldn't be back for a while: most folks didn't drive distances they could walk. And Matt also derived an ironic solace from the fact that he'd been so tightly tied up: it meant that the driver—that seemingly friendly asshole—didn't want him running off before he got back from wherever it was he'd driven off to.

That meant Matt had some time.

His escape plan was simple: to 'fall out' of one of the barn windows without knocking himself out, and then to make his way through the woods he saw outside. It would have better if his hands weren't tied behind him, but he figured he could still manage. Both end windows were low enough that by jumping he could fling himself through them. (Without being told, he knew all three barn doors were locked.) He hoped there was a highway nearby. He didn't want to be stumbling through a forest in the dark. Gagged like he was, he'd be unable to yell for help if he fell into a hole.

Dammit! If I just knew where he dropped my stuff. I could get to my knife and cut myself free!

Matt let it go. His rucksack was lost and as such useless to him. His head had stopped hurting now. He needed to get a move on.

Unfortunately, the nearer window had bars across it. The one at the farther end of the room was unbarred. It also had no glass in it; in this case a definite plus. Matt just hoped it didn't open onto a marsh filled with snakes. He could see trees out there, but had no idea what lay at their roots.

The real problem was . . . to reach the window, Matt had to pass by the pool. That wide pool with the jelly on its stone rim. That placid pool that scared him with its innocence. He'd have preferred not to head that way, but he clearly had no choice.

Shuffling slowly, he began crossing the barn. He went at a painfully slow pace. He was very conscious of not tripping himself up. If he hurried and fell over (not that he could hurry much), he would need to first roll back against the wall and right himself again before he could continue. So he went slowly.

Slow and steady wins the race, he told himself.

It was growing dark outside now. The windows and the holes in the barn roof still let in sufficient light to see by, but not for much longer.

Finally Matt reached the pool. Despite his hurry, he paused beside it. It was filled with muddy brown water. Try as he might, he couldn't see below its surface. His swollen-shut eye hampered his sense of depth: one moment it seemed like there was something down there, the next, it was just a trick of the twilight.

He studied the jelly mess on the stone rim. The transparent goop could have been frog-spawn, but it contained no eggs. There was also a huge amount of it, way too much for frogs to have made. And if frogs *had* put it there, how come they'd made no sound while doing so? There had been no croaking. All he'd heard was silence. And (now he admitted it to himself) he'd had a sensation of being watched. As though something nasty were drilling holes in his back with its eyes.

He put the creepy thoughts out of his mind. *I really need to get a move on. That crazy guy might come back any minute now.*

The jelly was piled around the bottom of the stone curvature. He was stepping in it. It was mixed up with the straw that covered the poolside floor, forming a sticky, icky surface.

But still, Matt found it impossible to leave the poolside. He was magnetized there by fear, understanding that once past the pool, whatever was in the water would be *behind* him. He'd not see it coming for him.

There's nothing in the water! Just get a damn move on! I need to escape from this crazy place!

Matt couldn't get a move on, however. *Something secreted this jelly. What was it? What was it!?*

His worries were interrupted by the sound of the returning pickup truck. Panic filled him. Suddenly it didn't matter *what* was in the water. What mattered was getting out of here alive. Without another glance at the pool, he began shuffling off again. The window of his escape was right ahead, maybe ten yards away. All he had to do was step over a few waterlogged cartons and he'd be free of this place. At the moment he'd gladly take his chances out in the woods.

Then, behind him, Matt imagined he heard a sudden spilling of water over the side of the pool again. Once more, despite his hurry, he froze and listened.

Yes, this time was no mistaking it. He was hearing water. Water trickling over the stones. Water splashing. Again he felt impelled to see what was behind him.

Slowly, ever so slowly, Matt turned around again. He didn't turn completely. He turned his body maybe ninety degrees, then let his head complete the arc.

He was just in time to see something slip beneath the pool surface again, leaving ripples and bubbles. But what was it? He thought he'd seen an eye, but it hadn't been any sort of a normal eye. The eye had been at the end of a brown stalk, like a snail's eye.

Maybe I just imagined it, he told himself, but . . .

But he'd not imagined the pile of transparent slime currently dripping over the side of the pool onto the straw. This time there was a lot more slime, as if the creature (what in the world was inside the water?) had come further out of the pool after him. *After him.* The pile of slime horrified Matt. The little hill of wet jelly assured him that whatever was in the water was BIG. BIG. Nothing *little* could have made such a heap in such a short time. How long had it been since he'd passed the pool? Eight or ten seconds at most?

Again he squinted vainly at the water. There was nothing to see, just a profusion of bubbles as if delinquent mermaid teenagers were chewing gum in some underwater high school.

Then he heard loud voices outside the barn. He listened carefully. One of the voices was his abductor's. The other was a woman's.

"Did you get it?" the woman asked. "I missed the last one. Jesse told me it was so . . . so . . . ."

"He's in there," Matt's abductor replied in his gruff voice.

"Who is it?"

"Some young kid who thumbed a lift. Said he was a student."

"A student?"

"Yuh. Dunno where he was studying though. His bags and ID are in the house, if you wanna look through 'em."

"Did you?" She laughed.

"Nah, I didn't. I had to come pick you up."

"Let's go see him. I want to see this one." Her voice conveyed intense anticipation. Matt imagined her trembling with delight, quivering like the jelly his gaze was riveted on.

She's delighted that they've got another captive. Another captive. I'm not the first person to find myself in these straits.

He realized he was being stupid, and immensely so at that, remaining here like this, peering at this pool while outside night fell, looking for a creature that was choosing to hide from him, and one which, even if it did show itself and proved to be aggressive, he'd be able to do squat against, tied up like he was. In a way, standing here like this was suicidal. If whatever was in the water suddenly grew emboldened and attacked him . . .

But it didn't. His worries now were primarily human.

"C'mon, let's go look in the barn," the excited woman outside repeated. "I wanna see who you caught this time."

On hearing this, Matt turned away from the pool and began hopping forward. Despite the clear danger that he might lose his balance and fall over while hopping, he felt he had no other choice; shuffling would be too slow. He needed to hop now. If they came inside he was done for.

"Later," the man gruffly told the woman. "I'm damn thirsty. Let's have something to drink first."

"Aw, I wanna see him now."

"Later, I said, Mary. Come on, let's go."

"Oh, alright then."

Matt sighed in relief and slowed down. There was no more need to hop like a frog. His heart was pounding. It was okay. He now had time to escape. In his experience, one drink usually became two or three and then . . . Whatever the case, Matt was certain that by the time the pair remembered him, he'd be far away from here.

He began moving forward again. Slowly, across the straw towards the barn window. Sweating inside his clothes while outside the world settled fully into darkness. Painfully short step after painfully short step. Dragging himself forward by the tips of his toes. Moving but seeming to remain at one point forever. Not daring to hop for fear he might slip and overbalance. Always conscious that something might be watching him, something horrible, something . . . hungry for human flesh?

However, two things proved Matt's undoing. And both of them were beyond his control.

First, the sound of the pickup truck's door slamming shut startled him. The couple's conversation had led him to assume that the truck door had already been closed. Clearly though, it hadn't been. Either that, or one of the couple had returned to get something from the vehicle.

The slamming noise was so unexpected that Matt leapt forward onto the flattened cartons in front of him, which he'd previously intended to go around.

The second thing that undid him was the flurry of startled rats that burst from under the cartons when he landed on them.

The rats' emergence startled Matt again so that he leapt back to escape them. He leapt far back, landing in the fringe of slippery straw bordering the pool. Next moment, he lost his balance. His feet slid out from beneath him and he fell backward. He wound up flat on his back, cracking his head against the pool's stone rim.

He lay there, half-unconscious. Thinking was impossible; the pain in his head was a migrainic universe unto itself. He lay prostrate in the ooze, trying to come to terms again with existence, his subconscious self trying to reassemble his fragmented psyche into an understanding that he was human. Only after this could the primal self-preservation instinct kick in and impel him to continue his flight from the danger that threatened him.

Slowly the pain cleared up. However, by then it was too late. As Matt's vision cleared he became aware of something staring down at him through two eyes which, yes, waved on stalks like those of a snail. He had the clear impression that the creature was wondering what he'd taste like. This impression was as sharp and startling as being stabbed in the belly with a knife.

As the creature watched him, the clear, spawn-like jelly squirted over him from somewhere beneath its eyes. The thick viscid jelly covered his head. It dripped down his face. It had that unnatural 'crushed bugs' smell. It stung when it got into the wound in his scalp.

The monster's eyes moved down, closer to Matt. He still couldn't tell what it looked like. It was too near to him. He however realized that it was immensely large. It was also brown and had very slimy skin.

Matt pissed himself from sheer fear. With the gag in his mouth, there was no way he could scream for help.

Suddenly, the creature lurched down. Matt felt something soft lifting his head and slipping beneath it. The next moment he was shrouded in darkness.

It took him several seconds to understand what had just happened. His head was now inside the creature's mouth! He couldn't see, but he could feel. Its lips were down around his shoulders now. Slowly, an inch at a time, it sucked him into itself. He felt its giant body squirm and contract as it pulled itself down over him, as it pulled him into itself.

Panic set in. He kicked his legs in an attempt to get free. All this accomplished was to help him slide quicker into the monster's mouth. His head was already covered in its vile jelly. The monster's mouth was an airless cavern. Matt couldn't breathe. The goop plugged his nostrils. He began suffocating.

He began praying fervently that the couple who'd gone off to get drunk would return now to look at him. He prayed that the woman's perverse curiosity would get the better of her, so that she'd insist her partner bring her out to the barn to peer at their captive.

It didn't happen. What happened was that Matt Seaver slowly vanished into the maw of the monster. He had no idea what it was that was killing him.

He died from suffocation long before it finished swallowing him.

CHAPTER 2

Allie

Alice 'Allie' Jackson had grown up in Cambridge, MA, a city situated north of Boston, just across the Charles River. Smallish, and with long blonde hair and blue eyes, Allie was the middle child of three, having both a younger brother Andrew, and an older sister Chloe.

As a child she'd loved toy cars, and had kept pestering her father to buy her bigger and bigger toy models. (He in turn had begged her mother to get her interested in the latest versions of Barbie instead, which even with the houses and clothes and the Hot Wheels Barbie car cost far less.)

Allie would also sit for hours in front of the TV watching NASCAR and drag strip races. She thrilled to the rush and the speed and the crash-and-burn of it all.

At age twelve she began racing Go Karts.

At age sixteen, she got her NASCAR license and began competing. Which had again threatened to put her father out of pocket, but he couldn't stop paying because she was so undeniably good behind the wheels of a car.

***

At age sixteen Allie won her first NASCAR race. For the rest of that day, she was walking on air, her own personal hovercraft. That victory—vindication of the hours she'd spent stomping the gas pedal of her pink 1986 Monte Carlo—was total unmatched euphoria. She'd been on top of the world.

***

Allie quit car racing at age eighteen because her parents insisted that she go to college and get an accounting degree.

Her older sister Chloe had gotten pregnant and married at age eighteen, to a thirty-year-old auto mechanic named Giorgio Cimini. Chloe and Giorgio had since moved south to the town of Dover.

Allie's parents were scared stiff that if they let their younger daughter "keep hanging around all those driver-boys," Allie would shortly fall pregnant too.

So away to Boston College Allie was dispatched. Even from school, she made as many stock car races as she could, and also participated in a few, but soon her studies took up all of her time.

Allie finished college like the well-behaved, well-brought-up daughter that she was, then, aged twenty-two, she got a job in Boston as a credit analyst with Eastern Bank. She worked with their Dorchester Avenue branch.

She figured she'd simply make money and marry one of the many young men vying for her affection. She'd never lost her love of driving though. She still followed all the races, both NASCAR and the Top Fuel drag races. She figured that if one day she made a large fortune, she'd start her own racing team.

But fate had other ideas about her future.

For about a year, Allie had been going steady with the Dorchester Avenue branch's assistant manager, a hot guy named Brian Kemp. Brian was tall, dark, and very handsome. Allie was very pleased with him. Her only problem with Brian was that she couldn't get him to commit to her. He said he loved her, but he kept pleading that they should wait "just a little bit longer" before getting engaged and married.

Like most businesses, Eastern had an unspoken 'no office romances' policy for its employees. Up to this point, Allie and Brian had managed to separate their private and professional lives quite well. Many people at the bank didn't even suspect that they were dating.

Then female trouble knocked on Allie's romantic door.

Their branch manager, Mr. Simmons, came down with lung cancer and was forced to retire.

The new manager, Valentina Ruzza, was a beautiful middle-aged woman. Valentina was looking to get married again. She instantly set her sights on Brian Kemp to fill the empty space beside her in bed.

Long story short, Allie lost the battle. Despite her good looks, nice figure, and winning personality, she was still young and inexperienced where men were concerned, while the older Valentina was *very* experienced in that female battle arena.

Valentina Ruzza was tall and had long black hair. Her complexion was flawless. She was busty too. She was always impeccably dressed and exquisitely turned out. She was more faithful in her use of the gym than evangelical Christians were at going to church. She was tanned and walked with the sort of swagger a catwalk model would die for. It was impossible to tell that she'd had four children and thrice been divorced. Her dark eyes sucked men in like a vacuum and her permanent red smile was to die or kill for. When she smiled, her teeth were so white, they projected laser beams at you.

Allie made the mistake of thinking 'love' would be sufficient to keep her man by her side. Valentina Ruzza, on the other hand, knew that while men often followed the leadings of their heart, that organ was also responsible for pumping the blood through their bodies. And she'd also discovered that men only had enough blood in them to work either their brain or their penis at any given time. Never both— if they were thinking, they didn't get erect; and if they got an erection, their brains stopped working. Also, so long as a man was sleeping with you, he loved you. The trick she'd discovered was to keep them both hard and hard at work in bed, so they had neither the time nor energy to think of another woman . . . not even the one they were engaged to.

Valentina dangled herself before Allie's fiancé like the Garden of Eden's forbidden fruit. To Allie's mind, Valentina was also the serpent doing the tempting. And, just like Adam, Brian bit the bait. He was as inexperienced with women as Allie was with men.

After a month of being "too busy to see her after work," Brian nastily broke off his engagement to Allie, leaving her in a flood of tears and feeling suicidal.

A week later, Valentina called Allie into her office and informed her that she was surplus to bank requirements. She thanked Allie for her services up to that point and handed her her termination letter.

Allie was too confused to protest. She got up and moved to leave. When she reached the door, Valentina called her back. "Alice?"

Allie swiveled like a zombie. "What now? Aren't I fired anymore? Or do you plan on sacking me again for not leaving your office fast enough?"

Secure in her victory over the younger woman, and buffered by her expensively purchased beauty, Valentina Ruzza pounced like a snake. She waved her perfectly manicured left hand at Allie, so Allie could see the flashing diamond on her middle finger. "I just thought you'd like to be the first to know that Brian and I just got engaged. We're thinking of making it a June wedding."

Allie lost it then. She flew across the desk at Valentina. They both collapsed back onto the floor under the impact. Then ensued a catfight of legendary proportions, with Allie grabbing Valentina by her perfectly styled hair and banging her head all over the rug, and biting at her face and neck and tearing her dress and scratching and screaming, while Valentina scratched and screamed and punched back weakly.

When Security arrived to haul Allie away, Valentina looked like a gang of dogs had savaged her. She was bleeding from nose and mouth and patches of her hair lay all over the rug.

Despite which, she managed a parting shot at Allie: "Brian was right to dump you. You've no class whatsoever!"

If the guards hadn't had such a firm grip on both Allie's arms, she'd likely have beaten Valentina to a pulp for that statement. The best she could do now was fight to free herself while her rival pretended to cry while hiding her smile of victory. Seeing that smile of female triumph, Allie belatedly wished Valentina's office was up on the fourth floor. Then she could have thrown her out of the window to break her neck on the sidewalk.

Still, Allie felt a victory too, even if it was just a small one. Valentina Ruzza no longer had the engagement ring on her finger. Allie figured it must have dropped off her hand while she'd been beating her up.

Brian arrived just as the security guards were hauling Allie out of Valentina's office.

He looked into the office, saw the bleeding and battered Valentina, then stared at his ex-girlfriend in disbelief. "How can you behave like this?"

She grinned a response. " 'Cos I just got fired, jerk. I no longer work here."

He shook his head and turned to step into Valentina's office. The security guards prepared to resume hauling Allie off to the back door.

"Hey, Brian, wait!" Allie called.

He turned back to her. The guards paused. They were amused and wanted to hear what she'd say now.

"Yes?" Brian asked impatiently. "Speak up, will you? I haven't got all day. I need to attend to Valentina."

After taking very careful aim, Allie kicked him in the balls. She kicked Brian's testicles as hard as she could, hoping she'd put paid to his plans to have kids with Valentina Ruzza.

Brian's mouth first opened in an exhalation of disbelief. Then the pain hit him and he grabbed himself between the legs and slowly— unable to scream as yet—crumpled to the floor, where he lay howling his lungs out.

Allie found the sight of him prostrate like that, all curled up like an aborted fetus, priceless. "Hey, Brian," she taunted, "congrats on your engagement to that old hag."

On the noise, Valentina charged out of her office. "For heaven's sake, get the little bitch out of here! What is wrong with you security people? Can't you see that she's crazy! Does she have to kill someone before you take her away to the madhouse?"

Allie indeed felt crazy. A great kind of crazy. She was laughing like a lunatic as security took her away.

In the end, no assault charges were pressed. The bank didn't want the adverse publicity. Also, Allie now realized that Valentina had played her like a mistressmind: she and Brian weren't even engaged yet. Allie finally understood that Valentina had planned this showdown all along so it would be impossible for her romantic rival to make any legal protests over being unfairly dismissed.

And now she had Brian all to herself.

Valentina claimed Allie had attacked her merely because she was incensed at losing her job. After taunting Allie with the engagement ring, she'd taken it off again before anyone else arrived to notice it. Everyone also assumed that Allie's 'engagement' statement to Brian was simply her nervous breakdown in operation.

By now Allie was in no mental state to hire a lawyer and plead 'constructive dismissal' anyway. She was too hurt. Without a job now to take her mind of her heartbreak, she spent most of her days in her apartment with the drapes shut and the TV tuned to the latest Kardashian soaps.

Even when she heard that Brian and Valentina had gotten engaged the next week, and that Valentina was already pregnant with Brian's child, and that the couple *were* planning a June wedding, Allie shrugged it off. (So that there would be no conflict of interests, Brian was also leaving Eastern Bank to go work with the Boston Consulting Group.) It wasn't important to Allie. Nothing was anymore.

After a month of moping over Brian's betrayal, Allie came to herself again. It was around this time too that her elder sister Chloe, who lived out in Dover, invited her to come stay with she and her husband Giorgio till she felt better.

That sounded much better to Allie than remaining in Beantown to be haunted by her bad memories. She gave up her apartment, gave away everything she couldn't carry with her in her car, hopped into her silver Nissan Sentra, and drove out to Dover.

CHAPTER 3

Grace, Barbara, and . . . Greg

As a young woman, Grace Barbanell had been madly in love with Doug Madden, but he'd married her younger sister Barbara instead.

Grace and Barbara Barbanell were both dark-eyed brunettes. Both women had been born and raised in Raynham, MA.

Barbara was by far the prettier of the pair; the one with the good figure, the sparkling personality . . . and the hunky boyfriends.

Grace, who was seven years older than Barbara but socially awkward, had been devastated by Doug Madden's deception (as she viewed it). Once or twice—before meeting Barbara—he'd kissed her and left her madly aflame with passion and expecting more from him. But it was never to be.

At the time Doug Madden showed up in their lives, Grace was thirty-five and Barbara twenty-eight. Tellingly, he'd chosen Barbara over Grace not because Barbara was younger and prettier, but because Grace had a 'bossy' quality about her that he could only see getting worse if he put a ring on her finger.

Devastated, Grace had gotten through Barbara's wedding purely by surfing on tranquilizers.

After this rejection, Grace had never fallen in love again. Nor had she ever forgiven Doug for slighting her. She'd hated Doug Madden from that day forward.

Two weeks after her sister's wedding, Grace Barbanell had packed up her bags and left town, moving the 40 miles north to Boston, so as to be a good distance away from Barbara.

In Boston, Grace had spent the next sixteen years growing old and bitter. She'd worked as a secretary for several high profile firms, where she was always the epitome of female efficiency. She'd never once dated anyone else. She was asked often—she was quite attractive after all—but turned all her suitors down. Her heart was locked up someplace else.

She spent her free time (when she could have been out having fun) hating Doug Madden and wishing for his death—so that Barbara would feel exactly how she felt. In all those years, the only times she ever saw her younger sister was on her yearly trips back to Raynham to share Thanksgiving with their parents. They rarely even spoke on the phone.

And so sixteen years passed. Then one day, Grace received the news that for over a decade she'd both longed to hear and had also dreaded: Doug Madden had died in a car accident. While standing on a street corner after having lunch near his office, he'd been smashed to death by a drunk driver who'd run a red light.

On hearing of Doug's death, Grace had fainted with the telephone still in her hand. *Nooo!* He couldn't be dead! He couldn't be!

She'd not felt the slightest thrill of the satisfaction she'd imagined Doug's death would bring her. Not in the least. She'd instead felt an intense horror, and when that subsided, an even more intense regret had taken its place. So she'd hated Doug and hated Doug . . . and for what? Maybe her hatred had even killed him. Didn't people say that if you willed a thing with sufficient emotion it would happen?

Doug, however, hadn't forgotten Grace. Or ever even stopped caring about her. Grace was utterly shocked to discover this. Doug Madden had left her *a lot* of money in his will. So much money, in fact, that his widow mistakenly assumed they'd been having an affair behind her back.

Barbara had gotten mad and cut off all contact with Grace.

The sisters found themselves once again estranged over Doug Madden.

Pretty, sexy Barbara had then remarried. However, her new husband Brad Jones was a con artist. Brad had made Barbara invest all her money in a scam lumber company. Brad Jones liquidated the company, then fled to Hong Kong with his secretary. His betrayal left Barbara (and by extension Greg, who'd only gotten $10,000 as inheritance—the late Doug Madden having reasonably expected his widow to care for their son with the million-and-a-half dollars he'd left her) as broke as a windowpane hit with a sledgehammer. Financially shattered.

Faced with losing everything she owned (she and Greg were about to become homeless), Barbara had no choice but to turn to Grace for help.

But would Grace ever forgive her? That was the question.

Abandoned by the man she'd loved with all her heart, Grace Barbanell may have grown old and bitter and withered worse than a prune, but working all those secretarial jobs had smartened her up as to how to make a proper use of her windfall. Grace had invested. And very shrewdly too. In the four years since Doug's death, she'd first doubled, then tripled the half-million dollars he'd left her. Then she'd doubled that triple.

Oh yes, Grace was wealthy now.

She'd received Barbara warmly. Of course she'd forgiven her, she said. And long ago at that. She bore her younger, prettier sibling no grudges. And as for the help Barbara required from her? Whatever were they sisters for if not to look after each other?

So, yes, Grace would happily help Barbara pay off her mortgage and finance the boutique she wanted to set up.

But she had one condition. See, she explained, she was a lonely woman now, growing older by the day and needing companionship, and she'd feel happy if Greg, her young nephew, would come live with her. She also promised Barbara (which had irrevocably sealed the deal) that if Greg lived with her, she'd make him her heir. It was, after all— she pointed out sweetly—his father's money she'd gotten rich from.

And that was how 18-year-old Greg Madden found himself living with his aunt Grace.

For a handout of two hundred and fifty thousand dollars, Greg essentially became Grace's son.

***

Greg and his aunt lived alone (sharing the housework) in a sensible two-story house on Corey Street in the Boston suburb of West Roxbury, with no-one in the least aware (definitely not Greg or his mother) that 58-year old Grace Barbanell was now worth close to six million dollars, or that that amount—by a slight shift in XTO Energy's fortunes—was about increasing to ten million dollars.

Truth be told, Grace wasn't nasty to Greg. Not intentionally. She gave him lots of pocket money, bought him a car—a Mazda3 Sport—

and paid his way through Nichols College over in Dudley, where he'd studied Economics.

She did, however, have her bad days when she snapped at him like a rabid dog. Those were the days when, on looking at him, she saw his father in his handsome features and reflected back on what she'd lost; on what Barbara had stolen from her.

(Greg quickly came to recognize her nasty days—those were the days when via slip-of-tongue she called him 'Dougie.')

Oh, he looks so much like his father, she'd think dreamily, remembering her youth, and how they'd once kissed on the back porch. She'd watch her attractive nephew happily out of the corner of her eye. But then, all of a sudden, her love for him would curdle into the blackest of hatreds and she'd feel like murdering him.

She had a gun upstairs. She'd actually considered killing them both. More than once. Greg never knew how close he'd been to death on at least five occasions.

And then, one fateful day, Aunt Grace actually, literally, kicked Greg in the ass because he'd messed up her smoothie. She booted his buttocks for all she was worth, filling that kick with years of tears and frustration.

See, Grace Barbanell had a thing about smoothies. She utterly loved them. "They're the sole pleasure of my life," she often claimed.

On weekends, she and her friends had smoothie parties. They had a smoothie club, the Graceful Blend, a group of enthusiasts who'd met online coming together in person to both debate and demonstrate their passion.

They had a club website now, and their numbers were growing.

The Graceful Blend smoothie club members would all bring their blenders and favorite ingredients over, and, like it was the *Come Dine With Me* cable show, they'd make and test each other's recipes, and award scores to one another. The winner got a prize of a hundred dollars. It was just honest, innocent fun.

The club members were a diverse mix. They weren't just the lonely older women that Greg had first supposed would be interested in smoothie manufacture. No, there were several businesswomen, a truck driver, a biker and his heavily-tattooed wife, a postal services worker and his tattooless wife, a police detective, a couple of 'criminals' and the Kims, three Korean-American sisters.

They made a motley crew indeed in Aunt Grace's living room and kitchen, and Saturday afternoons were always huge fun in the house. Even Greg enjoyed them. The oldest Kim sister, Jojo, once laced her smoothies with marijuana extract and got everyone stoned, including Detective Anderson. It was laughed off, of course, mainly because the whole club was giggling too hard to do anything else.

But then Aunt Grace kicked Greg. And Greg? Rather than merely overlooking the slight as the eccentricity of a sad old maid, Greg figured he'd hit Aunt Grace back where it would hurt her the most: in the palate.

Aunt Grace had been riling him up for most of that week, just little niggles, and he'd also been stressed out with work. (He'd just begun work at the Bank of America as a Portfolio Manager Associate.) For that combination of reasons, Aunt Grace's innocuous kick really pissed Greg off.

After ass-aulting him, Grace instantly turned away without apologizing, then went upstairs to her room. Five minutes later, she called Greg on his phone. "Please bring me up a smoothie, darling. Put lots of banana and nuts in it." Her voice was sweetness and cream again—she'd clearly forgotten she'd kicked him.

Greg though, hadn't. Still seething, he walked into the kitchen to make her "damn old-woman milkshake." Then just about to start up the blender, he'd been struck by an idea: *Oh, she wants banana and nuts, huh? I'll give the old girl some nut from my banana!*

(Later, Greg regretted what he did. Oh, he really did. He felt the Devil was in some way to blame for his actions. But right now, it definitely seemed to him the best way to pay back his aunt for her abuse.)

Grinning like a demon, Greg unzipped his pants, pulled out his penis and masturbated into Aunt Grace's smoothie.

He groaned in pleasure as his thick love milk spurted onto the diced bananas and hazelnuts, walnuts and yogurt in the blender. His semen looked like real cream. Then he zipped up his pants, blended the mix, stirred in some cinnamon to disguise any lingering smell of come, and carried the drink upstairs to Aunt Grace.

She was in bed. She looked beautiful. She received the tall glass from him like a queen. She sipped it and purred in delight.

She remarked, "Oh, you've added a new ingredient. I can just tell, darling. What is it?"

He did his best not to laugh. He regarded her aging face. So earnest. So like his mother's, only different. He got over his surprise at her noticing his semen addition. A woman whose passion in life was smoothies would be sure to notice one that tasted odd. She just didn't know how odd it was.

She was looking at him with an enquiring gaze. He smiled. "Oh, there's a little cinnamon in it, auntie."

Her smile soured a tad. "Don't patronize me, Greg. Yes, I can taste the cinnamon, but there's another, very tangy ingredient too. It's an unusual flavor, one I'm unfamiliar with. What is it?"

Greg grinned. He bowed. "That, most beautiful madam, is my secret. Only for me to know and you to enjoy."

She probed again. "Oh, but *I do* want to know. I must share it with the club. I haven't won once in the past two months. Okay, tell you what, darling—I'll pay you for the info, how's that sound?"

"No. C'mon, Aunt Grace, a secret's a secret."

She frowned and sipped some more. "Are you sure you won't sell? I'll really make it worth your while."

This was already worth Greg's while. Particularly when she secured the undrunk half of the smoothie into her little bedroom fridge for later.

He smiled tightly. "No."

Then, keeping a straight face with effort, he turned and hurried out of there. He hurried along the upper hallway to his own room. Once there, he locked himself in his bathroom and laughed till tears were flooding from his eyes.

CHAPTER 4

Anderson & Futana

A warm mid-summer day. Hillside Road.

The pair of plainclothes detectives sat in their unmarked patrol car, regarding the Watt residence. Anderson and Futana were parked on the opposite side of the road from the house, a split-level bungalow out east in Boston's Newton suburb, where the average home cost a half-million dollars and the average income was in six figures. A rich neighborhood full of bank executives and other moneyed folks. Lots of shade trees and well-kept lawns. Lots of high-maintenance housewives and airbrushed toddlers. Lots of high-priced SUVs and pedigree pets and Latino gardeners and expensive sprinkler systems and indoor swimming pools.

It was noon, but both of the Watt's family cars were still in their front yard. This fit in with the detectives' information that Fred Watt hadn't shown up to work today.

"He called in sick, so he should be in hospital," Laurie Futana said. "It's suspicious that he's at home now."

Her partner Tom Anderson, who was sitting behind the wheel, replied, "Not as suspicious as the fact that his wife hasn't answered our calls for the past hour."

Futana nodded. She was a pretty young blonde. She regarded the dark, middle-aged Anderson with cold gray eyes. "Tom, I really wish we didn't have to be so cloak-and-dagger about this. We'd surely crack this a whole lot quicker if more people knew about it."

He shrugged. "What else can we do? It ain't like we've evidence of any kind that there's foul play involved. So the captain says we keep our investigation under wraps. Keep our mouths shut. We interview this guy Watt to see if he knows anything. If he don't, then we move on. And remember, Laurie, this is the first break we've had in the case."

Futana winced. "It might not even be a break. The guy's an investment banker. Look at his goddamn house—both our cop salaries combined can't afford it, and you imagine he's got something to do with those stiffs that keep turning up?"

Anderson smiled at her. It wasn't a nice smile. But then, Tom Anderson wasn't a particularly nice man. His wife Nancy wouldn't have divorced him if he was. His kids wouldn't be angry with him either.

"It doesn't matter," he replied. "Lots of guys take camping trips out into the woods on weekends. Sometimes it's to get away from the office pressure; other times it's to escape the wife's nagging. Who's to say that our boy Watt here hasn't added some extracurricular activities to *his* camping?"

Futana slipped her service pistol—a Glock Model 22—from its holster and began examining it. She had large hands, but with well manicured fingers. She popped the gun's magazine out, frowned at its racked and glossy content of Death's favorite messengers, then slid it back in again.

"C'mon, man, quit joking," she said. "You saw the bodies and read the coroner's report on them. Their condition wasn't caused by a human being."

Her calling the recovered remains 'bodies' was stretching the truth a little. They both knew that. All that had been found were skeletons, each one as stripped of flesh as those in a plastic anatomy display. Though buried, all the skeletons had still been wet, covered in some kind of adhesive slime that the lab boys were yet to identify. Clearly not the work of a human being, but then, one never knew these days, Anderson thought. Real life kept showing signs of becoming one of those superhero mutant movies.

Anderson smiled/grimaced again. "Yeah, that's true." He waited while a white truck rolled past their car, then gestured forward at the Watt house. "Well, we don't know anything yet, except that Watt's wife called in yesterday and said she had info about something weird her husband was up to, then she hung up."

"And then the captain sent us two dummies to check it out," Futana said. "It's like he doesn't know exactly what to do with us both, so we get all the crank callers. Mark my words, Tom: we'll go in there now and discover she's just mad at him for chasing their maid."

Anderson rubbed his chin. A similar thought had occurred to him, that this was just a wild goose chase. But . . . "The Captain said Mary Watt used our code for this case. She specifically told the 911 operator her husband had something to do with 'Wet Bones.' That's why we're here. How'd she know we're working on a case having to do with wet bones?"

Futana grudgingly agreed with him. "Alright. I concede that that is suspicious. Let's go interview the man. Hear what he's gotta say."

"Yeah," Anderson agreed, opening the car door. He glanced back at his partner. "Hey, put your damn gun away. This is a friendly call."

She scowled, but holstered the Glock again. "Yeah, yeah, Tom, let's go. I won't scare the rich banker."

They locked their gray Ford sedan and walked over to the Watt residence.

***

No one liked Tom Anderson. Not his wife Nancy (who'd finally sued for divorce after 'twelve years of living hell' as she'd written in her petition), not his kids Billy and Amanda (who both had no idea why they disliked their father so much—he'd never, *ever* abused them: unknown to them, they'd merely picked up on their mother's reflected anger), and definitely not his work colleagues (who regarded Tom Anderson with a mixture of awe and dread; mostly dread).

Most people considered Tom Anderson to be an asshole. To their minds, the standard American concept of 'Asshole' was modeled on him. He was neat and well-behaved, and was hardly ever impolite, even under intense pressure, but he gave off a clear vibe of not liking you. Of possibly hating you and everyone else on the planet besides. He was unpleasant company. He completely lacked a sense of humor, and seemingly lacked a sense of humanity also.

Needless to say, he had very few friends.

As a husband, he'd been cool and totally unemotional. He'd however not been a bad husband. While still married to Nancy Anderson, he'd taken care of his family to the best of his ability. He'd always made the proper decisions where they were concerned, had done everything society expected of a spouse and father (in some instances he'd gone well beyond the call of family duty).

But nonetheless, throughout the time she was married to Tom, Nancy had felt like he was just waiting for her to make one major error and then he'd shoot her down like she was a rabid dog. She'd never been able to shake the feeling that at a deep down level, her nice, model husband hated her and wanted her dead. (Sort of like all those movies where clean-cut Mr. Middle America turns out to be a serial killer with the dismembered bodies of young girls buried in his basement.) Tom was hardly ever rude to her, and had never once hit her, but there was just this overall vibe of violence and hatred that he gave off.

Nancy, wanting to have kids, had been desperate to get married, and Tom had liked her and married her. Now, fifteen years later, he still liked Nancy (maybe even loved her if it was possible for him to love anyone), but she despised him with all her heart.

She'd broken down in court and begun weeping. The judge had considered the intensity of her emotions as sufficient proof of Tom's guilt. Just looking at Tom Anderson, Judge D. Velinski had known he was a 'quintessential asshole.' He known that 'the cold bastard' must have done 'a whole truckload of nasty things' to make this pretty woman cry so much. It hurt Judge Velinski—really pained him to the core of his being—that he couldn't sentence Tom to a long jail term for marital offences. Still, he'd done the best he could to make amends to the aggrieved ex-wife:

He'd awarded Nancy *everything*: the house, both cars, three-quarters of their life savings, and custody of both of their teenaged kids forever. Nancy even got Tom's prized fishing boat.

Tom had been left with just the clothes on his back. But he'd nodded at the judgment, left the court and jumped back in his squad car to go bust another felon. (He'd been working on an important case then. Stopping at court that morning for the judgment had almost thrown his arrest schedule off.) He'd not even frowned or acted pissed off.

He'd *not* been pissed off. That was the thing Nancy couldn't stand. That apparent inability to either feel or express emotion was what Nancy couldn't tolerate about Tom; how proper he always acted. How cool and normal he always was. How he refused to let his hair down and be human for even a second.

As she'd told the judge, living with him was like living with a robot. "Even in bed—ugh—it was just like using a vibrator!" and then she'd really begun crying her heart out.

So that was how Tom's marriage had ended. Tom rolled with the punches. He found a apartment and moved out of the house.

Tom hadn't seen his kids in three years. They didn't want to see him. Billy and Amanda both refused to even talk to him on the phone. It didn't bother him none. He paid their child support allowances, and sent them gifts on their birthdays and on Christmas. He figured they were just going through a 'puberty thing.' Something they'd grow out of in time.

At work, things were similar. The BPD would have *loved* to sack Tom Anderson, but he was their best cop. Bar none. It galled everyone that this guy whom they all hated—you saw the female cops, the police secretaries and dispatchers visibly cringe when he entered a room—was an almost perfect law enforcement machine. Dirty Harry, Judge Dredd, Axel Foley, Robocop, Chief Clancy Wiggum from *The Simpsons*, Starsky and Hutch, and John McClane of *Die Hard* fame; all those top Hollywood badasses rolled into one had nothing on him. Tom Anderson made more credible arrests than anyone else. He solved more violent crimes, busted more drug rings, got more convictions, and (ironically for someone so willing to use a firearm rather than negotiate a hostage release), saved more victims' lives. No one could understand it. You couldn't dispute the results though. Anderson was the best the force had and that was that.

Still, no one wanted to work with him. A detective was supposed to have a partner, but no one wanted Tom Anderson watching their back.

Finally, unable to get rid of him (Internal Affairs had tried six times to dig up some dirt on Anderson but had failed—in exasperation, they'd reported back that he didn't even download illegal mp3s online; he was apparently iTunes most reliable customer), Captain Larry Gillespie (who oversaw the Roslindale/West Roxbury district police station) was forced to partner Anderson with the department's other law enforcement outcast . . . Laurie Futana.

***

Born Laurence Clark Fortune, Laurie Clarissa Futana was twenty-eight years old, blonde, and transsexual. She still had her manly bits attached. She was too busy catching criminals to have the final surgery. That was what she claimed anyway.

Anderson doubted that was the real reason. To his mind, Detective Futana kept her penis intact simply to make people uneasy. Anderson thought Futana liked making straight guys squirm when she ogled their butts. And (Anderson figured), thanks to all the damned liberal legislation everywhere nowadays, there wasn't a damn thing he or anyone on the force could do about it. If you picked on Futana, she'd merely label you as homophobic. And, next thing, the LGBTQIA groups would stomp you into compliance. Talk about having one's cake and eating it.

Laurie Futana wasn't considered an outcast because she was transsexual. The BPD had several other transsexual police officers, both FTM and MTF, on the force. No, Detective Futana's problem was that she had an incredibly short fuse. Most times she was meek as humble pie, but when she lost it . . . she *really* lost it.

Just as folks considered Tom Anderson to the ultimate asshole, so similarly they considered Laurie Futana to be the ultimate bitch.

She was a good cop though. An excellent cop. Better than most on the force. Almost as good as Anderson himself. She was sharp, very intelligent, and an extremely hard worker, willing to put in hours of overtime on cases long after everyone else had gone to bed.

It was just that temper of hers that was the problem . . .

Long story short, Captain Gillespie was relieved to be able to pair Futana and Anderson together. It got them both out of everyone's hair.

He also made a point of giving the pair of them the hardest cases to work—those criminal cases that seemed impossible to crack. Or (as in this 'Wet Bones' instance) the weird cases that had everyone stumped. Time was no obstacle: the longer the pair of them were out of the office, the better.

Somehow though, the Odd Couple always cracked the cases, which gave Captain Gillespie sufficient justification to keep them working on all the X-Files kind of crime puzzles that reached his desk.

Anderson and Futana were polar opposites, but their combination worked. They just 'clicked' together, with their strengths and weaknesses balancing out. After a while they were like family. They worked together and socialized together, though they never became romantically involved with one another.

(Outside of his platonic dates with Futana, Anderson's only other private life consisted of his membership of the Graceful Blend smoothie club organized by Grace Barbanell. A strange hobby for a hard-boiled cop to have, everyone said. Yet more proof that he was an oddball.)

So that was them then: the grizzled old cop and the hotshot youngster.

The pair knew they were good for each other. They understood that they worked well as a team, with Futana's sensitivity balancing out Anderson's lack of feeling. Pooling their characters and mental resources had a synergetic effect on their crime-solving capabilities.

Anderson and Futana got on with being the best cops Boston had to offer.

It hadn't escaped their notices though that they got all the crank cases. All the crap no one else wanted. All the spooky stuff that might wind up giving you nightmares you'd never get rid of.

Like 'Wet Bones' for instance.

***

Wet Bones. That was what they'd elected to call this one. *Wet Bones*.

As she and Anderson walked up the Watt's driveway, Laurie Futana reviewed their current case in her mind:

So far, seven . . . no, nine (she was forgetting those two found near New Ashford) human skeletons had been unearthed at various locations in upper Massachusetts, all of them out west towards the New York State boundary. The skeletons had all been buried in shallow graves. Four men, three women, two kids. All the stiffs had been unearthed after heavy rains that triggered flash floods.

No one could tell, however, if the victims had been murdered. Or eaten. Or even more bothersome, when the deaths had occurred. Had these people died two months ago or two years ago . . . or two decades ago?

The reason for this confusion was the slime covering the remains. Futana recalled her sight of the first unearthed body. The slime on the bones had looked like a liquid cellophane wrap, a wet transparence keeping the woman's skeleton in a wonderfully gruesome state of freshness. All the other stiffs were in similar pristine condition. All had nothing in their braincases either, though their skulls hadn't been cracked open. Their brains had been dissolved away.

"It's the work of some sort of digestive enzyme," Dr. Stephanie Richards explained when they visited the State Police Crime Lab (MSPCL) in the nearby town of Maynard. "Whether it's natural or artificial though, is beyond speculation. I've sent several samples for analysis. I should have the results back in a fortnight." She'd frowned. "It should have been quicker, but we've a heavy backlog to work through."

The samples had consisted of cells scraped off several of the victims' bones. There wasn't much to salvage—all the victims' bone marrow was gone too—but forensics had done their best.

"Don't get your hopes up though," Dr. Richards had cautioned. "The samples will most likely be the victims' own cells, and you'll be back to square one."

That was three weeks ago. Anderson and Futana were still waiting for the forensic lab's reports. A lab assistant had mixed up the specimens and Stephanie Richards had had to painstakingly scrape up a fresh batch for analysis. Fortunately, due to the strange nature of the preservant gel there was no chance of sample degeneration.

Fingers crossed, Anderson and Futana were hoping nothing went awry with the test results this time.

But in the meantime, the pair had gotten on with their routine detective legwork, questioning folks in the towns closest to where the bodies had been discovered.

The word had gone out across the state of Massachusetts—leave these two Boston hardheads alone with the case; just render them any assistance they require. Then the State Police Superintendent had added one final request: "Everyone, keep this case under total wraps (no pun intended) until we know for sure what's going on here. That means absolutely no journalists."

The county police departments were only too glad to let Anderson and Futana have the Wet Bones case. As were the State Police. Those officers who'd seen the unearthed skeletons couldn't shake off the queasiness they'd felt on viewing the nylon-like wrapping of wetness that clung to them. They didn't want any part of whatever had done that. If these two Boston hotshots with major attitude problems wished to go poking around in the woods looking for the creature(s) responsible, they were welcome to the damn job. To everyone else, it seemed a suicidal undertaking.

Truth be told, at the offset of the Wet Bones case, Anderson and Futana weren't involved. They weren't state cops. This was a State Police investigation, nothing to do with the Boston pair. Ideally, they shouldn't even be operating outside of their West Roxbury/Roslindale police jurisdiction.

But with no leads forthcoming, and more important, no certainty that an actual crime had been committed, all the county police chiefs simply lost interest; they had more important things to do; as in actual *crimes* to solve and felons to track down. One or two people suggested involving the Feds, but the stumbling block there was the same lack of sufficient evidence of criminal involvement.

Still, someone had to keep up the investigation, just in case something of interest did turn up.

And then one night Captain Gillespie and the State Police Superintendent, Colonel Gilpin, were discussing work over dinner at the latter's house and the Superintendent mentioned the difficulty of investigating a case no one could hang a tag on. Captain Gillespie (once again desperate to get Anderson and Futana out of his hair) had quickly replied, "Oh, I got just the pair of guys for you."

And so it was that the case officially landed in their laps.

Wet Bones. Those eerie, scary bones.

There were other unusual points about Wet Bones: Six of the recovered skeletons had so far been identified from dental records. Three belonged to known Boston criminals: Ron Petrie, and the siblings Mark and Carol Loggia. This might have formed a pattern— maybe some criminal mastermind (maybe even the infamous kingpin Marko Velli himself, just out of jail) was disposing of his enemies in chemical baths.

But . . . the other three skeletons didn't belong to felons.

The two kids were the Fenton sisters. The fourteen-year-old twins had vanished three years ago while out camping around Bondsville with their friends.

The final skeleton belonged to a Canadian Catholic priest, Father Johannes Durant, who'd also gone missing three years ago. Father Durant had been driving down from his parish in Sherbrooke, Quebec to attend the Catholic Men's Conference in Bristol, Connecticut.

Considering these latter three victims, none of whom had the slightest of criminal connections, the suggested underworld link to the deaths became tenuous at the best.

As for the three criminals themselves, no one knew for sure when they'd vanished. Still, no one had seen either Ron Petrie or the Loggia siblings since January. Back then Mark had said he was driving west to handle some business in Ohio. Mark Loggia was a taciturn guy. No one thought too much of it when he'd not shown up again. He also had a reputation as being a mob hitman, so everyone just assumed he'd been killed. Same went for the others. Carol Loggia was a hooker who traveled a lot with her brother. Ron Petrie drifted from place to place and robbed folks for a living.

If you lived a life of crime and suddenly went missing, everyone simply assumed you were either dead or in lockdown.

The times at which the victims must have lost their lives also contributed to the confusion of it all. Three years ago for the innocent, seven months ago for the guilty; but all linked by the same inexplicable and tangled cord of a horrid slimy transition to the afterlife. So what had happened in between? Would they find other skeletons before they discovered what was going on? Maybe enough to fill in the two year gap?

Futana feared that they might. She feared there were several more bodies lying beneath unturned forest sod, just dying to be discovered. It was a very unpleasant feeling.

And there was also what Dr. Stephanie Richards at the State Police Crime Lab had said concerning the bodies:

"See, Laurie," she'd said, looking troubled, "that slime preserves the bones perfectly. Except that we know exactly when the priest and the twins went missing, it could have been just yesterday. That's how fresh their bones are."

Laurie Futana didn't know exactly what this meant, or was possibly shaping up to become. She did know, however, that she was growing increasingly worried by this case, even if Anderson wasn't.

She glanced at her partner as they ascended the Watt family's front steps. Yeah, Tom didn't look worried at all. He looked like he ate slime-covered stiffs for breakfast.

***

The Watt's front door stood between two pots of hydrangea shrubs. It was gray in color, a gray that matched the cloudless sky.

Anderson rang the buzzer. He and Futana heard it ring inside the house. They waited awhile. No one answered the door.

Anderson rang again. Same results. They heard no sound of anyone approaching.

Anderson looked at Futana. She shrugged back.

"Maybe they're screwing," she said. She pointed back at the two SUVs parked off the driveway—one red, one black. "We know for sure that they're both home, right?"

Anderson rang a third time. When that too brought no results, he banged on the door instead. "Hey, Mr. Watt, it's the police! We wanna talk to you and your wife! Ask you both a few questions! Hey, Mrs. Watt, can you hear us? Are you two alright in there?"

Still no reply. The silence began feeling eerie. Futana looked back at the road, at the few cars passing, the sunless sky reflecting on their polished tops. Nothing of interest out there. She turned back to the front door. Anderson was still ringing and knocking.

All of a sudden she felt chilled. She felt something eldritch in the air. For a flash moment, Laurie Futana felt that the air around the Watt building wasn't really air anymore. The air had become an influence; a malign breath of death with the power to influence the minds and wills of mere mortals such as herself and her partner.

This is crazy, she told herself. *We're just gonna ask this guy a few questions, that's all.*

Anderson stopped knocking and checked his watch. "It's twelve-thirty," he said disgustedly. "Where the hell could they both have gotten to?"

"I told you they're screwing. He's home sick and she's comforting his dick. It happens. We just caught 'em at a bad time."

Anderson scowled. He liked appointments to be kept. Punctual to the second himself, he expected others to return the favor by not wasting his time. "So what the hell do we do now, Laurie? Stand here like a couple of jokers till we hear them both gasping in orgasm?"

Futana shrugged, then tried to mollify him. She was supposed the one with the hot temper, not him. Anderson was supposed to be the 'good' cop, she the 'bad' one. The more they worked together though, the more the differences between them blurred. She was either making him better, or he was making her better. Or maybe emotional improvement wasn't the case here? Maybe they were each actually making the other worse? It bore considering.

"We could go wait in the car," she suggested. "Come back in ten minutes. By then they should be—"

They both heard it then—a loud thump. The noise had come from somewhere in the back of the house.

They looked at each other in surprise. Something about that noise hadn't sounded right.

Futana pulled out her gun. "Something's wrong for sure in there, Tom."

He drew his own Glock 22 and nodded. "Yeah, that sounded like someone falling down just now . . . but, they didn't yelp in pain afterwards, did they?"

Futana's reply was a nod. Anderson pointed his gun at the door lock. This was a shitty situation; the kind that made toilet-quality paperwork. *There'll be hell to pay if we get inside and nothing's amiss, if it's merely that the couple both fell out of bed in the heat of passion.*

But he wasn't taking any chances. *Someone might be really hurt in there.*

Before he could shoot the lock to bits, Futana pushed his gun hand down. "Hey, try just opening it first," she said. "I mean, just twist the knob?"

"It's certain to be locked."

"Not necessarily. With both husband and wife home, it's unlikely that they'll be worried about intruders." She stepped past him and twisted the doorknob. The door opened. She shrugged at Anderson. "Thank me, man. I just saved us both a whole friggin' lot of paperwork if nothing's wrong in there."

Anderson grunted something that might have been "Thanks."

Guns at the ready, they stepped through the door.

"Oh shit!" Futana exclaimed once they were inside the living room.

Mary Watt's severed head was sitting on the coffee table. The head, positioned in a pool of blood, was upright and facing towards the front door. Its eyes were closed. Mrs. Watt's head had been removed *after* killing her. What *had* killed her was clearly the deep ax wound that had almost split her skull in two.

"That damn son-of-a-bitch," Futana gasped. "That goddamn son-of-a-bitch." This was crazy. It also meant there was a whole lot more to the Wet Bones scenario than they'd originally imagined.

Beside her, Anderson scanned the living room for signs of Mary Watt's body. One of her arms lay on a blue sofa. They couldn't tell if it was her left or right arm though—all the fingers and the thumb had been chopped off. The rest of Mary's body was missing.

Futana gagged.

"Okay," Anderson whispered, "let's go find Mr. Watt. He's clearly got a whole lot of explaining to do." He gestured left, towards the dining room area. "You go that way, and check the kitchen too. I'll look down the hallway and in the bedrooms."

They separated.

***

In the dining room, Futana found Mary Watt's other severed arm. After taking a few seconds to determine that this was the left one (it too was missing fingers and thumb), she stepped through into the kitchen.

There was a whole lot of blood on the kitchen floor. There were bare footprints in the blood. There was blood all over the kitchen sink and counter. From the kitchen doorway, Futana could see two severed feet in the sink. Neither foot had any toes. Nearer to her, an open pot was boiling on the gas range, spilling steam into the air

Avoiding the blood, Futana stepped up to the gas range. She peeked into the pot.

Then she threw up all over the pot's contents. For a moment, the walls spun around her and she felt like she'd faint.

It wasn't the sight of the boiling fingers, thumbs, and toes in the pot that had upset her stomach beyond the point of no return.

No, there was something else cooking in there too.

Mary Watt had been pregnant. Maybe five or six months pregnant. And her crazy husband had cut the fetus out of her belly and cooked it along with her fingers and toes.

***

Tom Anderson made his way down the hallway to the rear of the house. It was clear enough where Fred Watt was: twin trails of blood led to the last door on the left. The door was open.

41

Anderson decided there was no point rushing in. He wasn't about saving Mary Watt anymore.

Like Futana, Anderson too now suspected that there was more to the Wet Bones case than they'd initially thought. *Or is there? This guy going crazy may just be a coincidence. But what kind of a damn coincidence?*

Gun held out in front of him, he paused a few steps from the open door. It was the couple's bedroom.

What remained of Mary Watt was laid out in bed. There wasn't much left. Just her torso with her legs attached. No feet. Her belly was ripped open.

Anderson had seen enough. "Hey, Fred, this is the police! You're under arrest for the murder of your wife! Come out of there with your hands up."

There was no reply from inside the bedroom, just an insane tittering. On hearing that, the grizzled old cop realized Fred Watt had snapped beyond the point of any repair. Exit wealthy investment banker, enter lunatic asylum resident.

"Come out of there! Show yourself, Fred!" He couldn't see the man, and wouldn't be able to unless he actually stepped inside the bedroom. He was certain Fred had an axe with him. His wife's headless corpse, lacerated as it was with deep wounds, was testament to that. He didn't know if the crazy man had a gun too.

Anderson wasn't looking to get gut shot again. His one experience of that was enough for two lifetimes.

"Come out of there, Fred, or we're coming in!"

Again came that mad tittering from the bedroom.

Anderson decided 'to hell with it.' No point going in there anyway. Better to just call for backup and let someone else handle the task of getting the unseen Mr. Watt out of his bedroom. They'd need to bring a straitjacket too.

What I'm gonna do now is close this door and keep a watch on it till the medics arrive. They can tase him and cart him away. Ain't no way this guy is going anywhere from here but straight to the loony bin. The state ain't gonna waste good taxpayer funds putting his crazy ass on trial.

Tom Anderson might have been an asshole, but he didn't believe in shooting anyone down in cold blood. Anderson followed the law to the letter, even in cases like this one, where he had a psychopath no one would give a shit about if he euthanized.

Meanwhile, Fred Watt was still laughing his crazy laugh somewhere inside the bedroom.

The sound was getting on Anderson's nerves. He took a final glance at Mary Watt's mutilated corpse. He winced. He stepped forward to pull the bedroom door shut. That should damp the sound of the laughter a bit.

Then he heard a noise on his right, from up the hallway. He spun towards the sound, then relaxed. It was Futana. Then almost as quickly as he'd relaxed, he was bothered again.

Shit, she looks sick. And why's she gesturing in horror like—

Then he got it and spun around again, back toward the bedroom door.

Oh heck!

Bloody axe raised overhead, Fred Watt was charging out of the door at him. The man was covered in blood. His eyes were swollen to bursting point; their pupils were tiny black circles, like dots painted on huge white and red marbles. He was frothing at the mouth.

That was all Anderson saw before he slipped on some blood and crashed to the floor with the madman on top of him.

Then it was a crazy fight for his life. His fall had taken him below the arc of the descending ax, but it had also smacked his head against the floor. Anderson ignored the pain. He flung his gun away, reached up, and grabbed the madman's wrists. They rolled around the hallway in a desperate fight for possession of the ax. All the while, Fred Watt kept slobbering spittle down on Anderson or spitting it up at him. And he kept on tittering.

Hell's bells, Anderson thought grimly, *where the hell is that goddamn Laurie?*

It seemed like an eternity before he heard the anticipated gunshot and felt the madman go limp on him. Then he felt fresh blood dripping on him.

Futana wasn't like Anderson. She didn't take no mess from no one. She'd simply shot Fred Watt in the back of his nutty head. Put the nutcase out of his misery. To her mind, anyone who could murder a pregnant woman then cook her baby didn't deserve the space he occupied on the planet. If Tom liked, he could dispute the rightness or wrongness of her actions (and yes, she *could* have simply knocked Mr. Watt out), but she didn't give a shit what Tom thought.

Besides, I just saved his life, didn't I?

She bent down and helped Anderson to his feet.

"Thanks, partner," he said.

He looked down at the dead man, then shrugged. "Couldn't be helped, I suppose." He gestured into the bedroom, waited till Futana got over her revulsion at the horrible sight, then asked, "You find the rest of Mary? I mean, what the hell did he do with her feet?"

She decided to spare him her gruesome discovery. "Just don't look in the kitchen, Tom. You'll hate what they were gonna have for lunch."

Anderson nodded. He remembered how she'd looked coming down the hallway. Oh no, he didn't want to see what had gotten her looking like that.

They placed the call to the station, then went to sit in the living room and wait for the boys in blue to come clean up the mess. They both avoided the sofa with the severed arm on it.

"You know," Tom Anderson said after a while, pointing to the severed head on the coffee table (which they couldn't move because it was evidence), "I'm not by any definition a superstitious man, but I can't shake off the feeling that Fred Watt didn't go crazy this morning by accident."

Futana nodded. "Me too, man. It's just too much of a coincidence—we're about to possibly get our first major break in the case and then this happens to the star witness? I'm thinking this mess *has* to be tied up in some way with those bones we've got. But how? There's no logical link I can see."

She remembered her eerie impression of the strange air outside the building having an influence on people, then shook it off. That was just ridiculous. "And," she went on, "what galls me about things like this is—we can't tell anyone what we suspect. If we do, they'll think we're crazy."

Anderson smiled. "Baby, they already think we're crazy."

"No, Tom, they think we're both assholes."

"Laurie, honey, I assure you they think we're crazy too."

"Crazy assholes then."

The two of them resumed staring at Mrs. Mary Watt's severed head. Independently, without voicing their thoughts to one another, both detectives agreed that there was something very creepy in the way the detached and cleft head was standing upright on its neck instead of falling over on its side . . . almost . . . almost as if it was using blood for superglue.

They theorized about what could possibly be going on. Neither of them left the living room, though Futana really wanted to pee. She was still spooked by what she'd found cooking in the kitchen. She didn't want to look in any of the toilet bowls, in case the dead housewife had been expecting twins. (She'd turned off the gas range, but left everything how she'd found it for the lab boys to analyze. Though what they could possibly conclude other than 'boiled fetus and mommy digits garnished with transsexual vomit' was beyond her.)

After a bit, she got up and walked around the coffee table. She squatted before the half-split head. She stared intently at the dead face. Mary Watt's face held a peculiar expression; one Futana found impossible to decipher. Maybe that was because the woman's eyes were shut. She wondered what secrets the destroyed brain held captive; secrets they'd now never have access to.

Futana felt better now. Death was familiar enough to her. It was the unexpected craziness of what they'd found here that had initially turned her stomach.

"I wonder what she'd have told us if she'd not been killed."

"Huh?" Anderson said, looking up from staring at the floor.

Futana pointed at the severed head in its pool of congealed blood. "Mary Watt. I wonder what she'd have told us."

"Most likely that he'd been cheating on her with his secretary. And that calling us was just a prank to get even."

Futana straightened up and walked back around the coffee table. "Maybe they'll find some evidence when they look through the house," she said while sitting down.

"Yeah, maybe."

"But maybe they won't. And maybe all this blood and death really is just a frigging coincidence. Shit! This just pisses me off."

"You know," Anderson said finally. "Once forensics arrive, I need to either go get drunk or go have a smoothie with Gracie."

Futana nodded. "Right now, alcohol sounds better to me than blended fruit. But let's go visit Gracie anyway. I'll come with you. Haven't seen the old lady in a while."

They resumed waiting.

CHAPTER 5

Greg

Greg felt there was something odd about Laurie Futana. Try as he might though, he couldn't figure it out. He liked her. The detective was a beautiful woman, tall and willowy and with great breasts. She also seemed to be a genuinely nice person.

Not like her partner Anderson. Like most people, Greg couldn't relate to the cold and taciturn Anderson. He didn't understand why his aunt liked the jerk so much.

Tom Anderson had joined the Graceful Blend smoothie club three years ago. He'd still been married to Nancy then. Joining had actually been her idea, to give them some kind of a social life. After the divorce, Nancy had quit coming. She didn't want to see Tom. Tom had continued with the club. He liked Grace. He sensed a kindred spirit in her. Her attraction for him wasn't her money; he had no idea how rich she was. Besides, he wasn't thinking of getting married again. One divorce was bad enough. But, whenever they sat and chatted after everyone else had gone home, Tom Anderson felt a sense of peace with Grace Barbanell that he didn't feel anywhere else.

As the detectives stepped past Greg into the house, he again tried to figure out what that elusive 'difference' about Futana was. Oh, she was charming and all, but . . .

He didn't dwell on it for too long though. Today he was pondering his own problems. And, boy, did he have big problems!

He saw both detectives into the spacious living room and served them Cokes. By the time he was through doing this, Aunt Grace had descended the stairs to greet the pair. Elderly and lovely, she was just graciousness itself. She shook hands with Futana, kissed Anderson warmly on the cheek, then went to fetch a bottle of wine and glasses

from the antique stateroom trunk bar that stood beside the TV. It was
8 p.m., the cops were off duty.

It was now that Greg noticed that both police officers had strained
expressions on their faces. They looked like they'd had a really bad
day.

He climbed the stairs to his room, put on some shoes and a jacket
and went downstairs again. He was leaving the house. He needed to
think; maybe have a drink somewhere quiet.

As he walked back through the living room, he heard Anderson
telling his aunt about some investment banker who'd hacked his
pregnant wife to death with an axe.

"Damn, the world's full of crazies," Greg muttered to himself as
he left the house.

***

Greg was baffled by the problem he'd caused himself. *If only I'd
suspected the fallout.*

What he'd considered a one-off joke on his 'evil' aunt had now
snowballed. Now Aunt Grace wanted smoothie 'specials' all the time.
Complete with his semen in them.

"I enjoyed that one you gave me yesterday so much, darling," she'd
said gently the day after. "And, don't forget that secret ingredient of
yours . . . Oh, I don't know what you put in that drink, Greg, but, oh
Lord, it gave it a donkey kick. I was tingling all evening."

Greg had tried to keep a straight face. He'd nodded to her, then
staggered out of the bedroom.

Descending the stairs that afternoon, he'd pondered her request.
Should I? No, I really shouldn't. She'd go crazy if she knew he'd fed her
his semen. He wasn't angry with her anymore. And besides, even if he
was, he'd already taught her her lesson.

He'd pondered on that too: What was the point of teaching a
person a lesson if they didn't even know what you'd done?

He'd decided to forget about it. It wasn't like he hated the old girl.
He'd just been angry because she'd kicked him like a dog.

He'd made his decision. No more masturbating into her drinks.
He'd walked into the kitchen and made Aunt Grace a normal
smoothie, with lots of nuts and fruit and vegetables. A delicious, rich,
and healthy drink.

It didn't work. The moment she'd tasted the smoothie, her lips twisted from her happy smile of anticipation into a scowl. She'd sipped the drink again, then stared angrily at him.

"It's wrong," she'd said flatly. "You didn't put the secret ingredient in."

"I can't duplicate it," he'd protested.

"I don't recall you making that excuse yesterday."

"C'mon, Aunt Grace, what if it was puppy doo-doo I put in it?"

She'd regarded him queerly for a second, then smiled coldly. "I don't care. I want the exact same taste as yesterday."

And Greg, rather than plead innocence or claim that what he'd served her the previous day had been merely a happy accident, had instead returned downstairs to the kitchen, gotten out his penis again, dialed up HARDX.com on his cellphone, found a hot scene of Mia Malkova being sodomized, and made his aunt another 'semen smoothie.'

And so it had begun. Aunt Grace had kept demanding for smoothies and Greg had (stupidly in retrospect) kept providing them for her. Doing so had originally seemed less trouble than refusing and putting her in a foul mood. After a while though (this had been going on for a fortnight now), Greg had also begun to derive a perverse pleasure from making the drinks. Feeding her his come felt almost incestuous in a way.

He took precautions not to be found out. He always insisted she go upstairs first, and also made sure to latch the kitchen door while 'working.' He explained these safeguards to Aunt Grace as his not wanting her spying on him. His secret ingredient had to remain secret. Thankfully, she always complied. (He wondered if she'd become addicted to what he was feeding her. Was that possible? Could a woman become addicted to the taste of semen?)

He also made certain to always use the same blender (tagged with magic marker). He didn't want to wind up drinking his own come.

Greg didn't make semen smoothies everyday. He couldn't: a man's body only had so much semen to give (and come wasn't something you kept in jars in the fridge).

Oddly, no matter what masking flavors he added—Ginger, nutmeg, coffee, cinnamon or even honey—his aunt could always tell when there was semen in her drink. Oh, it was driving her nuts that she didn't know what it was she loved so much. (If only Grace Barbanell had ever fellated a man once or twice in her life . . .)

Of course, also, Greg wasn't dating anyone just now, and being a healthy young stud, he had a lot of semen to offload. It had seemed good to be putting it to use somewhere. Making someone happy as it were. He'd felt happy himself seeing the wide smile on his aunt's face whenever she sipped one of his 'specials.'

***

Greg trudged slowly down Corey Street, towards Highland train station. He was lost in thought. It was quite a dilemma he'd put himself in. He wanted to stop doing this nonsense. He needed to stop doing this nonsense.

He hardly noticed the sidewalk he stepped on. He didn't notice the cars rolling by. His thoughts raged furiously, lions eating his conscience.

So, why the hell don't I just stop then! I'm not a pervert who likes wanking into women's drinks . . . but . . . whether I like it or not, masturbating into an unsuspecting woman's drink automatically makes me a pervert. I need to quit fooling myself that I'm a nice guy and—!

"Hey, Greg, wait up!"

He snapped out of his thoughts and looked around. It was Debbie Manning, literally the girl next door. Debbie was studying something or other at the Boston University College of Fine Arts; try hard as he might, Greg could never recall exactly what her major was. Debbie was a cute blonde. Once or twice they'd driven out for drinks in his car, but they weren't dating. She was just a nice, clean, all-American girl.

He waited for her to catch up with him. She was wearing a yellow shirt, white pants and flip-flops; and a short checkered summer coat over those.

"Man, where's your head at?" Debbie asked. "I've been calling you for almost a minute now, ever since you passed our house."

"Sorry," he apologized, "my mind just ran off with me."

She gave him a concerned smile. "Anything you wanna talk about? I'm all ears."

Greg just imagined telling Debbie Manning what he'd been doing at home, and her disgusted response. She'd probably never talk to him again.

He laughed. "Nah, it's nothing you can help me with. Just work stuff."

She nodded. "How's the job at the bank then?"

Her question reminded Greg of his aunt's attitude towards his Portfolio Manager Associate job at the Bank of America. Aunt Grace was totally against it. She said he was too good for such a job. She wanted him to work for *her* instead. She wanted him to be her secretary or personal assistant. Talk of someone being constitutionally unreasonable. Greg had no intention whatever of working for his aunt. She was too controlling already. He wasn't allowing her to get that kind of a foothold in his professional life as well . . .

"The job's cool," he replied. "The pay's great anyway." He changed the topic. "Hey, how're things with you? How's Eddie? I haven't seen his car outside your place for a while now."

She shrugged. "We broke up."

"Oh, I'm sorry to hear that."

She shrugged again. "Don't be. He was screwing my best friend." For a moment she looked distraught, but then she regained control of herself. "You know Angie, right? Well, I went over to her house to visit her—I couldn't get her on the phone—and found them in bed together."

Greg winced. He wished he'd not asked. Now Debbie seemed close to tears.

The conversation had stalled. Debbie was staring at him like she wanted him to say something. He stared back at her. She looked pretty like this, framed against the night.

"I . . . uh," he started, then stopped. He couldn't think of anything to say that wouldn't sound clichéd. "Hey, you wanna go have a drink with me?" he asked finally.

"Yeah, sure," she said and slipped her arm through his.

They walked along in silence. After a while Greg became conscious of Debbie's body beside his. How soft she felt when she innocently brushed against him. How warm her smile was, how blue her eyes were, how soft and lustrous her yellow hair was.

He wasn't interested in her though. He had lots of female interest of his own.

Despite which, they laughed a lot over their drinks.

It was only while tipsily walking home again later that Greg realized that being with Debbie had completely taken his mind off his worries.

He saw her to her front door. He did his best not to kiss her, but her lips were oh, so inviting. She looked like she wanted to be kissed, so he kissed her.

It was a very drunken kiss. When they separated they laughed.

"Sorry, Greg," Debbie giggled tipsily, "I really like you, but it's too early for me. You understand, right?"

He nodded. "Yeah, that's cool. We'll just be friends for now."

He turned around and staggered off home. *That's a really nice girl*, he thought. *A really nice girl.*

CHAPTER 6

Allie

Allie's sister and brother-in-law lived on Dover's Whiting Road.

Her brother-in-law's garage, the Hot Rodz Automotive Establishment, was right next door to the house, a short thirty yards walk away from the Cimini's cottage.

Chloe Cimini was an older and plumper version of Allie. She had the same straw-yellow hair and blue eyes, a happy disposition, and a sweet smile.

Giorgio was tall and thin. He was a quiet man who smiled sparingly.

Giorgio welcomed Allie warmly to his house, repeated that she was welcome to stay for as long as she liked, then vanished back into his oily world of engine tune-ups and overhauls, wheel alignments, vehicle-diagnostic computer systems, brake disk skimming, welding and sanding and dead sparkplugs, and everything else involved in returning recalcitrant modern automobiles back to sterling uncompromised roadworthiness.

The Cimini's house was a large one and comfortably furnished. Allie's bedroom was spacious and airy, and its windows afforded her an excellent view of the luscious green countryside. She settled in and got to work on purging her heart and soul of the remnants of Brian Kemp. She went for long walks in the mornings and evenings. She helped Chloe with her housework and her three kids.

She also helped Giorgio out in his garage. Mostly she handled his bookkeeping. Giorgio was terrible with figures. His accounts were a total mess. Allie spent days trying to figure out how much Giorgio's income tax was.

Occasionally, when the mood took her, she also got her hands dirty in a car engine. Staring up at the oily undersides of a hoisted-up Ford or Dodge was one way to get through a painful space.

Though the Cimini's both seemed happy enough with each other, Giorgio wasn't any kind of a model husband. On the day Allie arrived at her sister's place, Chloe was sporting a split lip. Despite which, to Allie's surprise, she seemed to be in the best of spirits.

A few days later Allie witnessed the couple having a violent screaming match in their living room, while their 2-year-old son Enzo watched from his playpen with a bemused smile on his face. Thankfully, no blows were thrown.

"Why don't you leave the pig?" Allie asked Chloe the next day. "I hate the way he keeps disrespecting you."

Chloe frowned. For a moment she looked really confused, as though the question wasn't one she'd ever actually considered. Finally she shrugged. "I love him, I guess."

But Giorgio was never rude or nasty to Allie. He was harsh at times, usually when she didn't hand him a monkey wrench or oil can fast enough when they worked on a car together, but that was all.

And he never once put the make on her. After a while, when she'd gotten her sexual confidence back, she found his behavior a bit odd for a brother-in-law. Other than when he was arguing with her sister, Giorgio never spoke much anyway, but wasn't he supposed to . . . ? He was supposed to secretly lust after her, wasn't he? Steal secret glances at her from the corner of his eyes, comparing her hot twenty-something body with her sister's saggy one, then look away just when she turned towards him.

But Giorgio didn't, he seemed happy enough with her fat sister. After a while, she forgot about it.

**

The Hot Rodz Garage was more of a mob front than a viable business. Allie quickly worked this out. Giorgio and Chloe and their three kids were clearly living much more comfortably than Giorgio could afford on the garage's earnings.

And they had lots of extra expenditure too. For instance, the family was planning a long summer vacation to Disneyland, and Chloe was talking of flying cross country afterwards, to Las Vegas, so she could gamble a little and catch some shows.

While balancing the garage accounts for Giorgio, Allie noticed that he had two kinds of clients. The first kind just dropped their vehicles off for servicing and repairs. The other kind sat in Giorgio's office to discuss 'business.'

Two of the second kind of client came around a lot. Their names were Tommy Collins and Dave Fontaine. Most times. Giorgio would put Allie out of the office to attend to them. She'd peer in through the glass window and see them all serious and making angry gestures at each other. Once she even saw Tommy hand her sister's husband a large bundle of cash—about $100,000 by her banker's estimation. On that occasion, Giorgio had put the money away and nodded. Then he'd said—she'd read his lips clearly—"Twenty-five percent or no deal." The trio had haggled a bit longer, then with smiles all around, shaken hands.

(One thing Allie did glean from what she overhead was that Tommy and Dave's outfit was called the Rectifiers. The name didn't sound particularly criminal, but, she considered, 'rectifying' could cover just about everything from torching a business competitor's store to shooting cheating spouses. Ugh!)

On weekends, when the garage was closed, Tommy and Dave would come over to the house instead. Sometimes Dave had a woman with him. Tommy, however, always came alone. He'd smile politely at Allie and make idle chat.

Tommy was slim and dark, with average looks. He looked tough and Allie didn't doubt he was as tough as he looked. Tommy Collins never said more than he had to; he could sit smiling or scowling for ten or fifteen minutes without saying a word. In that sense he was a copy of Allie brother-in-law. She decided that was part of the reason why Giorgio liked him so much.

Dave, on the other hand, was just *gorgeous*. That was what first struck her about him: how damn handsome he was: black hair, sexy eyes that seemed either green or blue depending on the light, nose and lips taken straight from a classic Greek sculpture, a strong chin, great even teeth. Dave was taller than Tommy, over six feet. He was muscular too. The way he filled out his shirts, Allie could only imagine what his chest and abs looked like. Best of all though was his mischievous, naughty-little-boy smile.

Also, unlike Tommy, Dave didn't economize words. He always had a lot to say, at least to her. She liked him from the first moment she met him and that liking soon veered dangerously close to star-struck infatuation.

Whenever they came visiting at the house, Allie would seat the guys, pour them drinks, then call Giorgio. She could tell that Tommy was interested in her—it was all over his face—but Giorgio had clearly told his associates to lay off her. Even Dave the womanizer—and God, just looking at him, she got all hot and bothered and desperate to be womanized—never hit on her. She was wary of him anyway. Brian had taught her a deep lesson—no man was ever using her and dumping her again. The next time she gave herself to a man, it had to be for real—she had to know he wasn't playing baseball with her heart.

On those weekend visits, Tommy and Dave never talked shop. They'd sit around and drink and joke with her, and afterwards depart with Giorgio and Chloe for a night on the town, leaving her to babysit her nephews and niece. Most times, after reading the kids their bedtime stories, Allie would have to dash into her room, lock the door, grab her little blue vibrator, and masturbate fiercely before Giorgio and Chloe got back—that was how hot seeing Dave always left her.

But then too, there was the desperate desire for her which she always read in Tommy's eyes; a desire with very little lust in it. That gave her a different sort of erotic heat—the slow-burning sort that promised/threatened to last a lifetime.

But a lifetime with Tommy Collins, of all people? Still, occasionally she wondered if he'd be good for her. But a crook? And how in the world would she ever explain her choice of him to Chloe and Giorgio?

***

"Tommy Collins isn't really a bad egg," Chloe told Allie one night, out of the blue while they were doing the dishes after dinner. Tommy and Dave had stayed for dinner, and they and Giorgio were currently out on the back porch, drinking beer and talking shop.

"How do you mean?" Allie asked, feigning lack of any real interest, though she knew that for Chloe to have brought the matter up, she must have noticed her interest in Tommy.

Chloe shrugged. "Tommy's alright; it's Dave you've got to watch out for. Davey thinks he's God's gift to women." She sighed dreamily. "If you don't watch yourself around him, he'll be in and out of your panties before you even realize you've been hit and run."

Allie looked sharply at her sister. "Hey! Don't tell me you've . . "

Chloe shook her head quickly. "No. No, I haven't. Giorgio would never forgive me if I did. But sometimes I'm tempted. You know?"

Allie regarded the shadow of lust on her sister's plump face. "Oh, I do understand. But . . ."

Chloe smoothly changed the topic. "But I was talking about Tommy. Behind all that macho posturing he does, he's got a really kind heart."

Allie had to laugh at that. "What's he do, sis? Rescue kittens from trees? Help old ladies cross the road?"

Chloe put some plates away then nodded. "He actually did something better. He—"

Chloe's older son ran into the kitchen then, seeking attention. Allie watched in amusement while Chloe kissed the little boy's bruised finger well again then shooed him back out to the living room.

Chloe straightened up and patted down her skirt. "Yes, where was I? Oh yes, Tommy Collins. He once saved a woman from getting killed in a parking lot." She nodded at Allie's 'interested' expression. "Yeah, he really did. This old lady Grace—she's really about sixty—was about getting in her car one night when some drugged-up punk sticks a switchblade to her neck and tells her to 'hand over the money, bitch.' "

Allie gasped. "So what happened?"

"Nothing would have happened, except that Grace Barbanell is a very feisty and tough bird—actually she's just stubborn—and wasn't about to give the mugger any money. She starts screaming and kicking and whatnot. The guy apparently decided to kill her to shut her up. He's a junkie looking for some fix money—he clearly wasn't thinking too much about right and wrong. One dead old bat won't bother him too much until the cops arrest him. Anyway, he'd already lifted his hand to stab Grace dead when Tommy grabbed his wrist." She sighed. "It turned out that Tommy knew the guy from somewhere. Tommy gave him some fix money and ran him off. Then he drove Grace home. She wasn't in any condition to drive herself: it was just sinking in that she'd almost gotten herself murdered."

Allie found the story a bit of an anticlimax—a criminal stopping a junkie from killing someone—but she didn't say so.

Chloe smiled. "And so it is that Grace Barbanell doesn't currently reside in a nearby cemetery." She dried her hands on a napkin. "Oh, isn't it just funny how life throws people together? Would you believe

Tommy and Grace are still friends?" She nodded at Allie's look of surprise. "Yes, they are," she said, leading the way back to the kids and noise in the living room. "Grace runs a smoothie club. Tommy's a member. He's been attending without fail for over a year now."

"A smoothie club? Tommy Collins? Wow—now I've heard everything." Whatever else Allie could imagine about Tommy Collins, sitting with a group of old women and mixing yoghurt drinks wasn't one of them. "And Dave, does he attend too?"

Chloe lifted her younger son Enzo onto her plump lap. She waved her daughter Nicola away from the television. She smirked. "Dave Fontaine? Oh, he ain't got the time. He's too busy chasing girls."

She winked at Allie. "Look, forget Dave, okay? He'll just break your heart all over again. If you're gonna place your money on either of them, Tommy's the safe bet." She winced. "Only thing is, if you do date Tommy, Giorgio's gonna be mad for sure. He regards you as his own baby sister now."

"I-I-I'm not thinking of dating anyone!" Allie blurted out.

Chloe just smiled back. Chloe wasn't in the least deceived. She'd seen the looks her younger sister kept giving Dave Fontaine. There was no doubt at all in her mind what those looks meant.

Hadn't she herself often felt exactly the same way about him?

CHAPTER 7

Anderson & Futana

"The Watt house was clean," Laurie Futana said. She placed a cup of coffee in front of her partner. "Any illegal crap Fred Watt was into was being handled elsewhere."

"Yeah, yeah," Anderson said, looking up for a minute from the screen of his laptop. "Only we can't actually prove that he *was* doing anything criminal . . . before hacking his wife to bits, I mean."

Futana sat facing him. She sipped her drink slowly. "Yeah, I get what you mean: Rich guy cracks from work-related stress, happens everyday." She gestured across the desk at his laptop. "What's that you're studying?"

He leaned back from the laptop. Outside their office, the police station buzzed with activity. He regarded his coffee for a moment. He studied the slow swirl of still blending colors that had resulted from Futana's stirring it, and also the vapor rising from it. He lifted the drink and sipped from it.

Futana didn't press him. She was used to Anderson now. He wasn't ignoring her; he was processing his thoughts. She waited.

Anderson drank half the cup of coffee then said, "I'm studying the background findings for each of our stiffs. There's gotta be a connection somewhere."

"Anything new so far?"

"Nah. Fifteen bodies so far—the oldest dating back to 2010: that Davies guy—all killed the same way."

"Not all the same. How 'bout that guy with the broken head?"

"Sammy McClursky?"

"Yeah, and the other guy with the broken arm? What's his name again?"

"Mack Irish?"

"That's almost establishing a pattern of violence."

"Nothing to go on there. There's too much separation between them. Irish vanished five years ago; McClursky just nine months ago." He finished his coffee then added, "McClursky likely *was* murdered—he was that kinda guy—but his death just as likely has nothing to do with what we're searching for; whatever killed or ate everyone else most likely just found his dumped corpse in the woods and snacked on it as well." He regarded Futana over the laptop. "Anything from Steph at the MSPCL yet?"

She frowned prettily. "No. Or maybe that should be 'yes.' "

"How'd you mean, 'yes?' "

Futana pouted and ran a pencil through her short blonde hair. "Well, she says those cells she sent for analysis came back positive for an animal. They weren't human anyway. The problem is, so far they can't match the cell DNA to anything in the zoological database."

Anderson didn't say anything for a while.

"No shit," he remarked finally. "The plot thickens."

"Like molasses it does. At least now we know it wasn't a chemical reaction that covered the skeletons in slime." She thought a moment. "Yeah, Stephanie also says the slime is corrosive—well it *was*, it's denatured now—like a digestive enzyme of some sort."

"Corrosive? A digestive enzyme? Aw, c'mon now. Don't tell me a giant runaway gator, no . . . a giant snail or slug—those exude slime—ate all those people? And it's gone undetected all this while?"

"That's what it looks to be adding up to. Anyway, once she's made a zoological match on the cells she'll let us have her full report."

Anderson frowned. "I don't like this. I don't like this one bit."

"Man, we've neither of us liked it from the get-go."

"Yes, but now . . . Laurie, this ain't just some wildlife problem we've got going on here. I can feel it in my bones. I know it's illogical, but . . . there's a goddamn human angle to this too. I just know there is. And not just 'cos of that Watt guy." He looked carefully at his partner. "Listen, Laurie, you and me both know how this works: Once Stephanie matches the animal DNA, it's off our desks for good. It'll become something for the wildlife guys to hunt down. And if they don't find whatever it is, the case will go cold."

"For a while, yes. Until more bodies turn up."

"Yeah, yeah," Anderson said impatiently. "But my point is, in the meantime, if there's a crime going on, it continues." He stared at

Futana to ensure she understood him. She did. Everyone knew how much Anderson hated crime.

"And," he went on, "what's to stop the perp from simply burying the stiffs elsewhere once word gets out? And *deeper* this time, so rain doesn't unearth 'em?"

"Yes, I get you, man." She checked her watch, then pushed her chair back and got to her feet. "Tom, you and I just got off duty. Let's go have a drink somewhere; wash the slime off our shoulders."

He got up and followed her out of the police station, his mind heavy with dark thoughts.

CHAPTER 8

The Man

While Detectives Anderson and Futana sat drinking beers in a bar, somewhere deep in the woods across the state of Massachusetts, a man was digging a pit.

Like Anderson had recently surmised, this pit was a whole lot deeper than the previous ones.

Once done with his labor, the man stood by the edge of the hole he'd just dug. He leaned on his shovel and waited to get his strength back. He wiped sweat from his brow with a dirty handkerchief. He was a big, strong, muscular man, but the digging, needing to be done quickly, had winded him.

"Yeah, four feet's deep enough," he muttered to himself. "It's just wet bones after all."

The man had had no knowledge that the police had begun finding the other bodies. But someone—the folks he worked for were very well connected—had called his brother with the info that a search was on. (They'd also heard that Mary Watt had ratted them out to the cops and had taken care of her too.)

And so the new policy of burying the skeletons at least four foot below ground had been instituted. It was too late to rebury the others—so long had passed since they'd died that the man had forgotten where they were. Besides, there were too many skeletons anyway, going back too many years. They were also spread over a wide area; inhumed in four different counties. Burying folks across the state wasn't like tending a regular cemetery where one kept a log of who was in which plot and planted tombstones to identify locations.

The man grinned to himself. He'd ranged far and wide; oh yes, he had. He'd buried folks as far northwest as Williamstown and Clarksburg, and (slightly closer to home) a few up north around

Nichewaug (near the Quabbin Reservoir) as well. The Wendell, Warwick, Spencer, and October Mountain State Forests, and the Wells State Park were particularly great places to leave bones. One just had to keep one's eyes open for Bureau of Forestry workers.

The interred skeletons numbered almost a hundred, if his memory served him right. Now that the cops knew of their existence, it was best to just leave them in the ground. The cops would never be able to prove anything anyway. He'd been very careful over the years, ensuring he never left any traces that could connect him to the crimes.

Finally the man felt recovered enough from his digging to head back to his pickup truck. This was parked amidst some trees, so no one driving past would notice it.

The man got out the package in the back of the truck. It was wrapped in black tarpaulin. Even a cursory glance told one that the package contained a human body.

He carried the package back through the woods to the hole he'd just dug. There he unwrapped it. He coldly regarded its gory contents. Once a living breathing person, now just dead bones. Joined white bones covered all over with transparent jelly, like someone had melted plastic bags over them. The creature had eaten all the flesh. The brain case was empty too. The creature's jelly had dissolved the brain till it drained out from the skull as a liquid to be absorbed, just like the rest of the body had been.

Knowing how corrosive the colorless jelly was, the man made certain not to touch the unwrapped body. The creature made two kinds of jelly: One was the harmless sort it exuded from its body surface and mouth. And then there was this second type—its digestive jelly—which it squirted from the walls of its gut after eating someone. Once it had absorbed the liquefied flesh, it vomited out the skeletons.

The man found one detail of the creature's feeding process particularly weird: the only reason that the wet bones afterwards maintained the shape of a skeleton—why they still held together— was because of the same jelly that had stripped them naked of flesh in the first place. It was crazy, he knew, but it was true. The jelly dissolved away all the ligaments that usually held joints together, but then it replaced those bonds with itself, behaving like a glue and keeping the consumed person's remains in one morbid piece. The man had pondered on this for ages. Finally he'd decided that the strange gluey action had to be a survival mechanism on the creature's part. Because, for sure, it would be a whole lot easier to eject one person from its body than a hundred different pieces of that person, and besides, what if one of the smaller bones (like a rib, for instance) got stuck somewhere inside the creature and tore it open?

At least he figured that was why its insides glued people up perfectly like that.

The man had once made the mistake of touching one of the regurgitated stiffs. The jelly had burnt the tip of his finger off. He still had no sensation in his right index finger. He'd learnt his lesson. Since then, he was extremely careful with the creature's internal secretions. Even while packing the corpses themselves, he first dropped the tarpaulin wrapping over the skeleton, then rolled them up in it. And even then, he wore gloves. Afterwards, before shifting the tarp, he always first hosed it down with water, to wash off any of the jelly that had accidentally gotten on its outside.

Now, he used his shovel to roll the skeleton into the grave. The skeleton wasn't very large. The victim had been a teenaged runaway he'd offered a ride on Route 32, down by the Connecticut border.

The wet remains hit the bottom of the hole. As was routine, they didn't separate on impact, the jelly glue held them together. He checked a minute to ensure the hole was actually deep enough, then began filling it up. Then he spread some dried brush over the spot to conceal it. Once done, he took a little time to catch his breath again.

Then he carefully rolled the black tarp back up and carried it back to his pickup truck. Tomorrow he'd hose it down again.

Then he drove back home, whistling a tune.

CHAPTER 9

Greg

Jojo Kim was 50% Korean, 50% American, and 100% geeky-freaky. She was thirty-five and worked in computers and IT—graphic designs and such like. In addition, her two younger sisters Kiki and Lulu had a rock band and she handled their video recordings and business deals for them.

Jojo Kim had that Asian-American hybrid sort of pretty, with an oval face and eyes that weren't as slanted as you'd expect. Her prominent epicanthic folds were her primary racial giveaway. Jojo was slim, with just the right proportion of bust and buttock to emphasize her femininity. She was tall, but not too tall. She looked more like a nineteen-year-old athlete than a 35-year-old digital witch. As though she were trying to subconsciously distance herself from the nerd/geek stereotype which naturally accompanied her computer work, most times Jojo dressed in black leather—jacket and skirt or trousers, with high heeled boots—and sunshades. She looked like Zen that had had an accident in a nightclub.

As far as Greg could tell, Jojo's father had either been a North Korean defector or South Korean spy, or both. Her mother had been a stewardess on the plane that brought him to America with a bullet wound in his leg. From Jojo's calculations based on the date of her birth, she'd established that her mother had gotten pregnant somewhere up in the air over the Pacific Ocean that same night.

Jojo Kim was a founder member of the Graceful Blend smoothie club. She and Aunt Grace were tight; in some regards thicker than thieves even. Except that Aunt Grace didn't appear to have a sexual bone in her aging body, Greg might have imagined she and Jojo were lovers. But no, it wasn't anything like that; the pair were just great friends.

Greg had major difficulties understanding how his aunt stirred up such intense loyalty in such diverse individuals: Tom Anderson, Tommy Collins, and now Jojo Kim—a cop, a crook, and a geek-diva. But he couldn't deny the facts: each of them really liked Aunt Grace in their own way, even that moody grouch Anderson, who didn't seem to actually like anyone else.

***

In the meantime, the status quo at home was being maintained. Greg was still making semen-injected smoothies for Aunt Grace. A suicidal undertaking to be sure, but one he seemed unable to extricate himself from. He felt trapped in a vicious circle—like a cat in a cat circle—unable to free himself from his own stupidity.

Every two days or so, Greg would lock himself in the kitchen with his tablet PC, open up a HD video of either Abella Danger or Phoenix Marie or Bridgette B., or Eva Angelina performing fellatio, and release his varying frustrations as sperm for his aunt to orally imbibe.

He kept telling himself that he'd quit soon. And besides Aunt Grace was happy. Keeping her happy was paramount.

***

Back to Jojo Kim.

The first time Jojo grabbed Greg's ass was after a Saturday afternoon smoothie party.

The guests were all leaving and they were alone in the kitchen. Aunt Grace was chatting at the door with Detective Anderson, whose loud voice was audible all through the house.

Jojo was helping Greg wash up. He turned to set four tall glasses on a tray to dry and next thing, Jojo squeezed his buttocks with both hands. In his surprise, Greg almost flung the glasses across the kitchen.

He turned back to find Jojo winking at him. "I like you," she said. "See you later, honey."

She turned and sauntered off. At the kitchen door she turned back and blew him a kiss.

Greg was confused.

***

Since their first drunken kiss on Debbie's doorstep that night, Greg and Debbie had started dating seriously. She was cute and fun and so far their relationship was going great.

Still, cute and seemingly girl-next-door as she was, Debbie Manning had her own kinky side too. Oh, she was really kinky.

Debbie had this thing about her where she loved fucking while looking out of the window. She'd be naked from the waist down, but wearing a T-shirt on top, so passers-by didn't suspect what was going on. What she'd then do was try to maintain as normal a demeanor as possible to any onlookers while simultaneously coming to orgasm. Greg found it very frustrating. He'd be hidden behind the curtain, pumping away, with only Debbie's bare buttocks and legs visible, while in front of him, she'd be busy waving to neighbors, yelling down at the street saying, 'Hi, Mr. Bates," and "Hey, Dad, don't forget what mom said about not drinking too much!"

She was a *sexibitionist?*

Debbie also had this crazy thing about bird watching during sex. While Greg was thrusting away behind her, she'd stare up at the sky and try to figure out which avian species were going or coming to and fro.

"Hey, baby, there goes a flock of doves! Wow, Greg, there's a woodpecker tapping on your tree!"

Since Greg never saw the birds in question, he had no idea if she was making them up or not.

Wanting to feel as much of her as he could while inside her body, he'd reach through the drapes and grip her firm mounds of pleasure with their soft but firmly swollen points. He'd squeeze gently. She'd stifle a lust-powered moan. Then, gently but firmly, she would pry his fingers off of her nipples.

"Hide yourself, man," she'd whisper back at him in her hoarse passion, "someone might see." Then she'd reassert control over herself as best she could. She'd resume counting the birds outside. "Ooh, here's a little one that just landed on your lawn, baby . . . It's soooo pretty . . . it's got yellow and black plumage, with a little white too. It's . . . it's singing, baby . . . warbling. I think . . . I think it's an oriole. Oh, baby, it's so pretty."

Greg, in turn, would content himself with his prime view of her pretty backside, and work on bringing them both to orgasm.

***

That evening, over drinks, Greg told Debbie what had happened with Jojo. At first, she acted amused.

"Ah, she's a cougar looking for a cub," Debbie said.

"Well she can look elsewhere on the prairie. Besides, she's not *that* old as to be desperate for a guy."

"Just avoid her. It's *your* aunt's house." Her tone became teasing. "What's she like anyway? Pretty?"

"Jojo? Yeah, she's good-looking, but she's always dressed in black leather, and—"

"Goth?"

"Nope, hard rock without all the studs and chains."

"She sounds hot."

"Yeah, she's hot alright. I find her creepy, that's the thing, and sometimes she smells of weird incense, like—"

"Hey! Back up a bit. Are you saying that if you didn't find her creepy, rabbit, you'd happily hop into bed with her?"

"Why would I do that when I've got you?"

"Oh, you're only going out with me 'cos I fuck you?"

"Baby, I *love* you. I'm not dating you just 'cos we sleep together."

"Oh, really? How about if we put it to the test then? How about I stop sleeping with you for two months? Let's see if that helps or hurts our relationship."

"C'mon, Debbie, don't take it like that. You know I—"

"See? I knew it. You men are all the same. If I wasn't putting out you'd be all over that middle-aged Korean witch like glue."

Greg wasn't sure if she was joking or not. He however knew he wouldn't be discussing Jojo Kim with Debbie again.

"Look, just forget it," he said. "I doubt she'll try it again—she'll be scared I'll tell my aunt. Besides, she was likely just drunk. Hey, did I tell you how she put canna-oil in her smoothie mix and got the whole club stoned silly? Including Anderson?"

"Jojo got Detective Anderson stoned?"

"You need to have seen it to believe it. And you know what sort of a hardnose Anderson is. It's a miracle we're not all in jail now."

"So how'd you work it out?"

"It was crazy. Anderson was like a space cadet—completely off his rocker, mouthing shit about being Kurt Cobain's father and stuff like that. I don't think that old guy ever smoked a joint before in his life. We got Anderson's partner's phone number from his cellphone and called her. Detective Futana's a different kettle of fish. She's cool and vibey. My aunt explained the situation—how Anderson was stoned out of his skull and in absolutely no condition to drive himself home. She came over and took him home."

"And afterwards?"

Greg shrugged. "Anderson never mentioned it. I don't think he realized what had happened. Or if he did, he was too embarrassed."

Debbie looked unconvinced. "He doesn't seem the sort to ever be embarrassed."

"No, he doesn't." Greg shrugged again. "I dunno. Maybe Anderson's just waiting for a chance to send us all to jail forever." Then he laughed. "In that case, we're all lucky he's so fond of my aunt. He'd never do *anything* to hurt her. And heaven help anyone who ever tries to."

***

Next Saturday, the Kim sisters arrived early at the house. Kiki (the youngest sister) and Lulu were going for a band rehearsal but they'd come to drop Jojo off first. Jojo owned a silver Porsche that moved like it owned the road. Lulu had her own car but preferred taking Jojo's as it looked much cooler.

The sisters' band was called Kimchi Chocolate Stereo (or just KCS). They played loud alternative rock and were on the verge of breaking into the big time.

For a three-minute period, while her younger siblings unloaded her stuff from the Porsche, Jojo and Greg were left alone in the living room. Aunt Grace was upstairs.

Seeing the coast clear, Jojo walked across to Greg (who was putting away a set of home decoration magazines) and grabbed his ass again.

"Kiss me," she said when he straightened up. "I like you."

Greg almost did. She looked so pretty that afternoon. She looked exquisitely hot as well, in her short black dress, fishnet stockings, and black peep-toed heels. (Looking at her, one would imagine *she* was the rocker, not her sisters.) But he was in a bad mood—Aunt Grace had yelled him out again that morning. So, instead of kissing Jojo's expectant purple lips, Greg said, "Hell no!"

Jojo became insistent. She held onto him and pulled him towards her. "Kiss me! Quick, before my sisters get back."

They could hear Lulu and Kiki arguing about something outside (those two were always arguing), then the slam of the car door.

"Get away from me!" Greg growled. Then he shoved Jojo. He shoved her hard, so hard she stepped backward, lost her balance and wound up in an armchair with her panties showing. In contrast to the rest of her black attire, her panties were green. Fluorescent psychedelic green. He'd never even suspected they made female underwear in that color. The front half of Jojo's panties had a discolored patch like she was really aroused, and the rear part, now clamped between her tight buttocks, had a dark stain on them like . . .

Greg felt repulsed by the dirty sight but controlled himself not to show it.

He refrained from laughing. He already felt terrible about pushing Jojo. What had gotten into him? One didn't shove women around; not even irritating ones; he knew better than to do that.

For her own part, Jojo initially looked furious. Her half-Oriental face twisted up like that of a cat about to strike. Then she calmed down. (Lulu and Kiki Kim had meanwhile made a detour into the kitchen to drop a few things off before joining them in the living room.) Jojo sat up, smoothed down her nightshade dress, then smiled at Greg. It was a bittersweet smile; she clearly hated him rejecting her so violently, but she equally clearly intended to be classy about it.

"Look, I'm sorry I pushed you like that," Greg apologized. "I don't know what came over me."

Still smiling, Jojo nodded. "Don't you ever lay your hands on me like that again or you'll regret it," she warned him. Then she laughed.

She got to her feet. She walked over and stroked his chin with her index finger. He stood there, trembling now, wishing her sisters would come in from the kitchen and rescue him—they were still arguing in there.

Jojo walked around him, trailing her hand around his body, feeling his muscles. Still amused, she said, "You should be nice to me, boy. I've got your balls in my hand, you know."

That startled Greg. "Huh? What are you talking about?"

She giggled softly. "Just be nicer to me from now on or you'll regret it. I might just stop cradling your testicles softly and squeeze them hard instead."

"Jojo, what do you—?"

Her two sisters walked in then, killing the conversation. Greg couldn't get out of there fast enough. In fact, he abandoned helping set up for the smoothie club meeting. He dashed upstairs, grabbed a jacket and his car keys, then hurried back down. In the living room he pulled Kiki away from yet another argument with Lulu (this time over who would sit close to the TV). He whispered to her to tell his aunt that he'd had to rush off to a friend's birthday party which he'd somehow forgotten about, and that he wouldn't be back till late. Then he ran out of the house, exiting the front door just as the majority of the club members were arriving.

In his haste he almost knocked Detective Anderson off the front steps. He was aware of Anderson's bemused scowl as he climbed into his sky-blue Mazda.

He drove next door to Debbie's house, told her they were going out, and waited for her to get dressed. They went to see the new film *Evil Nights of the Resurrected Dead*.

The film was cool, but Greg's mind wasn't really there: he was trying to understand what Jojo Kim had meant when she'd said "I've got your balls in my hand." Had she somehow discovered his 'secret' smoothie ingredient?

At that moment, the filmmakers threw in a jump-scare of the zombies abruptly breaking through a wall and biting off both of a security guard's ears. Debbie whimpered in fright and gripped Greg tight. While stroking Debbie's hair to comfort her, Greg decided Jojo was just bluffing to make him sleep with her.

But by now he'd decided he wasn't doing it and that was that. Any woman who wore fluorescent green panties was a danger zone. And besides, he really liked Debbie and wasn't about to do anything to hurt her. He wasn't going to cheat on her like her last boyfriend had done. Ms. Kim would have to find someone else to sexually satisfy her.

Later that night, while licking Debbie's anus while she watched the trees for owls and the sky for turkey vultures, Greg decided that it was high time he stopped messing with his Aunt Grace.

It wasn't all altruism. No, a guy only had a limited amount of semen in him. One could only come so much in a day. Debbie was healthy, hot, and horny. She liked making love, and on his part, it was hard to be interested in sex when you'd spurted it all into someone's banana and yoghurt milkshake.

So, yes, it was time to reserve all his love milk for where it belonged. Which was inside . . .

No, on reconsidering, Greg realized that this was a slightly flawed analysis: seeing as he and Debbie always used condoms while making love, it was rather time to reserve his love milk for *who* it rightfully belonged to.

And that was definitely his young, sweet and hot girlfriend, not his old aunt.

CHAPTER 10

Allie

That Thursday, Allie went with Tommy to a concert at Boston's Hole Faith Club.

"It's the half-Korean sisters from my smoothie club," he'd explained while asking her out. "They've got this band called Kimchi Chocolate Stereo—KCS—and they've written two songs about the club, one of them about Gracie."

"Are they any good?"

Tommy had laughed in response. "Yeah, they're great. Real intense, real loud. So, you wanna go with me? Don't think of it as a date. It's just to get you out of the house for a few hours."

"Is Dave gonna be there too?"

He'd shrugged. "I dunno. I haven't seen Dave since Monday." He'd grinned. "I think he's got a new girl or something."

Though disappointed that the gorgeous Dave Fontaine wouldn't be at the concert, Allie had said yes. She was glad to have somewhere to go. Her niece and nephews had started a loud howling when they'd seen her leaving the house without them, but she wasn't going to spend her life babysitting them.

Her sister Chloe had waved approvingly. "Have fun, sis." She'd tapped her ring finger and laughed. "Get that ring, girl."

At that, her brother-in-law Giorgio had looked up from his newspaper and grumbled his disapproval: "For heaven's sake, Chloe, don't you go putting ideas in the girl's head."

So now here they were. The Hole Faith club (one of two in Boston) was in West Roxbury. It was situated on Spring Street, on the south side of the Morrell Street turning and opposite the VA Medical Center. Allie had been here before, back in the day with friends from work, to see the bands Antichrist Underdog, Decibel Jezebels, and Witchgrrrl.

The Hole Faith was an eerie, spooky place. Gothic décor with lots of satanic and horror symbology—pentagrams and plastic skulls on the walls, fluorescent inverted crosses and such like. Allie recalled reading about a fire breaking out here in which some police officers had been killed. There'd been rumors of Satanism involved, but they'd fizzled out. The building had been restored since then. Now it looked creepier than before.

It also maintained its old welcome: *Hole Faith Club. Enter the Abyss here, you who dare; the pit welcomes all.*

A particularly confrontational advertisement, Allie thought, considering how the building's northeast side directly faced the Arabic Evangelical Baptist Church.

She loitered on the entrance steps while Tommy greeted folks: "Hi, Detective Anderson! Wow, and you brought Detective Futana with you too. I didn't imagine she rocked. She's always struck me as more of a jazz bar kind of foxy lady. You know, with Ol' Blue Eyes crooning sentimental ballads to her."

Tommy's got friends on the force? It was an amusing revelation and made Allie pay attention to the police duo. Detective Anderson was middle-aged, of average height, brawny, and with a jaded expression on his face like he'd seen everything twice over. He was smiling but it wasn't reaching his eyes. His smile looked like something he'd practiced in front of a mirror.

Detective Futana was a very pretty blonde. Tall and dressed in a chic red top and brown leather pants. She giggled as Tommy flattered her. For some reason, Allie found herself getting angry at the attention and compliments Tommy was lavishing on the tall blonde. It wasn't like she wanted him for herself, but he should know better than to praise one woman while escorting another.

Her attention wavered as the three turned to greet others. Apparently, almost the entire Graceful Blend smoothie club were in attendance today. A tall and attractive leather-clad Asian woman had a large video camera with her. Another, shorter, woman was dragging her husband after her toward the club entrance. "Move your ass, Dez," she was saying. "I want us to get good seats."

The band were already inside, doing a sound check. Rays of noise floated through the front entrance like distorted auditory vultures seeking prey.

After a while, Tommy gestured Allie over. She joined him and an elderly woman who was just alighting from a sky-blue Mazda3.

"I'd like you to meet Aunt Grace," Tommy said.

Aunt Grace smiled. "Pleased to meet you, Allie."

Allie shook the old lady's hand. It was pleasantly soft. Luxuriously so; she clearly had money.

Allie's impression of Grace Barbanell was of a rigidly controlled personality. On the surface, the elderly woman seemed a gentle soul, but Allie felt this was a deceptive impression. She sensed a cast-iron core beneath Aunt Grace's placid exterior; a fiery desire just begging to be thwarted. This wasn't a woman you wanted to anger. Angry, she might take things to extremes.

Though attractive, and well dressed in an expensive peach-colored pantsuit and high heels, Grace Barbanell gave off the stifled air of an old maid. She was polished in a way that neutralized rather than emphasized her sexuality. Her costly lilac perfume warned men to keep their distance. Even her impeccably styled brunette hair seemed forbidding.

Or maybe, Allie thought, *that's just my own youthful bias coming into play: I never really imagine people over fifty as having sex lives.*

"Alright, most beautiful auntie, we're ready to rock and roll."

The speaker had just joined them. He was a young man of about Allie's own age. No, she decided after looking him over properly, he was a bit younger than she was. He looked like he'd just escaped the travails and mischief of studenthood. Dark hair and eyes and wearing denim and sneakers. Handsome too, and there was more than a little facial resemblance between he and the old woman. This had to be Greg, the nephew Tommy had mentioned.

Tommy introduced her to Greg. They smiled at each other and shook hands.

Then Aunt Grace took Greg's arm and the four of them walked up into the club.

***

They sat upstairs in the gallery, two or three of them to a table. The lower floor was packed with a standing-room-only crowd.

The opening act was a sultry black singer named Manuela Costa. She performed a simple acoustic set, backed by a lone Spanish guitar.

Allie was envious: In addition to having a knockout figure, Manuela had the kind of voice that made men want to fuck her.

Manuela Costa finished and left the stage. Kimchi Chocolate Stereo came on next to loud applause.

"Ladies and gentlemen . . . KCS!!"

KCS were a five-piece. The band was comprised of three girls (one of whom looked strangely familiar to Allie) and two guys—the guitarist and drummer. One girl handled the keyboards, the other played bass. The third played herself, leaping up and down like a monkey on speed and shrieking like she was being murdered. Or was murdering someone.

Tommy hadn't exaggerated. The band was loud. Really loud. And the girls (they all sang) all sounded like they had throat infections.

"They're great!" Tommy enthused. He sipped his beer and stamped his feet to the beat.

Allie wasn't sure 'great' was the word she'd use to describe KCS. The band's sound leapt off the stage at her. She felt like the music was attacking her; trying to batter her into submissive fanbase pulp. She was adrift on waves of jagged rhythm, with vulturine chords waiting to feast on her corpse. But meanwhile, Tommy was nodding happily. She looked around to see if anyone else shared her opinion of the band.

On her left, Detective Futana was also nodding her head to the music. Her companion wasn't though. Detective Anderson looked like he was trying to make sense of what he was hearing, and failing.

She looked right, at Greg and Aunt Grace's table. Oddly enough, there the reverse was the case: Aunt Grace had a smile on her face and was tapping her feet and sipping from her glass of wine. On the other hand, Greg just looked bored. He looked as if, to escort his aunt, he'd made the sacrifice of leaving his extra-hot girlfriend at home and was now really regretting it.

"And now," the lead singer yelled, "we've some special songs for you great people in the audience! We're gonna play two of 'em. This first one's from our new album Psychic Diva Apocalypse. It's titled 'Aunt Grace.' It's about a real-life superwoman!"

At this announcement, a loud cheer went up from everyone on the balcony. The cheer was so loud that those on the ground floor turned to stare. As she looked down at the sea of upturned faces, Allie's gaze locked for a moment with that of a tall man with a shaggy beard and pale eyes. She felt the shock of a connection between them. She felt a momentary chill, as though an infection had been transmitted between them.

Then the eye-contact was broken. By now the band were counting in the song: "One, two, three—hit it!"

The majestic opening chords of *Aunt Grace* flooded Allie's auditory spectrum. The song had a crazy psychobilly groove to it.

Through the wall of noise Allie could just make out the lyrics:

"Aunt Grace owns a special place,
Up in yoghurt cyberspace.
And her drinks always have that kickass taste,
So there's never a slurp, slurp goes to waste,
Aunt Grace, Aunt Grace!"

Then, all of a sudden, Allie stopped paying her attention to the song and shifted it to the singer instead: *Damn if that isn't Lulu Kim on stage! Yes, it is Lulu!*

Allie and Lulu Kim went way, way back. Back in fact to her teenaged years and the night she'd won her first NASCAR race.

Wow, that had been some night. *Teens!* Allie giggled at the memory.

***

After Allie's first NASCAR win, she and her friends had held a celebratory party at her cousin Robbie Michael's house, because his and her parents were down in Florida for the weekend.

That night Allie had gotten so sloshed on Robbie's 'special' spiked punch that she'd fallen asleep in the toilet where she'd crawled to throw up. She'd nodded off with her head leaning on the edge of the toilet bowl like it was a pillow.

Then matters had gotten even dirtier. Lulu Kim—who everyone in their high school (including Allie herself) suspected of repressed dykedom, though no one had ever proved it—had crawled in after her. Lulu (who was even more drunk than Allie) had, on seeing the obstruction of a slouched female body in her way, somehow pulled her skinny athletic form upright and stepped around Allie, then . . . with Allie resting her head on the toilet bowl and Lulu desperate to ease herself, Lulu had pulled up her skirt, pulled down her panties, and then balanced her buttocks at a slant—the left one on the toilet rim, the right buttock on Allie's head. Then, maintaining that precarious position, she began to urinate.

Allie hadn't protested. The weight on her head had just felt like more alcohol filling her brain.

When quizzed later, Lulu said she'd thought Allie's blonde head was part of the toilet bowl rim. That was how drunk they both were.

In retrospect, Allie realized that Lulu Kim had actually done a good job of not pissing on her. She remembered watching the thick yellow stream of piss—and there was A LOT of it—rushing past her nose, looking like Fanta jetting from a soda fountain nozzle, while some instinctive thread of female sanity prevented her from sticking her tongue in it for a drink.

She did, however, stick her right thumb up Lulu's vagina, and began making thrusting in and out motions with it. She'd never been attracted to girls; she'd just wanted to find out if Lulu *was* a lezzie or not. It had taken some contortion not to get her hand drenched by Lulu's endless stream of pee, but she'd managed, approaching the dark-haired vagina from its anal direction with her right hand, which she'd been resting up on the toilet rim too. Touching Lulu's soft pubic hair had felt like she was scrubbing her fingers with a delicate brush.

Lulu hadn't reacted one way or the other to either the sexual penetration or subsequent in/outs. She was fully concentrated on her peeing. Balanced there on Allie's head, she'd kept up her pelvic miracle of urinating into the white crescent of space between Allie's face and the side of the toilet bowl.

When she was finished, Lulu stood up off Allie's face and thumb and pulled her panties up again. Then, about to stagger off to the living room and rejoin the drunken teenage revelry, she'd lost her balance. Her legs had given out, and she'd dropped onto her knees. Next thing, she was grabbing her stomach and vomiting all over the toilet rug.

Allie had stared bemusedly at Lulu, who'd finally wound up sitting on the floor beside her, her head balanced on the other side of the toilet bowl.

"Damn, girl," she'd said comfortingly, "you shoulda puked in the toilet. Now Robbie's gonna be mad at both of us."

Then, to finally confirm if Lulu was gay or not, she'd leaned forward and kissed her on the lips, their vomit coating notwithstanding. The act was a natural progression with their mouths so close together on the toilet.

Lulu had huffily shoved her away. "G'off me, ya repressed dyke—ur mouf stinks. Go lick a fish."

That said, they'd both passed out, to the strains of TLC's *Waterfalls*.

***

Remembering now, Allie chortled. Yeah, that had been one crazy party. Robbie's mother had been mad at them for the mess they'd made of her house. Robbie's father had been even madder at them because they'd drank all his booze: that punch bowl had had *everything* in it—whiskey, brandy, wine, sherry, vodka, rum, bitters—whatever his 15-year-old son could raid from the home bar.

Allie hadn't been welcome at her uncle and aunt's house again until she turned eighteen. As her Aunt Nicole had explained to her mother: "We don't want her in our home again until she can go to jail for trashing it."

***

The *Aunt Grace* song finished to massive applause.

"Aunt Grace, everyone—she's here, live in the flesh!" Lulu Kim pointed up at the gallery. Once again, all heads in the nightclub swiveled towards the rear balcony.

Greg helped Aunt Grace to her feet. She waved. At that moment Grace Barbanell looked truly gorgeous. She had a smile on her lips and tears in her eyes. Everyone cheered, the Graceful Blend smoothie club members loudest of all.

Aunt Grace sat back down. The audience looked back towards the stage. Lulu began introducing the next song. "Now, guys, this one's from our first album, *Social Messiah!* It's about that nutty Miller Family. *Americannibal!!!*"

"Eat eat, sweet human meat!
We're obsessed with the taste of roast flesh!
Delicious, Delicious,
We're so vicious, 'cos you're delicious!"

As the band resumed rocking, Allie got to her feet.

"I need to use the restroom," she whispered in Tommy's ear.

She slipped out into the corridor that ran alongside the gallery. She felt worried. For a second time, her eyes had locked with those of the burly man in the crowd. She didn't know if this was because he was looking at her, or because she was looking at him.

Well I wouldn't have noticed him looking at me if I wasn't looking at him, would I?

And even if he had been checking her out, what did it matter? She wasn't here alone. But there had been something nasty in his gaze. Something which, even at a distance, upset her.

Immersed in her thoughts, Allie completely ignored the fact that there were restrooms on the second floor. She descended the steps to the ground floor and walked round to the toilets there. Arriving outside the ladies' restroom, however, she met a long line of young women waiting to use the facilities. She considered waiting too, but several of the girls were smoking and the smoke made her feel claustrophobic. It hung heavy in the air, like fog or dissolving ghosts.

She decided to come back in a while. In the meantime she'd get some fresh air out in the parking lot. She turned and left the corridor.

Outside, she sat on the hood of Tommy's Toyota Camry and thought, while the moon shone down on her face. Tommy was parked around the side of the club, so that she was in relative solitude. The loneliness of the place fit her mood. She hadn't entirely left the concert ambience though. Her feet felt the bass vibrations of the band's music coming through the ground.

Life was a funny thing, it seemed to her at that moment. No one honestly knew where the River of Days was bearing them off to. Look at the Kim sisters, for example: from nerdy high-school brats who couldn't get laid, now the pair were rock stars. In the short silences between the songs, Tommy had explained that the band had just finished recording their sophomore CD and were now working on videos. That was the reason there were so many cameras recording them tonight; they were hoping to use some of the concert footage in the videos. The leather-clad Asian lady with the video camera whom Allie had noticed in the parking lot was their elder sister Jojo, who was also their manager.

And me? Allie asked herself sadly. *Six months ago I was on top of the world. I had everything a girl could want: a great career, money, and the guy I loved. And now, what have I got?*

She understood that she was exaggerating her case to convince herself of her misery. Considered objectively, things weren't anywhere near as bad at that. In her case the worst was definitely over. Ancient history, with no chance of an emotional archeologist unearthing the same mistakes.

Brian and Valentina Ruzza have broken my heart and gotten away with it. So what? Poop happens, right? All I need to do is pick myself up and get on with my life. I'm young and well-educated and . . .

Yes, that was being objective about things. But Allie currently didn't feel objective. Tonight her subjective judgment leaned heavily towards a healthy dose of self-pity. Tommy was nice, for sure, and she could read in his eyes that he liked her, but . . .

But what was best for a person wasn't always what they wanted.

If only Dave were here with me tonight, if only he'd been the one who'd brought me to the concert, and not Tommy. Then I'd feel a whole lot better and . . .

She wallowed for a while in her maudlin emotions; enjoying the dark pathos of desperation they cloaked her with like a widow's clothes and veil.

But then, suddenly, she became aware of a presence nearby. A dark and unpleasant presence.

At first she shrugged it off. The Hole Faith nightclub itself had an unhealthy ambience to it. The strip of lawn bordering the parking lot boasted sickly grass and flowers, as if the flora had grown from urine-drenched earth.

However, her sense of something bad in the parking lot increased. The night now felt grimy, as though the air had abruptly thickened and dirt had been added to it. It was an spooky feeling to have.

She didn't look around. She didn't want to. Just in case, there was actually something there to see which shouldn't be there. Just like how right now, she thought she heard someone breathing by the rear of the car.

Alright, it's time I was leaving here. I have to pee anyway.

Allie got down off the hood of the Camry. She was about walking away when a gruff male voice called from behind her: "Hey, lady, don't go. Hold on a sec."

She didn't look back. She didn't wait either. Waiting to talk to strange men in deserted parking lots at night was a sure-fire way to get kidnapped. Allie walked off as fast as she could. She prepared to run if he came after her. As she went she wondered what had possessed her to come sit in the dark out here, while everyone else was having a good time inside.

"Hey, wait!"

Yeah, right; like I'm naive or something? The corner of the building was only a few yards off. At first Allie heard the man coming after her. Heavy footsteps, their tempo speaking of a quick pace. But then, just when she was about breaking into a run and screaming for help, he seemed to give up. His footfalls ceased.

Around the corner she heard voices. A male voice saying, "Those Korean girls are so loud that I can't even tell if they're a good or bad band. Each song they play is just a stacked layer of noise. Whatever happened to good ol' heavy metal that actually made sense, huh? Stuff like AC/DC and Mötley Crüe and Judas Priest? Nowadays, each band I hear is louder than bombs going off. It's like they're fighting the Gulf War in there."

A laughing female voice replied, "You're just old, man!"

Allie turned the corner, and bumped into Detectives Anderson and Futana.

It took a moment or two for her to steady herself and get her wind back. She was panting really hard. By then Detective Futana had recognized her. "Hey, you're Tommy's date, aren't you? I saw you upstairs. What's wrong with you? Don't you feel okay?"

Allie nodded, her right hand tightly clutching her left breast to soothe her rapidly beating heart. Then she gasped out, "I-I-I th-think s-s-someone's after me. A guy. He's round the back there."

Detective Futana instantly had a gun in her hand. So fast, Allie imagined the blonde had done a magic trick. "Is that so?" Futana asked, her eyes turning cold. She nodded at her partner. "Let's go get the bastard."

Anderson nodded back. He too pulled out his gun. "Yeah, let's check it out."

While speaking though, Allie had heard a car start up. The detectives were still walking towards the edge of the building when a brown pickup truck drove past them.

Anderson looked at Futana. "You think that's our guy?"

She shrugged. "Might be." She stepped forward and looked around the corner at the side parking lot. She looked back at Anderson. "No one else back there, so I guess that's him leaving."

All three of them turned towards the pickup. The vehicle—a battered brown Ford F150—was already at the club gate. At this distance, the driver looked to be a large, bearded fellow. Allie thought it was the same man who'd been staring at her inside the hall, the one with the pale chilling eyes.

The most remarkable thing about the departing pickup truck was how muddy it was.

"That's a farmer's ride if ever I saw one," Futana said. "And believe me, I know how dirty they can get. I spent my teen holidays on my uncle's farm."

Anderson holstered his gun again. "Ain't that guy ever heard of a carwash?" he asked.

Allie knew what he meant. The mud was everywhere on the pickup truck, like splashed brown paint. The hubcaps were completely coated with it.

The truck was outside the gate now and pulling away.

Futana was still holding her service pistol. "Whatta ya say? Should we go after him?"

Anderson looked at Allie. "Did he hurt you in any way? Grab you or anything like that?"

"Or pull a knife?"

She shook her head. "No," she admitted. "He-he-he just scared me." Now she felt embarrassed. The man hadn't actually done anything wrong to her. There was no point in getting him in trouble with the police. It was just a misunderstanding. It had just been her nerves. And . . . and that strange ambience she'd sensed for a moment. That *evil* ambience.

Futana nodded at Anderson. "We can let it go then." She put her gun away too, then grinned at them both. "Alright, you two, I wanna finish watching the concert. I love this band—they totally rock!"

Allie followed them back inside, while Anderson groaned, "Laurie, my ears can't stand it!"

CHAPTER 11

The Man

Once certain the police weren't chasing him, the driver of the brown Ford F150 pickup truck turned the vehicle west. In five minutes he was on Route 135 and heading home.

As the man drove, his feelings were mixed. It was just too bad he couldn't hang around for the rest of the concert. The band had been great. A friend of his who knew their manager had gotten some tickets and given him one. He'd particularly liked that *Aunt Grace* track.

And that was when he'd noticed the girl: the blonde up in the gallery.

Then, when he'd looked back up at the balcony again, he'd seen her walking away from her table. He'd decided to take a chance on seeing if she was going outside. So he'd left the concert himself, hoping to run into her.

The man was disappointed that the young woman had run off. He'd just wanted to say hello and maybe get her autograph. He was certain he knew her from somewhere. She was a celebrity. She looked like a girl he'd seen on TV in the past; used to race stock cars with NASCAR.

But the way she'd taken off like the hounds of Hell were after her—damn, some folks were just crazy. Maybe that was why she'd stopped racing? (He'd not seen her onscreen for years.)

She'd almost gotten him in trouble though. Big trouble. He'd had to get out of there fast. And, on noticing the glint of metal from the police officer's guns as he'd driven past them, he realized he'd been just in time too. If those two cops had discovered what he was carrying in the back of his truck, there'd have been hell to pay.

He was well out of the Boston suburbs now, approaching the city of Framingham. There was little traffic on the road. He parked the truck and got out to piss. He stood there in the night, humming to himself.

Yeah, he thought, *I was real lucky back there!*

He zipped up again and returned to the truck. On a whim, he decided to have a look in the back of the vehicle. A heavy white tarp lay draped over the rear's contents. He slid the white covering aside and shone a flashlight on the two motionless forms it had hidden from view.

One of them was routine: another tarp-wrapped slimy skeleton en route to its unmarked grave in the woods.

The other body was still alive, a wino drugged on alcohol. He'd found the wino in the alley beside his brother's pet shop. There'd been no one else around, so he'd figured, 'why not?' and humped the old guy into the rear of his truck.

He grinned as he covered the bodies again. The creature would appreciate a snack. The creature's name was Boku Ke Houzz, but lots of times they called it just 'Boku.' It didn't eat much, maybe once or twice a month, but he liked watching it feed. He enjoyed seeing the terror on the victims' faces as Boku Ke Houzz swallowed them and they knew there was nothing in the world they could do to save themselves. That too, was why he generally fed them to the creature feet first. He loved watching their eyes bulge out in pain. This generally happened when they were almost completely swallowed; when their feet had just reached the creature's belly and it began secreting jelly on them to dissolve them. There had to be few things worse than feeling your flesh agonizingly turn to liquid while you were still alive and conscious.

He smirked as he climbed back into the front of the pickup truck. Sure, a few of the others didn't approve of his fun and games. They said he was being needlessly sadistic. The self-righteous pricks could go screw themselves. *He* was in charge of looking after the damn thing. He'd not wanted the job; but they'd insisted. And he'd been doing a damn good job of it too. For the past eight years since they'd brought Boku Ke Houzz in from SADE's Outerness, he'd been looking after it and feeding it its fortnightly victuals.

He laughed as he drove along the night road. The cops would have a cascade of heart attacks—major law enforcement coronary failure—if they ever guessed how many skeletons he'd actually buried in the past decade.

He began wondering how he'd gotten away with it for so long. (He was a simple man, and didn't really think too much. It was why he was so good at his morbid job of beast keeper. Anyone else would have had too much of a conscience to continue.)

But still, he thought, *I've been burying stiffs for ages and the police have only just cottoned on? Now that's just odd.*

No, he corrected himself quickly, *the cops never actually cottoned on—it was the blasted rain that flushed the evidence to the surface. If that hadn't happened, they'd still not realize a thing!*

Finally, as the man swung the Ford truck onto the dark side road that led to the woods where he intended burying the latest skeleton, an understanding came to his dull mind: *It's Boku that's doing it. The damn thing is protecting me!*

He was amused for a moment. But then he had a reality check. *Nah, it's not protecting me. The creature's really protecting itself. It doesn't want to go back to where it came from.*

With that knowledge in his mind, he reached his destination. He parked the muddy pickup truck, got down, and then got to work carrying the wrapped skeleton into the trees, to the new spot he'd selected for burials.

At this rate, he thought, *soon I'll have filled the whole damn Bay State with corpses.*

The thought amused him immensely. He hummed happily as he dug his hole. After a while, without realizing it, he began humming the melody to *Aunt Grace*.

CHAPTER 12

Dave & Petra

While Tommy Collins attended the KCS concert with Allie, Dave Fontaine was in bed with Petra Velli.

Petra Velli was the wife of Boston's top mobster Marko Velli.

Petra was currently flat on her belly with her legs spread while Dave slipped his penis into her vagina from behind.

Not into her ass. No. She'd made that very clear to Dave—he was to leave her anus alone no matter what erotic inspiration took him: "Marko's been in jail so long he's apparently forgotten what a pussy's for. Or maybe he turned gay in there and is trying to keep it in the closet." She'd pouted in anger at Dave's amusement at her comment. "No, don't laugh—I'm being serious here. All Marko wants now is my asshole. And he never goes gently back there either. You'd think I was some snitch jailbird he was trying to teach a lesson in respect. I don't remember when last I took a crap that didn't hurt like my rectum was prolapsing."

"Leave him for me," Dave had joked. "We'll be together."

Petra's eyes had narrowed. "Don't joke like that, Dave. I might take you seriously."

"Please, take me serious, baby. I frigging am serious."

"Then don't be. Marko would murder us both. In fact, if he even suspects that we're seeing each other, we're as good as dead."

"So we'll run away together then."

"Stop, Dave. Please. Just fuck me."

They'd left it like that and gotten down to the sex.

Now, with her squirming with pleasure under him, the threat of Marko Velli was all but forgotten. Dave concentrated on satisfying them both. He kissed her neck and licked her ears. She moaned and purred with contentment. He thrust deep into her sweetness, loving the feel of her soft buttocks on his thighs. He slid his hands under her body and gripped her breasts and squeezed.

"Oh, gosh," she groaned and trembled. "Oh, I just love you, Davey!"

Oh, baby, how I wish you did, Dave thought back at her as he felt his orgasm approaching.

***

Petra Velli was thirty-four. She was pretty, though a little out of shape after having three kids for Marko.

It was hard not to commit serial adultery when your husband was doing seven years in jail for various criminal offences; even when you knew how violent he was.

In this regard, Petra was living a charmed life. It was always the men she slept with who suffered.

Petra Velli wasn't the kind of woman who thought deeply about life. Though well-educated, she never concerned her mind with issues beyond the present, as in the immediate satisfaction of her social and physical desires. And so, in her mind, she never really questioned the chain of misfortunes that dogged those men who slept with her.

Men like Hulk Kowalski, for instance. Or Tricky Hansen.

Petra simply refused to think deeply about such things. If she had, she'd have quickly realized that her husband was engineering her lovers' episodes of bad luck.

Marko Velli was old-fashioned. He was dedicated to Petra because she was the mother of his children. For that reason, he was willing to overlook a lot. Particularly when he'd been in jail. But now that he was out again, all Petra's nonsense had to stop. Marko was sick and tired of it. In addition to his wife's serial sluthood showing her disregard for him, it also made him look silly in gang circles. It was annoying to be in a room full of hard men and find yourself wondering how many of them had fucked your wife.

Petra, however, wasn't smart enough to realize it was time to keep her legs closed. Besides, she really liked Dave Fontaine a lot. She thought she might even be falling in love with him.

***

They finished off the erotic session with Petra on top, squeezing her breasts together while she ground her crotch down on Dave. She came loudly, then collapsed on him, her body trembling from how good the pleasure had been. Damn, it had been good. All her nerve ends were tingling.

He came almost immediately after she did. He held her tight, feeling content at that moment, even if she didn't love him.

Love. Dave Fontaine was feeling an unfamiliar emotion. True love for a female was something he'd not experienced since high school, when Kate Sutton had broken his heart, ditching him for his best friend Justin on the night of their senior prom. Since then Dave had gotten his own back on the female of the species by seducing and leaving them. But now, looking at Mrs. Velli, her light brown hair spilling down over his arms to the bed sheet, he wondered what had happened. How had his plan to remain carefree and easy gone wrong?

So, just like that, you're hooked again, huh? Well, it's about damn time, I guess.

Petra fell asleep on him. Dave gently rolled her off his body. Then he got out of bed. He lit a cigarette. Then, naked, he walked to the bedroom window and looked out into the night.

They were in the Velli's beach house down in Quincy. Far off to the northeast Dave imagined he saw the Logan Airport control tower, perceivable now only as a pencil of stacked yellow lights. Every few minutes, sets of colored dots—red, green, and blue LEDs—lifted skyward like multicolored electric fireflies, destination unknown. At intervals, other lights settled down to earth.

Closer to home, Dave watched the beach and the ocean. The dark waves bore their elongated and fractured reflection of the moon left and right.

His thoughts drifted similarly. Every now and again, he looked from the window to the woman on the bed.

What the hell have I gotten myself into? But I'm crazy about this woman.

It wasn't her looks that had hooked him so bad. Yeah, for certain, Petra was a looker. But he'd had lots of other beautiful woman, so many of them that he no longer even remembered their names or faces. This struck Dave as a sort (or a symptom) of emotional disease, one in which partners were consumed with the regularity (and desperation) of pills to stave off . . . what? The death of his soul? He had to be using the women to buffer something in himself. Or were they his protection against loneliness? A parasitical, pathological, incurable loneliness? Or was he still scared of rejection? Was it that deep down inside himself, he still hadn't gotten over Kate Sutton dumping him at the prom? For sure, she'd made him a laughingstock that night, leaving his side and crossing the dancehall to start kissing Justin. And afterwards, the pair had left together, with Kate loudly asking Justin if he had condoms in his car.

But, Dave considered, *that was fifteen years ago. Surely I'm over that emotional hump now!*

He disembarked from that train of thought. He was looking at the bed again. Petra had just turned in her sleep. Now she lay on her left side, facing him with an arm hooked over the edge of the bed. She looked so pure and lovely. The picture-perfect representation of his heart's utmost desire.

He took a drag on his cigarette, then crushed it out in an ashtray.

Unfortunately, he sadly reflected, *the lady I love is married to the most dangerous man in New England. Why the hell couldn't I have felt this way about Manuela?*

(The beautiful black singer Manuela Costa had been Dave's last girlfriend. They'd split up when he began fearing for his life because of her crazy temper.)

Petra reached around in bed, feeling behind her. Her fingers probed the sheets, unconsciously searching for Dave. The lack of him beside her woke her up. She opened her eyes and stared at him. At first she smiled, but on seeing the hangdog look on his face her sunny hazel gaze clouded.

"Don't tell me you're still thinking of us running away together. Forget it, baby, it'll never work." She attempted another smile. "Please, light me a smoke, will you?"

He lit a cigarette for her.

She sat propped up on pillows. For a while she smoked in silence. The cigarette smoke uncoiled from her mouth like a snake's tongue. She liked Dave but he was oh, so unstable. If she made the mistake of leaving Marko for him, it wouldn't be long before he dumped her for another woman. It would be silly to set herself up for a fall.

He still looked upset though; and she didn't want that. He was a good lover, more patient in bed than her husband. Marko made love as though he was having a business meeting. His lovemaking (at least since he'd gotten back from prison) was abrupt and fast and furious.

It was fun too; but not always. And, to complicate matters, there was his current painful interest in her back door. She wondered how porn stars did it—those ladies seemed to love anal. They all acted like sodomy was even better than the real thing. Or was that all pretense? Just lies one built an erotic career on?

She felt in the mood to make love a little longer. She crooked a finger at Dave, demanding that he come to her. He however remained by the window, staring at her through hooded eyes, his feelings unreadable in his face.

He looks tormented, she thought. *Maybe he really is in love with me. At least he thinks he is.*

She sighed. She'd need to take the initiative now. *Else we'll become embroiled in another nonsense discussion about eloping. And that isn't ever going to happen.*

She stubbed out her cigarette in the ashtray on the nightstand. She got out of bed, stretched, and walked over to Dave. She leaned against him. He was stiff and unresponsive, his penis hanging despondently. She needed him in the reverse condition: body relaxed; penis stiff. She rubbed her breasts against him. She gripped his buttocks and danced against him and kissed his neck and chin. In a short while she felt him responding. His manhood woke up. It began rising to the occasion. When it was risen enough, she got down on her knees and took him in her mouth. He gasped. She sucked harder, stopping every now and then to swirl her tongue around the head of the turgid penis and lick the split on its underside. As she tended to his erection, her own excitement rose. Her sex became a seething puddle of erotic juice.

Finally she dragged the moaning man to the bed and slipped a condom on him. Then she got on her hands and knees. She slapped her ass with a hand. "I'm your bitch, dog; don't let me down."

He slid into her from behind. She let out a loud groan of delight. He began thrusting. She held on tight to the bedcovers and let herself go, merging with the ecstasy.

***

Afterwards, they didn't talk much. They had no time to. Petra had to hurry home. Marko was due back soon from a late night meeting.

"Honey," she said as they walked to her car—a red Audi A5 Cabriolet, "it's not as though I don't have similarly deep feelings of love for you. It's just that I'm not suicidal." She turned in the flower-lined driveway and planted a lingering kiss on Dave's lips. "Interpret the motion of my tongue, baby; I love you too. But . . . the only way I'll ever leave Marko Velli *alive* is if he dies." Before Dave could respond to that, she added, "And if seven years of prison food didn't kill the bastard, what will?"

"More like, *who* will, you mean?"

She got into the car. She looked out at him and laughed. "What? You're planning on being my hero?"

"I wish you wouldn't joke about it."

"Please forget it. Besides which, he's the father of my kids. I'd never forgive myself if I ordered a hit on him. Get in the car, Dave. Please?"

He got in and they left. The front gate was automatic; it opened and shut by itself.

She dropped him off at South Station to catch the Needham Line. He was going to join his friend Tommy at a rock concert down in West Roxbury.

"Look, Dave," she said as he was about getting out of the Audi, "please forget about killing Marko, okay? Put it completely out of your mind, alright, darling?"

He looked sad. "And us?"

"It's *because of us* that I want you to forget this madness about killing my husband. Lots of other guys—and I mean, really tough guys—have tried to murder Marko, both in and out of jail. They all failed. If you try, you'll fail too. Davey, honey, I don't want to lose you. I want us to enjoy what we have now for as long as we can."

She regarded him sternly. "So, do we have an agreement? No more planning to bump off Beauty's beast?"

He nodded. He creased his face into a tough-guy parody, and in an equally comic machismo-dripping voice said, "Oh, alright, dame. He lives, but only 'cos ya say so."

She giggled with delight. "Oh, come here, you!" She leaned over and kissed him again, her light brown hair fluttering in a gust of wind, her hazel eyes alight with delight. She really was fond of him. She really was. It was all just so tangled up and confusing; in her experience, illicit romances always were. But then, so long as Marko didn't find out, there was no danger.

Dave walked into the train station. Petra put her car in gear and drove off. She was pleased with herself. The sex had been great and she felt energized.

Of course, like all adulteresses, Petra Velli prided herself on being discreet where her extramarital activities were concerned. It never occurred to her that her husband might suspect she was cheating on him.

CHAPTER 13

Anderson

He got up, looked around, tried to remember if there was anything he'd forgotten. *No,* he finally decided, *I didn't come here with anything.*

"Are you okay?" she asked.

He smiled at her. "I think so. I've been distracted as hell since yesterday."

"Is it Laurie again? And that crazy case?"

He grimaced. "Yeah." His eyes flickered to the front door. He really had to leave this place, to leave her. How could he possibly tell her that she was the cause of his unease? No, he couldn't tell her he was worried about her—not because he didn't dare to, but because she'd likely take it the wrong way. She'd either interpret his concern to mean he pitied her (which she hated), or as intent to get back into her panties again (which he wouldn't mind doing—he loved what was in her panties—but there was no time).

He stared again at the front door, willing himself to leave the room, steeling himself to take those five or six steps which would remove him from this place where he no longer wanted to be.

Now she began to look concerned. "Tom, are you *really* okay? You're not acting like your normal deadpan self. Like the emotionless man I love."

He almost screamed at her, "No, I'm not okay, okay? Use your eyes, will you?" but instead, he favored her with a sad smile. "It seems like it's going to rain . . . I always feel crappy on days like this. It reminds me of the day Dad left home for Vietnam and didn't return. The weather was like this too, overcast like God was about filming the Second World War again. When the sky's like this, I can't help but think of bloody mud and trenches and dying soldiers."

Once again his eyes leapt to the door, and now, a kind of anxiety began bubbling in his mind . . .

***

Tom Anderson was dreaming. Like he often did, he was dreaming of his ex-wife Nancy. Most times these weren't pleasant dreams. However, sometimes in his dreams he and Nancy achieved the sort of emotional rapport they'd lacked in real life.

Without waking, his mind shifted to another dream, one in which he was kissing Laurie Futana. And then they'd begun getting naked together.

The horrible thing was that he'd forgotten her intersex status. He was about going down on her when he saw her penis. The damn organ was hard and curved and telling him that it really, really loved him . . .

***

Anderson woke up. He wasn't amused. He knew why he'd dreamt about Futana. It was that scene in the car when he'd dropped her off.

After the Kimchi Chocolate Stereo concert he'd driven her home. And then . . . she'd kissed him. On the lips. He'd parked outside her apartment block and turned to wish her goodnight. And that was when it happened. She'd slipped across the seat and planted one on him.

She'd looked like she'd thought he might kiss her back. But he didn't. Instead, he'd pushed her away. He didn't shove her. He just gently disentangled himself from her embrace.

"No," he'd said slowly. "We ain't gonna be like that, Laurie. No, we ain't. We work together; we don't fuck together."

She'd looked hurt. "Sorry, Tom, I couldn't curb the impulse. It's been ages since I kissed anyone."

"It ain't you, baby," he'd said to soften the rejection. "I never date any of my partners." Then he'd laughed. "Maybe if you quit the force?"

Which he knew wouldn't ever happen. Just like himself, Laurie loved hunting down felons.

Then, in a completely uncharacteristic action for him, he'd pulled her to him and kissed her. He'd kissed her deeply and passionately, just like he'd used to kiss Nancy. Then he'd gently disentangled himself from her again.

"Wow!" she'd said, a glowing expression on her face. "What was that about?"

"That's just to let you know that you don't disgust me in any way. I'm not turned off by you 'cos you're different or anything like that. I'm just not dating you on principles."

He'd laughed, and she'd laughed with him. She had tears in her eyes. But when she spoke again, she sounded pleased:

"Alright, Tom, I get you. Thanks. You're a great guy."

"I dunno know 'bout *great*; but I'm a guy any day."

She'd leaned over and kissed him again, this time on the cheek. Then she'd gotten out of the car and walked inside. She'd not looked back.

Now, alone in the darkness of his bedroom, Tom Anderson reviewed the evening. *Yeah,* he thought, *I handled that well. I really like the woman, but . . . well, I ain't about sucking dick just to have a politically correct romantic life. Oh no, I'm not.*

He got up, went to have a pee, then went back to bed.

CHAPTER 14

Anderson & Futana

"Do either of you guys know anything about cryptozoology?"

It was ten o'clock the next morning, and both Anderson and Futana were back at the State Police Crime Lab in Maynard. They were seated in Dr. Stephanie Richards's office.

The doctor was a brunette in her mid-forties. She was good-looking but severe, always wearing her dark hair pulled tightly back, and never wearing makeup. Her only item of jewelry was her wedding ring. A framed photo on her desk showed her husband and daughter.

"Cryptozoology? What the hell's that?" Futana asked, a puzzled look on her face. She was feeling good this morning; almost as though she could still feel Anderson's lips pressed on hers.

Stephanie Richards looked questioningly at Anderson.

He shrugged back. "You better just tell us what it is, Steph. I'm just as lost as Laurie."

She nodded at the two seated opposite her. "Cryptozoology is the study of mythological animals. Imaginary beasts. Cryptids, they're called." She sat back and looked at them both, giving time for her words to sink in.

"Imaginary animals," Anderson repeated.

It took he and Futana half a minute to work out what Stephanie was getting at. Then Futana asked, "You're telling us we're looking for Bigfoot? That a damn sasquatch killed all those people and buried their skeletons?"

"Yeah," Anderson added. "But, if it's Bigfoot killing everyone, how come all the slime on them then? Is he pooping on them, or what?"

Stephanie Richards sighed. "Guys, I wish this were that simple. Hunting Bigfoot would make your lives easy. What you guys are looking for can't even exist. Notice I didn't say *doesn't* exist—I said, it *can't* exist."

"Alright," Anderson agreed, "so the damn thing can't exist, but yet it does. So what is it exactly?"

"We don't know," Stephanie replied. "We've no idea."

There was silence across the desk for a moment. Then Futana asked slowly, "Steph, if you don't know *what* it is, how can you be so sure it can't exist?"

Anderson nodded his agreement.

The doctor opened a folder on her desk. She was obviously angry at this puzzle throwing her carefully organized scientific life out of joint. She tapped the top paper in the folder with a pencil. "How much do you guys know about human or animal DNA?"

For the next ten minutes Stephanie Richards took them through a long scientific discourse. Afterwards, they asked her questions.

On leaving her office, Anderson and Futana were certain of only three things: First, that the creature they were after was very large; second, that it was very deadly (the slime coating the recovered skeletons had been confirmed to be corrosive while still fresh); and third, that they had no idea what it looked like. None whatsoever.

Like Dr. Richards had painstakingly explained, they were hunting something that *couldn't* exist. Something that had just appeared out of the blue.

Something horrible and terrifying.

Something that was still out there feeding.

There was something else too. One of the more recent skeletons had been slashed with an axe. Once again though, because of the slime coating the bones, there was no way of telling if the wound had been inflicted before or after the woman's death.

Anderson hoped it wasn't before. Because if that was the case, it meant someone was keeping and feeding the damn monster.

CHAPTER 15

Greg

On Friday, Greg's mother Barbara came to visit.

That Friday wasn't a good one for Greg. Aunt Grace was having one of her nasty days. She'd chewed him out for—of all things—upsetting Jojo Kim.

Greg couldn't imagine what Jojo must have told her. He was certain she'd begun putting her "your balls are in my hands" plan into effect. Alright, let her, he thought defiantly; she'd soon discover that blood was thicker than water. Or would she? Aunt Grace really liked Jojo Kim. It would be the devil to pay for Greg if Jojo fabricated some story about him trying to rape her. It wouldn't be hard, all she needed to do was get her sisters to confirm her story.

That morning Aunt Grace called Greg "A dumb, no-good gold-digger," and also a "Shadow of a young man." She also called him a "Waste of your dead father's genes and *my* money," and most hurtful of all, she called him "Looks-for-brains," which Greg interpreted as being the male version of a 'dumb blonde.'

That 'looks-for-brains' crack really angered Greg. He resolved to make her a particularly potent smoothie that day.

For this particular smoothie, he went 'vintage,' using two Seka videos and a Jenna Jameson one as penile inspiration. The videos worked a treat. He was delighted at the amount of semen he spurted over the cherry, pineapple, apricot and pear mix in the blender.

He'd just finished blending the semen smoothie for Aunt Grace when his mother rang the doorbell.

Aunt Grace was out doing some shopping. Greg answered the door.

"Hi, mom."

"Hello, darling," Barbara said sweetly, kissing him on the cheek and stepping inside.

In the three years that her son had been living with her sister (it was now seven years since her husband's death.), Barbara Barbanell (she'd reverted back to her maiden name after her disastrous second marriage) had turned her life around for the better. The woman who stepped out of the black BMW sports convertible that afternoon was nothing like the scared person who'd run to Grace for help after being swindled out of her entire fortune.

Tall, sleek, well-groomed, and expensively dressed (she *did* own a flourishing boutique), Barbara swept up into the house. She'd come both to see her son (who hardly ever came over to Raynham to see her) and also to discuss some business with her sister.

Surrounded by a cloud of her perfume, Greg shut the door behind her and followed her into the living room. Then, feeling suddenly pressed, he excused himself to use the toilet.

Immediately he did so, Barbara got up to get herself a drink of water from the kitchen.

When Greg returned from peeing, his mother wasn't in the living room. Half a minute later he discovered her in the kitchen, drinking Aunt Grace's just prepared smoothie.

Unable to do more than nod miserably as Barbara swallowed the semen-tainted drink and licked her lips in delight, Greg swore off *ever* ejaculating anywhere outside of a woman's body again. He wasn't even going to masturbate again in his life. Not ever!

"Gracie's sure taught you a thing or two about making these things," Barbara said with a sigh of deep appreciation. With a final lick of her lips she downed the rest of the drink.

She set the glass down then asked, "Hey, dear, is everything alright with you? Why, you look positively miserable."

He didn't reply her quickly enough so she turned to examining the magnetic clips on the fridge-freezer doors. There were six of these: two blue turtles, a beer can, a shopping basket full of fruit, and two pink rabbits eating carrots. Beneath one of the rabbits was a long list of things to buy, mostly smoothie stuff. The list was written in Grace's precise secretarial hand, on pretty yellow paper with green lines. Barbara flicked the list with a finger. She'd given Grace the rabbit clamps; she'd bought a set of twenty a year ago and distributed the surplus to friends and family. Two more 'rabbits' hung from the side of the microwave oven.

She looked at Greg in amusement. "Are smoothies all you two ever drink? Don't you get the runs?"

Greg had now recovered himself. "Mom, we need to talk . . ."

"Barbara!" Grace's voice rang out then from the entrance hall. "Where are you, dear?"

Barbara patted Greg on the cheek. "Later, darling. I've got to go see the elder sister."

Greg watched her leave. Then he dumped the besmirched smoothie glass in the kitchen sink. *Well—thanks for ruining that for me, mom!*

Hearing his aunt's voice had just reminded him of how angry with her he was. His anger dented his resolve. Yes, he planned on stopping his messing with Aunt Grace's drinks, but . . . she definitely deserved at least one more dose of punishment, one last spurt of testicular humiliation . . . and after that he'd quit for good.

Yes, he was going to make Aunt Grace just one more 'special.'

But where to get more semen? He definitely wasn't up to masturbating again; Jenna Jameson and Seka had wrung his balls dry. Besides, it was too risky with his mother in the house.

Then he grinned evilly. Thankfully, he had a replacement: Debbie had slept over last night after they'd gone out clubbing. They'd made love twice at the window, with Debbie claiming she'd seen several great horned owls.

Carrying a disposable plastic cup, Greg left the kitchen. The living room was empty. He hurried up the stairs. His mother and aunt were in his aunt's bedroom. Aunt Grace's bedroom door was slightly ajar; the two female voices filtered through the crack. They were laughing about some loser they'd known as young women who'd just gone to jail for tax evasion.

Greg went softly now so they'd not hear him. He hurried to his room. There he looked in the trash bin for his used condoms. There were two of these: one for last night, the other for this morning. He sniffed the condoms. He inhaled their leftover whiff of Debbie's vagina with relish. But he had urgent business here. He untied the knots in both rubbers and emptied their contents into the plastic cup. He re-trashed the rubbers then headed downstairs again.

Passing his aunt's room (her door was still slightly ajar), he heard his mother say loudly, "A hundred and fifty grand should do." His aunt's reply was, "Seeing as you'll never pay me back, what do I get in return?" To which the answer was, "What more do you want? You've already got Greg."

He'd been about hurrying past, but now he froze.

"I'll give you three hundred thousand," Aunt Grace said. "But then it's agreed between us that he's my son now, not yours."

There was a short pause, then Barbara replied. "Alright, but . . . how are you going to do that?" Her voice held a tinge of amusement. "He's too old for adoption . . . oh . . . or are you going to insist that he change his surname? Greg'll never do that, Gracie; you know how much he loved his dad."

"Nothing like that. I *like* him having the Madden surname. I just want it understood between *us* that he's *my* son now."

"Do you want it in writing? A contract?"

"Don't be silly, Barbara. You just swear to me and I'll take your word for it."

"Oh, alright then. I really don't see though why you couldn't just have gotten married and had kids of your own. Or even have had a child outside of wedlock. Gracie, it's not the fifties anymore."

"There wasn't any other man whose kids I wanted, that's why. I'd already lost the only man I'd ever . . ." She began sniffling loudly.

"Oh, Gracie, you're not gonna start on that again, are you? Please just stop crying. Please stop. I'm really sorry about what happened back then. I never even suspected anything."

"Oh, alright. It's just so damn sad that we can't ever rewind the past. Okay, so back to today. Greg—I want him. Deal or no deal?"

"Oh, alright. Gimme the money and he's *your* kid."

"For good?"

"For good."

"You swear it?"

"Cross my heart and hope to die if I lie."

Greg padded away. He couldn't really comprehend what he'd just heard. *I'm twenty-one years old, this is the USA, and my mom just sold me to her sister for $300,000?*

It made little sense.

But on further consideration as he arrived at the bottom of the stairs, maybe it did make sense. Yes, maybe. He figured his mom was just stringing Aunt Grace along for another handout. Such a sale wasn't enforceable anyhow. *I'm a human being, for crying out loud, not a commodity. I'm not a tube of lipstick, or an eyebrow pencil, or a pack of panties or a corset that some woman just ups and buys as the mood takes her.*

He emptied the semen in the plastic cup over a fresh smoothie mix, this time of bananas, cherries, strawberries, and vanilla ice cream.

But . . . This thing with Aunt Grace perplexed him. He now understood that she was crazy. He didn't know what her obsession with owning him was. (Greg, of course, had no idea of the romantic battle for his father's affections that the two Barbanell sisters had waged a quarter-century ago.)

He ditched the plastic cup. He watched Aunt Grace's fresh smoothie blend with misgivings. *That woman is already ruining . . . I mean, running . . . my life. She's certain to get even more possessive now.*

Just then, his mother walked back into the kitchen. Barbara looked pleased. Very pleased.

Greg stared at her resentfully for a moment. Then he realized that she wasn't looking at him, but beyond him. She was staring at the fresh smoothie mix in the blender.

"Is it alright if I have some more, darling?"

He gulped in alarm. "Uh, no, mom, you can't have any more. We're about all out of ice cream, and . . . you've no idea how Aunt Grace gets if she doesn't get her . . ."

She was still staring at the blender and unconsciously licking her lips. Greg secured the blender in the fridge, then took a firm hold of his mother's elbow. Ignoring her resistance, he turned her around and pointed her towards the kitchen door. "Come on, mom, you can't have any and that's final. Besides, I need to talk to you about something."

He sounded so serious. She forgot the delicious-looking smoothie mix and looked at him. "Something?" She lowered her voice and whispered, "Is it about Gracie?"

He nodded.

"Outside then," she whispered, gesturing towards the front entrance. "Let's talk in my car."

He nodded again and followed her outside.

"So, what's bothering you about Gracie?" she asked when they were seated in the BMW. The top was down. The sun was warm on their heads. A cool breeze tousled their similarly brown hair. Any observer would instantly spot the genetic linkage between mother and son, particularly in the spacing of the eyes and shape of the nose.

Despite her concern for her son, Barbara Barbanell's eyes glittered with pleasure. While awaiting Greg's reply, she admired her hair in a compact. She knew she looked really good for fifty-two; not just attractive, but classy as well. In her line of business class was more important that beauty. Few women were truly beautiful. However, even ugly women could have class. You just needed to learn to emphasize what you had. And if you had *nothing*—a rare case indeed— you bought it off the shelves, and learned the right carriage and how to walk with confidence, and also the correct way to speak. You created the illusion of yourself for the world. Also, beauty faded with age. Class never did; you simply applied a touch-up coat of polish to yourself.

Barbara found her appearance satisfying. The scars of battle showed in her eyes, but the lines on her face were lines of triumph. Oh, she'd been through more than her fair share of bad experiences. But she'd survived. She was a survivor. And she intended to continue surviving the rat-race called life. And also to make a survivor out of her only child.

"Mom, I'm tired of living here," Greg said. "I can't hack it any more. Your sister—Aunt Grace—she's driving me up the frigging wall."

Barbara immediately stopped admiring herself and scowled. "You've no choice, darling. She *wants* you here."

"Hey, what about what *I* want? Doesn't that matter?"

"Greg, what *you* want is to inherit the two or three million she's got in the bank. That's a worthwhile ambition for any young man to have. Don't screw that up for us . . . I mean, don't screw that up for yourself."

Greg didn't reply. He'd been right then: his mother *was* simply stringing along her elder sister. The realization killed his resentment. His mother was smart; she was right. Greg wasn't a fool; a three million dollar inheritance wasn't something to be trifled with. Even at twenty-one, he'd already done the math—it was possible to slave one's entire lifetime and never earn that much money. And all he had to do to become a millionaire someday was keep a cranky old spinster happy. Oh, alright then. He could do that. The thought of the money almost made him love Aunt Grace.

"Look," Barbara continued, "at the moment she thinks of you as her son. She's gotten this madcap idea in her mind that she adopted you at birth. Don't do anything, and I mean *anything*, to shatter that illusion."

Greg noted how she'd glossed over mentioning the deal they'd struck for 'ownership' of him. He figured it wasn't worth letting her know he'd been eavesdropping then. But still, he wanted to see how truthful she'd be with him.

"Mom, what do *you* get out of all this? You're not just doing it for me, are you?"

She giggled and patted his cheek. "Not entirely, darling. But remember, it's just the two of us now." She sighed. "After my horrible experience with Bradley, I don't see myself ever getting married again." She looked him direct in the eyes. He was surprised by how beautiful she looked. "Greg, I've been through hell and high water since your dad died. O.K.? Once or twice I even thought of killing myself, taking an overdose of sleeping pills or slitting my wrists. But I never did? You know why not?"

He shook his head.

"Because I couldn't abandon you, that's why. This world's a cold, cold place, darling. You've no idea just how cold and hard it can be." She sniffled, then wiped a tear from her left eye." She looked cold and hard at him again. "What I'm getting at is—for years Gracie and I never saw eye-to-eye. We hated each other with a passion. Even our parents couldn't get us in the same room together. Now imagine what would have happened if she'd not opened her doors to us both. Imagine the life we'd have had if Gracie hadn't forgiven me." She reached inside her expensive purse and pulled out a check. "This is for three hundred thousand dollars. A gift to help set up my hair and nail and tanning spa, and that new Springfield branch I've wanted to open up since last year." Then she smiled bitterly. "But in exchange, she wants to be your mother." Barbara began weeping now. "Greg, I just sold you to her; I did."

Greg was surprised. He'd never imagined that she'd level with him like this.

He leaned across the BMW seat and took her hands in his. "Mom, mom, it's okay."

"Forgive me, son! Please forgive me! I just sold you to Gracie."

"It's O.K., really. It's not enforceable anyway."

Barbara got out a tissue from her purse and dabbed her tears away. "You mean it, darling? You're not mad? You really do forgive me?" She looked more than a little surprised that he'd not blown a fuse. One expected young people to do that; they were all emotion and very little common sense or foresight. One generally had to be middle-aged to have a proper overview of what was really important in life. She still looked worried though, with lines of concern etched in the pampered skin of her face. "You really do forgive me, dear?"

"Yeah sure, why not? You're just doing what you think's best for both of us."

Barbara sighed with relief. Next, she examined her makeup in a compact mirror to ensure her tears hadn't ruined it. On a whim, she also checked that she didn't have lipstick on her teeth. "You're right, she agreed quietly. "It's not enforceable. But you can't ever let Gracie feel that way. She might leave the inheritance to a charity—imagine her dying and you discovering she's willed all her money to set up a smoothie foundation."

Greg tried imagining that and succeeded. Yes, he could definitely see his aunt leaving her millions to set up an "Organization dedicated to developing the perfect smoothie." It was a perfectly terrifying thought—all that money converted to milk drinks and slurped away down thirsty gourmet throats. No! Greg wasn't going to let that happen. Definitely not.

His mother saw that he understood. "So you have to be nice to her, darling. I mean, *really* nice to her. Do whatever she wants you to." She laughed, her voice taking on a hard, brittle note. "Short of sleeping with her, of course. Call her 'Mommie Dearest' if that's what she wants. Whatever, just humor the old witch till we get what *we* want."

"Yes, yes, mom. But . . . mom, I've been doing some math . . ."

"Ah, my son the economist."

". . . She's only *fifty-nine*. How long do I have to do this for? I mean, I'm gonna have a wife and family someday, and I want a career now. She might live till she's eighty. That's still twenty years off."

Now it was Barbara's time to be silent for a while. "She won't live that long," she said finally.

"She won't?"

"No. Gracie's got a weak heart."

Greg savored the words. It was odd how his mother sounded both upset and pleased at the same time. "How do you know this?"

Barbara shrugged. "She told me, of course. She's got some condition that might stall her heart at any minute and that's it for her."

"Why doesn't she get a pacemaker fitted?"

"It won't do any good. A pacemaker only regulates the heartbeat. It won't prevent it from stopping altogether. At least not in Gracie's case, it won't." She looked reflective. "Apparently it's a variation of what killed our mom. I'm fortunate not to have it too."

Greg mulled on this. The cool breeze had lessened now, but the sun was shelved away behind clouds. His mother put her sunglasses on. She looked cool like that, an advert for glossy style.

"Surprised, darling?" Barbara asked.

"It's hard to believe. She seems so healthy."

"Bitching is her energy. It's her superpower and her driving force. Her very unhappiness is her reason to continue living. If Gracie ever falls in love with a man—if that sort of true joy ever enters her life—she'll likely drop dead the moment after their first kiss."

"But why's she so unhappy?"

"Forget it. Some women are born bitches. Some become bitches by force of circumstance. Some women just discover being a bitch is fun."

Greg recognized that she'd sidestepped his question. "Alright, mom, so she's dying. It might still take her quite a while to go."

Barbara pushed up her sunglasses to stare at him. "What's the matter now? You're not getting cold feet, are you?"

"I'm twenty-one. I've got an economics degree. I've got a great job."

"Quit your job. That's something else I discussed with Gracie. She wants you to handle her money for her."

"I'm not an accountant. I'm an economist. *Economist.*"

"Whichever. She either doesn't know the difference, or doesn't care. Don't you get it? She just wants you around her all the time."

"This is like being locked in a cage."

"Well, it's a very gilded cage. Gracie'll pay you thirty-six grand a year just to keep her company as it were, and you're already living off her. All you'll do is bank your salary."

"She's obsessed."

"You should be grateful that's all she is. She's rich enough to be much worse than obsessed."

"Mom, are you sure this is worth it? Does she really have as much money as you say she does?"

Barbara looked pissed off. She pulled the check from her handbag again and waved it at her son. "Three hundred thousand clams, sonny." She smiled coldly at Greg. "I'm sure she'd have paid a lot more for you if I insisted, but I decided you weren't worth it."

His face twisted up in anger at the insult, then he saw that she was laughing. She leaned over and grabbed his arm. "Oh, c'mon, darling, I'm just kidding. You know, of course, that you mean the world to me. Way, way more than Grace's dirty money. Problem is, we need her money." She saw he was still upset. "You're still worried about something, aren't you? No need to be. All we need to do is coddle her till she croaks, and you'll be swimming in it. Besides, I don't see what you're so upset about. That's the *second* Mazda she's bought you parked over there . . ."

"She hates my girlfriend," he said. (This was a lie: Aunt Grace absolutely *loved* Debbie. "Such a nice wholesome girl, and *so pretty*," she'd told him more than once.)

"So change her," Barbara flatly replied. "Find another girl to sleep with, one your meal ticket approves of. Boston is full of post-teenybopper females who'll crawl over each other to get into your bed." She winked. "If you inherit Gracie's millions, that is. Just remember the pre-nup before getting hitched."

Greg felt defeated. It was hard to place where his mother stood in all this. Avarice or concern? He decided it was both.

(It *was* both: Barbara Barbanell did love and care about her sister, but she cared much more about her son. [She'd not been lying that her concern for him was the only thing that had kept her from committing suicide after her awful second husband swindled her broke.] And then, there was herself too to consider. But above all Barbara cared about Grace's money remaining *in the family*. That was paramount. If Grace got married—or heaven forbid—got pregnant at this late age . . . And if she didn't have Greg keeping her company, that just might happen.)

"Alright, mom," Greg said. "Thanks for listening to me." Then unable to resist the temptation, he added, "And thanks too for selling me to the highest bidder."

She froze at the comment. Then she began laughing. She laughed and laughed. Her shades were back in place now. She laughed so hard that she began crying. The tears dripped down under her sunglasses in thin liquid lines. They ran and ran. He watched himself reflected in stereo over her eyes as her teeth shone in their circle of pink lipstick.

Her laughter was infectious. Greg began laughing too.

After their mirth had quietened, Barbara checked her makeup again. This time her foundation and mascara needed some repair. She worked on herself till she looked perfect again.

Then her phone rang in her purse. She got out the Samsung and checked its screen. Smiling, she raised it to her ear.

"Hi, Josh darling. . . . Oh, sorry I'm late. . . . No, no, I haven't forgotten; I'm over at my sister's place with my son. We're ironing out some family wrinkles. Alright, see you there soon."

She hung up and turned to Greg. She was still smiling, her teeth white and pretty.

"I've a date," she said. She kissed him and started up the BMW.

"A date, huh? Husband number three?"

Her smile dimmed. She shook her head sadly. "I'm afraid not, darling. Josh is a politician and widower. He's really nice, but sadly I'm no longer the marrying kind. Wedlock brings me bad luck, doesn't it?" She felt like she'd cry again, but she controlled herself. It wouldn't do to have to repair her makeup again.

Greg watched the BMW pull out of the drive. He responded to his mother's final wave as she swung the car left. The sleek black automobile sped off.

Then he stood staring at the house. Aunt Grace. It was all well and good for his mother to plan out his future like she had. He couldn't really fault her—it appeared she'd thought of everything and nothing could go wrong. But still, staring at the two-story house, where upstairs a neurotic nearing-her-sixties woman waited for him with a new lease on their relationship, he couldn't help but feel worried. Worried that fresh trouble was brewing for him.

He decided there and then (for the second time that day and for good this time), that he was never, never not ever, making Aunt Grace (or anyone else for that matter) another semen smoothie.

Come to think of it now, he concluded (not for the first time), *I must've been crazy to ever have begun doing something as dumb as that to start with. What the hell got into me? It wasn't any sort of a nice thing to do.*

He didn't feel like going back inside, so he walked next door to see Debbie.

***

A short while later, Greg was scrotum-deep inside Debbie and rocking back and forth with her. As usual, he was hidden behind the drapes while Debbie was bent out of the window, her succulent young breasts tightly packed in her T-shirt. She was groaning through her teeth while examining the sky for birds, so far without any success. So that they didn't accidentally part, the curtains were pinned together between their bodies. To each of them the other appeared to be behind a veil.

He could see her sexy top half through the drapes, but it wasn't the same. The drapes seemed to form as much an emotional separation as a physical one. He wanted to feel more of Debbie than just her ass. A woman was more than just a set of buttocks, no matter how lovely the buttocks in question might be. He reached forward through the curtains and grabbed her breasts. He got the barest of feels of their soft juiciness before she swatted his hands away. "No! Keep your hands inside! Someone might see you! Then they'll guess what we're doing."

Miffed, he returned his hands to gripping her waist again. He was just in time. At that moment, Debbie partly overbalanced and almost toppled out of her bedroom window.

She giggled back through the curtains at him. (Her home was a single story cottage; the primary danger of falling through the window was one of embarrassment.) "Take it easy, stud; you almost killed me just now." Once she'd gotten a firm grip again on the windowsill, she ground her buttocks back on him and resumed scanning the sky for birds.

"Oh, *there's* a brightly colored flock," she said. "You should see them, baby; they're really pretty. I dunno what species they are— they're so far away. Ooh, I think they're flying northward."

Greg paid no attention to her voice. He concentrated on the soft white curves of her buttocks. He focused on sliding himself into the wet cavern below and between them.

A few seconds later, Debbie yelled, "Hey, mom, remember to get the ice cream!"

"Alright, dear," came her mother's reply. "What flavor was it again? Chocolate?"

"Vanilla and strawberry, dammit! Write it down, mom!"

"Stop swearing, dear. It isn't ladylike."

Greg heard the family car start up and leave. He kept thrusting. Debbie had such a sweet vagina.

"I really hope she doesn't forget," Debbie said in a tightly controlled voice. "There's *always* something mom forgets; then I have to drive back to the mall to buy it for her."

Greg grunted something.

"But hopefully, today she won't," Debbie added brightly, her voice betraying the strain of keeping it sounding normal while she was in ecstasy. "Maybe today will be that one perfect day when my mom remembers to tick what she's already bought on her shopping list." She shuddered against him. "Oh gosh, I just love you, Greg. You do me so good, baby!"

Then she lost the fight with her self-control. She began gasping in orgasm and making soft squeals.

Greg didn't understand it. He found Debbie's 'looking/leaning out of the window during sex' kink supremely weird. Still it was fun. He couldn't dwell too long on it though. He was already coming himself. He dug his fingers into her soft butt, pumped as hard as he could, then fired his semen deep into the condom.

Afterwards, while they lay in bed, he asked her why she did it.

"Oh, it just works," she replied, nuzzling herself against him. "Using the window just frees something in me. Do you understand me, sweetheart? I find it impossible to climax in bed, but . . . making love at the window releases me in a special way. It's hard to explain. The best I can express it is to say that there at the window, I feel as free as a bird, like I'm up there soaring the sky with them." She gazed lovingly into his eyes and kissed him tenderly. "You understand me, don't you, baby?"

He nodded. "Yeah, I do."

She hugged him tightly. "You do? Wow, baby, you're just perfect for me. Oh, I'm so, so glad I've got you."

He nodded, quite bemused. He figured it didn't really matter; everyone was weird in their own way. And the more and more he knew Debbie, the more he loved her.

At least, he thought, *I've settled the Aunt Grace issue for good. I'm completely finished with that crap now. My mom drank my come? Ugh—that's just so gross! Utterly gross!*

CHAPTER 16

Mike & Lucy Hayes

Lucy Hayes was aware of a haze. Slowly the haze took shape, becoming the interior of a huge barn. Half-awake, she had the dispersing fog in her brain and a nasty taste in her mouth.

She stared blearily about, unsure where she was or what was going on.

There were a lot of people in the barn, all dressed up as though for a Halloween party. Everyone had on red diaphanous robes through which their naked bodies were visible. They were arranged in a semi-circle, around a long table draped with a black cloth patterned with magic symbols. One symbol occurred four or five times on the cloth: a gothic inverted 'A.'

This was unexpected enough to view on waking. But then Lucy realized something else was very wrong. Her husband Mike lay on the black-draped table. Worse still, Mike was both naked and tied up. A strip of duct tape sealed his lips.

A naked woman with long red hair was waving a knife with a crooked blade over Mike. She was dancing beside his head and chanting. Her voice was eerily hypnotic. Mike was still alive. Lucy could see his chest rising and falling. His eyes were shut though, and blood was trickling from his forehead.

Now alarmed, Lucy awoke fully. She'd just realized that she was herself tied up. Her mouth too, was duct-taped over. While unconscious, she'd also been sat upright in an angle. She looked around. She was propped up against a rusty old tractor. The dead machine stank of ancient mildew and recent rat droppings.

Her memory returned at a rush now:

It had been night. (It was still night outside, but Lucy didn't know if it was the same night). Their car had broken down on the Palmer

111

Road section of State Route 20, shortly after they'd turned off Route 19 in Brimfield en route to Springfield. After calling AAA for roadside assistance, Mike had stood angrily kicking the rear driver-side tire.

Lucy had remained in the car. She saw no point in exhausting herself by pacing up and down. Mike had gotten AAA, and they were on their way. That was good enough for her.

"Hey, darling, come inside and have a seat," she'd called out to her husband. "You're making me nervous walking about like that."

Mike had grunted a reply, which meant he wasn't about getting back in the car and sitting down. Lucy had shrugged; he could wear himself out worrying if he liked. She'd found an easy-listening playlist on her cellphone and put in her earphones.

Occasionally she'd peered out of the driver's window at the solitary passing cars. There weren't many of those. They'd stopped around the Brimfield State Forest. The world here was trees forever. She'd felt a momentary chill staring at that night-shrouded expanse of endless foliage. What if something bad was lurking out there? Hanging up in the tree branches and staring hungrily at she and her husband?

She'd dismissed her fears as childish. She'd relaxed and let Enya and Yanni soothe her.

She'd closed her eyes and hummed along with the songs. Then something had touched her hand. She'd jerked alert again in fright.

But it was just her husband.

"A pickup truck's pulling up behind us," he said. "I'm going to talk to the driver. Maybe he's from Triple-A."

She'd turned and peered through the rear window at the pair of arriving headlights. She'd nodded to Mike. He'd walked off. Lucy had returned to listening to her music.

That was all she remembered . . . no, there had also been a funny smell—almonds and fish oil? . . . something wet placed over her mouth and nose so that she was forced to inhale the funny smell . . . she'd kicked and hit out but instead of escaping had felt increasingly sleepy . . .

And now she was here, all tied up, and Mike was naked on that black table with the equally nude redhead swaying like a charmed cobra around him.

An intense and unrelenting panic filled her. She wanted to scream through the strip of tape over her mouth, to throw a tantrum of horror. But at the same time she wanted to fade into the surrounding walls and not see what was about happening to her husband.

The barn smelt old and musty. It smelt of blood and sweat; her sweat and the spilled blood of others. (She instinctively knew that other unfortunates had preceded her here; and that none of them had ever left here alive). She also smelt something else in the barn. This extra smell was something not earthly, a completely unfamiliar odor that nonetheless (like an inherited racial memory) unnerved her on a primal, atavistic level.

Lucy stared at the people around the table. Four men, three women, and the naked dancer. As the redhead danced, the people in red robes chanted an unnerving melody like a fucked-up Gregorian chant. The woman's ritual knife—its long blade curved like a road winding through the desert to a rendezvous with death—glittered with silver malice in the barn's harsh fluorescent lighting.

Lucy didn't want to look, but felt she had no choice in the matter. *That's my husband up there! If anything happens to Mike, I'll . . . I'll . . . !*

She didn't know what she'd do. She was close to freaking out with terror already. Mike still hadn't moved. His chest still rose and fell, so he wasn't dead, but that wound on his head looked really nasty, and it was still bleeding.

To Lucy's relief, the redhead lowered her knife. Her companions immediately ceased their chanting.

Lucy's relief was short-lived, however.

"It is time to feed Boku, our demigod from the Outerness," the redhead proclaimed. "Let the skinning begin."

"What!?" Lucy yelped behind her gag. "What!?"

Any doubts Lucy had about what she'd just heard were quickly put to rest. At the redhead's words, a man had shed his robe and stepped forward. He was very tall and very muscular. He was gripping a wicked looking knife. This one had no curved ceremonial blade. It looked as functional as hell.

The muscular man began skinning Lucy's husband. He peeled Mike as though Mike were an potato. Lucy watched as the man, his hands and forearms covered with spilling blood, removed the skin from her husband's chest in a single sheet. He held it up for the priestess's approval, then when she nodded, flung it over her head, behind her. Lucy watched Mike's skin sail through the air, a fleshy kite without a tether. She heard the skin smack on something unseen that sounded like water. She heard the slobbering sounds of something eating Mike's skin. Lucy instinctively knew that that unseen creature was what she could smell so strongly in the barn.

The redhead was grinning at the others. She had drops of Mike's blood on her shoulders and breasts.

"Great Boku Ke Houzz," she intoned, "accept our sacrifice and empower us to do evil, to dominate those who are good. Strengthen us in the service of our master Satan. For to him, the Inglorious One, whose son and servant you are, we bow in worship."

The muscular man resumed skinning Mike. Unable to tear her eyes from the horrible scene, Lucy kept watching. Mike's chest was already a peeled red mess, and the man was now working on Mike's belly, raising the skin, slipping his knife under it and cutting it free of the abdominal muscles.

Lucy had a vague impression that she should try to escape, but she didn't try. She knew that any attempt at flight she made would be futile. Instead, she watched her husband. She prayed for a miracle to save Mike, who was still unconscious. She was relieved that he couldn't feel what was being done to him.

It was at that exact moment that Mike woke up.

The man flaying Mike had just gotten all the skin off of his belly. The man was holding the bleeding sheet up and severing it near the pubic hair when Mike's eyes popped open.

Lucy saw the play of expressions on Mike's face: first confusion, then disbelief, then finally agony.

Mike's eyes bulged out in pain. Pain that his gag prevented him from expressing.

"Great Boku Ke Houzz, accept our sacrifice and empower our desire to bring our infernal father Satan, who is also your own father, to Earth to rule for a million years over the worms, both those who do not believe in your father's existence and power, and also all those who worship that one we hate, that one called the Son of God . . ."

And all the while, there was poor Mike screaming in silence, his eyes filled with horror and torment.

The knife descended again. More of Mike's skin redly separated from his flesh and bones.

Lucy had seen enough. She had heard enough. She fainted.

***

When Lucy awoke from her faint the ritual was just being concluded. A loud chanting was going on.

Through a headache and bleary eyes, Lucy stared at the black table with its tapestry of cabalistic symbols. There was a vaguely human-shaped mass of gore on the table. Red bloody meat. It was completely skinless, just a butcher block mess of stripped muscle. Even its face and scalp was gone. It had no nose, no ears, no eyelids, and no lips either. To keep it from screaming, a gag had been stuffed in its mouth after its lips had been shorn off.

Lucy goggled at all this, at first unable to come to terms with what she was witnessing. Her mind just refused to accept the sight. That thing . . . that bloody butchered mess couldn't be . . . it just couldn't be her husband. No, it couldn't be!

However, the terrible mess on the table was still alive. It was arching its back off the table. It was flexing its flayed limbs. Blood was trickling off its raw, exposed muscles. Its lidless eyes were staring around it with the extreme horror that only eyes can convey.

Mike! . . . Mike! . . . Mike!!!! Nooooooo!

Mike hadn't seen Lucy, which she was grateful for. Or maybe his mind was gone, and all he felt now was the agony of torment; the pain of Hell. She managed not to faint again, though she was unsure what was so great about remaining conscious.

"Now!" the redhead shrieked in an utterly bloodcurdling voice. "It is time to feed Boku! Let's feed our demon god!"

The Satanists/witches stepped back from the table. The man who'd skinned Mike and an equally tall and equally naked woman stepped forward. Both were blood-splattered, as if while Lucy was unconscious the woman had disrobed and helped the man finish skinning Mike. The nude woman had a tattoo—an inverted 'A' exactly like those embroidered on the black tablecloth—on her left thigh. The man had a similar tattoo on his right arm.

The pair lifted Mike off the black table and carried him past the priestess. Another two men carried the table over to the side of the barn. This removal of their sacrificial furniture freed up space for them, so they could arrange themselves in pairs behind the redhead.

"Great Boku, accept this offering of living red meat . . . !"

Removing the table also let Lucy clearly see what lay beyond it. The table had concealed a pool, a raised stone circle filled with brownish water. The water was placid, though a few bubbles broke its surface. Red scraps of Mike's skin still dotted the stones, which were covered with glistening piles of something like transparent jello that spilled to the straw-strewn floor around the pool.

The nude man and woman placed Mike's bloody trembling body at the edge of the stone circle. They laid him on his back, his head up on the pool's edge. Then they retreated and arranged themselves behind the others.

"Great Boku, accept this offering of sweet fresh meat!"

Lucy knew something horrible was going to come out of the pool and eat her husband. She just didn't know what it would be. However, when she saw the revolting creature emerging from the muddy, bloody water, it was worse than she could ever have imagined. It was immense and brown and it . . . it . . .

The creature Boku Ke Houzz quickly slipped its huge slimy mouth over Mike's head. Mike thrashed uncontrollably and he shit himself.

Patient as a snake, Boku gulped Mike down.

"Feed, great Boku, feed! Feed and bless us with your blasphemous glory!"

Its worshippers knelt and bowed their heads to the ground before it, arms outstretched ahead of them in reverence. The witch-priestess alone stood, her hands raised. She smiled as she watched her demon feed.

Lucy watched and watched. Her eyes were so wide open, it felt like their lids were stitched to her forehead and cheeks.

Slowly, the skinned man vanished into the monster. Blood dripped from its lips as it sucked him down inside itself. Its scary smell increased in the barn.

Mike's feet vanished into Boku. After this there was silence in the barn. The creature rested on the pool edge, dripping slime and regarding its worshippers with large black eyes that wavered on long stalks. Its blood-smeared mouth opened and shut like a toad's. It was silent. Finally its gaze swung towards Lucy.

"Boku is still hungry," the redhead intoned without turning around. "It desires the other sacrifice. Reposition the Blood Table and fetch the woman."

A soft murmur spread amongst her companions. Quickly, the malefic worshippers got up from the barn floor. The men who'd moved the table to beside the wall went to retrieve it.

The naked man and woman who'd skinned Mike crossed the barn towards Lucy. As they approached her, she saw the sadistic delight in their eyes. They'd clearly enjoyed what they'd done to her husband.

Shit! Lucy realized all of a sudden. *Oh no, and now they're gonna do exactly the same to me! Oh noooooo!*

The moment the man touched her, she fainted again. She was totally unaware of being borne over to the Blood Table and of being undressed then laid on it.

Lucy only woke up again when they began skinning her too. As the muscular man's knife slid into her chest, and blood squirted out and pain squirted in, she understood exactly how her husband had felt on the black table.

"Great Boku," the redhead witch-priestess intoned in great solemnity, "accept too this delicious sacrifice and empower us to do monstrous evil in this human world. Enable we, your wolf cubs, to devour the suckling lamb known as Man. Make him powerless before our vicious ravening. As we feed thee, reward us, Boku Ke Houzz. Fill our hearts with the darkest blackness and gift us additional infernal abilities . . . !"

Lucy Hayes hardly heard the woman. By now her eyes were almost popping out of her face from the agony of being flayed alive.

CHAPTER 17

Greg

Saturday.

The weekly smoothie party began promptly at 4 p.m. Everyone except Tommy Collins was there, including Detective Anderson and all three Kim sisters.

Jojo Kim smirked at Greg when he let her in, then she strode past him, clicking her heels and swinging her handbag. He was relieved: she didn't seem about to grab his behind again. All week long, he'd dreaded a repeat of last Saturday's scene. Particularly since his aunt had ordered him to treat Jojo better.

And I now belong to Aunt Grace, so . . . In the twenty-four hours since the Barbanell sisters had completed their commercial transaction concerning him, Greg Madden had sort-of come to terms with the new family dynamic. There was now a new gleam in his aunt's eye when she looked at him. He didn't know whether to be flattered or scared that she wanted him that much.

Debbie was out with her girlfriends buying clothes that afternoon, so Greg stayed around to help out with the Graceful Blend club meeting. When it finally kicked off at 4 p.m., he found himself seated beside Kiki Kim. Kiki instantly began telling him how hard her elder sister Lulu was to get along with, both as a music partner and as a human being. (Lulu Kim currently haunted the outer reaches of the large living room, video recording the meeting for the club website.)

Everyone was elated over how well the KCS concert had gone. Everyone loved the *Aunt Grace* song, and had profusely complimented her and the band on it.

Greg listened to Kiki. Occasionally he nodded understandingly. He had nothing to do for a while: everyone's blenders and bags of ingredients were either on the twin coffee tables or by their sides.

There was a level of secrecy involved in making winning smoothies here that the CIA would be proud of.

After exhausting the topic of her sister, Kiki started on how her boyfriend Slasher (who was also the guitarist in their band) kept annoying her.

"I really love Slasher," she protested, "but he's gotta stop looking at other chicks during our gigs. It really pisses me off, man. Sometimes I just wanna stop playin' and break my bass guitar over his head."

Greg nodded understandingly to this too. Kiki Kim was very easy to piss off. She was a bomb with a short fuse and everyone else was holding lit matches. She was also the most American-looking of the three sisters. As if their father's genetic potency had decreased with each successive impregnation of their mother, the Kim sisters showed a marked decrease in Asian characteristics from oldest to youngest, with Kiki Kim looking almost totally Caucasian.

Kiki began telling Greg about the song she'd written just last night. "It's called *Housefly Boyfriend*:

"Fly, fly, fly. Boy, you're like a housefly,
Zipping off a turd,
Spreading icky love germs around the world.
You're like that when you leave me,
Taking my emotional diseases,
To your other nasty girls.

"The song's about Slasher, you know. I just know Slasher's cheating on me. But I ain't caught him at it yet, see? But I got feminine intuition about it. And I *know*, see? Us girls can just tell when a guy isn't being straight with us . . . sticking his love spoon into other hair pies . . . Shit, Greg! I love him so damn much! I just want him to love me back equally as much too! I mean, check out Lulu and Zombie Joe: he doesn't cheat on her, everyone in Boston knows he doesn't." She lowered her voice to a conspiratorial whisper. "You know, maybe it's all that pot that they both smoke that's holding their relationship together? I mean, yes, I know it sounds crazy, but I've really been thinking about it, right? They're both so stoned all the time—it's like they're both half-dead—so maybe their sex drive is stoned on marijuana too; or what do you think, man?"

And so the first quarter of the meeting passed.

This Graceful Blend meeting was the quarterly face-off, when the two club members with the highest aggregated scores for the quarter would go head-to-head in a smoothie challenge. The winner got a thousand dollar prize and bragging rights for the next three months. Detective Anderson was moderating today. Since arriving he'd been tallying and re-tallying everyone's scores to see who'd made the finals.

Jojo had her camera with her. She'd later upload the champion's photo to the club's website. From time to time, Greg caught Jojo's eye. When he did, she'd laugh and look away. She was seated right opposite him, but today she had on tight black leather pants; so no psychedelic green panties on display.

"Alright, let's do this," Anderson said finally. He was dressed in a red Gold's Gym T-shirt and brown shorts. His T-shirt spread over his muscular torso. His shorts showed off his exceptionally hairy legs.

Today, Detective Anderson seemed in less of a bad mood than normal. No matter how happy the cop appeared to be though, Greg was keeping out of his way. Anderson still gave off that asshole vibe of needing someone to hurt.

"Get on with it, Tom," Aunt Grace called.

"Yeah, Tom," another woman seconded, "we're thirsty as hell over here."

"Alright, alright," Anderson announced in his gruff voice. "The face-off is between Gracie and Dez."

Aunt Grace smiled coolly, then smirked at her opponent. "You got no chance in hell, kiddo!"

Desmond Haggerty—a small nerdy man who worked with the USPS and whose wife Jenny was also present—smirked back. "Just you wait and see, old woman. Just wait and see what I got lined up for ya'll today. Jenny and I have been working overtime on our recipe."

"Pah," Aunt Grace spat back. "I sure hope it ain't your damn asparagus again." She grinned at Greg, then announced to the room: "*My* drinks are already made. Just you guys wait until you taste my smoothies, made with my nephew's secret ingredient."

Hearing that, Greg felt like he'd been shot. *Oh, God, no. No, she didn't!* However, the gleam in Aunt Grace's eyes as she stared at him was firm assurance that she had.

He began sweating, really sweating. Water seeped from his agitated nerve endings and beaded on his forehead. So much so that Detective

Anderson began looking at him worriedly. "Hey, son, you alright? You look real pale all of a sudden."

"My stomach," he lied. "Something I had for breakfast."

Jojo Kim laughed loudly at that.

The competition began. Desmond won the coin toss-up and went first. He and Jenny got the kitchen to themselves for twenty minutes. During that time the other club members watched TV and chatted.

Kiki Kim refused to let Greg leave the living room. She also had issues with Lulu's boyfriend Zombie Joe (their band's drummer). She felt his backbeat was too laid back; he wasn't keeping a tight enough groove with her bass; had to be all that pot he smoked.

She was also upset with the way Jojo kept editing her in the band videos:

"She keeps getting this horrid blue tint in my hair, like I'm Indian," she whispered to Greg. "And my hair's nothing like that, see?" She leaned forward so that her head was deep in his lap. Viewed from the wrong angle she appeared to be fellating him. "See? See? I'm a nice chestnut brown."

Greg endured her with nods and smiles. It occurred to him that Kiki might be stoned on uppers. It didn't really matter. Kiki had normal airhead worries: herself, herself, herself. He, on the other hand, had *real* problems. No . . . *surreal* problems. If someone worked out . . . Shit! He couldn't believe that Aunt Grace had saved up all the smoothies he'd made her this week and was about to present them to . . . Why the hell would she do that?

But the answer was obvious, wasn't it? She simply didn't know what his 'secret ingredient' was.

Desmond and Jenny returned from the kitchen. Each of them bore a tray of tall glasses filled to the brim. Each glass dripped fat beads of condensation. The glass contents were the color of lobster.

"Ah, goddamn asparagus again," Aunt Grace sniffed. "I knew it."

"This isn't *just* asparagus," Desmond sniffed back. "It's mingled with shrimp and marshmallow and—"

"Don't spill the beans, Dez," his wife Jenny said quickly.

Aunt Grace began laughing. "Oh, there's soybeans in your smoothie too? How creative."

"C'mon, Gracie," Anderson said. "No teasing. You know the rules."

"Oh, alright," she snobbishly agreed.

The Haggertys passed their smoothies around. Greg got one too. He sipped it delicately. It was insanely delicious. It had to win, he had no doubts about that. From the smiles and nods around the room, everyone else agreed with him too. Even Kiki stopped complaining for a while and looked delighted.

"Alright, Dez," Anderson said, licking his lips. "These are fantastic. Let's see what Gracie has for us."

Aunt Grace got to her feet. "I'll be just a sec." She looked across the room. "Jojo, please give me a hand, will you, dear?"

They left and climbed the stairs. Greg began sweating again.

The next ten minutes passed Greg by like he was reading a comic: Watching Jojo and his aunt serve the semen smoothies to everyone in little cups; Aunt Grace apologizing to everyone that there was so little of them—just three glasses; Aunt Grace saying, no, she wasn't revealing what gave them their distinctive flavor; her agreeing that, yes, there were strawberries and plums and mango in some of them; everyone including Detective Anderson drinking and beaming broadly afterwards; the loud expressions of approval from all gathered.

Greg was pulled out of his haze by Kiki Kim shaking his arm.

"Hey!—you made these?"

Greg nodded dully.

"Wow! They're really good."

Greg smiled. A self-preservation instinct now kicked in. He understood that it was in the best interests of his survival that he give not the slightest impression that there was anything weird about these smoothies everyone was so busy enjoying.

"So see," Kiki Kim began again, "what I really think is that for our band to be taken seriously, Jojo really has to step it up a gear, you know? My boyfriend Slasher agrees too: Jojo's got to be more proactive."

"Yeah," Greg agreed disinterestedly.

"She really needs to—"

"Alright, folks, it's time," Anderson announced. "You've all drunk both championship smoothies. Now we gotta pick a winner. Dez or Gracie? Who's this quarter's kickass smoothie champ?" He laughed. "Those were some great drinks—this is gonna be a close one." He gestured around the room. "Okay, you all know the rules: one vote apiece, and both Dez and Gracie can't vote. Oh yeah, Jenny, you can't vote either. . . . No, you can't—you helped Dez with his preparations."

"That's not fair."

"Fair or not, it's the rules." He did a count of heads. "O.K., that leaves twelve of us who can vote. No, no. Greg, you ain't a club member; you can't vote either. Alright, everyone, write your favorite name down."

That took a minute or so. Everyone got out pen and paper and wrote a name down. Anderson went round the room collecting the names. Standing by one of the coffee tables, he revealed each ballot to the room:

"One for Gracie, one for Dez; two for Dez, two for Gracie; three for Gracie . . . four for Gracie . . ."

Aunt Grace won by seven votes to four. Greg couldn't believe it. He had a sudden suspicion that all the women in the room had voted for his aunt. Excluding she, the Haggertys and himself, there were seven women and four men present. He also suspected that the reason the women had voted for Aunt Grace's smoothie over Desmond's had little to do with nepotism, and a lot to do with their subconscious recognition of the drink's human-generated content.

He felt disgusted with himself. Utterly disgusted.

The Haggertys instantly contested Aunt Grace's victory.

"Hey!—this totally unfair!" Jenny protested. "Gracie herself admitted that she didn't make them." She pointed angrily across the room at Greg. "Her nephew made them."

Aunt Grace looked sour. She'd apparently not considered this point. Or if she had, she didn't think much of it. "He's my nephew and . . . they were made in this house!"

"Greg should win then!"

"He isn't a club member! He shouldn't be competing in the first place."

"He *didn't* compete. *I* did."

The argument raged for five minutes. Greg spent the time listening to Kiki recite another new song lyric to him: "It's called *The Suicide Media Show* . . . first verse goes like this:

"I hate you leeches,
All you scheming bitches,
Trying to shame me to pieces,
Screw you bully girls, go to hell,
Go drown in the bad wish well.

All you voyeur vultures,
Rapist culture,
Stealing nude pictures from my phone,
Like rabid dogs with bones,
Bloody leave me alone,
Yeah, fucking leave me alone!
You make me wanna throw away my cellphone!

"Well alright, yes," she explained, "Lulu did the last verse but most of it's mine." (Lulu was still videoing the meeting.) "The song's about the sort of nonsense us young ladies have to put it with nowadays: people hacking our phones for nudie pictures, being Catfished on Facebook, cyberbullying, and stuff like that, you dig?"

Greg nodded on cue. He was staring across the living room at Jojo. Jojo had gotten to her feet and had her camera ready. She was waiting to snap whoever was declared champion. In the meantime she was smoking a cigarette and looking really bored.

Despite his personal issues with her, Greg agreed that Jojo Kim was gorgeous. Face-and-figure-wise, she combined the best of Asia and Caucasia. Outside of her freakiness, she was the sort of woman he'd love to be around even if they weren't dating. The difference in their ages could be overlooked.

In the end the quarterly smoothie championship prize was awarded to Aunt Grace. She was all grins and delight. She gracefully conceded that she hadn't really expected to win, but that she'd so much wanted to share Greg's recipes with everyone. She also said that she honestly thought Dez and Jenny's asparagus and shrimp smoothie recipe tasted much better than hers, and that she'd love for it to be featured on the club website for the next three months, in place of her drink. She also let the Haggertys have the thousand dollar prize. Everyone hugged and laughed and drank a little wine. Then, after posing for photos with Aunt Grace, everyone left for home.

"Damn, son," Anderson said to Greg at the front door, "that sure was one hell of a smoothie you helped your aunt make." He winked. "The ladies all seemed to love it. Any chance of you sharing the secret with an old bachelor who needs an edge?"

Greg laughed nervously. "If I told you that, sir, you'd have to kill me afterwards. Aunt Grace would anyway."

Anderson found that hilarious. "Yeah, Gracie's like the friggin' CIA, ain't she?"

Then he checked his watch. "Shoot, I'm running late as hell. I'd better be on my way. I'm supposed to pick up Laurie in Roslindale in six minutes."

Laughing his ugly laugh, Anderson shook Greg's hand and lumbered off down the steps. He moved like a happy bear. Greg watched him climb up into his white SUV and drive off.

Greg was relieved. That was the end of it for sure.

Except that, just before leaving, Jojo Kim grabbed his butt again. This time she squeezed it really hard.

"I own this ass," she gasped in his ear. "It's mine, boy. Poop and all."

Then she kissed his cheek and slipped out the front door after her sisters.

Greg watched her silver Porsche pull away with deep misgivings.

CHAPTER 18

Tommy & Dave

Tommy Collins and Dave Fontaine were drinking in Bowie's Bar that same Saturday evening when the front door opened and Lonnie Black walked in.

Both men immediately set down their glasses and sat up. An immediate air of apprehension fell on them.

'Black' as he was called, (in contrast to his partner Carrie White, who they could see seated outside in the blue Dodge Charger parked by the curb) was a certified psychopath. He and 'White,' who ironically was a negress (while 'Black' was Caucasian), were both sadistic nutcases. Much more significantly, the psychotic pair worked for Boston crime lord Marko Velli.

So what did they want here in Bowie's? That was the question.

Black looked around the bar. The bartender averted his eyes, as did those drinkers who knew of Black's underworld connections and all-round nastiness.

When Lonnie Black finally spotted Tommy and Dave, he strode quickly over to their table. He was carrying a plastic shopping bag.

"Hi, man," Tommy said uneasily. "What brings you—?"

He shut up as Black thumped down his bag on their table, making them both grab their beer glasses to keep them from falling over. Black was a tall, sallow man with the manner of a wolf. His partner White acted more like a snake.

"Special delivery from the boss for Mr. David Fontaine," Black said. He smiled coldly at Dave. "The boss says to tell ya that this is the only warning you'll ever get. And he's only giving you this break for two reasons: One, 'cos you guys handled that last job real well for him; and second, 'cos he don't want to upset Tommy here." He turned to Tommy. "The boss says to give your dad his regards when next you call him. He don't do all that modern Facebook and Instagram stuff and he's lost the old guy's phone number."

With that comment, he spun on his heel and walked off. They watched him go.

Then, just before exiting the bar door, Black paused and looked back. "Hey, Dave," he said in a loud whisper heard by everyone in the bar, "don't be so stupid as to open that package in here."

Then he was gone, out the door and into the Dodge, and he and White drove off.

When the Dodge left, Tommy heaved a sigh of relief. Those two creeped him out no end. They were Marko Velli's executioners. Both were completely loyal to the kingpin. Both were also completely ruthless. Tommy had heard rumors of some of the things they'd done on Marko's orders. What he'd heard would give anyone nightmares.

An example was what they'd done to Tricky Hansen, who'd called Marko a cheat after losing his new condo to Marko at a game of poker. Marko hadn't been cheating; Tricky had. Even that wouldn't have been so bad, but Tricky had then gone around town telling everyone that Marko had swindled him out of his house. There was also the rumor that Tricky had begun putting the moves on Marko's wife Petra.

So Marko had sicced his 'dogs of vengeance' on Tricky. Black and White had completely fucked Tricky up. They'd mutilated him. They'd sliced off Tricky's nose, ears, lips, and his eyelids. Then they'd chopped them up and ground them into a burger patty. Then they'd fried the face-burger up with onions and French fries. Then they'd made Tricky eat his face-burger.

Tricky Hansen was still alive, but even after all the plastic surgery, he still looked like a freak.

Yeah, the Black/White pair were complete sickos.

Slowly, the significance of Black's message seeped through Tommy's surprise.

The bar patrons had returned to their drinking. The ambience in the room wasn't the same anymore though. Now Bowie's Bar felt as though the air had been poisoned. Like the walls and furniture had had their life—their comfortable familiarity—sucked out of them. The atmosphere had soured like milk gone bad. Only the living—the humans—remained the same, and even they were somehow less vivid than they'd previously been; their wariness and worries had reduced their humanity by tangible degrees. Everyone's manhood and courage waited for him outside the door, to be retrieved again when they left the bar to return to their business. Even folks' drinks didn't taste as good anymore.

Black had that kind of effect on places. And he was just half of the duo. Had White entered Bowie's with him, the place would have felt like a mausoleum now.

Tommy turned from staring out at the street, and stared coldly at his partner instead. "Alright, out with it, man—what the hell have you been up to?"

Dave still looked shaken. All the color had drained from his face. Before Tommy's question, he'd been staring at the bag on the table as though it contained a diamondback. Tommy too seriously considered that possibility, that the bag's content was alive and waiting to bite whoever stupidly opened it up. But no, the brown package in the bag wasn't moving, nor was it making any rattling or rustling noises. The brown package also didn't look too big. Tommy concluded that it wasn't explosives either. Marko didn't do 'loud' stuff like that. Marko was a *silent* killer. And besides, the kingpin was just out of jail and trying to keep a low profile.

Still Tommy regarded the bag. A vague, disquieting meaty smell was coming from it. That smell . . . what in the world could the package contain?

"What have you done?" he whispered to Dave.

"It wasn't me, dude. The Devil made me do it."

Tommy's heart sank. So Dave was guilty as charged. Fuck. The last thing they needed was to piss Marko Velli off. Not himself though: Marko and his dad Vince went way back. At one time they'd even been cell mates in MCI-Norfolk. The pair were lifelong friends. Marko wouldn't do anything to *him*—at worst he'd exile him from Boston.

Not so Dave though. Only Dave wasn't the smartest chip off the block; he clearly had no idea what Marko was capable of. Either that or he thought the rumors he'd heard were fairy tales.

Tommy didn't know what Dave had done, but he had a suspicion. Dave still wasn't saying anything. Tommy finished his beer then got to his feet. He picked up the bag Black had dropped.

"Alright, come on," he said impatiently to Dave. "You heard the man: 'Don't open your gift in the bar.' Let's go sit in the car."

Outside in their black Toyota Camry, they opened the package. They were parked in the alley behind the bar so no one could see what they were doing.

Tommy pulled the paper-wrapped package out of the bag and ripped it open. Inside was a layer of cellophane which in turn contained yet another package—this one wrapped in some kind of stretch fabric. Tommy unwrapped that one also. It contained something very long and soft that was also a mottled brown and white color. One end of the object was bloody, like it had been severed off a body. Now they understood the reason for the addition layer of cellophane wrapping—it was to smother the smell of raw meat which now filled the air.

At first, Tommy didn't understand exactly what he was looking at. It was Dave who gasped and pointed: "Shit, man, that's a dick!"

Horrified, Tommy looked closer. The wrapped object was indeed a penis. But (he heaved a sigh of relief) it wasn't a human penis.

"It's an animal dick," he said when he trusted himself to speak without his voice shaking. "A horse or bull dick. Most likely a horse's." To his nose, the organ stank of blood and mare vagina.

Dave was visibly trembling now. "Are you sure? Are you sure?"

"Sure I'm sure, man. Just look at it—how huge the damn thing is. You think the expression 'hung like a horse' is a joke?"

Then he sobered. Marko Velli wasn't any kind of a joker. So why had he sent this 'warning,' as he'd called it? Moving the severed animal penis to one side in the paper wrapper, he studied the fabric it was wrapped in. The fabric turned out to be an XXXL-sized pair of men's briefs.

Tommy stared at the bloodstained briefs in disgust. Then he slowly turned and stared at Dave in equal disgust. "You goddamn pussy-hound. Out with it. Who the hell have you been fucking?"

Dave didn't answer. His gaze was riveted on the animal penis.

"Hey, man, answer me, goddammit. You already said the Devil made you do it. So he made you do what?" He gestured to the package. "The meaning of this is obvious, you dolt. It means, keep your goddamn dick in your pants. So where have you been putting your dick that pisses Marko Velli off so much?" He regarded Dave with a pleading look. "Please, please, please, don't let it be inside Petra Velli."

"It's Petra," Dave said.

"Shit." Tommy stared at Dave. He couldn't believe anyone could be so stupid. "You're banging Marko's wife?"

Dave nodded.

Tommy did some quick thinking. He decided that Dave was still alive, not because Marko was in a forgiving mood today, but because the kingpin wasn't actually sure an affair was going on. If the man had had any hard evidence . . .

"How long has this been going on?" he asked.

"Three months. It started just before Marko got of the penitentiary." Then his voice turned defensive. "It ain't my fault, man. She came onto me. I didn't know then that she was Marko's woman."

Tommy wasn't buying that crap from his friend. "Yeah, sure. And when you did find out, what then? She told you Marko likes threesomes?" He spat outside the car. "Well, as of right now, it's over. You guys are through. Just call the woman and break it off . . . before her husband breaks your dick off . . . and your damn neck along with it."

Dave stared back defiantly. "Hey, man, I like her a lot. Maybe I don't want to break our relationship off. Maybe we're in love, you know. And she keeps telling me he's abusing her."

Tommy didn't reply. He simply got out of the car and began pacing back and forth along the alley. He finally stopped at a wall and began smacking his head against the concrete. *Are you kidding me? Is this guy the mold they make idiots from, or what? Petra says Marko abuses her? So fuckin' what? Marko abuses life. He's a walking criminal offence! What does Dave plan on doing anyway? Take on the whole mob? We can't even take on Black and White!*

He calmed down. He could feel blood running down his forehead where he'd hit it against the wall. But the anger had left him now. All he felt now was a sense of smallness; of momentous insignificance in the face of monolithic stupidity and looming disaster. He walked back over to the car. He picked the underpants-and-horse-penis package off the driver's seat and threw it away in a dumpster. Then he got back into the car.

He sat there in silence. Not looking at his partner, not looking at the steering wheel either. Just looking outside of himself, wishing he were an ant or a spider or a gnat; some little senseless thing that could vanish into a crack in the wall. Vanish completely so it didn't have to deal with idiots like Dave Fontaine.

Dave seemed to realize that he'd gone too far.

"Alright, I'll break up with her," he said quietly. "I call it off."

"Yeah, you just do that," Tommy said. "You just make the hell certain you do that. 'Cos if Marko ever finds proof that you're sticking it to Petra—I don't even wanna be your shadow."

Dave gulped.

Tommy put the car in reverse and backed out of the alley. Dave had just ruined a good day for him. He'd initially planned on driving over to see Giorgio Cimini's pretty sister-in-law Allie (he really liked her), but this nonsense Dave had gotten into had totally wiped all thoughts of romance and seduction from his mind.

CHAPTER 19

Laurie Futana

The pickup truck paused at the crosswalk at the Corinth Street–Belgrade Avenue intersection to let a party of old women cross the road. It was a brown Ford F150 with huge tires and mud-splashed sides.

The mud caught Futana's attention; a truck this dirty was an unusual sight in the big city. There were crates stacked in the back of the pickup, along with two red plastic tanks that might have contained either oil or gasoline.

Laurie Futana was on Corinth Street, standing on the sidewalk outside Sullivan's Pharmacy and Medical Supply. She was waiting for Anderson to pick her up for dinner.

All of a sudden, she remembered seeing this brown pickup truck before: on the night of the concert, when Allie had thought the driver was stalking her. Futana was certain it was the same vehicle—there simply couldn't be two trucks this dirty in the state of Massachusetts.

Momentarily distracted, her eyes traced a mud pattern along the vehicle's left side to the driver's window. They'd not seen the man's face that night.

Now Futana got a good look at the man driving the pickup truck. On seeing him clearly, she almost pooped her silk panties. She stood trembling, her hands balled into fists by her side. She felt as though lightning had struck her.

She couldn't believe her eyes. It was Brian McArthur!

She blinked, then squinted, then rubbed her eyes to get the grit out of her field of vision. She was desperate to ensure her eyes weren't deceiving her.

But no, she wasn't mistaken in the least. The man with the short beard and long hair *was* Brian!

Bitterness and butterflies filled her belly as she remembered him properly. Remembered those twenty or so times (actually it seemed more like a hundred times) in her middle teens that Brian had dragged her out behind the tool shed on her Uncle Max's farm. Once out of both sight and earshot, he'd pull down her pants and briefs (she was still a boy then), and next, while muffling her protests with a big brawny hand, would stuff his hard penis up her butt.

"Ain't no girls on the farm today, boy," he'd groaned while abusing her the first time, "so how 'bout you giving my dick a hand? I know you're as queer as a mushroom fruitcake, Larry; but don't worry, I swear on my daddy's testicles that I won't let on your secret to no one."

Futana paused in her recollection. Feeling dazed, she shook her head to clear the memory cobwebs out. Seeing Brian again had her almost weeping with rage. And yet, mixed in with her anger was a kind of amusement. Back then, in between 'stuffings' (as she'd come to think of their sexual encounters), she'd finally worked out that Brian McArthur was himself gay. He was also scared stiff of his father Ken finding out.

Ken McArthur was a man's man, a no-nonsense chap who chased skirts for a hobby. If he'd ever found out back then that his son was queer, he'd have first of all kicked out all of Brian's teeth, then kicked Brian's ass thirty shades of bent, before finally kicking him out of their house. Ken and Larry's Uncle Max were drinking buddies. They also had similarly ugly homophobic personalities, so Brian had correctly figured Larry wouldn't dare tell his uncle what was being done to his teenaged butt. And teenaged young men generally didn't report being raped to the police. All that ever did was make you a laughingstock.

Back then, that first time, sixteen-year-old Larry Fortune had been embarrassed to discover that he'd liked the penile invasion in his backside. It had hurt, but in a great way: the penis in his ass had seemed to complete a missing part of himself. That first time, once Brian had entered him, he'd immediately gotten an erection himself. Brian had chuckled when his hand felt Larry's swollen member. Then he'd squeezed it hard, painfully so. "Yeah, I just knew a mommy's boy like you would appreciate some big hard cock up your ass."

Brian had stunk of sweat and dirt, which added to the dirty excitement of the fuck.

Then, while Brian had been humping him, Larry had ejaculated without so much as touching himself. With that penis up his behind rubbing on his prostate, his virgin come had shot almost six feet across the grass.

Wow, what a crazy way to lose one's virginity, Futana thought now, as, with the road at last free of geriatric women, the dirty Ford truck crossed the intersection onto Robert Street and picked up speed.

It wasn't going so fast though that she couldn't take down its license plate number. She didn't have paper handy, so she wrote it on the back of her forearm.

She smirked at the vehicle number on her arm. Cursive blue ink on fussily depilated smooth white skin. The guys at the state RMV would turn up Brian's home address soon enough. If she felt like it, she might even pay him a visit. Not to rekindle their sex life though. In that regard, the past *was* dead. She was her own woman now, not some rapist's toy boy.

Across the intersection, Anderson was just arriving in his white SUV, driving towards her down Robert Street. He passed the departing pickup truck without even a sideways glance.

Futana forgot about Brian and his truck. She began waving to get Anderson's attention.

CHAPTER 20

Allie

That Saturday night Allie was feeling less moody than was usual nowadays.

Earlier that day, she'd watched the NASCAR races on TV. Watching the cars speed around the racetrack had filled her with a vicarious, almost-forgotten thrill. For the first time in ages, she'd wished she was behind the wheel of a stock car and competing again.

Then later, after dinner, she'd sat up in bed with her laptop, looking through online job offers. She'd figured she'd been unemployed long enough. It was time to get back to work. It was time to pick up the pieces of her life again.

As she looked out of her bedroom window at the moon, her lips curled up in amusement. She'd just remembered the details of a phone conversation she'd overheard Dave Fontaine having during he and Tommy's last visit to the house.

That night's moon had been a prelude to this one, a thin white sickle hung in the sky like a party decoration.

Dave had been out on the back porch, phone pressed to his ear. Allie had been returning from the kitchen. The bursts of angry noise from the cellphone were what had called her attention to Dave's presence out back.

From the pained look on Dave's face and his soothing reply to each successive explosion of ire from the phone, she'd deduced he'd been getting an earful from one of his many lovers.

"Oh, now come on, baby," she'd heard him protesting. "What's with this endless jealousy trip anyway? . . . No, I'm telling you—I'm not with some other woman! . . . I'm not! I'm over at Giorgio's place and we're . . . Yeah, honest, baby, that's the truth. I'm telling you, I got my hot rod all revved up and ready to race down your sweet, sexy fun tunnel. . . . What? What's that mean? . . . Oh, I better not have given your love milk to some puta? . . . Now calm down, baby, it's nothing like that. I'll be home in a short while and you'll see what I got in store for you . . . Oh, it'll be hard alright; you've no idea how hard . . ."

Hearing that, Allie had vividly imagined some sultry raven-haired beauty, all hot and bothered, dressed in the skimpiest of negligees and pacing barefoot back and forth across Dave's driveway, angry as hell, but nonetheless dying to leap into bed with the man.

She'd sympathized with Dave's unseen victim of lust and desire. She'd wished she was the lady on the other end of the line.

But back to tonight:

Now she yawned. Life had been quiet since her scare at the concert, nothing to do except babysit and go shopping. Tommy had been supposed to take her along to his smoothie meeting that afternoon, but at the last minute he'd cancelled, saying he had to see Dave to discuss business.

Dave! Oh, Dave . . . !

She was still imagining how nice it would feel to be wrapped in Dave's muscular arms when she dropped off to sleep.

***

Allie dreamt. In her dream she was kissing Dave Fontaine and it was wonderful.

But then, her ex Brian Kemp appeared from nowhere and walked over to them. Before she could protest, Brian slit Dave's throat. Dave fell down dead.

"No wedding for you, ladies' man," Brian smirked at the dead man.

Then, once again before she could protest, Brian took over kissing Allie.

"Oh, I love you, I love you," he told her over and over and over, "I've missed you so much, sweetheart."

"I've missed you too," she gushed back, then continued kissing him. Kissing him was wonderful, even more wonderful that it had been with Dave.

But then, just as she was really getting into it, Allie felt someone yanking painfully on her hair and pulling her away from Brian.

Next thing she knew, Valentina Ruzza was standing beside her.

Valentina placed a knife to Allie's throat and slashed it open.

"No wedding for you either, little girl," Valentina smirked.

Allie collapsed to the ground, bleeding and dying. Valentina took over kissing Brian.

"Oh wow, how I love you," Brian told Valentina over and over and over. "I've missed you so much, sweetheart."

"You're the only one for me," Valentina replied, her eyes huge with happiness. "All my previous marriages and husbands were just rehearsals, so I'd be ready to be your wife."

"Oh, yes, yes," Brian said joyfully. "Kiss me some more, sweetheart!"

They kissed some more, then Valentina said, "I think I'll just fire Allie."

And next, she pulled out a gun and shot Allie with it. A blue flag emblazoned with the golden message "YOU'RE FIRED, ALICE JACKSON!" popped out of the muzzle of the pistol.

Allie began weeping. Dying and weeping. She was fired, fired, fired!

Then, the scene shifted:

Allie was floating in the air while watching a wedding: Brian Kemp and Valentina Ruzza were getting married.

As the new couple came out of the church, Allie began crying again. But as she wept, her tears turned into confetti and rained down over the newlyweds. The more she cried, the more her tears became confetti and rice and flower petals and colored streamers too.

She sneezed. The snot from her nose became a bouquet of roses that Valentina caught and threw to her bridesmaids.

Allie was so sad, so sad. She felt the sort of sadness world-famous suicides were made from. She would have killed herself if she wasn't already dying. She felt just so impossibly sad.

***

Allie awoke suddenly, abruptly. Sitting up in bed, staring out of the window at the sky. The moon had vanished from sight now.

Her horrible dream was swiftly fading, but it had already done its damage.

In contrast to her previously positive state of mind, all Allie felt now was depressed. The switch in her moods was so complete that she doubted she'd even been happy earlier that day. She felt as though she'd never been happy before in her life and never would be again. Her gloom was that intense and that overwhelming.

All the nasty feelings she'd thought she'd successfully purged herself of—the agonized recollections of Brian and Valentina Ruzza, and her rage at the unfair circumstances surrounding her dismissal from her job at Eastern Bank—all of these negatives now returned to taunt her. As though the dam of her self control had burst open, bad impressions flooded her vulnerable emotional plain.

Allie sat there in bed, silent beneath the weight of her gloom. From somewhere a little voice seemed to nudge her:

Just kill yourself, it said. *Just die—get your life over with. Nothing will ever go right for you again in this life. Dying will be so much better.*

Allie found something pleasant in the thought of ending it all. It wasn't the thought of dying itself that enticed her, it was rather the release which ending her life promised her.

She felt so negative at the moment that any suggested escape from these horrible feelings, no matter how drastic it was, had to be viewed as a positive.

Once dead, she'd never have to think of either Brian Kemp or Valentina Ruzza ever again. They'd be gone for good, just like she'd be gone for good. Viewed this way, suicide became a wonderfully tempting proposition.

Allie began thinking of the best way to kill herself.

A gun? Chloe had one. But how could she get the gun from Chloe tonight? Walk up to the couple's bedroom, knock on the door and ask nicely? Tell them: "Hi, guys, can I borrow that little Ruger pistol of yours for half an hour? I just wanna off myself with it, you can pick it out of the mess of my brains afterwards."?

No. That would never work.

She could use a knife though. Slash her wrists and expire in a bright red flow of blood. She'd need to make sure she cut herself deeply enough so that she actually died. If she didn't succeed in killing herself, she'd end up locked inside a padded cell, wrapped in a straitjacket and doped silly. Then she'd never escape how she felt now.

Do it, girl! her soft mental voice urged. *Killing oneself isn't cowardice; it takes a whole lot of courage to end your own life.*

And at that moment, overcome with waves of depression it seemed like she'd never surmount, Allie decided to do it. Yes, she *was* going to kill herself.

She decided that she'd quietly pad down to the kitchen and get one of Chloe's paring knives. Then she'd come back in here and run a bath, just like every movie suicide did. Then, taking her time, she'd slit her wrists and let herself bleed away into the darkness.

Everyone dies, she thought. *I'll just be heading over there early, speeding into the next life just like I used to race my pink Monte Carlo back then. My one regret is that now I'll never own my own racing team.*

It was that thought—that if she killed herself tonight, she'd never race in NASCAR again—that shook Allie out of her funk. Dying and leaving motor racing behind—and this because of two people who'd not just hurt her, but who also had most likely by now already forgotten she existed—seemed utterly inconceivable to her.

Hell no, that is so, so, so not happening! I've still got a whole lot of stock-car racing left to do!

She slowly got a grip on herself. It took about ten minutes, but by then she was herself again. Her abrupt suicidal state was over.

Now, Allie no longer understood why she'd been so depressed. Killing herself was once more the furthest thing from her mind.

She looked out at the night. Coincidentally, the clouds chose that moment to unveil the moon again. Allie smiled. The moon's reappearance in the sky perfectly suited the upswing in her mood.

Things were looking up for her, not down.

You're finished, the negative part of her mind said.

Oh no, I'm just getting started, she replied herself. *I'm over that jerk Brian. I'm over that aging slut Valentina. I'm my own woman, and I'm picking myself up, and I refuse to lose my mind over something as silly as a breakup with a man who wasn't even worth it in the first place.*

Defeated by her positivity, her voice of depression shut up then.

Allie fell asleep again, this time wondering what all the fuss had been about.

This time she didn't dream at all.

CHAPTER 21

Greg

The next morning, Aunt Grace, resplendent in a beautiful blue housecoat, descended the stairs like an angel and asked Greg to make her a 'special' smoothie.

"Sorry, auntie, no more specials."

"Why not, darling?"

"They ran out of the special ingredient at the grocery store."

Her lips thinned into a frown. "I see. When will they be restocked? Any idea?"

"I don't think they're gonna, Aunt Grace. The guy at the store was really upset 'bout it too."

"I see," Aunt Grace repeated. Then suddenly she smiled. "Hold on a moment, while I fetch my laptop. We'll have a go at ordering it online." She laughed, showing her even white teeth. "Of course, now you'll need to tell me what it is, so I can buy it."

Giggling like a schoolgirl, she turned and hurried up the stairs.

Greg sat and waited. He honestly didn't understand her obsession with this. But after what had transpired yesterday at the smoothie club meeting, he was damned if he ever did that nonsense again. No, he'd have to fake her out somehow. He tried to think of some obscure vegetable that would need to be ordered from the other side of the globe, from Ethiopia or Bosnia perhaps. He scratched his mind with a mental finger. Which countries were currently at war? If they ordered something from Afghanistan or the Democratic Republic of Congo, or Syria for instance, it would surely take forever to arrive. Or maybe it would be smarter to make an ingredient up. Even Aunt Grace couldn't buy something that didn't exist.

"No, please, don't get up," Aunt Grace said when she returned. She set down her laptop on a stool in front of Greg. It was an ultrathin Sony Vaio. Extremely high specs. (Aunt Grace knew zilch about computers. Jojo Kim bought everything for her, and Jojo made sure she bought her only top-of-the-range stuff.)

Aunt Grace woke the laptop up from sleep, double-clicked on an icon, then sat on the arm of Greg's chair. The scent of her freshly-washed body filtered to him from within her housecoat.

The icon Aunt Grace had clicked on wasn't a web browser like Greg had first thought. It was a video player application.

He watched in surprise. His surprise fast turned to shock. His shock quickly became horror.

He was watching a video of himself masturbating in the kitchen. His right hand, slick with spittle, moving fast and relentlessly over his swollen penis. The hidden video camera was of very high resolution; it captured everything: his hand, the intense look on his face as he strained to come, the slurping sounds the act produced, and his grunting. The video showed his ejaculation in slow motion, a broken arc of white drops—snowflakes falling horizontally—splattering the insides of the blender.

"You've really worked that out," Aunt Grace said admiringly. "Not a drop wasted. Just look at it, all that yummy nut for your favorite auntie."

His throat felt parched. He searched for words but found none. What excuse could he make? What explanation could he give? As judged by his own conscience, his actions were inexcusable. Which was why he'd decided 'no more.'

But . . . he didn't get it: If she knew, why was she still insisting that he make her smoothies?

"At first I was mad at you," Aunt Grace said. "But then I did some online research. And I discovered that semen has all kinds of wonderful health benefits for a woman."

Her hands were on his head now, her thin fingers caressing his scalp. Her fingers stroked his hair lovingly. He flinched and tried to turn to look at her.

"Don't you dare move, you dirty little shit," she said. "We're not done watching yet."

He was scared stiff. Her voice sounded eerie, almost erotic.

They kept watching, he and his aunt. It was a long video, a splicing of at least fifteen different recordings. Another day—another scene of him damning himself—then another, then yet another. Greg in jeans and T-shirt, in just shorts, in pajamas or naked except for a towel or bathrobe. The clothes and tone of daylight differed, his action remained exactly the same: him ejaculating into the blender, onto a mix of sliced fruits and vegetables in their white creaming of either yoghurt, milk, or ice cream. The smoothie components also differed: Once it was carrots and beetroots; once strawberries got the splattering of sperm, a pearly dripping over their crimson skins. Twice it was orange pulp, crushed ice, and mangoes . . .

He felt weak. He felt sick. He felt dead.

She was still massaging his scalp, combing fingers through his brown hair. She stroked his ears, tracing the pliant contours of their lobes with her soft fingertips. He felt a morbid satisfaction resonating from her.

"I'm sorry," he said without turning. He didn't dare to look at her.

"You should be. What kind of a son treats his loving mother like this?"

Greg made no reply.

"Answer me, Gregory: what kind of sneaky little bastard treats his darling mother this way?"

Aunt Grace might have been referring to herself as his mother because of her 'purchase' of him from her sister, but now the video was showing Barbara in the kitchen on her last visit, drinking the semen smoothie Greg had prepared. Greg wished the floor would open up and swallow him. At the moment, his whole universe had contracted to just two things: the screen of the Sony Vaio and Aunt Grace. Aunt Grace was a demonic presence hovering over him. He was Atlas; she was the weight of the world on his shoulders. The smell of her overwhelmed his senses. He felt both like burying himself in her for safety, and fleeing from her.

The video was just past showing him pouring the sperm he'd retrieved from the condoms into the blender. It cut to Barbara asking if she could have some more, and him refusing.

"What do you think Barb will say when she sees this? Huh?"

"You're going *to show* her?" Greg had by now accepted that he was screwed. His horror leeched him of hope. If his mother ever saw this, she'd . . .

"That depends, darling son of mine," Aunt Grace replied smoothly. She grabbed two handfuls of his hair and yanked painfully on them. "That depends entirely on you."

"What do you want?" It was a breathless question.

"Not much. Not much, my child."

"Who recorded all this?" Greg asked. He knew the answer, he just needed confirmation.

"Who do you think? You should have been nicer to Jojo, Greg. She's a lonely girl, that one, though a little weird. She just wanted some affection from you." She rapped his head painfully with her knuckles. "Keep watching. The video's almost done. We'll talk when it's finished."

Yeah, Jojo was right. She did have my balls in the palm of her hand.

The video had now shifted to showing yesterday's smoothie contest. Edits of Lulu Kim's recordings for the club website. They watched freeze frames of each club member with Greg's smoothie held to their lips. Then finally the video played a full one minute scene of Detective Anderson drinking his smoothie, licking his lips, and grinning.

The significance of showing Detective Anderson wasn't lost on Greg. One Saturday after everyone had left, Greg had heard him tell his aunt: "Well the way I see it, the USA's a free country. Homosexuality may be a sin, but it sure as hell ain't a crime. Folks can be as gay as they want . . . just so long as they take the hints I give 'em that I'm not into that scene. If a guy gets pushy and refuses to take a hint that I ain't into that rod-licking scene, I'll happily feed him his dick for breakfast."

Maybe it was because he was still upset about his wife's desertion, but the tone of Anderson's voice that day had left Greg in no doubt that the man would readily kill to protect his heterosexual identity.

And now, here was a video recording of Detective Anderson drinking Greg's semen.

The video ended with a black screen on which formed white dripping letters asking, "Why'd you do it, Greg? Why, huh?"

Aunt Grace burst into loud laughter. "Jojo's so damn funny, right? This line never fails to crack me up each time I see it."

Damn Jojo Kim, Greg thought. *Damn her straight to Hell. I'll kill the bitch! I'll . . . !* His anger fizzled out. He wasn't going to do anything to her and he knew it.

All this while he'd not looked at Aunt Grace's face. His entire interaction with her during his video ordeal had been via her voice and her hands. Her soft voice that contained a crazy passion. Her pampered hands that caressed him possessively, each tender stroke of her fingers transmitting subliminal messages of ownership to his skin.

Now he found the courage to turn and stare at her. "What do you want?"

She laughed and pointed to his crotch. "I told you—not a lot. I'm by no means an unreasonable woman. First off, go make me a special smoothie, with lots of personal nut in it. That shouldn't be a problem now that we both know your secret. When you're done, we'll discuss the other stuff I want."

"Forget it," Greg said stubbornly. "I won't."

"You will," Aunt Grace replied, a creepy smile now forming on her lips. "Oh yes, you will, my darling child. What do you think Tom Anderson would think if I told him you'd made him drink your semen?" Her delicate fingers gestured towards the laptop. "And showed him this too, of course."

"I didn't . . . You wouldn't . . ."

"I've got you by the balls," she said. "You've got huge testicles to pull this kind of a nasty trick on me in the first place. I like that. Now you're going to continue putting them to use for me. Consider this good old-fashioned American poetic justice."

He got down on his knees. "Aunt Grace, look, I'm sorry . . ."

"*I'm not.* I'm not even angry with you, darling son. Now get up, get off your knees. Get into the kitchen. Get hard like a man and make me another smoothie."

She frowned, as defeated, he rose to his feet again. "One more thing, darling son—there's no need to lock the kitchen door anymore. I'm not going to peek in on you—Jojo already did that for me."

Utterly defeated, Greg headed for the kitchen.

***

Aunt's Grace's demands were simple: First of all, Greg would continue making semen smoothies for her. They helped her complexion. All her girlfriends commented on how 'young' she looked nowadays. His protests fell on deaf ears. Likewise his endless apologies. No, she insisted, he *wasn't* stopping; he'd keep on with it, and if he didn't, well then, she'd just have to show his 'home movie' to both his mother and Detective Anderson, wouldn't she? And Jojo Kim would back up her story that they'd only found out *afterwards* what he'd been up to. And most important of all, he needed to remember that Anderson wasn't the sort of man to see the funny side of anything.

They discussed how often:

"Every day."

"It's too taxing. Besides, I've got a girlfriend now. Debbie will be sure to notice. Too much masturbation has diminishing returns in bed."

"Make love to her *here* then. Keep the condoms in the freezer afterwards."

They settled on thrice a week. And she expected an extra load of semen whenever Debbie slept over.

Aunt Grace promised to make Debbie really feel at home whenever she visited. "Like she's my own darling daughter."

Greg suddenly realized that she'd not raised her voice at him even once this horrible morning. At first, he found this change in her odd, but then he understood it: she no longer needed to shout at him; she now had him right where she wanted him: attached to her apron like a button sewn on it.

"You like Debbie, don't you?"

"Yes, auntie."

"Then do exactly what I want and she'll never know what a scumbag you really are." She snickered. "Just imagine the look on her face if she ever saw you . . ."

That was settled then. Greg figured he could cope for a short while, until he found a way to delete the files from her computer. Besides, his mother had assured him that her sister had a bad heart. Sooner or later Aunt Grace would croak and he'd inherit, amongst other things, her laptop. But there were the original video files with Jojo Kim to consider too. Those didn't really matter though. Once Aunt Grace was in her grave, Jojo was certain to part with the damning videos if he offered her enough money.

If Greg's primary problem had been resolved, there was still the matter of his employment to consider. Aunt Grace insisted on him quitting his job and becoming her personal aide. Greg, cannily envisioning the kind of stifling control that a quarter-century ago had convinced his father to marry Grace's younger sister instead of herself, refused. On this issue he dared call her bluff. She upped her salary offer to $42,000 per annum. He stoutly refused. She smiled and acquiesced. Okay, he could work outside the house, so long as she got her smoothies on time.

Greg spent the next two days trying to figure out where the video cameras in the kitchen were hidden. In the end, none the wiser, he gave up. It was obvious that Jojo Kim had removed them. Once again he cursed her. He utterly hated Jojo now. He considered it a real shame that murder wasn't legal.

(It would have upset Greg immensely to know that the cameras were still there in the kitchen, and right in plain view at that: they were the eyes of the rabbit-shaped magnetic clamps on both the fridge and microwave oven. Jojo had modified his mother's original gift to Aunt Grace into recording devices. Now, she simply switched the rabbits each time she came around and replaced their batteries at home.)

So life went on. Aunt Grace got her smoothies on time. Greg kept working at Bank of America.

***

Debbie never suspected a thing. She got fucked a lot at Greg's bedroom window now, which was perfectly all right with her: the view of the sky was better there than at home, where, because her house was a cottage, an ancient elm on the front lawn blocked the left view of the sky from her window.

Despite all Aunt Grace's efforts to set her at ease though, Debbie continued to find the elderly lady creepy.

"There's just something about her that frightens me," she told her friends. "You can just see that Greg's utterly terrified of her too. It's like she's using his scrotum as her handbag."

"You don't think they're *doing it,* do you? That'd be just utterly gross."

"No, it's not *that.* It's just that she acts like she owns him—she's overwhelmingly possessive. Worse than if she was his mother, even."

CHAPTER 22

Aunt Grace

At the age of fifty-nine, Grace Barbanell had finally discovered porn.

"What nice muscles he has," she thought creamily, while stroking her sex to the video of Greg masturbating in her kitchen. "I'm sure they're just like his father's were. Oh, I'd love to be held and squeezed by such muscular arms!"

She groaned with pleasure. Her hand moved faster between her thighs. She felt herself beginning to come. "Oh, damn that slutty Barbara for stealing him from me back then!" On her laptop screen Greg spurted a generous amount of semen over a mixture of chopped plums, strawberries, avocado, oranges and apples. Grace found the sight of the white love milk glazing the fruits incredibly erotic. Her orgasm hit her in waves. She dug her fingers into herself and moaned with ecstasy.

After her orgasm Grace settled down to think. As usual, once not reviewing her investments, all she thought about was Greg: how to keep hold of him. Greg was the center of her world. He was hers now (hadn't she just bought him from Barbara?), but she still didn't feel secure. Her younger sister was sneaky. *Maybe I should have offered her more money? Maybe I should have offered to buy her a house?* Grace couldn't help but feel that sooner or later, Barb (*what an appropriate name—she's always been a thorn in my ass!*) would return and spirit Greg away from her.

And then I'll never see my son again!

She managed not to cry.

She considered the positives of her situation. Oh yes, she had a firm grip on Greg now. Still, Grace was very worried. Her worries had a new focus. She was now concerned for Greg's personal safety. Now he was out of the house working, he'd be exposed to all kinds of dangers.

She didn't want anything bad to happen to him. There were crazy people out there. Drunken drivers like the man who'd killed his father, serial killers, muggers and road-ragers, serial shooters, terrorists. There were even crazy girlfriends, crazy would-be-girlfriends, and crazy ex-girlfriends. Her son Greg was very handsome. It would be easy for some young woman to become obsessed with him and start following him around. And if that obsessed young girl found a handgun somewhere . . .

That's why I like Debbie so much: she's such a nice girl. She also knows her place: she's not scheming to take Greg away from me. Well, I don't think she is. Not yet anyway. Besides, she lives right next door, where I can keep an eye on her. If she ever becomes too much of a clingy nuisance, I can always pay she and her parents off . . . I know her father needs money, he'll convince the girl to lay off my son.

Her thoughts darkened. *But Greg going out to work is very dangerous too. Yes, yes. There are lots of desperate, clingy girls working in offices nowadays, all of them desperate for a young man to own and control. Greg is mine, all mine, not theirs! Oh my God! Offices are really dangerous now . . . what with all the psychos out there—someone could get angry with management and bring one of those semi-automatic rifles to work and shoot everyone dead! It'll be much better—a whole lot safer—that Greg work for me. Here I can keep a sane, motherly eye on him!*

She was filled by a sudden rush of panic at the thought that Greg might be hurt. In her mind's eye she saw someone murdering him and herself being left all alone in the world; just a miserable old woman with a lot of money. Lonely, lonely, lonely.

Her fear was a hand painfully squeezing her poor heart. *No, Greg, no—I'm gonna take care of you, honey. Yes I will. Mommy will look after her little boy. Yes she will.*

Alright, she thought when her heart had ceased pounding, *that job of his has to stop. Now, how do I fix that?*

She considered the problem for a good while. Like his father, Greg was stubborn. He'd not listen to her if she commanded him to quit his job. She'd already insisted on it; he'd adamantly refused to comply with her demand.

So what do I do? What, what, what? Oh, in this case it's best I help him lose his job. Then he'll have to work for me. Now, how do I accomplish that? There has to be a way!

Thinking so hard had stressed Grace out again. To relax herself, she turned back to her laptop. She searched along the video timeline for one of her favorite scenes—Greg ejaculating over some pineapple chunks; she utterly loved the way his hard penis twitched as it spat out its load. Almost immediately she felt aroused again. Her body was wet and ready. She slipped her hands between her thighs and once more pleasured herself.

It was while having another deliciously creamy orgasm, that the solution to her problem came to her.

CHAPTER 23

Greg / Tommy

The next morning Aunt Grace informed Greg that she felt her smoothies tasted best if the 'nut' came *fresh* from the source.

"At most five minutes, darling. Not more than that."

He gaped at her. He'd imagined their stalemated situation might continue for years. Now it was already getting worse, and in just how many days?

Aunt Grace laid down the new law. She demanded that Greg not leave home till she'd woken up and he'd prepared her early morning smoothie for her.

"I'm serious, sonny—I want my drinks within five minutes of you making them. Nothing beats fresh love cream to make my skin gleam."

"C'mon, auntie, don't do me like this. You know I've got to get to work."

Aunt Grace generally got out of bed at nine or ten in the morning. Greg's protests again fell on deaf ears.

In the end Greg gave in. He stayed at home to make her her smoothies before heading for the office. He got sacked at Bank of America.

Of course, seeing as he couldn't tell Debbie the real reason he'd been late to the office for five days running, she assumed he'd been slacking.

"Listen, baby," she protested during their next 'bird watching' encounter, while he ejaculated into her and her eyes trailed a solitary gull that had strayed too far inland from the sea, "I need a serious guy in my life. How the hell can you throw away a good banking job like that when lots of us young people are unemployed? You gotta be serious, man."

Once he'd lost his job, Aunt Grace repeated her request/demand that he come work for her. Greg again refused. But by now his resistance was growing weak. He began seriously considering her offer:

Maybe I should just become her PA like she wants. But what about personal independence? She's already telling me where and when to ejaculate. If I agree to work for her, she may upgrade to telling me where and when to pee and poop. No, I'm not having that.

He considered simply going AWOL. Running away. Vanishing from town for good to some unspecified destination where no one would find him. In another town (maybe on the other side of the country) he'd be able to begin again. But . . . there was the small matter of the three million dollars he stood to inherit on his aunt's demise. His mother would never forgive him if he screwed that up, if he let Aunt Grace's money slip out of his—no, *their*—hands. For that matter, he'd never forgive himself. Three million wasn't an amount one joked with. (Greg had no idea that his actual inheritance was thrice the amount he thought it was.)

Besides, by now he was deeply . . . no, *madly* in love with Debbie Jerrica Manning and had no desire whatsoever to abandon her. That would be pure cowardice.

So no, he couldn't just desert his aunt. He needed to find another way out of his troubles.

***

"You're serious that you want a job with us?"

Greg nodded. "Man, you've no idea how serious."

Tommy Collins nodded. He and Greg were seated in Bowie's, the same bar where a week ago, Lonnie Black had delivered that gory package to he and Dave. He'd not seen Dave since then. He really hoped Dave had broken things off with Petra Velli. Any other course of action would be total stupidity.

"I'm thinking I can't cope with this damn 9-to-5 grind," Greg went on. "It's weighing me down, man. It's cramping my style. I need to open up, get out from under the white collar enslavement regime. See, you and Dave; now you guys have got a free lifestyle. You do your own thing. That's what I want too."

Tommy winced. "Hey, man, your aunt won't like it, you know. You should hear her talk about you. She's got plans, plans, big plans for you—she wants you to be state governor and all that noise."

"She's an old lady. What the hell does she know about modern life?"

Tommy smiled wryly at that. "She's a *nice* old lady," he corrected the younger man. "A *nice* old lady. That's the difference." Then he laughed. "You should meet *my* aunts. You'd run screaming and drown yourself in the Wakatomika Creek. Believe me, my dad flees the house whenever my mom's sisters visit. He just can't cope with those ornery women."

"Yeah, yeah," Greg agreed, raising his beer to his lips, "but still, Tommy, I can't live how Aunt Grace wants me to. You should understand that, man. I think you do."

Tommy Collins drank some beer and pondered the younger man's words. Tommy was thirty-five, fourteen years older than Greg.

He'd seen a lot of shit in his time, most of it crappy shit. It wasn't true that if you lived on the wrong side of the tracks you knew more about the world than those on the straight and narrow. People (mostly folks who had good life experiences) liked to believe that, but it was complete bullshit. That saying/concept/impression that some eighteen-year-old hooker had seen more of 'Life' than most people experienced in their entire lifetimes was just a crock of shit. Except 'Life' consisted of getting high and almost OD'ing on heroin, getting fucked by twenty anonymous men a day, and getting beaten up by a pimp with the regularity of a flyweight boxer in training. Nah, Tommy thought, that doctrine is bullshit. 'Life' wasn't being homeless and hungry and continually hassled and busted by the cops, all because you were too silly/stubborn to go work a proper, decent job. 'Life' wasn't having to deal with folks' sexual perversions to earn a living . . . simply because, the majority of people alive didn't have sexual perversions. You couldn't be a minority and claim moral superiority. No, that experience was the dark side—life's underbelly. 'Cos if being a junkie hooker or pimp was the reality of Life, then what was everyone else living, huh? And how come all those 'real living' folks took the first exit out of that so-called 'Life' into the mundane everyday world, first good chance they got to get out? And then, once out of that hell, they did just about everything they could to never return there again?

Just like he had?

If that sort of crappy, desperate, bottom-feeder existence was 'Life,' then Death was the great doorway to hope.

"Hey, man," Greg said, "Dave said you guys call yourselves the Rectifiers. Other than to insist that you don't get involved in any crimes, he was very hush-hush about it though. So what's the deal?"

Tommy frowned. "Yeah, no crimes, man. We don't touch anything criminal. I've been down that route—heck, I grew up living it back in Dresden, Ohio. Vince—that's my old man—was . . . still is . . . a major league drug baron. I grew up helping him bag and sell the stuff."

Greg gaped at him. "For real?"

Tommy nodded. He snapped his fingers at the bartender for another beer. There was no danger in talking business here in Bowie's. This place was a mob hangout. It was safe. Though people did venture in off the street at random, the bar had an intentional seediness to it that discouraged non-underworld patronage.

Tommy laughed at Greg's disbelief. "Ah yeah, for real, man. In our house back west, we stacked boxes of marijuana up to the ceiling and filled suitcases with heroin and coke packages. And there were more pills in the house than in a Walgreens pharmacy. Buyers drove in from Columbus, Zanesville, and all the other big towns to pick up their shit. I began working with my dad and his friends immediately I graduated high school." He frowned at the memory. "I mean, Greg, you ain't never seen that many greenbacks in your life. Never. Our house was like the fucking federal reserve. Cash flowed in, dope flowed out, then cash flowed out and dope flowed in."

"Why'd you quit then?"

Tommy's beer had arrived. He took a long sip of it. "Reality hit me," he continued. "Reality literally handed me my guts on a platter of blood." He paused for effect, then explained: "I was handling a coke purchase for my dad in NYC, up in the Bronx, when this black guy stabs me in the belly with a goddam hunting knife. Stabs me, then rips the knife up. When he pulled it out again, my guts all spilled out. No kidding—my intestines emptied out of me like they had an appointment to make across town." He frowned. "The bastards took our two hundred grand and left."

"How'd you survive?"

"Sheer luck, bro. My girlfriend at the time—sweet kid named Lucy—had come along with me 'cos she was running away from home after burning her parents' house down." He saw that Greg was going to interrupt him with a question about that, and waved the enquiry off. "Don't, man, it's too complicated. Lucy was just . . . ha ha ha! Well, that night I'd asked her to stay out of sight while I handled the drug buy, so the guys who'd double-crossed me had no idea that she was around. Once they'd gone, Lucy came in and dragged my butchered ass to a hospital." He raised a finger. "Lying there in hospital with my belly stitched up, I saw the light. It was like the Angel of Reason walked into my hospital room and told me, 'Tommy Vincent Collins Jnr., you either get out now or this shit's gonna kill ya.' So that's what I did. When my dad came to see me in the hospital, I told him I couldn't hack it anymore. He agreed and I moved up to Boston."

"What happened to the guys who double-crossed you? Were they caught?"

Tommy smirked. "Yeah, but not by us. See, those guys were working for a black dealer named Huggers. They double-crossed him too—took his coke, took my dad's money and split. That black dealer was even madder than my dad was, 'cos the guys who'd ripped him off were fucking with his western connection. So he and my dad had a conference, and he assured my dad that he'd take care of the pair. No 'buts' about it."

"And what happened?"

"Both guys got killed before Huggers could find 'em." He frowned. "One of them got into a bar fight over a woman, somewhere down in West Virginia. The other guy slashed his throat with a broken beer bottle. He bled to death before the ambulance got there. The second guy—the one who'd stabbed me—was found in an abandoned Bronx warehouse, tied up and with a bullet in the back of his head. Someone had executed him. Craziest thing is, the money and drugs weren't ever recovered." He laughed coldly. "Both Huggers and my dad are still mad about that." Then he looked grimly at Greg. "Believe me, kid, hearing about those deaths scared me more that getting slashed up myself. If I'd wanted out before, now I really wanted out. I could just see how that would have been me if Lucy hadn't ridden along with me out east. I mean, even after getting patched up by the surgeons, I left three feet of intestine on the operating table."

Tommy shrugged. "And so I got the hell out of the crime game. However, when I got up here to Boston, I needed to earn some money. So . . ."

***

Yes, Tommy Collins had decided to give up the criminal life for good. But the thing was, he liked the glamor of underground living: the easy money and the glossy women who accompanied that money.

So now he existed as a fringe dweller, living in the barely-legal shadow of the law, a lot like a guy who only ever fucked seventeen-year-olds, but ensured he only fucked them on the night before their eighteenth birthday.

Tommy called his group the Rectifiers, because they fixed, or 'rectified' situations for people. If you'd been screwed over (or even if you felt you had but weren't entirely sure) you took the case to Tommy and he looked into fixing it for you. For a fee, of course.

For instance, there was the case of wealthy Boston socialite Lois Kane, whose ex-husband had threatened to publicize several very explicit videos of her bad behavior. In those videos, Lois and a few friends had apparently been doing their best to level a hill of cocaine about a foot high. Lois Kane had had so much cocaine powdered on her face that when viewed in combination with the bright red lipstick smeared left and right across her bony cheeks, she seemed to be wearing clown makeup.

Lois had been referred to Tommy. Tommy and Dave had doped Mr. Kane, then posed him naked in several compromising situations with a bowl of crack cocaine and Dave's fourteen-year-old sister Lisa (who got a brand new Apple laptop and an iPhone as payment for her part in the drama). The pictures and video were then handed over to Mrs. Kane, who warned her ex that if he dared expose her, she'd expose him too.

So now both exes each had something damning on the other, if they were stupid enough to use it. And from what Tommy had since heard of both, they just might be.

The Rectifiers had clients on both sides of the law. Boston kingpin Marko Velli had even hired them on occasion.

As had Anderson and Futana's police boss, Captain Gillespie himself, in an extremely delicate blackmail matter concerning a stripper he'd unwisely spent the night with. Misty Daye wanted $100,000 in cash, or she'd take her story to the tabloids. The Captain would have paid up, but there was no guarantee that if he did, Misty wouldn't soon be back for more money.

For a while the Rectifiers had no idea what to use as leverage. One couldn't shame a stripper and violence wasn't part of their game.

But then, Dave discovered that Misty was two months pregnant. More important, she'd told friends she intended having the child. After that, all that was required was a trip downtown by Tommy to see an old friend who worked in a morgue.

Later that week, on arriving home at 3 a.m. after a hard night's dancing, Misty Daye found a specimen jar on her coffee table. The jar contained a preserved human fetus, one about six months old. Misty instantly fainted. When she recovered from her faint, she saw the printed note that had accompanied the fetus into her home. It had been placed under the jar. The note read:

Lay off, bitch. Take a good long look at this bottle. The next time you see one of these, it'll contain not just that brat you got inside you, but your entire womb as well. Signed, friends of the blackmailed top cop.

Needless to say, Misty Daye instantly got the message. She desperately wanted to be a mother and decided a hundred thousand dollars wasn't worth losing her womb over. She immediately called Captain Gillespie on the phone. (Her 3:50 a.m. call got him in trouble with his wife, who imagined a mistress was calling.) Weeping profusely, Misty apologized and promised to never, not ever, mention what had happened between them to anyone else.

After she'd hung up, she sat and stared at the fetus in the jar, wondering how to get rid of it.

Finally the ghastly thing went into the kitchen disposal.

***

"Wow!" Greg said. "I'd no idea that's what you guys did."

"It's not always stuff like that," Tommy replied. "Most times it's mob stuff we handle."

Greg frowned. "But you said . . ."

Tommy laughed. "No, nothing like that. We're out of the actual game. But we've got a certain credibility in mob circles, so . . . alright, I'll give you some examples. One thing we do is transport things.

Never drugs or guns though. It's mostly money that we carry. Say a guy here wants to send a half-mil to some other guy in Chicago, but doesn't want to pay it through the bank so the IRS don't get curious as to both how he earned it and why he ain't giving Uncle Sam his rightful share . . . well, we move it for him." He waited for that to sink in. "Yeah, and another thing we do—and you'd be surprised how often it happens—is hostage retrieval."

"What the hell is that? No, man, no need to explain; I think I know what you mean. Just how do you get involved?"

Tommy shrugged. "Again, it's a gangland thing. Someone's wife or favorite kid gets kidnapped and we take the ransom money over and bring them back *alive*. Usually during hostage negotiations, tempers flare and everyone starts shooting themselves, so we act as mediators. Sometimes the kidnappers specifically request that we handle it, 'cos we *never* double-cross anyone. Now, once it's over, they can all kill themselves if they like, but during the switch they'll give us their hostage and we'll give them their money; clean—no cops involved and no backstabbing either." He smiled with satisfaction. "To date, we've handled twelve kidnapping cases and no one's gotten killed yet."

"Wow!" Greg said.

All the time he'd been speaking, Tommy had been sizing Greg up. He wondered if the kid had the balls for the job. Looks were deceptive. Some guys looked like they could handle a poopstorm, but let the poop actually start raining down and they helped it along by crapping their pants. Other guys didn't look like much, but once the chips were down, they held up their own end remarkably well. He couldn't tell which type Greg here was. But he could see the boy was still interested.

"You still want in with us?" he asked Greg.

Greg nodded. "More than before. I'm certain I can hack it." His expression turned curious. "How about guns and stuff? Do you guys carry?"

"No, we don't. That's part of the deal with us, see?" He laughed softly at Greg's surprise. "It's less dangerous than you imagine. No one in gangland fucks with us. First of all, because they don't want trouble with my dad—who's a known badass all along the East Coast. Second of all, because they don't want any trouble with Marko Velli."

"Marko who?"

"Work with us and you'll soon know. Mr. Velli runs Boston crime; he's top underground dog in New England. He's also one of my dad's closest friends and an even bigger badass that my dad. So no, we don't need guns. Everyone we deal with knows it—we ain't coming in armed, so if you pull anything funny it's on you. Anyone messes with us, there'll be hell to pay."

"That's a relief to hear."

"Yeah, but it's still scary, you know? Who's to say that some shithead junkie won't be tempted to pull a heist on us for some fix money?" He grinned. "But still, it pays well. Better than the 9-to-5 grind any day."

There were more people in Bowie's now, mostly lunchtimers. Greg had long ago finished his beer, but he had no interest in ordering another.

"So, am I in?" he asked Tommy. "Pleeease, man, gimme a tryout with you guys."

"Hmmm." Tommy appeared to think on it for awhile, though he'd already made up his mind. "Yeah, alright," he said finally. "But we'll try you out first with a little job; ease you in slowly, see if you can handle the heat." Then he shook his head. "But not right now. At the moment, there ain't anything happening for us that we need another member for. So you gotta wait till something opens up. Once that deal comes, you'll have your tryout. Then, if you're tough enough for the Rectifiers, you're in."

Greg grinned. "Thanks, man. I won't let you guys down. You'll see."

A broad smile on his face, Greg got up and walked over to the bar to fetch fresh beers for them both.

***

Afterwards, Greg felt relieved. As far as work went, his aunt no longer controlled his destiny. He had Tommy's word that he'd be inducted into the Rectifiers once the right opportunity presented itself.

But still, he had to do something about Aunt Grace. This thing with making her endless semen smoothies was bound to backfire sooner or later. It was merely a matter of time before it did.

Short of slowly poisoning his aunt with antifreeze, Greg saw only one way out of his dilemma:

***

In the fortnight since she'd figuratively almost pulped his balls, Greg had seen Jojo Kim just twice. Each time he'd scowled at her and pushed past, hurrying out of the house as the Kim sisters arrived for the Saturday smoothie showdown.

Greg utterly hated Jojo now. He had no idea what he might do if left alone with the woman for even five minutes. It would likely be something very bad. Something that would make national headlines.

Jojo, however, seemed to consider the entire farce a huge joke. There was absolutely nothing Greg could do to her and she knew it. Each time they met at the front door, she made a grab for his ass and laughed.

The first time, he'd dodged her hands. The second time, he'd not been fast enough. She'd gotten a firm hold of his buttock cheeks. She'd dug her fingers in with incredible strength. Holding him in place in the doorway. He'd stood there facing her sisters, who were arguing while unloading Jojo's silver Porsche. She was behind him; Lulu and Kiki couldn't see her grip on him. He'd wanted to elbow her in the face. He'd wanted to hit her. He'd wanted to do something painful and bloody to her. Instead, he'd stood there meekly as though paralyzed, her fingers digging painfully into his buttocks.

She'd whispered, "I still want you, boy. I really do. Be nice to me—you won't regret it."

By then her sisters were climbing the front steps. She'd let go of him. He'd limped off hating her. His ass had ached for the rest of the afternoon.

So, yes, Greg utterly hated Jojo Kim now. But it also seemed like she was his only hope of salvation.

CHAPTER 24

Greg in Kimland, Pt. 1

The Kim sisters resided in a light-blue two-story building over on Wolfe Street. It was their father's place, but since he was never in the country, Jojo acted as caretaker for the house.

Lulu and Kiki moved in and out of the house as the whim took them. Sometimes they lived with their boyfriends, sometimes rented a place of their own, sometimes they squatted with friends. They were rockers—young and adventurous (not to mention occasionally stoned)—and putting down roots of any sort was something they only thought of as occurring far off in the future.

***

Greg rang the Kims' front door. It was brown, with a white transom and a wreath of plastic laurel curled around the spyhole.

He'd called ahead to say he was coming. He'd not said why. Jojo had replied "Yes, come over" with very little fanfare. She'd sounded as amused as ever.

Lulu opened the front door. The middle sister. 26-years-old. Short hair, brown almond eyes. She wasn't as good looking as Jojo, but she was prettier than Kiki. Kiki resented that—it gave her something additional to bitch about.

Lulu looked at Greg with a blank expression on her face. She neither smiled nor frowned. That deadpan expression was her thing. Generally, the only time Lulu Kim ever really acted animated was when she was performing on stage. Then, she behaved like she'd been plugged into the electric grid. But afterwards, as if she'd used up all of her current supply of 'zest for life' onstage and needed awhile to recharge her batteries, she slipped straight back into 'impassive chick' mode again.

She said, "Oh, it's you, man. Come on in. I'll tell sis you've arrived."

He followed her into the living room. Kiki was there with her boyfriend Slasher, who was sucking on a beer. Kiki was sitting in Slasher's lap and making a phone call. Lulu's boyfriend Zombie Joe was there too.

Lulu pointed out a seat to Greg, blew a kiss at Zombie Joe, and vanished up the stairs.

Greg nodded to both guys. Slasher shook his beer at him; Zombie Joe gave him a thumbs-up. None of the three of them said anything. Both boyfriends had long blonde hair and wore T-shirts, ripped denim pants and studded boots. There was a open acoustic guitar case beside Slasher as if they'd been rehearsing a tune before Kiki got on the phone; possibly even her new *Housefly Boyfriend* song.

Zombie Joe looked stoned. He always looked stoned. That was how he'd gotten the 'Zombie' tag in the first place. Kiki said he got stoned to slow him down so he could keep pace with Lulu.

Kiki was saying, "Hey, pops, don't you dare forget my caviar this time. And I want the genuine Black Sea Beluga stuff, not something you bought in a shopping mall. I . . . Oh, and greet Auntie Galina for me. . . . Okay, bye—love you, pops." These words were spoken with the arrogant confidence of the last-born child who knows beyond a shadow of a doubt that she's the apple of her aging father's eye.

(Greg knew a little bit about this: Since being flown out of South Korea thirty-six years ago with a bullet in his leg, Mr. Kim had continued to work as a spy, this time for Uncle Sam. According to Aunt Grace, even Jojo was confused as to her father's actual role in helping implement American foreign policy. A case in point: At the moment the old man was in Russia, wining and dining [and possibly bedding—their mother having died five years ago] an aged millionairess—Galina Tokareva—said to be descended from Peter the Great. This rigmarole had to do with influencing President Putin on some minor detail about the Urals crude oil exports. Politics indeed made strange bedfellows.)

Kiki hung up and began kissing Slasher. She had a desperate way of kissing, like she was scared to press lip to lip, or didn't really want to kiss him (maybe she was too angry with Slasher to actually want to express intimate affection), but she felt it was a social obligation she needed to perform, both to reassure herself that Slasher was *her* boyfriend, and to remind everyone else around them of that fact too.

Zombie Joe closed his eyes and began humming *People = Shit* by Slipknot. (Their own band KCS was so heavy, they made Marilyn Manson seem like Justin Bieber by comparison.)

Lulu returned, a deadpan statuette. From the hallway entrance she crooked a silent finger at Greg.

"Upstairs," she told him when he joined her. "Second bedroom on the left. Sis says you two wanna talk in private."

Greg climbed the stairs.

***

Jojo Kim's bedroom was large. It was also very strange. The walls were bright blue. The ceiling was the same fluorescent green as his past glimpse of her panties. The floor was pink, and seemed coated with rubber. There were two rubber-upholstered chairs and a psychedelic orange closet. The windows had yellow curtains.

Jojo's bed was big and round and completely red. Red sheets, red pillows. It seemed to be a waterbed.

The room had a thick smell of incense to it. Joss sticks smoked in wall holders.

Greg took all this in as peripheral input. From the moment he'd opened the door his eyes had been riveted on Jojo herself. She was naked, without a stitch of clothing anywhere on her. She lay in the middle of the round bed, on her back with her legs slightly parted and her knees raised. The crimson bed seemed like a pair of giant female lips about to eat her.

Greg stared at her. Naked, she was alluring. Deliciously hot. Slim and sexy. Her small breasts were pert and perfectly fit her figure. Her nipples were large chocolate sweets. Her belly was a taut expanse of salon-browned flesh. Her hips were wide, her thighs toned, her legs sleek, her feet pampered and exquisite.

"Do you like what you see?" she asked in a matter-of-fact voice.

She dipped her hands between her thighs and pulled her southern lips apart. Greg caught his breath at the appearance of the black aperture in the middle of the pink. She was wet, smeared with her body's white cream. He began hardening in his pants.

Through a huge exertion of willpower he got a grip on himself again. No, *I'm not here for that. I'm here to discuss business. I'm here to discuss my future.* He looked around quickly. He saw no cameras. This wasn't her studio. That was a relief. Greg hated video cameras now.

"I feel like killing you," he told Jojo.

"Yeah, I know," she replied. "It'd be so easy to do in here, wouldn't it? All you have to do is leap up onto the bed, wrap your fingers around my throat, and squeeze with all the hatred you feel for me."

The way she said it; she made it sound so simple. He considered murdering her in exactly the way she'd just described to him.

She continued speaking: "You won't dare though. I'm your only hope to escape Grace's clutches and you know it."

"Why did you do it? Why?"

"Your aunt was curious. She paid me to find out what you were putting into her smoothies." She shrugged. "Hey, don't shoot the messenger. You were just silly. That was a nasty thing to do to an old woman who loves you."

"Yes, yes, and now she's making my life a living hell because of it. I need you to help me get my damn life back."

"You're so ungrateful, man; you dig that? Gracie loves you like a son." She laughed as she said this. "She'd do anything for you and you know that."

"Yes, but she's trying to do way too much. And lots of sons hate their mothers." His voice assumed a pleading tone. "Listen, Jojo, just help me, will you? I'll do whatever you want in return."

"Whatever I want? Well, fancy that. This is definitely an improvement over how you've been treating me for the past two months. Alright, if you'll do *whatever* I want, it's a deal. Now, take your clothes off and then come to bed."

"To bed?"

"Get naked and come make love with me."

Greg got naked. Walking to the bed, he became aware that the pink floor was a sort of rubber rug. It sank under his feet like a cushion. At several spots near Jojo's bed, the floor showed faded stains. Something had splattered there and not wiped completely off. Greg began to get a bad feeling. He hoped that that wasn't blood on the floor. He'd just promised to do anything she wanted. Had he just set himself up for some violent S&M play?

Still, he was young and Jojo was beautiful. Once he joined her on the red bed he had no trouble getting an erection. He felt no guilt towards Debbie: he was doing this for Debbie. He was here now so that he and Debbie would have a blissful future together without the eternal specter of his aunt's damning revelations threatening their happiness.

For Debbie, Greg was willing to do whatever it took.

Jojo stroked his erection for a while, then pushed him down towards her crotch. "Eat me," she demanded.

Greg got down to licking her sex. She was very clean. She was also very tasty down there, as though she'd been eating lots of pineapple in anticipation of his calling on her. He teased her clitoris with his tongue and sucked on her labia. Jojo moaned and ground her sex against his mouth.

After a while she pulled him up. "Put it in," she gasped.

"Do you have a rubber? I didn't bring any."

"Forget the damn rubber. I won't get pregnant. And I've drunk enough of your semen already to fall sick if I was destined to."

He positioned his body over hers and slid his penis inside. He began thrusting inside her.

The sex was strange. He felt as though her body was both welcoming and rejecting his penis. Jojo's body moved against his with a strange reluctance; as if he was hurting her. Or, as if she didn't really want what she said she wanted. Still, it was nice. He didn't think Jojo came. She made noises of pleasure and was wet and juicy and very tight around his erection. She seemed to enjoy the fuck, but she never let herself go. He could tell she wasn't completely into it. She was there, but gave off a vibe of needing 'something extra' to get her off. He was certain of that.

Very strange.

He came, emptying himself into her. Ejaculating all his months of hatred and frustration and anger into her sweet vagina. His dislike of her exploded out of his manhood in delicious spurts of wetness. It was almost as good as with Debbie.

His arms gave out and he collapsed on her. She sighed loudly and went limp. Not orgasmic limp but starfish limp.

Something wasn't right. Greg just knew that this wasn't what Jojo wanted from him.

"How was it?" she asked him.

"You were great," he said. "It's a relief not to have to think of smoothies during orgasm."

"I like smoothies too," she said in a sultry voice. "but not today. Today was for you, baby, so you could see what you've been missing. Next time, it'll be for me. You'll make me a smoothie too then, a large one full of your love cream." A fire entered her gaze now. Her eyes shone and she licked her already wet lips.

Her voice turned cold. "Okay, now listen. Where sex is concerned I've got a serious hang-up. For some reason that my shrink can't figure out, I can't come normally. You must've have sensed that just now."

"Yeah, I did," he admitted.

"I enjoy sex as much as the next woman, but the orgasm just won't come unless . . . So I need you to help me come; with no complaints. If you do what I ask, with no questions asked, I'll erase your aunt's copies of that video and get rid of the originals too."

"What do you want me to do?"

She told him. He stared at her in total disgust. "What? You want me to poop on you?" He was appalled. Even hardcore BDSM would be preferable.

She wasn't fazed by his disgust. She didn't even appear to notice it. "That's what gets me off," she said. "Yes, yes, yes, Greg, I've got a scat fetish—I can't have an orgasm except someone shits on me, and then fucks me in the shit. Like I said, even my shrink doesn't know why I've got this hang-up."

He examined her face to see if she was pulling his leg. But no, Jojo was clearly serious; no way was she having fun with him.

"You do it for me how I want you to," she continued, "and I'll hack into Gracie's laptop and delete everything she's got on you. And I'll erase my own copies too. You'll be clean, so long as you don't go wanking into another old woman's drinks afterwards."

"I don't get it—she *still* wants to drink them."

"She's obsessive, that's all. Listen, man, forget Gracie for a moment. Do we have an agreement or not?"

Greg thought on it for the longest minute of his life. *She want me to take a dump on her so she can get off.*

Jojo let him think. Greg knew he had no choice. She knew that too. He had to say yes. If he'd remained angry with her, if he'd not slept with her first, he might have stayed indignant enough to leave her presence. But having sex with her had mellowed him out. Now he was able to consider her request rationally and overcome his prejudices towards her fecal fetish. He also realized that the self-disgust resulting from what she wanted him to do would pass.

Still, he had one major fear about her request:

"Okay, let's say I agree to this, is this a one-time thing, or will I be expected to put in a repeat performance from time to time?"

"That's entirely up to you. Once is all I'm asking for. But who knows, you may enjoy it—then you're welcome back anytime."

She smiled while saying this; as though all she wanted him to do to her was to give her cunnilingus again. Greg managed to smile back. Inside he was thinking: *Enjoy crapping on you? You must be out of your pretty mind, pretty woman!*

"Deal," he said.

She smiled broadly. Alright, then! Now, let's see, when? Today's Wednesday. Gosh, I'm busy all this week with promo stuff for my sisters' new CD—I won't even be at the smoothie meeting on Saturday, none of us will. But how about next Friday . . . no no, Thursday'll be better." She looked at him, her eyes agleam with a desperate lust that had him pitying her. "Is next Thursday good for you? Some time after lunch hour? We'll have the house to ourselves—Kiki and Lulu have a rehearsal that afternoon."

He nodded grimly. "Any day of the week is fine. Until I get Aunt Grace off my neck, I'm serially unemployed."

"Good, good, now listen."

"I'm listening."

"You're new to this, so I'd better tell you how I want it done."

"Yeah, sure."

"First thing: don't you dare tell anyone about this. If word of my scat fetish gets out because of you, I'll string you up by the balls."

"C'mon. I'm no longer thirteen. But damn, you're just so dirty. No one would ever suspect that a beautiful woman like you . . . I mean . . . you hardly ever even find stuff like this in internet porn."

"Yeah, right. You're just looking in all wrong places then. How do you think *I* found out it worked for me? Mills and Boon? Harlequin Romances? Wise up, man. Okay, now here's how you prepare . . ."

CHAPTER 25

Anderson & Futana

It was shaping up to be a hell of a strange morning. Shortly after getting out of bed Tom Anderson received a phone call.

"Is that Detective Anderson?" a high-pitched voice asked.

"Yeah, speaking."

"This is Mary Watt," the woman said. "If you want to know about Wet Bones, drive out to the old Hourigan Farm at Oakham in Worchester County and have a look around. You'll find a lot to interest you there."

"Mary Watt?" Anderson asked. "H-h-how . . . ?"

But the phone had already gone dead on him. He called back several times with no response.

First thing Anderson did was write down the farm address the woman had given him so he didn't forget it.

Then next, he sat quietly for five minutes, bouncing thoughts through his brain.

Mary Watt hadn't just called him. Mary Watt couldn't have called him.

Mary Watt was dead, butchered by her husband.

But if the dead woman hadn't just called him, then who had? This couldn't be considered a crank call, not when the woman had used the 'Wet Bones' code name.

His first thought was that the caller hadn't actually been a woman. Her voice had sounded more like a transvestite's, a male faking female speech. Or had it been his partner, Laurie, playing a trick on him?

No, Laurie wouldn't do that. And besides, Laurie's voice was already surgically feminized. She sounded naturally female.

Anderson called the station. He gave them the caller's number and asked for a quick check on who it belonged to. Then, he went off to have a bath and make himself some breakfast.

The call from the station came while he was having his second cup of morning coffee. Anderson calmly received the news that the phone number he'd enquired about belonged to the recently deceased Mrs. Rosemary Susan Watt. He thanked the officer who'd called with the information, then hung up. He finished his coffee and then phoned Laurie Futana.

"Girl, you're not gonna believe this . . ."

***

They headed out alone, with Anderson at the wheel. Just they two in their unmarked squad car. It was the same as with everything else on this case: that 'being alone' bit. Like no one else on the police force gave a flying turd what they were up to.

"What are we?" Futana fumed while Anderson drove. "The Incognito Squad? We head out to this place without even backup?"

"Who's gonna believe a dead woman called me? Even I don't believe it. But the call did come from Mary Watt's cellphone. So . . . so we handle this alone. If we happen to find something out there, then . . ."

He let it hang. Futana filled in his thoughts. They'd been working together so long, she used almost the exact words he would have:

"Tom, even if we do find something out there, they'll put a shrinkwrap on it and stow it away in the station freezer. And that has to do with what Stephanie Richards told us about the damn cryptizoogy, cryptical thingies."

"Cryptids. Unknown, nonexistent, or mythological beasts."

"Yeah, yeah, whatever." Her beautiful face squeezed up into a pissed-off mess. She began tapping angrily on the glove compartment door. "So the monster can't exist and now a corpse calls you and tells you just where it can be found. Who are we, huh? Mulder and Scully? I don't even like that damn show. I tell you, man, this is getting infuriating!"

"Just cool it. We'll go in armed and keep well away from harm."

"More like we'll go in forearmed and get all four arms bitten off."

"Stop playing drama queen. It suits you."

"Well, here we are, I think. Shit, looking at this place, man, it don't seem like anyone's been here for the better part of a century. And . . . and we're still out in the dirt road."

Anderson nodded. "All the better to eat folks in, I guess."

***

The Hourigan Farm had long ago fallen into disuse. Its front yard was overrun with weeds. The grass grew as high as the knee. In some places it was even higher.

Anderson and Futana parked outside the low fence, out of sight of the farmhouse. They entered the rusty ancient gate. The main farm building stood fifty yards off, connected to the front gate by a long-overgrown gravel driveway. Behind it the tops of several barns were visible. The front yard had a smattering of fruit trees. Not enough, however, to provide any useful cover for the detectives.

Guns drawn, they moved quietly towards the farmhouse. It was imperative that they not scare off whoever or whatever was hiding here. The bushes on either side of the grassy drive rustled with hidden creatures, little animals unused to having their serenity disturbed. A stink of rotting fruit pervaded the air, tainting the morning.

"We're not the first ones here," Anderson whispered. "Someone else has been using this road."

"How'd do you mean?" Futana whispered back.

Anderson pointed down. "The grass is flattened."

Futana saw what he meant. "Yes, it's bent over because someone's been driving over it." She paused a moment. "But there's more, man: the blades of grass aren't dead. They're all flattened but still green."

"Yeah, meaning either that whoever's been using this place hasn't been using it for long, or they don't come here often."

"The way the grass is still bent over, I'll lean more to the first likelihood," Futana said. "Either that or someone drove over them just this morning."

"There's no car."

"The guy might have left. His departure would flatten the grass yet further."

"Why are we still assuming *human* involvement? Stephanie's told us it's some damn cryptid beastie doing the damage."

"Yeah, sure. But how'd it get out here to the farm? And . . . and if there's no human involvement, how come dead Mary Watt felt involved enough to phone you from the afterlife about it?"

Anderson had no reply to that.

They stepped off the drive and hid behind a large oak tree. From this place of concealment, twenty or so yards up the driveway, they studied the farmhouse.

The stone building had boarded-up windows. It was draped thick with ivy. In some places creepers formed a canopy between the trees and the house. Those structures closest to the main building were in similar derelict condition.

The oak tree concealing the detectives was on the right side of the yard. From here Anderson and Futana could see behind the main house. There were two large barns and a small wood-and-brick shed back there. All three buildings stood on the left. Both barn's doors had fallen off due to age and disrepair. The shed door was still intact but wide open. They didn't notice any vehicles.

Staring at the crumbling old buildings gave Anderson a bad vibe. "We gotta figure this out some more," he told Futana.

She shook her head. She pointed her Glock 22 towards the house. "There's nothing to figure out, Tom. Whoever's using this place is either still here or gone." Unlike Anderson, Futana was raring to get started. "We'd better split up," she said.

He shook his head. "No; too dangerous." He pointed beyond the farmhouse. "You wait here behind the tree. Stay out of sight while I go peek into the barns. If I notice anyone I'll call ya. If they're empty, I'll search a bit for evidence, and signs of our monster."

She frowned. "That sounds unsafe too."

"We've no real choice—it ain't like we got the manpower to cordon off the area. What I'm thinking here is—if I walk past the house to go check the barns at the back, anyone hiding in the house is gonna try to get away. They see me holding my gun and they'll figure it's the police. Then you can stop 'em leaving. Or if there's more than one person, you fire a warning shot and I'll come running. Then we cuff 'em and radio for backup."

She mulled it over. "Assuming the punk hasn't already seen us."

"It'd be hard for him to—seeing how all the front windows are boarded up." He raised a finger to make a further point. "Then afterwards, once certain all the barns are empty, we can both search the farmhouse. That way we can't be ambushed."

"Why not search the farmhouse first?"

"If someone in the barns hears us breaking in a door in the main house, they'll be over the fields and far away before we can get out to stop 'em."

She nodded. "Alright, we do it like you say." She grinned. "Sure you don't want me to go search though? You're an old man, you ain't got either the reflexes or stamina that I do."

Anderson shook his head and set off at a jog. He saw no point in moving secretively; he was fully exposed now, there was no cover between the oak tree and the farm buildings.

Futana watched him go. Suddenly she felt intense misgivings. Yes, Tom's plan made logical sense. The problem with it was, that despite their suspicion of human involvement in the Wet Bones case, they weren't actually looking for *people*. They weren't after homo sapiens. They were after a *monster*. A monstrosity of some kind. A terrible thing, the shape of which they had no idea of.

And if Tom ran into the monster in those barns . . .

She was suddenly scared for him. *Shit, Tom don't go in there!*

But he'd already reached the farmhouse. He turned, gave a thumbs-up, then ran quickly past it and vanished from view into the first barn.

Now all she could do was wait. She didn't plan on waiting forever though. The first hint she had that he was in any danger, she'd dash over there.

***

Anderson looked around the barn interior. There was nothing in here. Just bales of ancient and rotten hay in one far corner and two busted plows in the other. And lots of startled field mice that scurried for cover the moment his silhouette filled the doorway.

He felt both frustrated and relieved. Relieved because . . . well, they weren't actually looking for people, were they? They were after something non-human.

Their quarry had no definite form in Anderson's mind. He realized he might even be looking at the damn thing and not recognize it for what it was. It could trap him, swallow him up in an instant.

171

And as far as people were concerned? Anderson was well aware that even if there were folks living out here on the farm, that didn't automatically make them villains. They might just be squatters. Illegal, sure, but that didn't make them murderers. To make a proper arrest, he and Futana would need to unearth incriminating evidence concerning them. And that might or might not exist.

But meanwhile, the damn monster is real. And I've no idea what it looks like.

He walked through the barn and peered out of its far window. The view was prosaic. Overgrown fields as far as the eye could make out. An abandoned orchard to his left, close enough to smell the rotted fruit; either apples or pears, his nose informed him. A few houses in the far distance; other farms perhaps. Beyond those, a wide spread of picturesque hills.

Nothing suspicious or relevant to their investigation.

He turned to start back towards the barn entrance. Then he heard a sound. He stopped and listened. He heard it again. It was coming from the next barn. It wasn't a loud sound, but it sounded eerie in a familiar way. A muffled dull thud that repeated twice and then ceased.

Taking care now to avoid making a noise, Anderson hurried to the entrance. Outside he waved to Futana. She waved back, then ducked back into hiding. Anderson made his way over to the next barn.

To his surprise, this second barn was also empty. Its main contents were some old wooden feeding troughs and a stack of large pipes. Anderson walked inside. He stood in the middle of the barn, surrounded by the stink of the past. He turned in a slow circle, his ears alert for the sound he'd heard in the other barn. But there was nothing. That eerie thudding had stopped. He didn't understand it. Were his ears playing tricks on him now?

Just to make sure, he walked over to the wall next to the first barn. Except for a rusty box of old horse-shoes, there was nothing there.

That left just the third building on the row. The old shed. Pig shed, tool shed, tanning shed; whatever it had been. Maybe it had just housed the well and pump.

Anderson stepped outside and waved to Futana again. The sky was overcast now, heavy with clouds like it was going to rain. The wind too had cooled. He hoped the rain waited until they'd left the farm. He didn't want his new shoes ruined by mud.

And so why the hell didn't you wear sneakers when you left home? You knew you were going to a farm, didn't you?

Ignoring his own accusations, Anderson peeped into the shed.

Unlike the first two, this building wasn't empty, occupied only by impressions of the vanished past.

No. On the left side of the shed stood a wooden work table. Half of a skinned corpse lay on the table. The other half of the body lay in red pieces in a metal bucket.

Anderson was so surprised by what he was seeing that he failed to react when a brawny arm shot out from behind the door, grabbed his gun arm, and yanked him into the shed. Before he could spin around to defend himself, he was hit in the head with something hard that knocked him senseless.

***

Futana saw nothing of what happened to Anderson. She'd been staring back towards the road when he vanished from view. Just before he'd leaned into the doorway, she'd heard a vehicle behind her, approaching along the old road. On hearing the loud rattle of its engine, she'd ducked around to the other side of the oak tree, then turned to look at it, in case it was coming here to the Hourigan Farm. In that case, it would most likely be the criminal they were after. However, the nearing vehicle—an open farm truck piled high with fresh vegetables—had merely rolled past the Hourigan place, headed out for the main road.

By the time Futana turned back towards the farmhouse, Anderson was out of sight. She resumed her original sentry position and settled down to wait again. It was taking Anderson about six minutes to search each barn, almost as if he was attempting to become friends with the roaches and rats that lived in each, so he could ask them if they'd noticed anything suspicious lately.

She smirked. Maybe Tom's eyes needed that much time to adjust to the dimness in each building. She'd told him he was getting old.

***

When Anderson revived, he discovered he was both tied up and gagged. Also, his pants and underpants were down around his ankles. He didn't get this last bit. It made sense to him that criminals would tie him up, but why the hell would they pull his pants down too?

He was bent over the table next to the half-corpse, secured so he couldn't straighten up. His suit was completely messed up from the spilled blood everywhere. The skinned body was a woman's—it had no penis or testicles. He now saw what had been making the thudding sound: there was a meat cleaver stuck in the dead woman's right buttock. Anderson dully noted that the person chopping up the corpse must have been hitting it extra-hard for the sound to have travelled past the intervening building to the first barn.

He tugged and kicked against his bonds, but they held firm. This guy was good at tying people up.

He heard footsteps. "Hey, you're awake!" The voice was gruff.

"Hmmmph!" Meaning "Let me go!" which he knew wasn't about happening.

Anderson had one hope though: This guy who'd knocked him out clearly had no idea that Laurie Futana was also nearby. If he did, he'd have taken care of her first before tying him up. Or had he? No, he couldn't have. There was no way he could approach Futana's hiding place without her seeing him coming.

The main problem Anderson envisaged now was how long it would take before Futana decided to come looking for him. Anderson stared at the skinned set of buttocks beside him. *It had better be long before I start looking like that.*

Meanwhile his captor was talking. The man remained out of sight behind him: "Hey, cop, I hope you don't mind, but I've never fucked a cop's ass in my life; so I'm gonna sample yours."

The statement was so unprecedentedly absurd that Anderson felt his ears weren't working right. Then he got angry. *What? This son-of-a-bitch plans on raping me? What!? Hey, that's a crime, you asshole! Rape's a crime!*

"Now, easy now, let me just open ya up a little!"

Anderson heard a spitting sound and then fingers were being roughly inserted into his anus. He yelled in fury but the gag muffled the sounds. He kicked and flailed but it was useless. He was expertly bound.

The hurtful probing went on for almost a minute. Then the fingers were removed. Anderson's relief was short-lived. Almost immediately, he felt his unknown assailant grip his hips. "And now, let me ride this law enforcement ass, cowboy."

Anderson did the only thing he could. He tensed his ass as hard as he could. No way was anyone slipping any penis up his rear. Hell no! In his mind he began cursing his partner:

Dammit, Laurie, where the hell are you!?

Meanwhile, his clenching of his anus was working. His would-be rapist was getting frustrated. The man began swearing:

"Shit, you damn cop, loosen your asshole. Your ass feels like a rock—ain't nothing sexy about that! Relax your hole goddammit and let my dick in. Oh, you ain't gonna? Oh, we'll see about that. I'll just have to help you along now, won't I?"

Next thing, whatever had knocked Anderson out the first time hit him in the back of the head again. He faded into the darkness for a second time.

***

Laurie Futana decided she'd waited long enough. As far as she could tell, Anderson had found something of interest in that third little building. His not reappearing though, spoke of him being in trouble.

She left the cover of the tree and hurried forward.

In the time since Anderson entered the shed, it had started drizzling. The oak tree had been keeping Futana dry, but now she had no choice but to make her way through the falling drops of water. She went quickly. Amongst other reasons for her haste, she'd styled her hair just yesterday and the rain was certain to mess up her new hairdo. She saw a flash of lightning in the distance, heard the accompanying rumble of thunder.

As she passed the farmhouse, a sudden wind blew wetness into her face.

Once past the farmhouse, Futana began running. The rain had suddenly increased in intensity. She however wasn't worried about her hair anymore. She was now really worried about her partner.

Oh, Tom, what the hell's happened to you? Once again, her ambiguous feelings for him bubbled to the surface. He was impossible to like, but she found it equally unthinkable to dislike him either. His male vitality attracted her like iron to a magnet.

She'd reached the shed. To escape the rain, she pressed herself against the shed wall, beneath its cracked eaves. Now was the time to go slow. She didn't intend to get ambushed by whatever had Tom, in case something *did* have him in its slobbering clutches.

Gun held ready to fire, she eased her way along the wall to the door.

Then she kicked something that made a ringing metal sound. She looked down and winced. She'd kicked an old can hidden in the overgrown grass.

Like the proverbial 'empty vessel,' it had made a loud sound though. She realized this when a moment later, she hear a startled male voice saying, "Shit, cop, don't tell you've got backup! I ain't even put it in yet!" Then she heard the disorganized sounds of a scramble.

She dashed to the door and looked into the shed. She was just in time to see someone leaping out of the far window.

"Hey you! Stop or I'll shoot!"

She ran inside, towards the window to stop the man. But then she caught sight of Anderson. Seeing him, an intense worry flooded her. His head was all bloody. Abandoning all thought of apprehending the fleeing suspect, she hurried over to Anderson and examined him instead.

He was alive but unconscious, lying beside . . . Ugh!

We've certainly struck pay dirt here, she thought on seeing the skinned buttocks and legs that occupied the rest of the table Anderson was tied over. The cleaver stuck in the right buttock struck her as classically brutal.

Then she forgot the corpse and contemplated something even more intriguing. Why were Anderson's pants down? She looked closer, daring to part his buttocks for a proper inspection. Wow, she'd never imagined Anderson had this much hair on his ass. The hairy brown eye of his anus stared back at her.

Staring at her unconscious partner's bare behind, Futana suddenly understood what had been about happening. She felt horrified. *Oh, the guy who ran away was about raping Tom!* She was relieved that it hadn't happened.

But then the unthinkable happened.

At her moment of understanding, a wind of lust seemed to swirl up from the barn floor and fill her brain. The lust smothered her thoughts. It was thick like Vaseline, altering her perceptions of right and wrong.

Now she looked differently at Anderson's buttocks. They seemed to be waiting just for her. Prepared just for her. His ass hole looked so inviting.

She'd not had an erection in a long time (her hormone shots prevented them), but now she found herself hard as a bone (*Fitting,* she felt, *since we're tracking bones anyway. Though in my case it's a wet boner.*) Her erection was damned uncomfortable.

"Forgive me, Tom, for what I'm gonna do to you," she mouthed in anguished desire for his body. "I really *can't* help myself."

Moving in a sensual daze, Futana pulled up her skirt and let her hard penis out. She spat on it and pushed it against Tom's anus. The hole was tight and unwelcoming. She persevered. She imagined the sphincter opening like a door, admitting her inside his body like a close friend. She was undeterred in her efforts. Slow and steady was how one deflowered a virgin. She pushed harder. The hole gave slightly, then a little more . . . and then she was inside him. Fully inside his body. She quickly found a sweet rhythm in his rectum and stroked back and forth.

He made no sound as she used him, gave no indication that he was anywhere else than in La-la-land.

It didn't take long for her to come. It had been ages since she'd had sex. After a minute and a half of vigorous thrusting (*Damn, is Tom tight or what!*) she ejaculated inside him. She gritted her teeth and trembled against him and tried not to scream with delight. She'd intended to pull out of him before coming, but the sensation was too intense. She lost control of herself and let Tom have it all.

Then she pulled out. She rolled her eyes as her semen spilled out of his ass and ran down his hairy legs. There was so much of it!

Then reality hit her: *Oh my gosh, what the hell have I just done? What do I do now?*

Anderson was still out cold. Futana wiped her penis off and packed it away again. Then she hurried out of the shed. Ignoring the rain that was now coming down in torrents, she ran around the building, in the direction that she figured the man who'd knocked out Anderson had taken.

***

Anderson regained consciousness. He could hear that it was raining. He was still tied up and gagged. He had a splitting headache. His ass ached like . . . like . . .

Shit! Anderson was suddenly fully awake. *That son-of-a-bitch! He . . . he . . . !* There was no point thinking it through. He could feel the wetness between his buttocks and on the back of his legs. It had happened: he'd been raped by his captor.

Anderson had an impression of his body rocking back and forth against the table while he was unconscious. Of something fat and hard being stuffed where it ought not to be. Of a terrible wetness flooding him where the sun never shone.

Shit! Where in the hell is Laurie? Still watching for me under her damn oak? Scared to mess up her hair in the rain? God damn that silly woman! Get your ass in here and untie me!

Tom Anderson wasn't like most men. The indignity he'd just suffered didn't fill him with a crisis of confidence. He viewed his having been raped as a crime committed on his person. Nothing more than that. Besides, horrible as it must have been, he didn't remember it happening—the dubious benefits of unconsciousness. He could put it behind him. He however hated crimes and criminals with a passion.

Right there and then, he coldly decided three things:

First: He wasn't telling anyone that he'd been raped. Laurie would know, but that couldn't be helped.

Second: He was finding the man who'd sodomized him, if it was last thing he did in his life.

Third: When he found that man, he was going to shoot him dead. The guy was a sicko anyway—why else had he been chopping up a skinless dead woman?

Those three things settled in his mind, Anderson settled into a moody calm and waited for Futana to come and untie him. Even without another man's unwelcome semen smeared all over you, it was undignified being trussed up like this.

***

Laurie Futana ran through the rain looking for the fugitive. She didn't find him. She knew he was long gone. Nonetheless, she kept running anyway.

In a sense she was running away from herself. Fleeing from accepting what she'd just done to Anderson. In another sense, she was purifying herself from her crime, letting the rain cleanse her from her sin against him. Fuck her hair.

And in a third sense, she was establishing her alibi that she'd not been the one who'd come in his ass.

Finally though, drenched through and through, she made her wet way back to the shed. She had to untie Tom. She couldn't just leave him there with his bare ass in the air. She stifled an inappropriate giggle. She dressed herself in courage and walked into the shed.

Anderson was awake now. She crossed over to him. She tried not to stare at her trail of come on his hairy thighs, those white worms of semen wriggling down his legs. She was just going to pretend that nothing had happened to him. But what if he found her silence suspicious? It was a possibility. But also, knowing Anderson, he'd appreciate her not saying a thing about how undignified he looked.

First thing she did was ungag him.

"Where the hell have you been?" he growled. "I found the damn perp in here and the bastard knocked me out."

She had her story ready, revised and adjusted to perfection while running through the rain. There would be no holes in her tale. "Tom, I was just getting here, when I heard noises. I peeped in and saw this guy . . ."

"A big guy?"

"Yeah, quite big. He was dashing off through the rain. I peeped in, saw the corpse on the table and followed him. He just kept going . . . then I slipped on some grass and . . . by the time I got up, he'd vanished."

"You hear a car, or a bike? Any kind of transportation?"

"Nothing. The punk disappeared almost like a magic trick."

She pulled the cleaver from the corpse's ass. She slashed Anderson's bonds with it. She first freed his hands, then, while he worked the circulation back into his wrists, she released his feet from their constraints.

Bending over to slice through the ropes around his ankles, she smelt her semen on him. Some of it was splattered like spilled milk in the stretched crotch of his pants. Again, she couldn't help smiling. She'd had him!

But then, she immediately felt terrible again, chastened and wracked with guilt. *Good heavens, how could I?* She still didn't understand why she'd raped him. All of a sudden the intense desire for his body had been in her head and she'd been unable to control herself and . . . shit!

"You need to change your pants, man," she said. "Looks like you pissed on yourself."

He grunted. He'd been wiping the blood from his head with a handkerchief and feeling the bumps. He hoped he didn't have a concussion: that son-of-a-bitch had hit him extra-hard. Though relieved that Futana was pretending not to notice the obvious, Anderson couldn't see what she found otherwise amusing. He shoved her away.

She maintained the masquerade, looking across the shed like nothing odd was going on.

He wiped his buttocks and legs clean with the bloody handkerchief, then bent and pulled up his trousers.

Futana watched him closely while he zipped up. She felt very nervous. But, he didn't seem to realize that anything nasty had happened to him. Other than wincing while shifting his weight from left foot to right, he seemed exactly the same man who'd left her by the oak tree. She found that remarkable. In fact, she found it amazing how cool her partner was currently acting.

She felt intense relief that she'd gotten away with what she'd done to him. And it really looked like she had. If Anderson at all realized that he'd been sodomized while unconscious, he clearly thought it was the runaway man who'd done it.

Anderson finished buckling his belt. He frowned at Futana. "Well, that damn tip paid off, didn't it?"

She returned her mind to cop mode. The grim look on his face made it easy for her to pretend that nothing inappropriate had happened in the interim. "Yeah, I guess. But . . . if we consider this logically, we've got a problem."

His face squeezed up. "Run the problem by me."

She tapped the butcher table. "Well, this might be a completely different crime. This guy clearly isn't the Wet Bones maker. I dunno why the hell he's chopping this lady up, but we weren't about finding her skeleton in one piece and all slimed over with cryptzoogy goop."

"Cryptids, Laurie. Please try and remember that—the damn things are called cryptids."

"Yeah, sure. Cryptid goop then. And, hey, there's no need to bark at me like I'm your dog or something. I'm not the one who tied you up." She didn't mean to be nasty by replying him like this: she was just maintaining her alibi.

Her faked irritation bypassed Anderson like rain streaming off a duck's back. "Well, you sure could have gotten in here sooner," he growled back. He shifted weight on his feet again. He winced again. "Shit, my damn hemorrhoids are acting up again. The damn things are killing me! But yeah, you make a good point. This guy ain't our guy." Then he frowned. "But if he ain't who we're looking for, why did the ghost on the phone ask us to come out here?"

"That is the question to be answered." Futana looked outside. The rain was waning now. The sky was lightening. The wind had died down, letting the falling drops of water settle to the vertical again from their previous forty-five-degree slant. She even saw a suggestion of a rainbow.

It doesn't freaking matter now, does it? I'm soaked through and through and my hair's ruined.

She removed her jacket and tried wringing the water out of it. Then she gave up in disgust and looked back at Anderson, who was by the shed door, retrieving his gun from where it had fallen.

"What do we do now?" she asked. "Call the station?"

He shook his head. "Later. Let's search the farmhouse first."

***

Guns at the ready, they forced open the rear farmhouse door. A musty smell greeted them. The smell of bygone years and long-vanished people. Dust lay thick everywhere. The windows were draped in cobwebs. Spiders scuttled over the floor like they owned the place.

"We're not going to find anyone in here," Futana said on an intuition. "Look at the floor—no footprints except ours."

"You're right," Anderson agreed. She *was* right. The building was in a pristine state of neglect and abandonment. It seemed no one had entered it for years.

WOL-VRIEY

They retreated back out into the drizzle. Back to that final gory shed. There, they put their guns away. Anderson placed a call to the station. Then, while waiting for Forensics to arrive, he and Futana looked through the shed.

There was little in there of interest. Just the chopped-up woman, several buckets and knives, a large and bloody circular saw, and the portable gas generator that had clearly been used to power it.

"That runaway guy's fingerprints have to be all over this place," Futana said. "It's only a matter of time before we know who he is."

"Time?" Anderson retorted. "Time. Laurie, my patience is running thin. It seems like we've been working this case forever."

She blew him a kiss. He was a handsome mess. The blood trickling down his face made him look folklore heroic. "We *have* been working on this case forever, Thomas darling. It's been how many months now? Hey, when *did* the Captain hand the file over to us? Beginning of spring, wasn't it? Or was it in April?"

Anderson flipped the question off. His ass still ached and it wasn't putting him in a good mood at all.

Futana ignored him. She pointed to the woman's remains. "I wonder who she was?" She bent and peered closely into the bucket. "She's a mess. Wet and sticky and in a zillion pieces. Besides, no skin means no fingerprints. And the bastard bashed her teeth in, meaning we can't identify her from her dental records."

"I found something," Anderson said.

Futana left off studying the body parts in the bucket. She crossed the room to where Anderson was crouched beside the generator. He pointed to what he'd found. She squatted beside him to study it.

Half of a business card lay under a patch of straw. The card was old and faded, but they made out the name 'McArthur' and the letter 'P' on it. What looked like a telephone number beneath the letters had been eroded by mud.

"McArthur P.," Anderson said. "At least we've got a name."

"It may not be connected to this," Futana objected. "We'd better let Forensics decide."

Anderson grunted a reply. He left the card where it was. There was the outside chance it had fingerprints on it. If those prints were the same as those in the rest of the barn it would be an additional lead to identifying their man.

"You know what annoys me the most about this?" he asked when they'd both straightened up again.

"What?"

"There's no damn beastie here. No footprints, no slime, no smell of one. Zilch!"

"Try calling the ghost back again. Ask her where the monster is."

He grimaced. She was uncertain if this was because he thought her comment silly, or because his anus was hurting. "You're joking, right?"

She shrugged, then gestured about the shed. "It's worth a try. It ain't like we've got anything else to go on at the moment, is there?"

He scowled at her, but got out his phone. While he dialed, Futana studied the shed. She wasn't letting Anderson see it, but that card they'd found had startled her. She however thought her suspicions highly unlikely: *That card can't possibly belong to Brian McArthur, can it? And this is happening after I saw him at the concert and afterwards? Is he suddenly back in my life again?*

It seemed too much of a coincidence that that scumbag from her teen years had returned to haunt her again. But the evidence appeared to indicate just that: The surname; the fact that they were out on a farm; and most worrisome of all, the fact that he'd been about to rape Anderson.

This last detail seemed conclusive. To Futana's mind, there couldn't be many people who fit the bill—it'd be like searching for a toothpick in a haystack, and even then you'd need to go to a homophilic city like San Francisco or Minneapolis and *really search hard*, to find another scumbag named McArthur who made a hobby out of raping men.

At least till I did it for him, she thought glumly. *Brian fucked me and now I fucked the man he was about to fuck.*

She decided to keep her suspicions to herself. A fingerprint check would confirm or refute them easily enough.

She looked over at her partner. Anderson was staring at his cellphone in disgust. He saw her staring at him and shook the device at her. "All I'm getting is: 'the goddamn number you've called can't be reached at this time.' "

"Well, what do you expect? You are calling the afterlife. They likely run on a different schedule from us living folks."

He didn't get that she was making fun of him. He really had no sense of humor. That in turn greatly fascinated her.

He grimaced. "Yeah, alright. Hey, look, let's get back to the car. I gotta sit down. My ass hurts like my hemorrhoids are raping me."

With Futana walking behind Anderson so that he couldn't see the embarrassed expression on her face, they made their way back to their gray Ford.

They walked fast. The rain was picking up again.

CHAPTER 26

Allie

Allie went shoe shopping in Boston, on Back Bay's Newbury Street. It was a mistake.

At first the day was fine. It was a lovely midsummer morning and she found several great pairs of shoes.

But then she stepped into a café called the Thinking Cup and ordered a coffee. She sat by the café window, watching the street, watching the shoppers hurry to and fro.

And then, just when she was feeling perked up and raring to resume hitting the stores for more bargain buys, the young couple at the next table began kissing.

"Oh, Brian darling, stop it, please," the young woman being kissed pleaded, in a joyous whisper that assured Allie that she actually wanted Brian to continue with what he was doing for as long as possible, and if possible, even intensify his public efforts at romancing her. "Darling, everyone will guess that we're newly married."

Her husband Brian, a muscular man with a black mustache, was grinning at her as though he'd won the lottery.

Next, the new bride—trendy clothes, freckle-faced and with fashionably cut ginger hair—looked shyly at Allie and then away again.

That look of hers, laden as it was with happiness, almost ruined Allie's day.

Allie determined to salvage her day. She left her coffee half-drunk, left the Thinking Cup and walked off.

She glanced back once at the newlyweds. Brian was kissing his blushing bride again.

Laden with her bags of shoes, Allie retraced her steps up Newbury Street, in the direction of the Boston Public Garden. As she went she pondered what she'd just witnessed. Maybe it was just her paranoia, but she seemed to be surrounded by Brian's nowadays. They were everywhere she looked.

She was almost reaching the parking space where she'd left her car when a silver Porsche slid abruptly up to the curb ahead of her. A man and woman in black leather clothes got out of the car. Almost before they'd straightened up, the Porsche was in motion again, skidding away from the sidewalk like it was being driven by a maniac.

But by then Allie had recognized the young woman who'd gotten out of the silver car as Lulu Kim.

The young man with her (whom Allie didn't know, though she thought he'd been part of Lulu's band at the KCS concert at the Hole Faith club the other night) was staring after the departing Porsche as it skidded to a halt at the red light at the end of the street.

"Damn, baby," he said, "your younger sister is either gonna kill someone or die in a car crash if she keeps driving like that. Ain't she ever heard of speed limits?"

Lulu noticed Allie too. "Hey, girl," she said in a slow voice that sounded almost synthetic, "great to see ya again. Sorry, I couldn't wait to chat after the concert. Jojo was in a rush . . ."

Allie nodded. Lulu seemed stoned. Her pupils were quite dilated.

Lulu introduced the young man: "Hey, man, this is Allie Jackson—the chick I told you about from high school. Allie, this my boyfriend Zombie Joe."

"Just call me 'Zombie,'" he said, extending his hand to shake hers.

She shook hands. Zombie Joe had long blonde hair and a mustache. He had a spaced-out look in his blue eyes. His black jacket was sleeveless, revealing a red spiderweb tattoo on his left shoulder.

Then all of a sudden, a look of horror entered Zombie Joe's eyes.

"You okay, man?" Lulu asked in a flat voice.

"Yeah, but shit, I totally forgot—today's my old man's birthday. I'd better call him right away."

Allie waited politely while he dialed. "Hi, dad, yeah, it's Brian." He began singing: "Happy birthday to you! Happy birthday to you!"

Allie could only stare at Lulu's boyfriend in shock. Another Brian? Was there no end to Brians in her life? *All I want is to be able to forget him!!!*

Zombie Joe stepped away from them to the edge of the sidewalk, laughing and chatting on the phone.

"So," Lulu asked Allie, "how are things with you, girl?"

"So, so. I'm job hunting at the moment."

"Any luck so far? Any good offers?"

"Not really. The one or two I like don't pay much, so I'm still looking. I'm mostly searching online though."

Lulu nodded her deadpan understanding.

Allie was thinking hard. She had to know, so she asked: "Say, Lulu, your middle name isn't by any chance Valentina, is it?" Allie was certain that if Lulu Kim shared the same name as her romantic adversary, she'd break down right there and then and start crying inconsolably.

Lulu Kim didn't even look surprised at the question. "Nope, though you're eerily close. It's Brianna, actually. Why you asking?"

Allie gaped at her, at first too surprised to be upset. She glanced over at Zombie Joe, then back at Lulu. "You're serious? Brianna? Brian and Brianna?"

"Yeah," Lulu replied drolly. "Weird coincidence there, ain't it?" She gestured over at her boyfriend, who, phone held to his left ear, was pacing up and down by the curb. "Joe . . . Joseph's actually his *middle* name, but Zombie Joe definitely sounds better than Zombie Brian, you gotta admit."

Allie couldn't reply. She immediately concluded that there was a divine conspiracy intent on preventing her from escaping the past.

"Hey, Allie, are you alright?"

Allie nodded. At that moment though, she felt a hundred states of mind away from alright. She felt like murdering someone. Preferably whoever was responsible for her plight. She figured that would be God. But God was too far away to reach and strangle, so his creation would have to do. . . . She'd gladly blow up the world at the moment, if doing so would deliver her from the curse of Brians; and now *Briannas* also.

She had an epiphany that this was how non-religious terrorists—anarchists—were made, when innocent everyday men, and hardworking honest young women like herself that a miserable destiny simply wouldn't leave alone finally decided they had no other recourse that to disrupt the spinning wheel of fate by blowing up a thousand strangers in an airplane or a skyscraper or at a rock concert.

She stared at the passing pedestrians now with an unnerving fresh insight, realizing that their lives hung on a thread; that everyone on the street was at her disposal, living messages she could dispatch to

God whenever she felt like.

She was certain she was right about this, that she was now a potential political lunatic. Allie knew that if she had a knife on her right now, she'd slit Lulu's throat with it, then stab Zombie Joe also, just to make her point to God to stop messing with her.

She'd . . . she'd . . .

She suddenly realized that Lulu Kim was speaking to her. "Sorry, what were you saying?"

". . . So that's what I mean: our band needs a hook—some special angle to attract fans. Jojo's working round the clock to find us one. But everyone—particularly Kiki—is just so impatient, you know? I keep telling Kiki that we gotta be patient, 'cos most young people today are into all those reality shows like American Idol and The Voice and we're a rock band, not limp-dick pop noise like that."

Allie nodded. She realized that Lulu hadn't even realized she'd not been paying attention to what she'd been saying.

"What brings you two around here?" she managed to ask, gesturing from Lulu to Zombie Joe, who'd just rejoined them. Once more, just like on the night when she'd had the nightmare that had left her feeling suicidal, she was getting a hold of herself again. It took a little doing, but by concentrating on her companions and on the varied expressions on the faces of the many passersby, she was able to shift her thoughts from killing someone to being a sane and productive member of society again.

"We're supposed to collect some DVDs from Brian Thompson," Zombie Joe explained, pointing left. "His office is upstairs there. Jojo and Manuela need the discs for—"

"Shit!" Lulu exclaimed loudly, ending her boyfriend's explanation. "Here comes Kiki now to pick us up again!"

She leaned forward quickly and hugged Allie, who, on hearing yet another *Brian* mentioned had entered into a kind of stasis. "Listen, we gotta run, okay? I can't wait to exchange phone numbers at the moment—Kiki's gonna start bitching the moment she parks the car if we're not ready to go—but let's hook up on Facebook, okay?"

Allie managed a nod and a smile. She watched Brian and Brianna walk away from her and enter the building beside them to meet with another Brian. She turned away just as the silver Porsche again screeched to a halt by the curb. She dully noted that Kiki Kim looked pissed off behind the steering wheel.

Hefting her shopping bags, she resumed her walk to where she'd parked her Nissan Sentra.

Allie didn't even flinch when a thin woman dashed in front of her in hot pursuit of a runaway toddler who seemed intent on following someone else's dog into the road.

"Hey, Brian, come back here!" the harried mother yelled after her unconcerned puppy-struck offspring.

Yeah, God, today's been a great joke on me, Allie thought as she staggered up the road. *An absolute divine comedy at my expense. But I assure you, Almighty Sir, that I'm not amused in the least. Not one little bit.*

CHAPTER 27

Debbie

Greg was making an 'Aunt Grace smoothie'—chocolate ice cream, banana, apple, coconut milk, and something that looked suspiciously like egg-white. He'd just switched off the blender.

Debbie sniffed the blended mixture. "This smells delicious. Can I have some?"

To her surprise, Greg looked horrified. He grabbed the blender away from her. "Oh no—not from this one. Aunt Grace goes ballistic if each glass isn't full, so I gotta have accurate measures."

"She's that particular?"

"She's worse." He looked around the large kitchen like the walls had ears, then whispered, "She's almost nuts about the composition and quantity of her smoothies. Every single ingredient's got to be in there in the exact amounts, or she starts throwing pre-geriatric tantrums."

"I want some too," Debbie insisted. Her insistence was merely an emotional test. Greg was her boyfriend. He was supposed to care about her feelings, not those of some old hag. He was supposed to take care of her.

He smiled. He noticed her pouting and kissed her. "Hold on. I'll make another just for you. Let me just put this one away in the fridge for Auntzilla."

He put Aunt Grace's drink in the fridge, then, still bent over there, enquired, "What flavors do you want? We've got strawberries, cranberries, grapes, grapefruit, oranges, apples, pears, plums, mangoes, beets, papaya, watermelon, carrots, kiwis . . . walnuts, hazelnuts, almonds, monkey nuts, dates . . . chocolate . . . everything imaginable. Hey, baby, come choose for yourself. I don't even remember what some of these fruits and veggies are called."

Debbie walked over for a look. "Wow, baby, you aren't lying about having *everything* in here." The large fridge was packed with fruits and vegetables and different types of yoghurts and milks. And according to Greg, there were sixteen different flavors of ice cream in the freezer compartment. One would think smoothies were all Aunt Grace lived on.

How on earth doesn't she get the runs?

"Strawberries and bananas," she decided. "And some grapes."

Greg got the required ingredients out of the fridge and arranged them on the kitchen counter. He rinsed out the blender, then started slicing the bananas into it. Then he paused and grinned at Debbie. "Hey, admit it: the real reason you came over is 'cos you wanna birdwatch, right?"

She giggled and struck a sporty pose with her hand on her hip. "Well yes, I do wish to continue my ornithological studies from your bedroom window too. Wow, just before coming over I spotted two Baltimore cardinals—oh they were such a pretty scarlet color, like flying streaks of nail paint . . . You know, maybe we should go camping, somewhere out where there's a pond, and then we'll do it in a tent while watching the blue herons feeding! I've always dreamt of lovemaking in the wild. Just imagine all that open sky dotted with all those little fluttering bundles of warm avian feathers. Just imagine your stiff pecker pecking deep inside me while all those noisy woodpeckers are pecking happily away at their barks . . . and the sparrows . . ."

She realized he was staring oddly at her and calmed herself a little. "Sorry, I got a little carried away. . . . But . . . but actually . . . I really just felt like being with you, baby."

"Oh, I love you too, Deb." He kissed her, then resumed preparing her fruit selection, taking his time to remove the seeds from the grapes.

And then she noticed how, all of a sudden, his face appeared to collapse. Just like that, his expression went from happy to sad, with no stops in between.

The abrupt alteration really perplexed Debbie. There was something going on with Greg. She was certain of this, that her boyfriend had a problem weighing heavily on his mind nowadays. Greg was normally a cheerful sort. But for the past week or so—no, now she thought back seriously on it, she dated his sudden sadnesses back to when he'd lost his job—he seemed to be living under a dark cloud.

She'd been meaning to ask him about it, but her schoolwork kept getting in the way of them having a long meaningful conversation about how depressed he'd lately seemed. Clearly though, it was time for her to investigate what was bothering her boyfriend. It was time for them to have a serious heart-to-heart talk about this.

But then he finished making her smoothie and he was smiling again and she forgot all about it, till next time.

CHAPTER 28

The Coven

That same night, while Anderson and Futana both awaited the results of the forensics examination of the Hourigan Farm, a burial ceremony was taking place on that same premises.

***

The cops had long since left, taking away the corpse and leaving a web of yellow—'Crime Scene Do Not Cross'—barricade tape everywhere. The chopped-up body currently lay in a Boston morgue, where the coroners were reassembling its head so they could attempt a digital reconstruction of the woman's missing face. In the meantime, they'd also sent a request to Missing Persons for the particulars of any adult human female who'd been reported missing within the past week. The deceased woman hadn't been dead for more than forty-eight hours. The medical examiners assumed she'd been kidnapped not too long before that.

Also, they'd been able to conclusively link the woman's corpse to the Wet Bones case: the chunks of her head and shoulders were covered with cryptid slime. The only difference was, this slime wasn't the corrosive kind.

"Like the damn thing began eating her, then spat her out again," Futana had told Anderson on hearing that. "Maybe she tasted off or something."

He'd scratched his chin. "Yeah, which means that once we get our fingerprint match, we've solved the case."

"Don't get your hopes up," she'd whispered. "This case has a way of fucking us in the ass."

She instantly regretted saying that. He didn't comment.

***

Out on the Hourigan Farm, the time was almost 1 a.m.

A hundred yards from the farmhouse, eight naked people stood around the man who was to be buried. He too was naked. He was also still alive. He was lying on the wet grass and was bound hand and foot. He'd been well beaten; there was a lot of blood on him.

"Please!" he pleaded. "Don't do this, don't kill me!"

"You betrayed us," the redhead high priestess intoned. "You betrayed our coven. You betrayed Boku Ke Houzz."

"I didn't mean to do it. I don't know what got into me!" The victim was sweating bullets. "Please—the Devil made me do it!"

This last statement provoked loud laughter all around. Those gathered were witches and Satanists. They were reasonably certain the Devil had had nothing to do with him betraying them. After all, didn't they all work for him? Weren't they all here even tonight doing his bidding? Handing down *his*—Lucifer's—prescribed justice?

***

The man about to be killed was Desmond Haggerty, a founder member of Aunt Grace's Graceful Blend smoothie club. His connection to the Wet Bones case was simple: Mary Watt (who'd been butchered by her husband Fred when the coven had invoked the Graveyard Wind that drove him insane) was Desmond's younger sister. She and her husband had both been members of this same coven. Mary had called the police when the high priestess had insisted that her unborn child would be sacrificed to Boku Ke Houzz.

Angered by his sister's death, Desmond had gotten hold of her phone and called Detective Anderson, using a 'magic voice' app to feminize his voice.

Desmond's wife Jenny had no idea of his occultist activities. She currently thought he was out getting drunk with an old college friend who was passing through town.

Desmond now regretted ever joining the Abyss Club. His childhood interest in the supernatural had led him to a really sticky end. The call from the high priestess had seemed routine enough. As was usual, she'd called him just after closing hours. She'd asked him to come out to the Hourigan Farm. It was an emergency, she'd explained: they'd had a security breach. The police had raided their 'abattoir' and they needed to dig up a few bodies before the cops found them.

Desmond had felt there was no way anyone could possibly connect him to the leakage of coven information. He'd lied to Jenny and driven over.

And now here he was. Looking up at his judges . . . and executioners.

How the hell could I have been so naïve as to think I'd get away with it? he pondered. Yes, Desmond had wanted revenge for what had been done to Mary, but . . . *But I really should have known better. The coven plays for keeps. And they've got access to forces well outside the range of normal human experience. I knew that! I knew that! Shit!*

Now, Desmond stared up at the eight who surrounded him. Two of the women spat down on him. One of the spitting women was an up-and-coming porn star. She had a shaven head and crotch. She had massive F-cup breasts. From his prone position her breasts looked like zeppelins. Desmond however felt not the slightest twinge of arousal. The porno actress smirked at him. Then she squatted over his head and pissed on him. Right in his face. It took her a long time. Her split crotch hung over his face as her stinky water fell on him. She had an inverted 'A' tattooed over her clitoris. The porno actress thoroughly drenched him with her urine.

As though taking their cue from her, all the male coven members began pissing on Desmond too. Then the women took turns as well.

None of this bothered Desmond in the least. He was fervently praying he got out of this alive.

***

"You called the police on your sister's cellphone," the red-haired priestess coldly accused him. "The cops missed it while searching the house; you later found it under the sofa."

"No!" Desmond pleaded. "It wasn't me." He couldn't stop blinking: the porno actress had pissed in his eyes.

In response to this denial, a man stepped forward and hit Desmond in the side of the head with a mallet. He didn't hit Desmond too hard. The witches wanted him to remain conscious. They wanted him to properly appreciate his fate. Desmond lay there limp at their feet, his eyes rolling in his head. By now, large flies had begun buzzing around his urine-drenched body. Desmond was aware that he stank like a public urinal.

"Don't lie to us!" the redhead priestess shrilled. "You used a voice changing app, so he thought Mary was the one calling!"

"How could you possibly know that?" Desmond was desperate.

"A stupid question; but I'll answer it. Satan told me."

"And now the cops have that other woman's corpse," a man said. "The one Boku didn't eat 'cos it was already gorged on her husband and her skin."

The coven members' voices rained down on Desmond as relentlessly as their urine had:

"And they almost caught the Butcher too." This was an angry woman's voice.

"Yeah, Dez, you snitch S.O.B. I really should fuck your ass for that; sodomize your asshole, asshole. You sold me out."

"No, you won't sodomize him. We've no time for that now. We're here for business, not pleasure."

"Shit! They raided us. The first time ever."

"And it's all your fault, Dez. Now we'll have to move our abattoir from here. And this was a great place. No one ever drives down this way."

"I'm sorry. Forgive me!" Desmond's protest was weak and bloody. He was guilty. He knew he was guilty. All he could hope for was mercy from the cold hearts behind these stony accusing faces. "Please, forgive me!"

His plea brought laughter from the witches. Then the high priestess said:

"We are not Christians, Dez. It is Jesus who forgives sins, not our master Lucifer!"

To this statement there was much assenting laughter.

"Fuck you assholes, then!" Desmond screamed. "I hope you all BURN IN HELL!"

This brought the loudest round of laughter from the witches.

And then the witches killed Desmond Haggerty.

First they taped over his mouth so that he couldn't scream or protest. Then they rolled him into the grave they'd previously dug for him, out in the abandoned wheat-fields about fifty yards back from the abattoir shed. (The grave had been prepared with a bed of firewood.) And then two male acolytes each poured two cans of high-octane gasoline over Desmond.

After which the high priestess threw in a lit match.

"Ash in the night," she solemnly intoned. "Corpse pyre burning bright. Evil Master Lucifer, accept our ghastly offering with infernal delight!" There was no excitement in her voice. This was merely a job. Whoever got excited over throwing away the trash?

The witches sat and chanted spells of worship to Satan and watched Desmond burn. Unlike their leader, the rest of the coven enjoyed his death immensely. The man writhing beneath the orange flames was wonderful entertainment, a spectacle worthy of the ancient Roman coliseum. They enjoyed the cringing pain in Desmond's eyes before those eyes popped from the heat, loved seeing the unreliable man's skin burn and crack and turn to ash and his blood vessels explode in geysers of redness that in turn evaporated into clouds of thick black smoke. They loved watching his burning body squirm like a worm as it cooked; loved how it thrashed in pain before the fire roasted the brain. They relished watching his muscles blacken and shrivel away on his bones as if by a magic trick. They delighted in watching him shrink as he dried up.

Several of the witches toasted marshmallows in the fire. They loved the meaty taste the smoke gave the marshmallows.

It took an hour for the traitor to be reduced to a blackened husk.

After which, the witches filled in Desmond's grave and drove away.

CHAPTER 29

Greg

On Saturday, the Graceful Blend club members heard that Desmond Haggerty was missing. Because of this news, the meeting was rather subdued, with Aunt Grace also complaining that she felt a little under the weather.

***

The next day—Sunday—Aunt Grace fell ill and had to be hospitalized. She was admitted into the Carney Clinic, a private medical establishment over in Dorchester. Very expensive—the best. Visiting her there on Monday, Greg was reminded that his aunt was rich.

She had a stomach virus, the doctors explained. She was okay, but they were going to keep her at the clinic for observation for a few days.

Greg was disappointed. He'd been praying she had something terminal. Something long-lasting and excruciating like cancer. Something to make her suffer like she was making him suffer. Her death would be the end of his problems.

But no, Aunt Grace clearly wasn't about exiting his life any time soon. When he saw her, she looked radiant in her hospital bed. Weak, but angelic in a way.

Her private hospital room was as luxurious as a hotel suite.

He sat beside her and took her hand in his. "How do you feel?"

She frowned. "I'm fine, dear. I really miss my smoothies though. If I could just have a big one to drink, I'm certain I'd be as right as rain in no time at all. But the doctors say I mustn't even *taste* anything milk-based until my stomach's fine again. So enjoy your rest, my darling child, 'cos once I'm back home again, your balls are going to be working overtime."

Her last statement was made with utmost seriousness and a solemn tone of determination in her voice, and while licking her lips in clear anticipation, as though she could already taste the semen-soiled drink on her tongue.

Greg left her bedside determined to *really* satisfy Jojo Kim. Scat fetish or not, he'd had enough of this.

***

Still, Greg had to admit that not everything about his life was bad. One of the good things was Debbie Manning, with whom he grew more enraptured daily. He wondered how he'd been blinded to her charms for so long.

But then I wasn't in the market for a girlfriend, he reminded himself. *Ann had just left for Nebraska and I was pining for her.*

They were currently upstairs in Greg's house, making love at his bedroom window. As was usual, Debbie was in front of the drapes, Greg behind them. Debbie had on just a black X-Men T-shirt over her breasts. Greg, who couldn't be noticed from outside, was only wearing a condom. Debbie was up on tip-toes, gripping the sides of the window frame with both hands, while Greg filled her hot body from behind. She stared at the sky, counting the birds. "Ooh, baby— wow, today the trees around here are full of goldfinches and blackbirds."

Whenever she couldn't see any birds, she watched the street, keeping a straight face while waving to passing neighbors: "Hey, James! See you in class tomorrow! Tell Michelle I'm still not talking to her!" "Hello, Mr. Nolan!" Occasionally her self-control failed her and a mousy squeak betrayed her pleasure.

Greg was used to it now. Overlooking the oddity of their sex life, he made love to the pair of soft buttocks presented to him. He also watched carefully to ensure that she didn't lean too far out of the window, as she was wont to do while climaxing. If Debbie fell out of his bedroom window, she was going down onto the concrete steps below. If she also broke an arm or leg, it would take them both quite a while to live down the resulting notoriety.

But still, she was sweet, her sex elastic around his manhood. Her trembling legs were long and supple. There was something magical about how she rolled her buttocks against him. He noticed she was leaning back against the curtains, pressing herself against his chest. This was unusual for Debbie; normally she leaned as far forward as she could; to better view the sky, she said.

Oh, Debbie was so sweet. Even with the drapes separating them, her body felt really nice against his.

Greg wasn't far from exploding. Then he was going to freeze the semen and preserve it for Aunt Grace's return. Depending on how long she remained on admission at the Carney Clinic, he might even build up a substantial semen reserve before she returned home.

"Shit!" Debbie exclaimed suddenly, falling backwards through the drapes. Suddenly she was all there with him again; not just the half-woman he'd grown used to copulating with, but the completeness of her—her musk and loveliness, her creamy shoulders and arms, her blonde hair full in his face.

The momentum of her retreat was so sudden and unexpected that it knocked Greg back towards the bed. His erection remained inside her, but bent at an uncomfortable angle.

"What happened?" he asked worriedly, just managing not to topple onto the bed.

"A bee almost stung me!" she gasped, pointing to the drapes, beyond whose translucent expanse Greg clearly made out a hovering black silhouette. Next, the dark silhouette was joined by two more.

"Damn things," Debbie griped. "And I was just about to come too."

"You're still gonna come, baby." He turned their bodies towards the bed, and gently bent her forward over it. He lovingly pushed her up onto the sheets and arranged her on her hands and knees.

"I want the window," she protested. "I wanna see the sky while you're filling me!"

"The bees own the window now, honey, except you feel like having your face pollinated."

"I wanna feel myself soaring," she groaned in pleasure, feeling him slide his hands inside her T-Shirt and grasp her breasts. "I can't come otherwise."

"There are windows in your mind," he said while gently running his fingers over her nipples. "Just close your eyes and imagine you're outside." Not bothering whether she was paying heed or not, he'd already resumed moving inside her. He trusted to the feeling to calm her, to make her move with him. "Imagine you're soaring with the birds, baby. Imagine you're a bird yourself. Imagine that you're a seagull or a sparrow . . . oh, Debbie! . . . Imagine you're flying . . . Oh, baby—I'm coming!"

She was coming too, eyes closed like he'd suggested, her mind soaring far up into the clouds. It was one of their best orgasms together.

***

"I had a dream," Debbie said afterwards. "It was weird and very frightening."

"What about?" Greg asked. He felt relaxed now. For the moment his problems had vanished. They were lying on their sides, cupped together like pink spoons.

"You'll laugh at me if I tell you," she said over her shoulder.

"I promise not to."

"Okay then. It was very simple. You and I were out in the woods together somewhere having a picnic, and then you turned into a huge wolf—a horrible ugly creature—and ate me. And while eating me you were slobbering at the mouth and laughing." She shuddered and turned a little to stare at him. "It was really vivid; you know how real some dreams can seem. I woke up covered in sweat. In the dream I was screaming and begging you to let me go, but you wouldn't. You kept eating me up."

He stroked her hair. "That sounds horrible. Thank heavens it was just a dream. Don't worry, baby. You've nothing to fear from me. I'll never in a million years do anything to hurt you."

Smiling, she turned fully around and kissed him. "Thanks for not laughing at me."

"I love you," he said.

"I love you too," she said back. "Oh, I just remembered: any news of Mr. Haggerty yet?"

"Dez? No, he's still missing. His wife is climbing the walls in panic that something bad's happened to him."

Debbie shuddered. "I really feel for her, you know. It must be utterly horrible for your husband to head off after work to see a friend, and never be seen again. I really hope they find him soon."

"I hope they do too," Greg said. "Dez was such a nice, funny guy. I still recall that last smoothie contest between him and Aunt Grace. It'd be a real shame to not have any more of those."

They made love again. Still on the bed, the bees refusing to give up their ownership of Greg's bedroom window.

***

Afterwards, while Debbie had a bath, Greg remembered his discussion with Tommy Collins, over his being admitted into the Rectifiers. He smiled. He had Tommy's word on that. It was merely a matter of time.

For the first time in ages Greg actually felt optimistic about his prospects in life.

He figured he owed it to Debbie to wipe his slate of transgressions clean. He didn't want to saddle her with his baggage. As much as Jojo Kim's request disgusted him, he was going through with it. His love for Debbie firmed his resolve. He was doing it for both himself and for her. For their future together.

And then, with Aunt Grace no longer milking him dry physically and emotionally, he'd be able to concentrate on the new job with Tommy's Rectifiers. That job promised to be a lot more fun than working in an office.

There are times when the stars all seem to be aligning correctly in a man's life. For Greg Madden, this was one of them.

He grinned at Debbie's rendition of the *Spiderman* theme in the bathroom. Yes, things were definitely looking up now!

CHAPTER 30

Allie

The next Wednesday night, Allie's life turned on its head.

Allie had just gotten off the phone with Sylvia Platt, a friend of hers who worked at Eastern Bank. Sylvia had been telling her that Brian Kemp and Valentina Ruzza had gotten married the previous Saturday, and that the pair had just this morning jetted off to Paris for their honeymoon. Sylvia had been their chief bridesmaid.

After Allie's expected recriminations of "What? How could you, when you knew what she did to me?" and Sylvia's profuse apologies and hanging up, Allie sat down and took stock of her life.

She logged into Facebook (she'd been absent for ages) and saw that it was true. Brian and Valentina's wedding was uploaded there in all its photographic glory. And even with her prominent baby bulge, the middle-aged Valentina looked hotter that ever in her blue dress, as though what flowed through her veins was seduction, not blood.

'Hearty Congratulations to Mr. and Mrs. Brian Kemp!' the post read.

The wedding post already had four thousand 'likes.' Seeing that amount of support for her past adversary; Allie felt momentarily flattened.

Allie had thought her emotional wounds healed. She'd imagined she was over her shattering heartbreak for good. And this despite her several setbacks; setbacks like her Night of Suicidal Thoughts (the night she'd dreamt of Brian and Valentina's marriage), and her Dark Day of Repeating Brians (the morning she'd met Lulu Kim and Zombie Joe while out buying shoes). She'd done her best to put the past behind her. She'd really worked at reclaiming her life.

In truth, she *was* healed, but seeing as she didn't yet have a replacement man of her own to flaunt at anyone who reminded her of how she'd been betrayed, and seeing as how her ex was having a happy ending to his infidelity, she suddenly felt very depressed.

She wasn't crazy depressed, but still, she felt very likely to do something crazy (like blowing her brains out) if she didn't immediately clear her head.

Realizing her current state of vulnerability to life-shortening suggestions, and feeling the need to be away from her room for a while, she decided to go for a walk.

By force of habit, instead of leaving by the front door, Allie departed the house by the side entrance. Stepping out into the night, she headed towards the garage. She wasn't actually thinking; she was merely driven by her need to be out of the house. Any direction would do, so long as it led away from her home base and her cellphone.

She walked fast, haunted and pursued by the Ghosts of Relationships Past, propelled by a surge of desperate emotion which, if not channeled into wearying physical activity, could either result in her leaping for joy at being delivered from her bad relationship, or in her leaping in front of a train from being traumatized by being so wrongly used by those she'd trusted.

She walked; heading for the road though not really conceiving her destination as anything other than a vague mental location.

But then, again from force of habit, instead of walking past the garage entrance to join Whiting Road, she turned inside the building.

She stepped past the red Chevrolet hoisted on the hydraulic auto lift, trailing raised fingers dreamily along its shiny lacquered surface from trunk to hood.

It was only now that she was fully inside the garage, surrounded by space and machinery, and breathing in the odors of oil and gasoline, that she realized what she'd done and looked around in surprise, finally realizing where her feet had unconsciously brought her too.

Good gosh, I need to get a grip on my emotions. If I'm this distracted, it's a wonder I didn't walk straight out into the street and kill myself.

It seemed impossible to Allie that in her blind rush to escape her thoughts of Brian's monster betrayal, she'd come all this distance unaware. She felt she now understood how a sleepwalker must feel, on surfacing from a midnight haze in an unfamiliar place that might even be their own living room, but rendered momentarily unrecognizable by its very unexpectedness.

She looked around.

The garage was empty, but she heard voices coming from Giorgio's office, and the office door was open. The office drapes that faced the street were shut, most likely meaning the business currently being transacted in the office wasn't of the sort one wanted passers-by witnessing.

She was curious. Besides, at the moment, her greatest need was for a distraction of some kind to occupy her mind, and this promised to be a distraction.

She walked quietly over.

She paused beside the office door and listened. She instantly recognized the voices: her brother-in-law was in there with Tommy and Dave again. More gangland goings-on to discuss, she figured.

She considered walking silently away, back out into the night, but something—on later reflection she concluded it was a neurotic death wish triggered by her depressing phone chat with Sylvia—made her pause and listen.

Tommy was smoking. Allie could smell the tobacco fumes from where she stood.

"Listen, Giorgio," Tommy was saying, "we got a serious problem, man. We need a wheelman for this weekend's Springfield job."

"A driver? But you guys already got a driver. What happened to Ronnie Briscoe?"

"Ronnie won't be driving anything for a month. He's in hospital with the moon-landing flu or something just as dumb sounding. Last time I looked in on him he looked like he was dying."

"How about Ray?"

"Ray's too much of a crack-head. We need someone who'll keep his cool."

"I'd recommend Carlo Motta then," Giorgio said. "You guys know how he's cooler than ice cubes."

Tommy replied in a subdued voice: "Yeah, Carlo'd be perfect, but we can't use him, man. He's part of Marko Velli's crew and Dave is humping Marko's wife. And you know how Marko acts once Petra's involved."

On hearing this information, Giorgio turned and gaped at Dave, his mouth hanging open with shock. When he finally found his voice, it was to growl: "Are you suicidal? You're balling Petra Velli? Hell yeah, I know the woman's a bimbo, everyone knows that, but . . ."

c'mon, kid, think with your brains sometimes. Thinking with your dick will just put you in an early grave."

Dave didn't say anything. He just looked embarrassed. So, yes, Allie realized, the bad little boy had clearly been filling Petra Velli's panties (whoever Petra Velli was) while her husband wasn't looking. Oh, but how she wished he was filling her own panties instead! She'd make him so welcome in them, he'd never want to leave!

Tommy said, "I've been telling him that over and over, Giorgio, but he just won't listen. I even reminded him of how Mo Stevens went missing right after Petra kissed him at Joey Falcone's party."

"That's right," Giorgio added soberly. "The city cops are still looking for Mo to question him over that Worcester bank robbery." He frowned. "The harbor fish ain't though. They're really good friends with Mo's rotting remains now, and from what I hear, they really admire his concrete boots." He peered hard at Dave. "Listen, boy, steer away from that Velli tramp, or else . . . you're as good as dead."

Tommy looked at his partner in disgust. "He says he's in love with her," he told Giorgio. "He's got this pipe dream in his head of saving her from her evil husband and running off to live in Canada."

Giorgio shook his head. "Love, huh? Don't be a damn fool, Davey. Love's put more young men in the grave than anything else in history except war. You're safer just remaining your old playboy self. See, *no one* loves Petra Velli. She's a sexual hit-and-run machine. She ain't got any brains in her head either—they're all between her legs. Listen, if you're gonna fuck her, you drop what you got in her manhole and get the hell away before Marko's any the wiser." He looked at the ceiling a moment before continuing: "The last person who 'fell in love' with Petra was Hulk Kowalski." He looked sourly at Dave and Tommy. "Guy didn't always look like that, you know."

They both knew Hulk Kowalski. Hulk's nickname came from his weird deformity. Kowalski was all bulged-out and swollen everywhere; he looked as if he'd been inflated by ten or fifteen bicycle pumps at once, like someone had just injected a propane tank full of air into him. He just looked inflated like that.

"Yeah, I've wondered about that for ages," Tommy said. "What did happen to Hulk?"

Giorgio sighed. "It was Marko that fixed him up like that. He found out from jail that Hulk had been entertaining his wife in bed.

Well, Hulk's related to Marko—they're second or third cousins—anyways Marko didn't want to cut his head or nuts off 'cos of their family ties, so he had Black and White dunk him in the ocean without a diving suit on. You know how crazy those two are, right? So, Black and White strap an oxygen tank on Hulk's back, tie his hands together so he can't swim off, tie barbells to his feet so he won't surface before they pull him up, then float Marko's yacht out into the Atlantic and drop the guy overboard at the end of a long, long line. They wait like maybe an hour or so, by which time his body's gotten used to the underwater pressure down there, then they haul him back up again. But, see, they haul him up *very fast*, too fast for his body to depressurize safely. So all that compressed gas—I think it's the Nitrogen that's done him like that—expands while it's still inside his muscles and it swells him up everywhere like that Hulk monster chap on TV—only difference is he ain't painted green. Worst case of the bends ever. He don't just *look* fucked up now either: his body's in constant agony. The guy now lives on painkillers. And the doctors still can't find a solution for him. They say the nitrogen is wrapped around his muscles in crazy balloons . . . Looks like he'll be looking like that for life." He looked pointedly at Dave. "And Hulk's a *cousin* of Marko's; I mean, he's *family*. What you think Marko's gonna do to *you*, if he finds out you're feeding Petra your wiener?"

Tommy gulped. Outside the office, the eavesdropping Allie gulped too. Gosh, now that was an utterly nasty way to get even with someone.

Tommy stole a look at Dave to see if the warning had registered. It clearly hadn't. Dave still looked adamant, like he thought he was Superman and Petra Velli was Lois Lane in danger.

Giorgio had noticed it too. "Nah, there's no point talking to you, is there? You *do* think with your dick." He returned his attention to Tommy. "Yeah, Carlo's out then. Marko's more petty than that rocker guy Tom where his wife is concerned."

"Yeah, for real. There's no telling that he won't ship us to the cops for revenge if he hears about the score we got planned."

Giorgio shook his head. "Forget the police—Marko don't ever snitch on no one; he didn't get where he is today by telling tales. No, what I'm worried about is him shipping Dave out into the Atlantic somewhere to go work as an underwater salesman for concrete footwear."

They fell silent, staring at themselves for awhile. Then Giorgio asked. "So, who then? What's the job anyway?"

"Some inheritance papers a friend wants destroyed. His old man just died and according to him, the old guy was almost nuts and willed most of his money to his cats. Can you believe that? Twelve million dollars, and our guy only gets a hundred grand and the house; and he's expected to look after the damn millionaire cats too."

"So he's paying us twenty of that hundred grand to destroy the will before it's read. We'll get a lot more, of course, once he inherits the money. But for now that's all he's got in the bank."

"It's a dicey plan your friend's got going, man. There's gotta be more copies . . . how many locations you guys gotta hit? And if it's a lawyer's office, there's sure to be surveillance cameras . . ."

Outside, the eavesdropping Allie had heard enough. She strode into the office and confronted them. "I'll be your wheelman," she said. "I'll drive you guys, but I want a third of the take."

After saying this, she sat down on the edge of Giorgio's desk and waited. She didn't really understand why she'd walked in on them and made this proposal. But listening to them speak, she'd felt a deep excitement stirring in her breast. And besides, she realized that here was a chance to drive again; to *really* drive.

After Tommy and Dave had gotten over their surprise at what she'd said, they both burst out laughing. Giorgio wasn't laughing though, he just looked angry.

"You?" Dave finally asked Allie. "You? What do you think this is: a trip to the mall to buy lipstick and pantyhose?"

"I said, I'll drive you," she repeated calmly. Suddenly, she was on familiar ground. Lots of guys had doubted her ability behind the steering wheel. She'd always proved them wrong. This time would be no different. She noticed Tommy wasn't saying anything though. He was smiling at her, and had an odd glint in his eyes.

"I'll do it," she repeated. "But I want a third of that twenty grand you're making."

"What the hell for?" Dave asked.

"I'm broke. I need a job."

"You work for Giorgio."

She could see that Dave still wasn't taking her seriously. "He don't pay me too well," she retorted. "Just room and board, and I got expenses." Then she looked at Tommy, who she'd long ago worked out was the leader of the duo. "What do *you* say, man?"

Tommy seemed to think a bit, then he turned to Giorgio. "Is she any good?"

Giorgio sighed heavily, like the world would shortly come crashing down on his head. "Oh, she's good alright; behind the wheel she's likely better than both Ronnie and Carlo combined." Then he groaned. "I was worried about this happening when she started working here in the garage. Shit, her sister's gonna kill me!" He slumped forward as if in resignation to his marital fate.

"Don't tell her then," Allie said.

She looked from Tommy to Dave.

Tommy was nodding and lighting himself a fresh cigarette. Dave was still smirking at her. "Girl, you sure you got the nerve for our kinda work?"

She laughed; it was the usual test the guys gave you—they thought if you didn't have nuts, you didn't have guts either. She gave Dave her usual retort: "My ovaries are bigger than your balls, man. Try me on for size."

Dave's eyes went wide at her reply, then he began laughing. Tommy blew out a series of smoke rings, then said, "Alright, we'll try you out for the Rectifiers . . . tomorrow. If you're as good as Giorgio says, we'll cut you in on the weekend deal.

"Aw, man," Dave groaned, "but . . . a *female* wheelman? Dude, we're gonna be a laughingstock!"

Allie didn't say anything. She ignored him. She kept her eyes on Tommy. He had a big smile on his face now. She could tell he was amused by Dave's discomfort at her joining them.

Tommy turned and addressed Giorgio, who'd just pulled out a bottle of sherry and was pouring himself a drink. "If she can drive like you say . . ."

Giorgio now looked like he had a migraine. "Oh hell, the girl can drive alright. She used to race with NASCAR."

On hearing this, Dave looked at Allie with newfound respect.

"You cool with her working with us?" Tommy asked.

Giorgio sipped his sherry, and offered the others the bottle. They declined and he capped it and set it aside again. "Yeah, sure, sure. I'd rather she goes with you guys than some punks I don't know from

Methuselah." He winced. "But what the hell am I gonna tell Chloe? She'll think *I'm* the one who put Alice up to this."

"I already told you, Giorgio—don't tell her." Then she looked shrewdly at Tommy. "I get my third of the take?"

He took a puff of smoke. "Nothing tomorrow—we're just trying you out. But if we like you enough, you'll get twenty-five percent on the weekend job."

"Hey!" Giorgio protested. "Don't shortchange the kid!"

Allie was grateful for that. "Yeah—I want my money," she said in as tough a voice as she could manage. She knew she could make a noise here because Giorgio was family. Elsewhere, she'd not have dared.

Dave seemed resigned now. "It ain't that, Giorgio. Tomorrow's job ain't paying us much. Just a grand—beer money—to run some dogs out to Brimfield. And the weekend job . . ."

"Either give the kid an equal cut or I ain't lettin' you have her," Giorgio insisted. "I already told you she's better than both Ronnie and Carlo put together."

Tommy nodded slowly. "Well, okay," he told Allie finally. "You got your equal share of Saturday's job and any future ones." Then his eyes turned cold again. "But only if you don't screw up in the nerves department. Then you only get a quarter. We need to be sure you can handle yourself in a tight situation."

"Don't worry," Allie assured him, "I got nerves to spare." She gave him her most winning smile. "Alright, I'll prove it to you. Let's go for a test drive, okay? I promise not to bounce your balls off."

***

Tonight, Tommy and Dave hadn't brought their regular Rectifiers' ride along. The vehicle Allie would be driving was a white RAM 1500 pickup truck.

"This is ours too," Dave explained. "It's better than the Camry for handling large shipments of stuff, but most times it's parked in my garage so the cops don't tag it. We'll be using it for tomorrow's job. Just like the Camry, it's also outfitted with secret compartments for storing valuables in. But we'll just carry the dogs in the back. It's just two of 'em."

She nodded. It didn't matter to her. One combination of engine and wheels was as good as another.

They sat together in the front of the truck. Tommy sat right next to her on the bench seat. Dave was out by the passenger door, dangling his arm from the window.

Allie felt great as she drove the RAM. It handled like a dream. Magic transmission. Her few doubts on the wisdom of entangling herself up in Tommy and Dave's crooked business blew away on the wind.

"So what's the deal with tomorrow night?" she asked Tommy. "I mean, why carry two dogs so far out of town for so little money?"

She saw him smile in the darkness. "Jesse McArthur's an old acquaintance of mine who owns a Boston pet shop. The dogs are for his older brother, Brian. He's got a farm out there and says something's been killing and eating his sheep."

"Yeah, sure. I get that bit," Allie agreed. "But still, you guys don't strike me as the selfless type."

Tommy's lips squeezed into a thin line. Allie wondered if she'd said too much.

There was silence in the truck for a moment, then: "We're not being entirely altruistic," Dave explained from the window seat. "Once we drop off Brian's mutts, we'll make a short detour to Springfield to discuss the next job after Saturday's."

She nodded. "You guys work a lot?"

Tommy said, "It's like the weather report: sometimes there's a downpour, sometimes a drizzle, sometimes a drought of opportunities." He lit a fresh cigarette then said, "You handle this quite well for a chick. You been driving long?"

"Since I was twelve. I used to Go Kart race." She glanced across at Dave who was tapping his fingers on the far end of the dashboard. Oh, yeah, Dave was so impossibly hot. She wished he was the one sitting next to her. But if he was, maybe she'd be too aroused by now to concentrate on her driving and just crash the pickup truck.

Tommy nodded at her reply and lapsed into silence again. Allie expected another question from him, but it didn't come, so she shrugged and concentrated on the road ahead. She was in a happy place here in the truck with them. The RAM ate up the road like it was hilltop grass.

They were rolling through the town of Foxborough when Tommy asked Dave: "Dude, what was Manuela going on about yesterday? I thought you guys broke up ages ago. I could hear her yelling at you over the phone."

Damn," Dave replied in a mock-horrified tone, "Manuela is crazy, man, as in Grade-A Acapulco loco. She says she wants us to get back together again. But me, I ain't having it. Oh no, man. Manuela's either gonna fuck me into the grave, or shoot me there one night when I'm asleep. I've known lots of women, but that one? She's so possessive, you'd think her dad ran away from home immediately after he'd dropped her off for her first day at school." Then he scowled. "You know, maybe he did, I dunno. But, man, if he did, then it's a real sad legacy he left behind for fun-seeking guys like I."

"You can't blame her, man. The lady's just scared that you'll treat her like before, then dump her for some other woman again." He laughed and tapped Allie's arm. "Maybe even pretty Miss Cimini here."

Allie laughed. "My surname's actually Jackson," she corrected him. "C'mon, man, get it right: I'm Chloe's sister, not Giorgio's."

She was intrigued by this new direction of their conversation. She knew Manuela Costa, the utterly gorgeous black Cuban singer who'd opened up the KCS concert. In addition to her lovely face, Manuela had boobs and buttocks to spare. It boggled Allie how Dave could have that woman in his bed and want another one. For a moment, she stopped concentrating on the road ahead and pondered the nature of the human male. What exactly did men want in their women? Manuela Costa was talented, and looked great too. She doubted it was really the singer's purportedly terrible temper that had separated them. Allie knew lots of bad-tempered women, some of them real termagants, who were still with their men. And yet, despite all her good points, Manuela and Dave Fontaine had broken up, and Dave was now sleeping with the married Petra Velli.

In this case, the fault clearly lay with Dave. Allie had no doubts about that.

Oh, men were just dogs! Still, that didn't stop Allie's nipples from stiffening whenever Dave looked her way.

And she'd not missed Tommy's compliment on her looks either. Yet another thing to get horny over. She didn't understand it though. Just looking at Dave got her hot; but with Tommy, she got hot too, but she didn't even think she liked him that way at all. And that despite her sister's encouragement to date him.

Allie rolled the pickup truck around a curve. She was taking it easy; restraining her natural urges to put the pedal to the metal and burn rubber down the highway. It would be so easy to showboat and show them everything she could do with a car.

Yeah, and immediately get pulled over by the police. That'd be a great start to your new job.

There was a whole lot she was capable of behind a steering wheel that her two male companions couldn't even suspect. She suppressed a grin at a memory: once, while aged fourteen, she'd made her driving instructor Mr. Russell literally poop his pants with her daredevil driving displays.

So, yes, she wished to impress her companions, but not at the expense of attracting police attention. There wasn't anything incriminating in the back of the vehicle but that wasn't the point. As a rookie in Tommy's Rectifiers, she didn't want to appear unprofessional. She already understood that part of her job was keeping them all as unnoticed as possible.

"Look," Tommy went on as the road straightened out again, "I mean it, Davey, you really should consider getting back together with Manuela. She's just scared of your womanizing. It hurts a woman when you treat her like that." He nudged Allie's elbow. "Back me up here. I'm right, ain't I?"

Pleased to be inserted into the conversation, Allie nodded. "Yeah, no woman likes being cheated on."

"See?" Tommy said. "Miss Jackson agrees with me." His voice turned serious. "I'd rather you were dating Manuela again than still sleeping with Mrs. Velli. At least that way you won't have Black and White after you."

Dave rolled his eyes in mock horror. "Scared? Dude, did I hear you say Manuela's scared? Hey, I'm the one who should be frigging scared here." He leaned across Tommy to stare at Allie, and added, "Do you know that, while we were dating, Manuela chased my previous ex-girlfriend Brie down the stairs with a baseball bat because Brie Becker turned up on my doorstep with a positive pregnancy test result for me." He laughed. "You should have see the way she was wielding that bat, like she was gonna hit a home run on Brie's head."

Allie was interested. "So what happened?"

Dave settled back into his seat. "Oh, nothing. Brie made it out to her car alive and zoomed off. Then Manuela stalked back upstairs, dropped the baseball bat, yelled at me for thirty minutes, then gave me a blowjob."

"I mean," Allie asked, while wishing she could be the one giving Dave a blowjob, "what happened to the baby Brie was pregnant with? Or was she just faking in an attempt to win you back?"

Dave laughed. "Oh, she really was pregnant. She aborted the kid, said she didn't want to have to cope with Manuela's ceaseless melodrama if we got married."

Allie's relentless ardor for him cooled a bit. "And you don't care?"

"Sure I care." He was smiling though.

"You don't sound like you do."

"Well, I'd have liked to have been a daddy, but . . . I guess it just wasn't meant to be. Not with Brie anyway." Then he shrugged. "Shit happens, I guess."

Gosh, what a jerk this guy is," Allie thought. Still her heartfelt disapproval of him wasn't stopping her panties from getting wet.

"Just to be on the safe side, so that Manuela didn't break my legs while I was sleeping," Dave added with a loud laugh, "I removed the baseball bat from the house. I hid it in the back of this pickup truck— it was the only place I could think of that I was certain she wouldn't look." He jerked a thumb behind them. "Ha ha ha—it's still back there now."

Allie glanced at Tommy in the jump seat. He wasn't saying anything. She imagined she read disapproval in his eyes.

But Allie wasn't certain Tommy fully disapproved of his partner's casual behavior towards women. She was immediately on her guard against him too. No, he'd not given her any indications of being as flighty in romance as his gorgeous friend, but, as the old saying went: 'birds of a feather flocked together.'

Little else of consequence was said after that until Tommy finally reached his decision about her. "Alright, you'll do. Turn the truck around and head back."

CHAPTER 31

Anderson & Futana

The connection seemed random, but was nonetheless troubling. Had Jenny and Desmond Haggerty not been members of the Graceful Blend smoothie club, it might never have been made.

While discussing Desmond's disappearance, Jenny Haggerty told Tom Anderson about the tragedy of her husband's younger sister's recent death . . . and mentioned that her name was Mary Watt.

Jenny explained that neither she nor Desmond had ever mentioned his sister's passing during their smoothie club meetings because each time Dez thought of how violently Mary had died, it in turn filled him with a correspondingly violent rage: he got literally red in the face, apoplectic with anger and an insane desire for bloody revenge. It always scared her horribly to see him like that.

And on Anderson and Futana's part, once told by Forensics that no incriminating evidence had been discovered in the Watt residence, both detectives had summarily discarded the link's importance to the case. They'd made no inquiries at all about the victim's next of kin.

Indeed, Anderson still imagined that Mary Watt's ghost *had* actually called him using some paranormal linkup from beyond the grave.

Futana, who was wary of she and Anderson being made to look even more silly than she believed they already did, had angrily vetoed his suggestion that they visit a medium to try to contact the dead woman again.

But now . . .

Once Jenny Haggerty threw Mary Watt's name into the morbid mix, Anderson put two and two together, summed them up to twenty-two instead of four, and decided that a look through the Haggerty's residence might yield something of interest to he and Futana's Wet Bones investigation.

To his hardboiled cop mind, too much of a coincidence was always a bad thing.

Of course, the distraught wife thought he was merely seeking clues to her vanished husband's whereabouts.

***

"Ah, yes, *sane* police work again," Futana cattily remarked. "Not like going over to visit some crank who'll assure us she's raising the miserable lately-departed from their slumber until we find the smoke and mirrors she's fooling us with."

"Yeah, yeah," Anderson retorted, "you're always skeptical till it works. And I *still* think it was a good idea."

"Yeah? Well, this is a *better* one—just doing the normal detective work the city pays us to. If we find a clue, then we find it; and if we don't, we don't. I ain't looking to get ridiculed. This way I know for sure that I'm not going to be writing any reports explaining how Madam Zaza"—she made wavy fortune-teller-like gestures with her fingers—"told us Mary Watt's angry ghost needs appeasing with chicken blood. You want my suggestion, man?" Heels clicking, still gesturing in a parody of a medium, she paced back and forth in front of Anderson. "Just wait till your phone connects to the afterlife again. If Mary calls back with fresh info on the monster, we're good to go."

"Hey, give it a rest, woman. I already agreed with you that we won't consult a medium."

"Just rubbing my thoughts in like Vaseline into . . . that thick skin of yours, just to make extra-sure you realize how serious I am about this."

After this statement, Futana decided she'd said enough on the medium issue. Just now, she'd almost said "like Vaseline into your ass," instead of what she'd intended. And if that wasn't a dead giveaway of a Freudian slip, she didn't know what was.

Anderson and Futana were currently in the missing Desmond's study, having a look through his books and work paraphernalia. Jenny Haggerty was downstairs making them coffee.

Anderson looked up from the files he was examining on Desmond's desk. "I'm not even sure what we're looking for . . . but I've a hunch the size of Massachusetts that there's a clue in here somewhere."

Futana nodded. "I feel exactly the same as you do." She gestured to the bookshelf. "He's got way too many books on occult shit to not be guilty of something. Too bad his wife doesn't know the password to his PC. She walked past the computer desk and sat on the windowsill, looking out at the Haggerty's lawn.

Another wealthy suburban residence, she thought. Possibly another suburban tragedy. They were still looking for Desmond's car. The three Haggerty kids were at school. Futana wondered how they'd been feeling since their daddy hadn't come home.

At least in this case, we don't have blood all over the walls, and a kid on the boil.

Anderson's abused anus began aching again. "Hey, daydreamer," he growled at Futana, "make yourself useful." He indicated a thick leather-bound card holder. "Have a look through all these business cards. Just might be something in there."

Futana picked up the folder and began leafing through it. "Hey, you having any luck with those files?"

"Nah, it's just bank statements and bills and receipts." He heaved an angry sigh. "I hate to say it, Laurie, but we may be barking up the wrong tree here."

"I don't think so," Futana replied. "I think we're barking up the right tree."

Anderson looked at her sharply. "What have you found?"

She slipped a card out of the leather wallet and handed it to him. "Strike you as familiar?"

As Anderson stared at the card, a cold clammy feeling set in the pit of his stomach. "Well, I'll be damned." He looked at Futana. He heard Jenny Haggerty coming up the stairs with their coffee, so he lowered his voice. "It's the same as that torn-up old one we found over at the farm."

She nodded. "McArthur Pets and Pet Supplies. Now we know the full name of the establishment. And now we've got both the address and phone number too."

Anderson nodded grimly back at her. She could practically read his mind: he didn't like the association between a tub of chopped-up woman and a shop that sold pet food.

Jenny Haggerty entered the study then. She was a pretty little housewife just beginning to fill out with middle-age. She wore a white summer dress; the heat had sweated up her armpits. "Here's your coffees, officers. I hope they're sweet enough." Her face was pinched up with worry. She looked exhausted; out on her feet.

"Oh, I'm sure they're fine," Futana replied, accepting a cup from her. "Thanks."

"Hey, Jenny, you got any pets?" Anderson asked, an unreadable expression on his face. "Any cats or dogs or hamsters?"

She shook her head. "No, nothing like that. We'd love to have some, but Kristin our firstborn is allergic to fur. She breaks out in the most horrible rash if she so much as strokes a cat."

Anderson gave Futana a veiled look. She understood that too. It meant this wasn't looking good at all.

"Have you discovered anything helpful?" Jenny asked the two cops. "I mean, why the pet question?"

"Unfortunately no," Anderson replied. "We're just checking up on all possible leads. We found this card for a pet shop among Dez's stuff, and were wondering . . ."

He handed the card to Jenny. She took it from him and studied it. She looked puzzled for a moment, trying to connect the printed words to a memory archived in a dusty vault in her mind.

Then she frowned. "Oh, this is very strange."

"What's strange?" Futana asked, sensing that they hovered on the edge of some pertinent revelation.

"This card is," Jenny replied. "The name on it is McArthur. You see, the friend Dez left to see that night was Jesse McArthur. Until now the man's surname completely slipped my mind. All I could remember was 'Jesse.' " She paused a few moments, staring at the card some more, then added, "The really odd thing though is that Dez said the man had driven in from out of town, from Maine—but this is a Boston address."

She looked at both cops in puzzlement. They stared back, both almost as puzzled. Both police officers, however, now had no doubt they were on the right track.

Anderson smiled coldly. In fact, his expression seemed more like a frown than a smile. "Don't you worry, Jenny," he said in a voice that sent chills down Jenny Haggerty's spine with its relentless intensity, "we'll get to the root of this."

"If there's any foul play going on, we'll fry the bird," Futana added. Her face was only a few degrees warmer than her partner's.

Jenny smiled nervously. "Please find my Dez for me," she pleaded. "I miss him so much and . . . and the kids are going crazy since he's been gone. They keep screaming for their daddy."

She fell silent, seeming to crumple up with misery, as though her loneliness were a compactor that given sufficient time would squash her into nothingness.

His scowl not once leaving his face, Anderson politely drank his coffee. Then he got up and nodded to Futana. "C'mon on, Laurie, we've got a pet shop to go check out."

They took the pet shop card with them. Watching them leave her house, Jenny Haggerty had the impression she was watching a storm brewing, a human thunderstorm.

CHAPTER 32

Anderson, Futana & Stacy

The pet shop was situated down on the lower end of Dorchester Avenue.

Anderson and Futana's relief at finally being on the right track was short-lived. McArthur Pets and Pet Supplies had been sold. The shop's new owner—a tall redhead in her late thirties named Stacy Lovejoy—told them that Jesse McArthur had moved out of town.

"I'm not really certain, but I heard he moved down to Connecticut," she said. Around her a menagerie of little animals bustled noisily. Puppies, birds, mice and newts all went loudly about their caged businesses, while the hamsters and snakes slept through the din.

Anderson found Ms. Lovejoy charming. Futana found the woman creepy; she thought there was a coldness to her that seemed out of place with so much animal warmth about. Almost like she was a serpent and ate the pets on display.

They thanked Stacy Lovejoy and left. Both were frustrated to have run into a dead end.

"Well, I guess Jesse McArthur did drive in from out of town then," Anderson said as they got into their car.

"I don't trust that woman," Futana said. "Something's wrong about her."

"I don't trust her either," Anderson agreed. "But then, I'm paid not to trust anyone. You are too." He yawned. "Look, Laurie, forget her, the pet shop ain't running away. Besides, it's time for lunch. Thai or Chinese?"

"I really don't trust that woman," Futana repeated. "She's a redhead. They make great femme fatales."

"Give it a rest already. I'm hungry. Look, we'll have the guys in the records department run a search, see if they can find out where Jesse McArthur moved to. Then—"

"Hey, slow down, man. This place—Carney Clinic? Isn't this the hospital where Grace Barbanell's on admission?"

Anderson slowed the car. They were nearing the Dorchester–Gallivan intersection. "Yeah, it is. Wanna stop for a moment and say hello?"

"I guess. Yeah, let's. Just don't start telling her about police business like the last time we were over at her place."

"It keeps the old girl happy, and I like to see her happy."

"I really don't get why you like her so much. I wish you liked *me* even half as much. I'm sure you jerk off to her at night."

Anderson steered the car off the road and into the Carney Clinic parking lot.

***

As soon as the two detectives left her pet shop, Stacy Lovejoy made a phone call.

"Jesse, it's Stacy."

"Hey, Stacy! How are you, baby? Or should that be *high priestess?*"

"Cut the formality, man. You know that shit's only for the coven. Jesse, the fuzz were just here asking about you. I think it has to do with Desmond."

She filled him in on the details of the cops' visit. He laughed. "Nothing to worry about. I was out of the state on the night you guys torched him. Got a perfect alibi—I was down in the Big Apple, in bed with a hot stripper."

Stacy felt more than a twinge of jealousy. "That's a relief."

"The other problem is if they track Dez's calls for that night. *You* called him, didn't you?"

Stacy nodded to herself. "Yeah, but I used one of the phones from Boku's recent dinners—that married couple from last month; and I did it from out of town. So at best they'll be tracing a dead person calling a missing person. It's a loop. Dammit, poor law enforcement can't ever win, can they?"

They laughed over that. Then Stacy asked hopefully, "I miss you, Jesse, I wanna see you. Are you coming up soon?"

He laughed. "Yeah, either tomorrow or the day after. I'll be in town for a week; my brother says he needs some stuff. Security dogs to keep intruders off his property. He said he already talked it over with you. Say, have you still got those police dogs—those German Shepherds?"

"Yeah, we discussed it but didn't reach an agreement. He said it was club expenses. I still maintain it's personal, but the coven don't mind feeding them. So . . . how many German Shepherds does Brian want?"

"Two for now, and a whole lot of dog food for 'em. At least till they get used to eating our brand of stuff."

Stacy grinned into the phone. "Okay, man, I can do you a fantastic deal on those; $1,000 each and I'll throw in collars and leashes for both. But, hey, you know I don't deliver if it's outside of Boston. Club biz or not, it ain't cool to have the high priestess running errands for acolytes. Besides, that place of yours is over an hour's drive away. I don't even like going out there for our ceremonies."

"Cool, cool. I've already taken care of that for you."

"You have?"

"Yeah, I remembered in time that you don't like long drives. Some guys I know will handle the delivery—I've already set it up with them."

"Jesse, is it safe?"

"Yeah, with these guys it is. They're a reliable bunch who don't ask silly questions. I for one don't want any mutts in my car. Big dog equals big dog poo. I don't care how house-trained they are, there's no guarantee they won't dump on my expensive leather seats if the feeling takes their canine asses."

"Hey, Jesse—you're not bringing your damn stripper along with you when you visit, are you? 'Cos you know if you are, I sure as hell don't wanna see you."

"No no no, baby," he said soothingly. "She was a redhead too, but nothing like you. You've got way better tits for one thing . . . for another, you're a red hot witch . . ."

Stacy smiled at his flattery. While listening, she whispered a spell and watched as the skin of her right forearm suddenly became hairy and her delicate fingers lengthened into claws. She grinned at the transformed limb. Ha ha! If Jesse dared bring his stripper to Boston, she'd rip the bitch to shreds.

It wouldn't be the first time either. Both of Jesse bringing some tramp to her house for a quick screw and of herself ripping the woman into pet food.

All of a sudden Stacy Lovejoy felt peckish. She licked first her lips, and then her chin with the extraordinarily long tongue that had accompanied the transformation of her arm, said tongue dangling between canine teeth that were much longer than the human norm. Then, leaving her arm in its animal condition, she turned, left the pet store, and headed upstairs to her kitchen, where she had some nice, raw, wet bones just dripping with marrow in her fridge.

CHAPTER 33

Petra and Dave

"Marriage is a funny thing," Petra Velli said. "Sometimes I'm uncertain if I love or hate my husband. Other times it's both—I look at Marko and I can't tell the difference. I feel like fucking him but also feel like unloading a shotgun in his face." She dragged slowly on her cigarette. "But then, I think of our kids. If I killed Marko, I'd be robbing them of a father."

She searched Dave's face with her eyes to see if he understood.

Dave nodded. It was Wednesday afternoon. They were once again at the Velli's beach house, lying face-to-face on an white airbed. They'd positioned the mattress in front of the French windows to the upstairs living room. This location gave them an excellent view of the beach. Petra appreciated the view; she enjoyed staring at the endless water running out to the gray horizon. Dave was more interested in Petra's body, her luscious curves providing him all the view he needed. They were stranded in the interlude between physical exertions.

"It isn't that I wouldn't love to leave Marko," Petra said. "But if I did, where would I go?"

Dave decided she was talking to herself. Sex had calmed her body, and now, forgetting he was here with her, she was unburdening her soul to the air. She didn't know where she'd go? Oh, but he'd asked her more than once to elope with him, but she'd repeatedly refused.

"I'm a prisoner," Petra said. "Fully provided for, living in comfort and luxury, but nonetheless a captive. That's the one thing no one mentioned when I was marrying Marko—that one day I'd be unable to leave him."

"Yeah, right," Dave said. "So you won't leave the guy, and you don't love him either, but you won't let me knock him off. So what else?"

"Marko Velli is an army. No single man can defeat him."

Dave smirked. "Sweetheart, I can raise an army of my own. Your old guy wouldn't stand a chance."

She saw that he was serious. She giggled and blew a smoke ring in his face. "No, no, no. I already told you, we don't kill Marko—the guilt would finish me off. I'd wind up in a nuthouse, crazy for life. You wouldn't want that now, would you? So, no, *we don't* kill him, even if he's such a horrible little man. He gave me kids and I love them, and they love their evil daddy, and they'll hate me if I kill him." She sucked on her cigarette and blew another smoke ring in Dave's face. "So we don't kill him."

"And us? What about us? I'm desperate to have you, baby!" These words were spoken with raw, unmistakable urgency and intense masculine despair.

"You and I, we just fuck. You already have me. You've been having me a whole damn lot. Even more than Marko has been. You and I have fun here. Lots of fun. Marko isn't ever fun. Not even in bed. Mind you, he's not bad in bed, baby, he's just always in a hurry."

She giggled mischievously, then added, "I like to think that Marko and I have a fifty-fifty relationship in bed: He fakes foreplay, I fake orgasm."

"I don't think you care about me like I care about you," Dave protested, as petulant as a child being punished with a lack of candy. It hurt him, really hurt him, how languid she was about the state of his heart. Couldn't she see that he meant what he said? Didn't she realize that he was willing to take on her husband's entire mob just to have her? Dave wanted to show her that he wasn't scared of anyone. Not even the dreaded Marko Velli.

She sat up and hugged her knees. Her expression turned serious. "I care a whole damn lot about you, baby," she said. "I just don't care to become a corpse. I like making love with you and corpses don't make love."

"Oh, come on." *Here it is again*, he thought, *she's playing me again.*

She read his expression correctly. "No, it's not what you think, baby. I mean what I say—I . . . we . . . can't do a thing." Her cigarette was finished so she lit two more and handed him one. Then she smiled sadly and said, "Did you ever hear about what happened to Barrymore?"

"Who's that?"

"That's my point, baby— Barrymore's no one anymore. But five years ago, Barrymore was the big deal in northeastern mob circles. He was a Philly dope baron who tried to muscle in on Marko's territory while Marko was in prison. When Marko got tired of Barrymore messing with him, he gave Black and White the nod to do a job on Barrymore's daughter Katie. The next Friday, Katie was kidnapped from her school. No one had any idea where she was. The cops couldn't find her; neither could the mobsters.

"Then a week later, Barrymore received two packages from São Paulo, Brazil. One contained a plastic bag full of wet bones—a complete skeleton." Petra pulled on her cigarette. She held the smoke deep in her lungs, then released it slowly through her nostrils. "As if that wasn't bad enough, the second package contained a DVD recording. The DVD showed Katie Barrymore naked and hanging in a large, half-filled aquarium. She was suspended there by large hooks stuck in her shoulders. The water reached up to her waist and . . . the water was filled with piranha."

Petra gagged; more smoke spilled from her nose. "It was horrible, Davey. The video recorded the messy, bloody process of the piranha eating away Katie's legs and crotch down to the bones . . . while she screamed uncontrollably. She just screamed and screamed—it was a god-awful, ear-splitting racket. They'd rigged their setup in such a way that the water kept flowing, washing the blood away so that it didn't mess up the view. So you could clearly see those horrible ugly fish ripping away the poor kid's flesh. Ugh! Then, once Katie had died from all that pain and blood loss, two masked figures—one male, one female, clearly Black and White—dropped the rest of her into the tank for the fish to eat too. Believe me, by then there was nothing left of the poor girl below the waist."

"Ugh!" Dave looked sick. He began choking on cigarette smoke.

"Barrymore instantly suffered a coronary," Petra continued. "The loud-mouthed fool never even finished watching the DVD—he collapsed halfway through the viewing. He was rushed to hospital, has been stuck in a wheelchair ever since. I hear it's his wife who runs their business now."

Petra looked pointedly at her lover. "Needless to say, no one from the City of Brotherly Love has tried to muscle in on Marko's turf since then. And that was Black and White's doing."

"Dammit," Dave said. "I've heard rumors about those two but I never imagined they were that sadistic."

"They're worse than you can imagine. And keep quiet about this, baby. Almost no one knows how it happened. *I* only know because I'm Marko's wife. Black and White kept the kid in our basement for two days before stowing her away on a ship bound for Brazil."

"And you let them?"

She shrugged. "Marko's orders. I couldn't possibly refuse. Besides, I had no idea they were going to kill the girl. People were getting locked in our basement all the time, mostly drug dealers' wives and girlfriends held to put leverage on their men, or hookers who needed teaching a lesson. Once or twice it was a judge's kid, blindfolded and scared, and with no idea what was going on. As far as I recall, they all got sent home alive. So, when Katie Barrymore was leaving, I assumed that she too was being returned home, after her daddy had agreed to cease being a pain in my husband's ass."

She smiled coolly at Dave. "Now, do you understand why I'm not interested in running away from Marko? I'd rather have the FBI or terrorists after me than Black and White."

They remained like that for a good while, each mulling on their private thoughts.

"Okay, okay," Dave agreed finally, in as macho a voice as he could manage, though his testicles had practically crawled up into his stomach on hearing her tale. "So your husband lives to fuck you hastily another day. But it ain't 'cos I'm afraid of his damn checkerboard trolls. It's just 'cos you said so, babe. Personally, I'd love to bump him off just for what he did to that Barrymore kid. Aw, come on now! The girl never even knew him!" He stubbed his cigarette out with deep feeling.

"Crime ain't a game for dreamers, baby."

He frowned. "Is that how you see me? A dreamer?"

"Oh, don't be like that, baby!" Petra pouted, then finished her cigarette. She smiled languidly at Dave, then reached down and took his soft penis in her cool fingers. She began stroking him back to hardness. "Let's forget all the bad men. And the bad women too. Just make love to me again, baby," she cooed at him. "Let's have more fun. I never knew cheating on one's husband could feel so good."

Dave had no reply to that. Once he was hard again he rolled over on her and slid himself into her welcoming wetness. He began thrusting slowly, shoving his manhood as deep as he could inside her, trying to fill her core with insight of the depth of his love for her.

She groaned and clutched him tighter and tighter. "Oh shit, baby! Oh, don't you agree? This is so much better than us plotting to kill Marko. Oh, you HARD man! Oh, yesss!"

Dave agreed with Petra. Making love with her like this was much better. He just wanted it to last a lifetime. He'd take the chance if she would. They'd take the kids and leave.

But . . . the specter of Katie Barrymore cautioned him and he instantly discarded the plan. Better to just have fun like she said.

After a while, Petra rolled on top of him. She took control of their lovemaking, guided their synchronized erotic motions. He admired her body as it writhed above his. She was a wonderful sculpture in flesh. Imperfect because age had caught up with her. Beautiful in her own flawed way. Her large breasts dripped the sweat of her exertions. Her nipples stood proudly erect. Her lustrous brown hair reflected the sun like a pool of spilled honey. Her ivory skin glowed with the burnished sheen of life. Her pink lips parted wide with ecstasy, uttering choice syllables of erotic nonsense, baby talk which nonetheless made perfect sense to his similarly attuned mind.

Oh, how Dave loved her!

She gasped out her orgasm, rolling her crotch deliciously over his. He held her buttocks tight, digging his fingers into their soft meatiness. He tried to bury himself inside her. He wanted to lose himself inside the fathomless depths of her vagina. She was the Atlantic Ocean and he the Titanic.

It was really good. Dave felt himself about to come.

It was then that Petra Velli gasped in horror. She flung the fingers of both hands to her mouth and gasped loudly. Then she dropped down flat on top of Dave.

"Hell!" she groaned in a scared voice. "It's Black and White! They must be here looking for me! Marko must be wondering why I'm not answering my phone."

Dave was already ejaculating. The urgency in her voice merely assisted the semen in exiting his testicles. The semen jetted out of him as if it was scared of losing its place in the future of the human race.

Petra was fighting to get off him and shut the curtains, but Dave held her down. He didn't let her go. He gripped the squirming woman tightly until all his sperm was out of his body and inside hers. Then he permitted her to roll off him.

It was only now that Dave began feeling scared. The feeling of terror rose up from the sweaty airbed and smothered him. *Black and White? Those two psychopaths? Oh, heck—man, I gotta get out of here!* Dave would rather take on Marko's entire army than that pair.

Again he remembered what they'd done to Barrymore's teen daughter. The image of ravenous piranha stripping a screaming young woman bare of skin and flesh rose up red and bloody in his mind.

Shit!

Dave rolled over on the airbed. Being careful to keep his head down, he peeked out into the front yard. Yes, Petra was right. Black and White were just getting out of their blue Dodge. Once out of the car, Carrie White turned and pointed to the beach house, up at the French windows.

The dread pair began walking towards the house. They approached leisurely, laughing. A tall white man and a small black woman. Only you had to reverse their skin colors to get their names right.

A thrill of panic went through Dave.

He resisted the urge to leap to his feet and start dressing. If he did that, they would certainly see him. If they saw him, all hell would break loose. So, instead of jumping up hurriedly, Dave slowly crawled back over the airbed. Then he sat in a chair beside the TV and began pulling his boxers on.

Petra was already dressed and busy tidying herself up.

"You've gotta go, baby!" she pleaded. "Don't you dare wait and fight with them! He who fucks and runs away lives to fuck another day!"

Dave had no intent of waiting. He didn't even have a gun on him. (Not wise, sure, but that was Tommy's law: the Rectifiers never carried arms.) Still, a guy had to show some pride. If he acted scared, her opinion of him might plummet like Wall Street on a bad day.

"Yeah, okay," he drawled in a tough voice. "I'll go if you say so. Sure I'll leave, baby, but only 'cos you're insisting on it. But really, I feel like staying and teaching those two punks a lesson in violence they can relay back to your husband."

Petra looked at him in horror. She didn't suspect he was merely bluffing. She was convinced he was serious. "Davey, please, just go! Please, I'm begging you not to make a scene. Do it 'cos you love me!"

"Sure, sure, I'll go. But how the hell am I gonna get downstairs? That's the problem, baby."

Petra had a ready answer: "What we'll do is—I'll go out and talk to them, keep them from coming in here. Then you can climb over the balcony railing and drop to the ground. Hide in the trees till they're gone; then you can come back inside. That way, even if they search the house, they won't find you." She gave him a concerned look. "Don't try leaving, baby. Remember the fence is electrified."

He nodded. It was a good plan. It was an easy drop, just a single floor. He just hoped Black and White wouldn't insist on checking this upstairs living room before he got a chance to effect his escape.

Petra kissed him then slipped out into the hallway. Dave waited, timing his move. After a while he heard voices in the hallway. She'd waited for them to climb the stairs before showing herself. Dave appreciated her brains: if she'd gone to meet them downstairs, they might still notice him dropping to the ground.

"My phone?" Petra was saying. "Oh, the battery ran down and my car charger's blown; I need to order another from Walmart." She sounded as cool as a martini, as if she had a college degree in lying. "What's the matter anyway? . . . Junior got a tummy ache at school and his dad's worried? . . . But . . ."

Dave dropped silently into the bushes and made his way along the side of the house.

It was while he was crossing through the trees that he tripped over a stone and slid into a hole.

As he fell to the ground, Dave felt his ankle twist. Then his ankle snapped like a gun going off. The sound of the bone breaking was so loud that he imagined they'd have heard it inside the house. Quickly, to keep from screaming, he stuck his hand in his mouth and bit down hard.

Dave managed to pull his leg out of the hole and crawl into cover beneath a large clump of azaleas and rhododendrons. Then all he could do was lie there, gritting his teeth in agony amidst the dense floral perfume and curious bugs, and wait for Black and White to get done with Petra and leave the beach house, so that she come could take him to the hospital. It wasn't just her son who needed a doctor now.

He wasn't worried about her getting rid of the psycho pair. Petra was a smooth talker. They'd believe whatever she told them to make them leave without her.

Then Dave remembered his partner and tomorrow night's job.

Shit, Tommy's gonna be so mad about this!

CHAPTER 34

Greg in Kimland, Pt.2

2:37 Thursday afternoon.

I can't believe I'm actually going through with this, Greg thought as he parked outside the Kims' house. *I'm here to shit on a woman.*

Since his first visit here a week back, the perverse gravity of Jojo's demand had receded in his mind. Particularly since Aunt Grace had been in hospital. Now that the hour of fulfilment of their pact was here though, the disgusting immensity of what Jojo expected of him preyed on him like a vulture.

"Eat a lot all week," she'd said. "Lots of meat and protein. And no wanking or sex all week either. I want a full load—I'm making my own smoothie afterwards." She'd giggled after saying this. "Thank fuck Gracie's in hospital, huh?"

Yes, thank fuck indeed, Greg thought as he climbed the porch steps. He rang the front door bell.

This time it was Kiki Kim who let Greg into the house.

"Can you just believe this?" she asked as she shut the door behind him. "Lulu ran off to the studio. The biatch took Jojo's hot ride. She left me to finish off chores at home. And she knows full well that they can't start the damn rehearsal till I get there. How are they gonna rehearse without the bass guitar? Besides, our rehearsal ain't until four anyway. I think she just wanted to go screw that freaking Zombie Joe of hers."

Still lamenting her older sister's behavior, Kiki sat Greg in the living room then hurried upstairs to tell Jojo he'd arrived.

***

Upstairs. The bedroom was the same as last time: pink rubber floor, red bed, green ceiling, yellow drapes now tightly shut, incense smoking on the blue walls. And Jojo . . . Jojo waiting in bed naked again. Jojo grinning in delight. Jojo's dark eyes burning with a fire he'd never seen in them before. Her nipples already erect and demanding his attention.

Once he was naked, she handed him two pills. One was Cialis, the other a large green lozenge. "It's a laxative. It's mild, but it'll flush you out in fifteen minutes tops."

He nodded. He'd be relieved to empty his belly. He'd eaten so much over the past three days, he felt totally stuffed. And then there was the additional factor that, since yesterday, even when he'd felt like emptying his bowels, he'd doggedly refused to do so. He was going to do this right; he didn't want to arrive at Jojo's with a depleted poop consignment, with nothing left in his belly to excrete.

That had been easier part of his preparations. Explaining to Debbie why he couldn't see her till Friday had been more difficult. But seeing Debbie would mean sex and he couldn't make love to her: Jojo wanted a full load of come from him for her celebratory smoothie. And he intended to give her that too.

He'd used Aunt Grace's stomach virus as his excuse.

"I don't see why you even care," Debbie said testily. "No, no, I don't mean it like that, baby. She's your aunt and of course you have to care about her . . . but you're always going on about how she's controlling your life. I imagined you'd be glad that she's finally out of the way for a short while."

They'd been seated in McDonalds, drinking cokes.

"I don't care *that* much. I'm just pretending to. It'll look bad if she suddenly dies and I've hardly ever been to see her at the hospital, won't it?"

"Yeah, I guess. Hey, and why've you been eating like a pig for the past few days anyway? You're stuffing yourself like you're Oliver Twist's entire starving orphanage."

"I've got a sudden craving, that's all. I'm eating for both of us . . ."

"That's the lamest excuse for gluttony I ever heard. Next thing you'll be saying you're preggers, that's why."

"Debbie darling, please, please, please overlook my overeating. The main thing is, I can't see you till Friday."

"But . . . why? I don't get it. I live next door to you. I can just walk on over." She'd placed her soft hands over his on the tabletop. "Sweetheart, I'll really miss bird-watching from your bedroom window."

"Friday, baby. Trust me. I want you even more than you want me. You know that. Hey, tell you what—we'll bird-watch together all weekend."

"Yeah, okay. Oh, alright—Friday then. But I'm sleeping over at your house that night."

"Of course, babe. Saturday and Sunday nights too if you like. We can watch for the owls together."

That took care of Debbie. Jojo would have her damn semen smoothie. It didn't matter—this would be his last ever. An event of this magnitude demanded celebration; it was acceptable that he went out with a bang. Yes, this final nut would be a mega-nut. He hoped to ejaculate so much for Jojo, she'd have enough come to make a dozen drinks if she so desired.

And now, here he was with Jojo. Since entering her psychedelic bedroom, he'd been looking around for cameras. If she was recording this . . .

He saw no evidence of any video cameras: no tiny isolated tubes, no suspiciously glittering lenses, no glass balls on silver stalks, no oriental statuettes with rotating heads; nothing that could prove calamitous to him.

They got down to it. Greg was surprised: It wasn't like he'd expected it to be. He'd thought he'd just shit on her and that would be it. But no, it started off exactly like normal intercourse. They did a lot of foreplay. They kissed. Jojo kissed him with the hunger of a starving animal. She went down on him, sucking his penis with almost prostitute expertise. He went down on her, licking her vagina with relish. The incense in the room gave their intercourse the characteristics of a dream.

By the time the laxative got to work on Greg, his penis was so hard from the Cialis, it felt like it would never go down again.

By then, he'd almost forgotten what he was here for. He winced as the first warning spasm went through him.

"Shit!" he yelped. "I think it's about to . . ."

She didn't gasp with delight like he'd expected she would. She merely smiled. She kissed him passionately then instructed him first to stand, then to squat over her. She lay under him, gripping her breasts, teasing her swollen nipples between index fingers and thumbs.

"Now just let it out," she instructed softly. "Relax and let it all out on me." She reached up and grabbed his penis. "Shit on me, baby!"

"But the bed!"

"It's shitproof!"

Greg let it out. Jojo stroked his erection while he pooped on her.

The combination of sexual pleasure and bowel evacuation was impossible to put into words. Greg could feel the excrement squirting out of his body. He looked down. He watched the feces plop on Jojo's tanned skin, splattering and fragmenting like huge brown raindrops falling on parched desert sand.

Then Jojo let go of his erection. She began smearing the shit over her belly and breasts. Now she began gasping. She writhed over the bed. She slithered up and down between his legs so the shit dropped on her exactly where she wanted it to fall. Finally, mewling like a cat in heat, she turned over on her belly and made swimming motions on the bed like she was propelling herself through the excrement.

The room smelt of shit. The smoking joss sticks, however, rendered the odor much less pungent and offensive than it might otherwise have been.

Greg's penis was still hard. The Cialis had seen to that. And beyond that, he now found a perverse excitement in what they were doing: the joy of experiencing a taboo act; the pleasure of exploring the forbidden. As Jojo writhed and moaned and touched herself, he dropped down so he was kneeling on either side of her hips and let himself go. The laxative really kicked in then—he blew out a brown liquid mess all over her buttocks.

It was only now that Greg realized that Jojo was herself pooping—she'd also taken a laxative pill. Her excrement was a flow of bubbly brown lava erupting from the anal peak between the Oriental mountains of her tight buttocks and traveling down through the erotic landscapes of her tanned and trembling thighs to pool and smear into a dirty lake on the rubber bed.

"Yes, yes!" she moaned in ecstasy. "Now fuck me in the shit!"

As per her instructions, he rolled on a condom first. She wanted to drink his come afterward, his clean virile come. The excrement was smeared down the back of his thighs but his penis and scrotum were free of it.

Once he had the condom on, he rolled Jojo over. She'd been masturbating hard with both hands beneath her. Her palms and fingers were messy with excrement. Now she removed her hands from her sex and grabbed his manhood instead. She pulled him down hard on her.

She stabbed herself with him. Shit-greased vagina. Shit outside her, shit inside her now too.

"Oh, yes," she groaned as he filled her. Her eyes gaped wide into his. And this time, Greg saw, there was no faking in them. Jojo was here, here, here, right here with him. She was crapping herself silly, adding her mess to Greg's mess. But that wasn't important now.

What *was* important was that Jojo was going to make it, she was going to come. She was going to reach her sexual peak, and at that moment of her fullest pleasure—with the dirt and smell and the fecal mess smeared all over her, all over them both, with more spurting unheeded from his ass as he thrust into her—at that supreme, sublime and exquisite moment, there was no obscenity in what they were doing. At that moment of ultimate physical focus, it was just sex; nothing more, nothing less.

The mess was there, the smell was there, but Greg understood that this was merely sex—freaky, messy sex—but just a man and a woman in bed all the same.

Jojo began coming. During her orgasm she gripped him with her excrement-covered hands, wrapped her messy legs around him and screamed. She began weeping; the tears poured from her eyes like they'd never stop. She leaned up and kissed him. She kissed him like she was trying to suck out his soul. He kept thrusting into her. His belly hurt and more shit wanted out of his rectum, but he was HARD and he kept going. She was deep and sweet and the smell in the room was normal to him now—incense, and lust and poop.

Then, as her orgasm began fading, he came. The semen blew out of him. At the same moment he shat himself massively.

Jojo saw the expression of the 'little death' in his eyes. She felt him grow larger inside her, then stiffen. She gripped him hard, as hard as if her survival as a human being depended on it.

She was satisfied, satisfied, satisfied.

Then it was over. Greg lay on his back on the bed. He was covered with shit. His own shit. Her shit too. The smell was dirty perfume.

Toilet perfume. There was so much of it, he'd ceased noticing it. He might just as well be covered with chocolate.

Jojo rolled over and kissed him. "Oh, thank you! Thank you so much." Her lips and tongue were possibly the only clean part of her left. Everywhere else was a stinky brown. He figured he looked exactly the same as she did.

She looked down at his penis. It was still HARD. The bulb at the tip of the rubber was filled to bursting with semen.

"Ooh, there's so much of it!" she gushed like a little girl.

Greg watched dully while she carefully rolled the condom off. At a point he bent to the side so she could get it off without spilling any of his ejaculate. His belly ached but he thought the laxative had finished its work. He hoped it had.

Mild, she'd said? Then what would a 'heavy duty' laxative feel like? Jojo had to have used those too before to be able to tell the difference, right?

Jojo got off the bed. Naked and covered with feces, she padded to the bedroom door. Greg dully accepted that this was how the dark stains had gotten on the rubber rug.

The backs of Jojo's legs were a twin brown. Her legs looked like chocolate bars—inedible chocolate bars. She opened her bedroom door and yelled, "Kiki! Hey, Kiki, are you still fucking home!?"

He heard a voice reply, then a few moments later, saw Kiki Kim appear in the doorway.

"Sis, is that poop on your boobs?"

"Huh?"

"Sis, you got shit on your tits!"

"Yeah, so what? Like *you* haven't seen shitty tits before. Look, stop fooling and put this in the fridge for me, will you?"

"Ugh, there's poop on it! I'm not touching that. Ugh, you stink worse than an unflushed toilet."

"Hey, goddam take it from me. Pour the come in a glass then. Ditch the rubber."

"Who's poop is this? His or yours?"

"Don't be fucking sexist. It's unisex, gender-equal shit."

"How come *I* get to do this shit?"

" 'Cos you're the youngest sister and Lulu and I are both jealous that dad loves you more than he loves us. Wise up, kid, why d'you think Lulu ran off to rehearsal early today? You know she's always late."

Greg watched this verbal exchange with little interest. They were crazy, that was all. He understood everything now with crystal clarity. All three Kim sisters were crazy: Jojo with her poop-fetish, Lulu with her blank-faced stares, and Kiki with her endless bitching about everything and everyone. Maybe Korean and American DNA simply didn't mingle well.

Kiki hissed. Then she peeked around Jojo and blew Greg a kiss. Then she left with her condom-load of semen held out at arms-length.

Yeah, Greg concluded. *The three of them are crazy.*

Jojo shut the door and walked back over to the bed. A besmirched black-haired beauty. A poop goddess.

Greg was still hard. Jojo pointed at his erection and giggled. "That's just such a lovely sight for a lady to see. Alright, now I'm gonna ride you, man. I want that dick deep inside my ass. No need for a rubber this time." She climbed on the bed and grabbed his penis. "Hey, man, I might shit on you, but don't worry about it, alright? You hear me, man?—if I dump on you, don't you worry about it at all."

Seeing as he was already covered with shit anyway, Greg found that impossibly funny.

She got on him and rode him to two more orgasms. She did shit on him, but not much.

Afterwards, she left him in bed and, still dressed in poop, went downstairs to the kitchen to make her smoothie. So as not to dirty the floor outside her bedroom, she wore massive flip-flops. Each huge slipper was the size of a snowshoe.

On returning, she offered Greg a sip of the drink. He politely declined.

"Ah, baby, you taste so good," she enthused after a long gulp.

"I need to use your bathroom," he said.

She gestured languidly at the room's other door. "Be my guest, man. Use whatever soaps or creams or perfumes you like in there."

Leaving Jojo sipping her smoothie on the shit-covered bed, Greg walked into her bathroom.

Now that everything was over, he was trapped in an anticlimax. It felt as though he'd shat his essential self out along with the feces. He realized it was the laxative that had drained him. That had to be why Jojo was taking it easy outside now with her smoothie.

Jojo's bathroom had a similar pink rubber-mat floor as her bedroom. Its walls were done in a horrible lime-green that made Greg feel like throwing up. Her bathroom contained both a regular bath, and, set in a corner, a glass-enclosed shower stall. Between bath and shower stood a tall, ornamental glass soap cabinet set over a red sink.

Eyeing the sink, Greg considered drinking some water to rehydrate himself. But the sight of the mess on his hands stopped him; there was no way he was trusting them anywhere near his mouth until he'd really cleaned up.

So instead, he stepped under Jojo's shower and turned on the hot water. As the hot jets of water hit his flesh, stripping away the caked layer of smelly brown, he felt much better.

Then he searched the shelves of the intricately designed glass cabinet beside the shower for a bar of soap.

He was surprised. He now realized that when Jojo had told him to use 'whatever he liked' in her bathroom, she hadn't merely been playing on a figure of speech: Jojo had an impressive selection of bath salts and soaps. Her soap cabinet contained diverse bottles filled with a rainbow of liquids, and soap bars of differing shapes and sizes and scents; including several that were shaped like animals. She even had some that looked like strings of beads.

The most perverse soaps, however, were the ones shaped like penises. There were seven or eight of these, and in different colors and sizes too. Some of the phallic soaps were a little worn down, as if Jojo had been using them on herself.

"She definitely takes cleaning up afterwards very seriously," Greg muttered to himself.

Thankfully, the hot water was really purging the shit off his skin. Staring down at the icky brown mess on the shower stall's bright orange floor tiles, he couldn't believe how much of it there had been stuck to him.

He finally settled on a soap bar shaped like a frog. It was very realistically molded and a dark green in color. The frog-soap bar foamed easily under the water.

Greg got to work purifying himself.

He spent half an hour showering himself clean.

CHAPTER 35

Greg

After a farewell kiss with Jojo, who'd by then exchanged her empty smoothie glass for a joint, Greg drove back home. Contrary to his expectations, he didn't feel disgusted with himself. Rather he felt a deep sense of a mission accomplished.

It's a real pity, he thought while steering his way through the late afternoon traffic, *'Cos Jojo's such a beautiful lady. It's just the shit . . . I guess shit really does happen.*

Just as he pulled into his aunt's driveway, his cellphone rang. It was Tommy Collins. Greg parked then accepted the call.

"Hey, dude, what's the news?" he asked.

"You free tonight? I got a major problem you can help with."

"Fill me in, man. I'm all ears."

Greg listened to Tommy's explanation of Dave's broken ankle. He decided he wasn't shedding any tears for the guy. This was his own big opportunity. And damn, was he excited about it—he'd not expected he'd get his break into the Rectifiers this fast.

So thanks, Dave. Sorry 'bout your bad luck and all that, but your loss is my gain. At least you got laid first.

"So, are you up for it?" Tommy asked. "Sorry, dude, that it's on such short notice. We're gonna do a test run tonight—gotta make a delivery out of town—then on Saturday it's the big one."

"Count me in," Greg replied without hesitation. "When and where do we meet up?"

"Great. Meet me at Bowie's Bar then. I'll pull up outside at 9 p.m."

"Sure, man. I'll be there."

Greg hung up, left the car, and walked towards the house.

He was grinning as he opened the front door. Today wasn't just turning out alright, it was getting better by the minute.

CHAPTER 36

Allie, with Tommy & Greg

Allie was surprised when, that night, Tommy turned up with Greg in tow.

She regarded the pair in surprise. She had no idea what Greg was doing here. On their previous meeting, he'd not struck her as having criminal leanings. *But then, neither did I either.*

She forgot Greg for the moment and looked at Tommy instead. She let her puzzled gaze ask the obvious question.

He met her eyes evenly. "There's been a slight change of plans, baby," he said. From the tone of his voice she could tell he was wrestling with intense exasperation.

Her eyes widened. "What happened to Dave?"

"He broke his ankle."

"Broke his ankle? How?"

Tommy laughed before replying. "The dumbass broke his ankle jumping out of Petra Velli's window. Dave's lucky to be alive. Shit, I always warned the fool—if you're screwing another man's wife, take her to a motel. If that married woman happens to be Petra Velli, ensure that the damn motel you take her to is out of town; out of the state even."

Allie grimaced at how blasé he sounded while making the comment. She wondered if she'd misjudged him. Maybe the pair were actually birds of a feather. That was that then, though; no more handsome Dave tonight. Too bad; she'd been looking forward to seeing him.

"Where is he now?" she asked.

"At home with a cast on his leg, watching a football game," Greg said.

"I'm wondering if someone ratted on Dave," Tommy said. "According to him, Marko couldn't find Petra at home and sent Black and White over to their beachfront house in Quincy. That's where it happened." He frowned. "Dave suspects Manuela Costa might be the snitch."

"Why would she do that?" Allie asked.

"Simple. She might be trying to get back at Dave for scorning her."

Allie found the logic of that highly dubious. "By getting him killed? How exactly does that help her romantic intentions? I thought you said she's trying to rekindle their relationship? That'll be impossible to do if he's dead."

Greg shook his head too. "Yeah, man, Allie's right: Manuela can't get back together with Dave if he's dead. I doubt she had anything to do with it. Blaming her for what happened to Dave is just chasing shadows. Besides, from what you told me about this Marko guy, if he knew for sure about their affair, Dave would be hog food now."

Tommy nodded. "Yeah, there is that to consider. Bad luck for Dave then."

"Yeah, bad luck indeed," Greg agreed with a cold smile.

That resolved, Allie focused on the business at hand. Her eyes on Tommy, she tilted her chin toward Greg. "He's coming along too?"

"Yeah," Tommy replied. "We need backup and Dave's out for at least two months. Greg'll be doing the Saturday job with us too."

Allie regarded Greg coolly. *There just may be too many of us newbies in on this caper*, she thought.

Greg seemed to read her mind. "Don't worry about me," he told her, a look of determination in his eyes. "I got both your backs. I ain't gonna fuck it up. You can rest assured on that."

Allie nodded back at him. This was getting surreal.

I used to be an accountant and now here I am, driving a getaway car. And Greg, from what I've heard of him, also has a degree in money.

But the way Greg had spoken, he'd been calm, like he'd done this before. However, she was willing to wager money that he hadn't. But then, one never really knew.

She gestured at both men. "Alright, whatever. Now, where the hell are those dogs we're delivering?"

"Outside in the truck," Greg said.

***

Ten minutes later they were rolling out of Dover, headed west for Brimfield. The dogs—two huge German shepherds—were riding out in back, tongues lolling out of their mouths to catch the wind.

Along with the dogs in the back, they were also carrying a rucksack of dog food and some other stuff for Brian McArthur.

The very name 'Brian' was angering Allie already. Oh, not another one of *them*. Right now, she totally abhorred and completely detested all Brians. She hoped tonight wasn't about becoming a replay of her dreadful Dark Day of Repeating Brians.

The guys were silent for most of the trip. Allie concentrated on her driving. Despite her tough front she was nervous; she didn't want to screw this up. At the same time, doing something forbidden— entering the criminal world (even though according to Tommy, the Rectifiers didn't commit crimes, rather, they made things right for the criminally aggrieved) held a compelling fascination for her.

***

"Hey, here it is, turn left here."

Allie made the turning, off of Route 20 onto Dearth Hill Road. She instinctively hated the road's name: 'Dearth' sounded too much like 'Death' for comfort.

After a while of heading south, they turned west. If Dearth Hill Road had sounded bad, this new turnoff was in fact worse. This road, which appeared to be nameless, was one of those outback kind of nowhere routes.

The further she drove down this turnoff, with the thick woods leaning ever more and more over the road at them, the more convinced she became that they were heading into the middle of nowhere. The road wound back and forth. It wasn't particularly long, but she'd slowed the truck almost to a crawl now so that they wouldn't overshoot their destination, and this made the journey seem longer.

Yes, the more the road curved and the denser the surrounding woods grew, the more certain Allie in turn got that they were all going to end up as the victims of some inbred lunatic in a rabbit-head mask with a huge chainsaw.

She didn't let the others see her fear though. Tommy had hired her because he thought she was tough. Well she'd thought she was too, but she couldn't shake off her gut feeling of trouble waiting for them at the end of wherever they were headed to. The chill fingers of fear gripped her tightly.

"Hey, doesn't this damn road ever end," she growled after a bit. Neither man replied her. Tommy kept smoking. Greg was staring sideways at the woods, as though he had friends hiding in there. She shrugged, maybe the guy had bigfoot relatives.

"Here it is . . . I think," Tommy finally announced.

***

They'd arrived at a farmhouse, an ugly old two-story stone building, thirty or so yards in from the road. On their approach up the road, the truck headlights had showed their destination clearly. Behind the main farm building stood three large barns. Way off to its left, Allie made out the reflective form of a greenhouse, though most of its glass was shattered.

The ground floor farmhouse lights were on.

Farm or not, the place gave Allie the creeps. The bad feeling she'd had while driving here had reduced now they were finally out of the tunnel of trees, but not by much.

On Tommy's instructions, she parked at the foot of the driveway. Then she turned to face her companions. Now her nervousness got the better of her and she asked, "Why the hell would anyone want to live out here in the middle of nowhere?"

"It's a farm," Greg replied drolly. "I guess they ran out of space to keep it in the city."

She ignored the joke. "You know what I mean, man. Hey, Tommy, what's the deal here? This place is so far off the beaten track that there doesn't seem to be a beaten track. I don't even think it's on Google Maps. Even this road we're on is overgrown with grass. So why would—?"

"You ask a lot of questions, baby," Tommy interrupted. "Just zip your pretty lips for a bit. We'll be in and out of here before you know it." Then his gaze softened a little. "And keep out of sight, just in case there's trouble. There shouldn't be any, but you never know with these backwoods types. Trust me, I don't like the looks of this creepy place any more than you do."

Allie shut up. She nodded. She adjusted her seat back and down so she wouldn't be seen from the house.

They left her in the RAM. Tommy let the dogs out of the back of the pickup truck, and then he and Greg led them up the short driveway to Brian's house. Greg was also shouldering the rucksack that held the other stuff they were delivering to the guy.

Allie watched the front door. It opened, and a large hillbilly sort of guy in overalls stood framed in a rectangle of light for a moment. Then Tommy and Greg stepped through the door and it closed again.

Allie settled down to wait. She thought of turning on the radio for some music to keep her company, but then she remembered Tommy's warning about remaining unnoticed. Also, her original worry about this place had returned to bug her now. So she sat in the darkness, keeping herself entertained by thinking of all the great times she was going to have driving her new companions to their different jobs.

The pay was also a great incentive. Consider this weekend's job: $6,500 for two or three hours of work, and with the possibility of more money to come? Not bad . . . So the police were wrong: crime really did pay.

But Tommy insisted the Rectifiers weren't criminals. That was good then. Allie didn't really see herself as a crook anyway.

CHAPTER 37

Marko Velli

Thing is, Boston kingpin Marko Velli wasn't a troublesome man. He was ruthless, sure; and most definitely a calculating S.O.B.; and a violently murderous fellow to boot, but he didn't go around stirring up hornet's nests simply because he could.

No, Marko wasn't anything like that. He was like the Arizona desert rattlesnake minding its own business sunbathing until you stepped on it. Or the Bengal tiger similarly sleeping until you trod on its tail. Marko was the mad dog that you didn't take by the ears even if you'd had all the rabies shots available in the USA.

Marko minded his own business; he went his own way. Until you pissed him off, that was. Then he struck back with the fury of the angry rattler, the savage brutality of the woken tiger, and the rabid insanity of the dog out of its senses.

And at the moment, someone was pissing Marko off. Really, really pissing Marko off. And that was a suicidal thing to do.

The Boston crime lord—a pale-eyed, stocky man pushing fifty—was angrily pacing his bedroom. Its extreme luxury was lost on his disquieted mind. The lights were off; the room had shadows for furniture.

He was watching his sleeping wife, who lay in their bed nude as a baby and illuminated by rays of moonlight.

His mouth squeezed up. *Dammit, she's still screwing that piece-of-shit!*

Petra had been clever. But everyone slipped up sometime. You had to, it was too much hard work maintaining a 24-hour subterfuge. Petra disliked hard work anyway; she had an army of maids to do everything for her.

Marko didn't mind having a lazy wife, but he drew the line at having a slutty one. He remembered being young and his playmates taunting him because his mother was a hooker. He'd hated that.

As a kid, he and his mother had lived in the Croatian seaport of Rijeka. They'd been church-mouse-poor after his sailor father had died. Marko no longer resented his mother for her slutty behavior. He understood now that she'd had to spread her legs back then to put food on their table.

His wife didn't, however. He was taking exquisite care of her. And she repaid him by sleeping around like she was on the streets?

Marko looked at Petra with intense bitterness. It embarrassed him to even remember how he'd confirmed her infidelity:

She'd given him crabs.

I'm the number one mobster in goddam New England and my wife gives me pubic lice!?

He recalled his confusion over the genital itch that wouldn't cease no matter how much soap he washed with, his visit to the clinic two days ago, and finally, his red-faced disbelief when old Dr. Harper had diagnosed him with an STD.

His wife had given him crabs. Dr. Harper had assumed Marko had contacted the crabs from an unhygienic call girl. Marko hadn't disabused him of the notion; he'd not used a hooker since returning from jail; Petra was the only woman he'd slept with.

Marko had accepted the doctor's prescription for an anti-lice shampoo and left the clinic.

Since then he'd been seething. He'd kept his temper under control though.

But now . . .

Marko figured he needed to somehow drum it into Petra's head that she was going to have to stop screwing around.

He wasn't going to kill her. That was out of the question. He didn't want his kids to lose their mother, but . . . he figured he might just cut off one of her legs. The problem then would be that if he disfigured her, he'd not feel like sleeping with her anymore. And what use was a wife you didn't fuck?

Arrrgh! Marko didn't feel like sleeping with Petra at the moment, anyway. Not after the damn genital lice she'd given him, clearly gotten from donating her vagina to that young punk with more dick than brains. The punk had no idea that up to now he'd been living purely on Marko's goodwill. He was still alive only because of his friendship with Tommy Collins. That and that alone was why Marko had even bothered to send Dave that crude 'horse penis and boxers' warning.

Marko was certain it was Petra who'd hit on the kid, and not the other way around. But in the final analysis, the punk was as much to blame for their having an affair as his wife was.

Even if that young man has dick-for-brains, he should have respect for his elders too! Viewing the underworld as a dog-eat-dog society, the silly little puppy should have kept away from the Big Dog's bitch.

Well it didn't matter anymore. Marko had made up his mind. Enough was enough—the crabs had decided it. The crabs meant that even after being warned off, Dave Fontaine was still fucking Petra.

Marko picked his cellphone off the nightstand and quietly left the bedroom. By his phone, the time was twenty minutes to midnight.

Out in the living room, with a cold drink in his hand, Marko Velli made a phone call. It took a while for the phone to connect. Then Lonnie Black's drowsy voice came over the line. "Boss? What's up?"

"That job we discussed last weekend. The Fontaine kid. Do it."

Black yawned loudly, then asked, "What? He *still* ain't learned his lesson?"

"Nah, the punk still clearly thinks I'm a porno producer using my wife for casting. Do it exactly like you guys suggested."

Black laughed. "Alright, boss." Then he yawned again. "I'll get hold of White and we'll handle it. We'll let you know when it's done."

Marko hung up. He sipped his drink. He didn't envy Dave Fontaine, but the idiot had brought his fate on his own head.

There were some things that a man tolerated and others that he didn't and never would. It was always wise to know where to tread and where to draw the line. Marko thought about himself; of his rise in mob circles. No, it hadn't been smooth sailing. Sure, he'd made his own mistakes during his years as a young punk, but one mistake he'd never made in all his time as a mobster was screwing another man's wife. Even though he wasn't Sicilian, Marko prided himself on carrying on the old Cosa Nostra spirit, and in that world there were two things you never did: you didn't snitch and you didn't fuck another guy's woman.

And since he hadn't done that nonsense himself, Marko Velli saw no reason why he had to tolerate such behavior from others.

He remembered his discussion with Black and White about the best way to fix any young fool who might be considering raising Petra's skirts. He recalled the sadistic looks on the faces of the pair as they'd outlined procedure after procedure, each more sickening than the last.

After they'd left, Marko had felt relieved. He'd also felt like he needed to take a long bath to wash their stench off him. Lonnie Black and Carrie White creeped him out too. There was something very horrible about those two. There had to be when they made a profession out of murder for pleasure. Sure, murder occasionally had to be done, but when you got kicks from doing it, you needed your damn head examined. That was the Velli philosophy of death anyway.

No, Marko didn't envy Dave Fontaine at all.

He finished his drink then went back to bed. This time when he considered his slumbering wife, he smiled. Then, knowing the solution to his problem was in competent hands, Marko fell peacefully asleep.

CHAPTER 38

Anderson & Futana

"Bingo!" Laurie Futana exclaimed as the printer spat out its printout. "Yeah, finally we've got our man!"

Anderson looked up from his coffee. He was dog tired and wanted to sleep. It was almost midnight. They were still in the office solely because of their commitment to solving the Wet Bones case. Any moment now, the coffee Anderson was drinking would become ineffective against his nervous system and he'd crumple to the floor, a quivering mass of exhaustion that could only be resuscitated by eight hours sleep in a soft bed.

"What you got?" he asked.

She stapled the pages together then waved the printout at him. "The name of the perp from the Hourigan Farm. The fingerprint matches just came in."

Anderson was instantly wide awake again. He was anxious to get even with the man who'd sodomized him. Not even the deepest exhaustion was getting in the way of that.

"His name's Brian McArthur," Futana said. "Brother to Jesse McArthur."

"Lemme see that," Anderson growled.

She handed over the printout.

Anderson coldly regarded the suspect's printed face, then scanned the file. "Brian Philip McArthur. Age: 37. Six foot two in height. Incarcerated for violently raping a man . . . spent five years at the Old Colony Correctional Center in Bridgewater, was released eight years ago. . . . Hmmm, he seems to have kept his nose clean ever since."

"Last registered home address: 2284 Dorchester Avenue. His brother's house. That's the building that houses the pet shop. Only"—

Futana raised her eyes to meet Anderson's—"he doesn't live there anymore."

"Huh? How d'you know that?"

She explained about how she'd seen Brian in his muddy truck a few days after the concert. "I didn't stop him then 'cos I had no idea he was involved in any of this, but I'm certain that truck came from a farm. It was too dirty to be a town ride."

"So we start checking farms then."

"I took down the truck's number," Futana said.

He looked surprised. "Why'd you do that if you didn't suspect him of anything?"

She looked embarrassed for a moment; she wasn't about telling him of she and Brian's sordid sexual past. "Oh, just a girl's intuition thing. The damn vehicle was such an eyesore, I figured it had be breaking some public decency law or the other. I wondered if there was someone you report stuff like that to who could force him to wash it." She shrugged. "Anyways, what's important is that I got the truck's number. In the morning we'll send it to the RMV; they may come up with an address different from that of the pet shop."

Anderson nodded and studied Brian McArthur's printed face some more. The guy had a shaggy beard and looked as mean as an angry coyote. Anderson smirked at the man. *So you like raping people, huh, Brian? Well, once we meet up again, you're gonna realize you fucked the wrong guy! I'm the damn law around here, Brian-rapist! No one commits a crime against my ass and gets away with it!*

Futana could practically read Anderson's thoughts on his face. She suppressed a shudder. *Oh, I'm so, so, so glad it's not me Tom's thinking that angrily about!*

Anderson kept eyeing Brian McArthur's mug shot. Futana imagined him burning the wanted man's image deep into the synapses of his brain. Indelibly deep.

Time hung in stasis in the police station. The only sounds on their floor were those of air conditioning and the pacing of a few other night birds, insomniac detectives like themselves with cases of violence that couldn't wait till morning.

Anderson still wasn't saying anything. To his partner, he seemed frozen in his hatred of Brian McArthur.

"Hey, man, there's more," she said. "There's a whole lot more dirt to this than just Brian."

Anderson slowly pulled his gaze away from the printout. Futana shivered again. There was murder in her partner's eyes. She felt incredibly guilty. She was oh so relieved that he believed Brian was responsible for what had been done to him. And she intended to help his misbelief along. She found it complicated though: just the barest memory of how tight his anus had felt around her stiff penis threatened to make her hard again. It had been so wrong and yet so right!

She said, "There were several other sets of fingerprints in that farmyard work shed. Most can't be matched—no criminal records . . . but one set could. And . . . you're not going to believe whose those were."

She flipped the printout over so Anderson could see the person's face.

Anderson whistled. "Stacy Lovejoy. I don't believe it."

"I told you I didn't trust that woman," Futana said.

Anderson read through Stacy Lovejoy's file: "Kleptomania, shoplifting, prostitution . . ." Then perplexed, he looked up at Futana. "Suspected but unproven child abuse and infanticide . . . ? *That* woman? What is this shit?"

Futana nodded grimly. She flipped the page again so he could confirm what she was about to tell him: "Apparently Stacy Lovejoy is a practicing *witch*—if you believe any of that damn mumbo-jumbo. And not of the sweet and kind, environmentally-friendly 'Wicca and white witch' variety either. Our girl's into Satanism and black magic— all of that 'wicked airhead' nonsense."

"So . . . ?"

"Well, she had a two-year-old daughter Cathleen . . . Cathleen Horner, father's name . . . who vanished one night. The poor kid was found two weeks later . . . dead and rotting in a dumpster." Futana grimaced in disgust. "Someone had sacrificed the child. They'd slit her throat and drained all the blood from her, and also sliced a pentagram into her flesh."

Anderson scanned the page. "And Stacy walked free because she'd clearly had nothing to do with it: she'd been over at her sick mother's that night, leaving the daughter at home with a babysitter . . ."

". . . Who said the house was broken into at midnight by three masked men who snatched the child. The babysitter was the next door neighbors' kid. She didn't know a thing. She even got beaten up for her efforts to protect the child. The kidnappers broke her arm."

"This stinks," Anderson said. "It stinks worse than unflushed shit."

"I couldn't put it better myself. Anyway, that's Ms. Lovejoy in a nutshell." Futana picked up her cup of coffee from their desk and sipped from it, then waved a finger in the air at her partner. "Now, even if we're going slow, we *are* slowly resolving things. Things are beginning to, if not exactly fall into place, at least form recognizable patterns. Forgive the pun, but we're putting meat on our wet bones."

"That's a good one, Laurie. Meat on wet bones, huh?"

"Yeah, man. Alright, so back to our main suspects. Now, we know Jesse McArthur is *supposedly* down in NY nowadays, so that possibly rules him out of things. But Stacy definitely knows something about those corpses."

"At least about the dead woman in the barn," Anderson pointed out. "We can't reasonably assume more than that."

Futana tapped the desktop. "Yeah, okay, but let me finish. What I'm trying to say is, Stacy knows something, but . . . well, we can't prove anything. She may even know where Brian is. Getting her to admit it, however, is the problem."

Anderson nodded slowly. His gaze strayed to the printout again, then he looked back up at Futana. "Yeah, I get you. If we pull the woman in for questioning, she'll simply deny everything. She's got a logical link to both brothers—she bought Jesse's shop—and so can reasonably claim accompanying him out to visit his brother on the farm for some reason. She could say she just wanted to find out where he got his pet food supplies from."

Futana nodded. "You do get it, man. This is a tricky one and we don't want to blow it. We put pressure on Stacy and she'll start destroying the evidence before we can get a search warrant . . . and . . ."

"Yeah, go on. I'm listening."

"And . . . we can't have her doing that, mainly 'cos at the moment we're still unsure what the actual link between herself and Brian and our Wet Bones is."

Anderson got up. "She may start destroying the evidence anyway. She knows something's up now. She knows we didn't come by looking for Jesse 'cos he won the lottery or 'cos it's his birthday."

"You still tired, man?" Futana asked.

"No. Why?"

"I suggest we go stakeout Ms. Lovejoy. Maybe, just maybe she'll slip up tonight."

Anderson finished his coffee. He checked his wristwatch. "It's almost midnight."

She grinned at him. "My point exactly. Midnight is the Witching Hour. I can't think of a better time to catch a witch."

Anderson smiled coldly and they left the station.

CHAPTER 39

Allie, Tommy, & Greg again

Allie suddenly broke out of her reverie. *Hey, where they hell are the guys?*

She checked her watch in the darkness. Tommy and Greg had been gone for forty minutes. Even if they'd sat down to have a couple of drinks with Brian, they should be back by now.

And strangest of all, though she strained her ears hard, she couldn't hear any sounds of a conversation happening inside the house.

Now *that* was really odd.

Allie might have waited longer in the pickup truck, except that the guy's name—Brian—kept nagging at her. At the moment, she REALLY distrusted Brians. And this one had looked huge and mean, not like her wimpy ex. She was suddenly scared of what he might have done to Tommy and Greg in there.

Besides which, she was also tired of sitting waiting out here in the truck like an also-ran.

After another five minutes of mounting impatience, Allie got out and went looking for everyone.

She might have been scared and worried, but she wasn't a fool. Before heading up the driveway to the old stone farmhouse, she first searched the back of the truck for the baseball bat Dave claimed to have hidden there from his ex, Manuela Costa.

He hadn't been lying; the bat was in there, one of those aluminum ones. She also found a tire iron, but compared to the baseball bat, it seemed puny, not as likely to do sufficient damage if wielded by a woman.

Armed with the baseball bat, she reached the front door.

Standing there on the front steps of the farmhouse, she was aware of a weird smell about the place, something not quite wet and not quite dry either. It smelt like an animal of some sort, but not any she could place. Maybe it was Brian's sheep? The guys had said he was a farmer. But no, she didn't recall any sheep she'd encountered ever smelling like this.

Acting on a sudden intuition of danger, Allie chose to forgo knocking on the front door. Instead, she padded sideways along the stone front wall to peek inside the living room windows.

The living room was empty. Yes, she saw, they *had* been drinking, but where was everyone now? There was a bottle of Wild Turkey 101 bourbon on a round table and two half-filled glasses, but there was no one in sight, not even the two dogs they'd brought over.

Then Allie noticed something VERY odd: There were two neat piles of clothes on the living room couch. A closer look revealed the clothes as being Tommy's and Greg's, what they'd each been wearing on the trip over. Their shoes were on the floor too, with the socks tucked inside them. Tommy's last cigarette lay still burning in an ashtray.

Allie's first thought—that the trio of men had gone off to have sex—she instantly dismissed as silly. *What? Two straight men coming all this way out here into the boondocks to have sex with a guy they'd never met before?*

No, that wasn't it at all.

Allie was convinced beyond all reasonable doubt that something was VERY wrong.

So scared now that it was taking her all of her willpower not to simply run back over to the truck and drive off, Allie slowly stalked around the house in the darkness, looking for Tommy and Greg. Stealthy as a mouse hiding from a cat, she peeked into window after window. The night was dark, the moon obscured by clouds, but sufficient light spilled from the farmhouse windows for Allie to see by.

She finally found everyone in the barn next to the farmhouse. And at first she didn't believe what she was seeing.

This first barn was connected to the farmhouse by a concrete walkway, at the end of which Allie now stood peering in through a rotted double door.

The barn interior was well lit. It was a massive stone chamber, with a ceiling of sagging beams and several empty windows. It had a similar double door on its farther side and a nearby, smaller door on her left.

The building housed an ancient broken-down tractor and some rusty old pipes and crates. The barn floor was covered with straw.

And . . .

Allie now saw what was responsible for the heavy smell she'd perceived from the front door of the farmhouse.

What on God's green earth is that?

Once she understood clearly what she was seeing, Allie's free hand flew to her mouth to stifle her fears. She recoiled in shock, horror, and most of all . . . *revulsion.*

There was a GIANT worm in there. At first she'd imagined it was an anaconda, but the thing was so damn immense as to defy her imagination. Allie couldn't believe worms grew that large. The worm was dark brown, its nauseating body pinched into segments by wide black bands. It seemed as thick as her torso. It was covered in transparent slime.

Brian McArthur had Tommy stripped naked and was feeding him to the giant worm. The sight was so unexpected as to cause Allie to stand gaping there in the barn entrance.

The monster worm was coiled around a pool in the middle of the barn. Indeed the disgusting creature was so long and large that its coils formed a wall around the pool. The slime bubbled out from lines of hair-ringed pits in its skin. The slime filled the barn with a smell that nauseated Allie with its alienness.

Tommy (whose hands were tied behind his back) was entering the worm feet-first, while Brian supervised and helped push him into the grotesquely stretched annelid maw.

Worst of all, Tommy was still both alive and awake. He was gagged, but his eyes were open, and he was shaking his head, though weakly.

The worm shook its slimy head too and sucked Tommy in up to his thighs. It waved its eyes on their thick feelers and bent them to stare at Tommy.

Allie's heart fell. *Oh no—where's Greg?* She imagined the worst, that he was already inside the worm's belly and dead.

But a hurried look around the barn revealed Greg to still be alive. He lay on his side by the right wall, with some blood on his forehead. He too was both gagged and bound hand and foot. He was staring desperately around while struggling weakly.

Brian was talking to himself, or maybe he was talking to Tommy and Greg?

Allie slipped her shoes off. Then, barefoot, and with her baseball bat held ready, she stalked into the barn. It was either take action now or run away screaming. She was *utterly* terrified of the worm in there, but something—a reserve of courage she'd never before suspected she had—impelled her forward to attempt a rescue.

In addition, her hatred of *Brians* had suddenly overloaded, and just like in Valentina Ruzza's office at Eastern Bank, she was mad again.

And a mad Allie wasn't someone anyone wanted to tangle with.

Brian McArthur was still facing away from her, attending to his grisly business. As she snuck up on him, she now made out what he was saying:

"So, ya see, boys, that's just how it is. Boku Ke Houzz here is tired of just eating dogs and sheep now. It prefers *real* meat. You know—human meat." He cleared his throat. "Boys, we've been keeping a low kidnapping profile 'cos of nosy police investigations—I don't wanna snatch someone and discover they're an undercover cop with a tracker on 'em. But Boku was getting restless, you know, and the coven kept bugging me to find a solution so it don't die on us. Me, I figured the creature could wait till the cops got through with their goddamn snooping and the heat was off, but everyone else said no, though none of 'em ever give me a hand with finding folks for it to feed on.

"See, Boku ain't from Earth like we are. It's from Hell, one of Lucifer's favorite kids apparently—all it ever eats is raw flesh. So anyways, I asked my younger brother Jesse to send me some *proper* meat for it. It took us a while to figure out a safe supply, but then, just this morning, Jesse and I put our heads together again and figured that well, since you two scumbags were bringing my dogs over anyway . . . well, I guess you can figure out the rest of it . . . Yeah, we both agreed it was safe enough to feed Boku wastes of space like you two—ya, know, crooks—people no one's gonna miss when they don't turn up to work on Monday, 'cos assholes like you, you don't work anyway, do ya? All you do is leech off hardworking folk like me an' Jesse and other American taxpayers—"

Then Brian noticed that Tommy, who'd previously been struggling nonstop to get free of the worm's mouth, was now gaping in amazement at something behind him. He began turning round to see what it was.

Powered by rage and fear, Allie whacked Brian in the face with the baseball bat. She hit him so HARD that the shock of the bat's impact with his head seemed to dislocate her right shoulder.

She had sufficient time to see that the bat had completely flattened Brian's nose, then, with bright red blood spurting all over his mustache and lips, the huge man collapsed to the ground.

She stood there breathing heavily for a moment. Then, after prodding Brian with her foot to ensure that he was out cold, she stepped over him to help Tommy.

The huge worm was still hard at work swallowing Tommy Collins. Its mouth was almost covering his crotch now.

In utter disgust, Allie glanced back at the unconscious Brian. Now that she had time to think, just being near the worm's bulk terrified her. It was larger that it had looked from the door, and some of its segments had short tentacles that ended in little claws. In girth the creature was much thicker than her body, almost twice as thick. Its alien stench threatened to knock her out. In addition, just the sight of all the slime it kept secreting made her gag. Watching that transparent goop ooze from the monster's body was the stuff of nightmares.

The worm watched her with alien eyes full of evil. It looked like it would curse and damn her if it could, and hated the fact that it couldn't speak because its mouth was full of Tommy. Brian had said this monster came from Hell. At the moment Allie believed him. Nothing native to Earth could possibly be this horrible.

She got a grip on herself. She stared down at Tommy, then back at Greg. The relief on both their faces was priceless to her.

She stepped forward into the worm-slime. She had no choice, the transparent mess was all over the floor here, so much of it that it practically *was* the floor. She hoped it wasn't caustic or poisonous; Brian had been standing in it, but he had thick boots on. She however, was shoeless. She figured though that in this case, even wearing her shoes—slip-ons with open backs—would have made scant difference.

The slime was as warm and as sticky as it looked. It reached up to Allie's ankles. The goop felt so chillingly unnatural against her flesh that she almost backed out of it. But she steadied herself for what needed to be done.

First of all, she pulled the gag out of Tommy's mouth.

"Hi," she said next. "Whatever you do, don't you dare crack that joke about me taking my sweet time getting here, or I swear to God that I'll lay you out too."

Tommy nodded. At first he seemed unable to speak, like he'd been so scared he'd forgotten how his mouth worked. She glanced under him, curious to see if he'd pooped himself from fear. If he had, the worm had eaten the evidence.

"Thanks," Tommy finally wheezed. "I've never been so happy to see anyone in my life."

She smiled tightly back at him. Then she set her mind on the puzzle of how to get his legs out of the giant worm's mouth. It was still swallowing him in short, abrupt gulps. Several of its clawed forward tentacles were assisting the feeding process.

As Allie watched it, it swayed its eyes on their stalks, so it was watching her too. Its huge eyes were evil lamps hypnotizing her into giving up.

Screw that, Allie thought. She placed a foot against the worm's mouth and tried pulling Tommy out. That didn't work in the least. The problem was all the slime everywhere: despite having a firm grip on Tommy, she had zero traction for leverage—her feet kept slipping over the straw. She was having to consciously watch her balance, lest she go skidding away across the barn. And meanwhile, the monster seemed to have an inbuilt ability to grip its food extra-tight to prevent it slipping from its mouth.

"This ain't working," Tommy said.

"No, it ain't," she agreed. She stopped to think. *Maybe I should untie his hands . . .*

But she realized there was a problem with this plan too: even if she untied Tommy's hands, he looked too weak to be any help in freeing himself. Merely talking seemed to be tiring him out.

And also, she'd just thought of another problem: She'd read somewhere that snakes were helpless while eating. Did that apply to worms too? If it did, then this one, massive as it was, couldn't attack her so long as it was swallowing Tommy. But that wouldn't be the case any more once it had vomited him up. And those hooks on the ends of its tentacles looked sharp.

Confused for a moment, she let go of Tommy and paced left and right through the slime.

Tommy watched her pace. He clearly wanted to offer some helpful suggestions, but just as obviously couldn't think of anything. In addition, Allie now realized that Tommy looked sort of groggy; as if now that the immediate danger was past, he was having difficulty remaining awake. A glance over at Greg revealed him to be in the same sleepy condition. For the first time it occurred to her that both he and Tommy might have drugged.

As Allie paced, the worm's horrible dusky eyes tracked her. Its slimy segmented body tensed, then it began shifting its head purposefully left and right.

Suddenly, Tommy's legs slipped two inches back out of the worm. Then an additional three inches of him slid from its mouth.

At first Allie was relieved that her work was being done for her. Then she grew worried again. The worm's current behavior presented a disturbing puzzle: why would it suddenly stop trying to eat Tommy?

Right or wrong, it looked to her as if the beast was puking up Tommy so it could attack her instead.

There was just that 'outlander' look in its eyes that set her on Red Alert.

A sort of reasoning panic gripped her. Scared, she hefted the baseball bat again, took aim at a spot between the monster's eyestalks, and hit it HARD.

She whacked the damn thing even harder than she'd hit its crazy keeper.

The giant worm twitched once, then went completely limp. A flood of smelly jelly oozed from its brown hide. She'd knocked it out cold too. As though it were still retching, Tommy's legs now slid completely out of its mouth. They were covered in clear, but stinky saliva. They didn't look digested yet.

Tommy lay in the goop looking dazed and breathing hard.

Before untying her companions, Allie first searched around for some rope and tied Brian up. Just like he'd done to them, she bound his hands tightly behind his back. His nose was a shattered mess through which bubbled a bloody froth. She doubted the doctors could ever fix his nose.

She spat on him. *Shame on you, Brian, you really earned this ass-whipping.*

Ten minutes later, she had both Tommy and Greg free. Tommy spent five minutes cleaning the worm jelly off his body. (She saw now that Tommy had a long jagged scar extending all the way from his breastbone to his pubic bone.)

"You got here just in time," he informed Allie once he was recovered enough to make proper conversation. "According to Brian, once that goddamn thing's finished swallowing someone, it secretes another internal goop that dissolves your flesh." He spat towards Brian. "Son-of-a-bitch!"

"Wow, girl," Greg said the moment she ungagged him. "To get us out of this mess, you're more badass than Mike Tyson."

She'd brought their clothes from the house, and also the bottle of Wild Turkey they'd been drinking from.

Both men shook their head to the offer of booze. "The bastard put knock-out drops in it," Tommy explained. "That's how he got us in here."

"Yeah," Greg confirmed, shaking his head to clear it. "One moment we were all laughing, then next . . . the room began spinning."

"He told us he didn't put in too much though," Tommy spat. "He wanted us conscious when the worm ate us. Can you believe that?"

"The idiot claims it's a demon—a demigod from Hell. He and his friends have been worshipping it, feeding it human sacrifices. How stupid can someone get?"

Tommy's face clouded with anger. To Allie, looking into his eyes now was like staring at Death personified. "That bastard Jesse McArthur set us up," he growled. "I'll get even with him if it's the last thing I ever do. Feed *me* to a giant worm? Shit!"

The return of his moodiness cheered Allie. It meant he was feeling okay. But she was still very aware they were in danger. If the worm revived . . .

She studied it carefully. No, she'd not killed it. Every now and then, its muscular brown segments twitched, and it shifted. When that happened, its stink increased, as if it was farting in its sleep. Its eyestalks dangled limply across its head. Both stalks trembled as if conveying pulses of energy to and fro. It didn't wake up though. But it would soon, she knew, and heaven help them all if they were still here then.

She looked away from the monster to see Tommy watching her. "Forget the damn thing," he growled. "I'll shoot it if it bothers us. Brian's got a shotgun in the house."

She nodded.

Greg was fully dressed now. He gestured at Brian, who was just coming to. "What I don't understand is where this guy found a worm this big. The thing's a frigging monster. And did you hear what he was saying about it being a *god?*"

"He kept calling it *Boku Ke Houzz*, saying it comes from somewhere in Hell called *SADE*. Man, what the hell was that about?"

"The world is full of crackpots—it's all that crack and pot they smoke."

"Alright, what now?"

"Hey," Allie interrupted before Greg could reply again, "where are the dogs?"

Tommy pointed. "In the side room over there. I think he really wanted them to feed to his damn worm anyway. I doubt he's got any sheep at all out here."

On the floor, Brian McArthur stirred. In addition to the blood all over his face, his dark hair and beard were also dirty from the floor now, flecked with sawdust chips. Tommy kicked him in the groin. Brian rolled over on his side and began jerking in pain. A series of loud grunts announced that he was waking up.

"Hey, wake up, you stinking S.O.B.!"

Allie left them and went to look for the dogs. To her relief, both dogs were fine. The room stank of worm, though, and one of the German shepherds had a bone in its jaws that just might have been a human thighbone. There were other bones scattered around the room and several dry red smears on the walls.

Grimacing, she left the dogs in there and returned to Tommy and Greg.

In her absence the men had gotten down to stripping Brian. They already had his boots and pants off, and they'd gagged him with his socks. From the spilled booze on the ground by his head, it seemed like they'd also doped him with his own whiskey. She noted in passing that the man had a small but elaborate black tattoo—an inverted 'A'— on his upper left thigh.

Allie looked down at Brian. His scared eyes stared back at her. "What do you plan on doing to him?" she asked.

Greg grinned at her, then pointed ahead to the pool, where Brian's giant worm was just reviving. Its stunned eyes glowed like purple lamps. Each eye wavered on its stalk like a drunk. "Brian? Into his pet he goes."

"Yeah," Tommy agreed. "We're the Rectifiers, right? Well, we're about to *rectify* Brian's miserable existence."

"Ha ha ha!" Greg laughed.

Allie thought of protesting—being eaten alive was a horrible fate for anyone to suffer. But she didn't protest. She felt little pity for Brian. If she'd not stopped him, he'd have killed both her male companions. He'd have killed her gang. Allie felt it deep in her heart: The Rectifiers—Tommy and Dave and apparently Greg too—were 'her crew' now.

In the minutes since she'd rescued the two men, she'd sensed a shifting in her power relationship with Tommy Collins: from just barely tolerating her on the job, he now respected her as an equal. Greg too, but she was less concerned about his opinion; she hardly knew the guy.

Aw, screw Brian, she decided. *The worm is still hungry. At least it saves the dogs' lives.*

Once they had him stripped fully naked, Tommy and Greg hefted Brian McArthur over to the pool and offered him as a sacrifice to his pet or his god, whichever of the two it was. Allie let them handle it. She wasn't about stepping into that gooey mess around the worm pool again.

Brian's eyes were beseeching them, and he was grunting weakly through his gag with pleas for mercy, but they ignored him.

Once they had him laid out for the worm, Tommy prodded it with the baseball bat till it properly revived, then they retreated and watched it eat Brian.

Brian went head-first into the worm. It was bowel-loosening to watch him vanish into it, all slimed-up like a bleached turd being absurdly sucked back into an anus. Fifteen minutes later, as if the giant creature was making up for lost time, only his legs projected from its mouth. Thankfully, he'd stopped wiggling ten minutes earlier. Now, they beheld the belly-bound Brian-bulge in the beast's body with bemused bewitchment. For the moment the monster had stopped secreting slime. (They didn't know that it could only secrete in one direction at a time—either inward or outward, never both at once.)

With the feeding giant annelid as a morbid background, they sat on some crates and discussed what to do next:

Tommy had gotten his cigarettes out and was having a smoke. "We gotta get to Boston; get Jesse too before he realizes what's happened and goes into hiding," he said.

Greg groaned. "Shit. We gonna drive all the way up to Boston tonight?" He looked to Allie for support in his dissent.

Yeah, she decided, *he definitely considers me his equal now.*

She shrugged. "Man, we've got no choice. He ain't gonna email himself here, that's for sure." (This crack was intentional payback for Greg's previous joke about there being no space for this farm in Boston.)

Tommy blew out a smoke ring, then laughed. "Man, I frigging love this girl. I gotta marry her someday!"

Allie restrained from preening herself. It seemed wrong to do so with Brian's feet poking from the worm's mouth just a few yards away. The thick bulge in the worm's body was definitely man-shaped now.

Greg nodded. "Okay, I guess you're right. But, what are we gonna do about the dogs?"

"We take 'em back and give them to Giorgio," Allie suggested. "He's been saying for ages that—"

"Shush," Tommy interrupted her. Then, pressing a finger to his lips, he whispered, "Listen."

They listened. A car was just pulling up outside.

Greg grinned. "Oh no, it can't be—God doesn't like me *that* much."

But it was Jesse McArthur. When Jesse walked into the barn five minutes later, they were waiting for him. (In the intervening interval they'd hidden Brian's clothes and boots behind the old tractor in case Jesse recognized them.)

Jesse McArthur was a small fat man. He looked so sneaky that Allie wondered how Tommy could ever have trusted him in the first place.

"Hey, Brian, you fed those two lowlifes to Boku yet?" From their hiding places behind several stacks of crates, Allie and the men watched him smile approvingly at the human-shaped swelling in the worm. "Yeah, I see that you have. Hey, bro, where are you? Hope you got my money ready! And I told you, the price is eight hundred bucks for each of the suckers, or I won't ever send you any more!"

They stepped out of cover.

Tommy grinned at Jesse. "Hi, bro, how you doin'?"

Jesse was still putting two and two together and working out who the worm had actually eaten when Allie whacked him across the brain with the baseball bat. Jesse's eyes instantly crossed like he was looking at his nose and he slumped to the ground.

"Another McArthur bites the dust," Allie quipped, a rush of adrenalin lifting her spirits.

She didn't, however, have the heart for what happened next.

***

After forcing a large amount of his older brother's drugged liquor down Jesse's throat, Tommy and Greg stripped him naked too, removing all his clothes except for his boxers.

But, no, they weren't feeding him to the worm.

"C'mon, you guys, just shoot him and let's leave this damn place," Allie protested. Behind them, Brian's huge pet seemed to be asleep and dreaming of digesting its master. "Hey, tell me where in the house Brian's shotgun is and I'll fetch it for you."

Greg nudged her and grinned. "You're joking, right? Just *shoot him* after what he did to us? And you did just hear him say he's planning to send more people down here too, right?"

Allie couldn't dispute that Jesse had something nasty coming to him. She just didn't have an inkling of how nasty it was going to be.

First they gagged him with his socks, and bound his arms and legs like they'd done with Brian. Then, while Allie watched aghast, Tommy methodically broke Jesse's arms and legs with the baseball bat. He took his time with it, smashing first the bones in both Jesse's upper and lower legs, then repeating the process on his upper and lower arms.

By this time Jesse was awake and moaning piteously, his eyes bulging like he was seeing a vision of God. Tommy, on the other hand, had a look in his eyes like he *was* God, God Almighty dispensing justice to one of His most hated sinners. His eyes were colder than a snowman, his frown grimmer than the Grim Reaper's.

Despite all of Jesse's broken bones and distorted limbs, there was scant blood in evidence, except for a dribble down his right thigh, where the broken femur had pierced through the skin. Allie understood that Tommy had been very careful that this be the case, but why?

Then Tommy and Greg dragged Jesse into the room with the two German shepherds. Jesse was mewling pathetically now behind his gag, begging for mercy.

Tommy left Allie and Greg in there with the dogs and headed over to the farmhouse.

Once he was gone, Allie pleaded with Greg. "Stop him. This is punishment enough."

Greg shook his head and laughed. He was in too much of a malicious mood to heed her plea. (Unknown to Allie, he too was trying to prove to Tommy that he was as badass as they came.) "Oh no, girl, we haven't even gotten started with this bastard yet."

Shuddering at the sadistic look in his eyes, Allie waited for Tommy to return. One thing was certain: she wasn't about leaving to go sit in the truck and wait there for them to come out after they were done. That might erode their newfound respect for her. There was no way she was letting them think of her as inferior again.

So she waited, her eyes occasionally flickering down to the naked man on the sawdust strewn floor, his mangled limbs all bent out of shape. Jesse seemed to be in a place beyond any mere experience of pain—beyond space and time possibly. Both German shepherds were lying in a corner, uninterested in what was happening. One of the dogs yawned at her.

Tommy soon returned. He was carrying a knife, and oddly enough, one of the large boxes of dog food that they'd brought over. The really odd things he had with him though were a rusty shoemaker's awl and some thread. Somehow, the sight of the awl spooked Allie more than seeing the knife did. What on earth was Tommy going to do with the awl? Blind Jesse with it?

For a moment, the barest flicker of humanity returned to Tommy's face—he no longer looked like God on the Day of Judgment.

"You don't have to see this," he told Allie. "Go wait out in the pickup."

She really wanted to leave, but instead she held his gaze and shook her head. "I'll stay. Get on with it. Just hurry up."

He nodded, then seemed to grin. Then he turned back to Jesse. Jesse had just shat himself, which was now making the dogs look his way with interest.

They got to work on Jesse. Working in a straight line down the middle from ribcage to crotch, Tommy carefully slit Jesse's belly open, cutting through the skin and separating the muscles and connective tissue till his guts were on red display. Jesse, with tears streaming down his cheeks, was trembling like a fish being gutted while still alive. His gray boxer shorts slowly grew dark with absorbed blood.

Now Allie really wished she'd taken Tommy's offer to leave. He'd been right—she definitely didn't need to see this. But it was too late now, so watch it she did.

Tommy finished making the abdomen-length incision. Then, while he held Jesse's belly open, Greg filled it with dog food.

"W-w-what are you doing!?" Allie protested.

Greg grinned up at her from his squat position. "What's it look like, lady? The dogs are gonna be hungry soon; we're just leaving 'em something to eat."

Alice Jackson may have fought a giant worm tonight, but understanding what her crew had planned for Jesse was just too much. She began puking against the wall.

Tommy looked over at her, shrugged, then went back to evenly distributing the dog food amidst Jesse's guts. He spread it left and right with his hands so it mingled with Jesse's intestines.

Then, when he and Greg were satisfied, they stitched Jesse's belly up again with the awl. Their victim's thrashing while they did this was almost worse than when they'd been slicing him open.

Then they both stood up and regarded Jesse with amusement. He looked like a corpse who'd revived midway through his own autopsy—a pregnant corpse. With zero surgical experience between them, Tommy and Greg had made a haphazard job of repairing the cut. Patches of dog food lay visible in the open pockets between the stiches in Brian's belly, as though his separated skin was a too-tight shirt the overweight man was wearing. Streamers of blood trickled left and right along the sutured incision as if it was a weeping eye.

"There, the dogs'll be fine now," Tommy said.

Allie had just gotten through wiping the vomit off her mouth. But seeing Jesse lying there, with his limbs all broken, with blood all over his belly, and with the horrified understanding on his face that the German shepherds were going to have to rip him open to get to their food, almost made her start throwing up all over again.

She stood hunched forward over the baseball bat like a geriatric crone over a walker.

"What the hell?" she said finally, in an unconscious quest to rescue Jesse McArthur from his fate. "I still say we take the dogs to Giorgio."

"Look, Allie, we'll come back for them in a week," Tommy said. "They'll have eaten their fill of Jesse by then."

"I'll find them some water," Greg said. "I don't think he'll pee enough for them to drink."

"Yeah, do that, man," Tommy agreed. "I need to wash my hands too."

Allie nodded dully. "Yeah, sure. I need to pee too."

And she needed some toothpaste or mouthwash also, to get the smell of vomit off of her breath. Alright, she'd had enough; she really had to leave this room of horrors right now, or she'd start throwing up again.

Then she stiffened. Jesse's bloody boxers had ridden up on his thighs and she'd just noticed something strange. She mentioned her observation to the others:

"Guys, hold on a sec."

Greg and Tommy immediately gave her their attention. "Yeah?" Tommy asked.

Allie pointed. "Have a look at that tattoo on his left thigh. That inverted 'A.' "

"What of it?" Greg asked.

She explained: "Guys, Brian had one exactly like it, and in almost exactly the same position. When I saw Brian's, I didn't think much of it; everyone's got tattoos nowadays . . . but this guy has exactly the same mark. And now that I've studied it in more detail, I think it means something. There's something creepy about it."

Both men studied Jesse's tattoo. "Has to be a brother thing," Greg said finally. "Yeah, I agree it looks creepy. But they're a pair of creeps anyway."

Tommy smirked. "It's an 'A'! Ha ha! Don't you guys get it?"

Allie frowned. "Get what?"

With a grin, Tommy delivered the punchline: "C'mon, guys. On this guy and his brother, I'm sure the 'A' just stands for 'Assholes.' "

They all had a good laugh over that.

Allie managed to stopped laughing. She glanced at Jesse and winced. The man was squirming like a worm on the floor, his terrified gaze darting in turn from their trio to the pair of massive dogs, who'd now definitely begun sniffing the air in his direction.

"Guys," she said, "yes it's an 'A,' but it's *upside down*."

Greg grinned. "Let me ask you, Allie: did either Brian or Jesse here strike you as winning awards for being smart? They were worshipping a worm, for chrissakes, a damn worm."

Allie looked at Tommy. He shrugged back. "Dude has a point, babe. I suspect they tattooed the letter upside down simply 'cos it was easier for them to read that way. Either that or they thought it looked cool and cryptic." He snapped his fingers airily and gestured to the door. "Hey, amigos, let's get outa here. The dogs are starting to look hungry. I think they're merely being polite—waiting for us to leave before they tuck into their dinner."

This comment brought a wild moan of terror from the bound man on the floor.

After Greg had filled a metal pail with water for the dogs, they left the now loudly weeping Jesse McArthur locked in the room with them.

Outside, the monster brown worm was definitely asleep in its puddle of ooze. Allie could hear the horrible thing snoring.

CHAPTER 40

Allie, mostly

At first, driving back along the same winding road that had brought them to tonight's nightmare, Allie was literally speechless.

She wasn't sure which she was more confused over: whether the fact that in this day and age, the two McArthur brothers would conspire to feed people to a giant worm they owned, or the ruthless brutality of her two partners' retribution.

She was also surprised by her own violence. Well, that was self-defense, she reasoned. She managed a small smile amidst her turbulent emotions. And the man's name had been *Brian* after all.

She also still wondered about the McArthur brothers' tattoos. Regardless of what Greg or Tommy said, she was convinced that her instincts were right: there was definitely something esoteric about those tattoos. The memory of them made her uneasy. Two brothers who weren't twins wearing exactly the same design? It wasn't really the duplication that bothered her—Greg was right in that regard; they were siblings after all—but the intricate style of the depicted 'A' left no doubt in her mind that the symbol meant something. What did it mean though? Had she and her friends stumbled onto some kind of cult? A worm cult? 'A' just might mean 'Annelid.' It seemed crazy, but on this crazy night, it also seemed very possible.

At the moment, neither of her companions was saying anything either. Tommy was chain smoking. Greg was checking the text messages on his cellphone while humming something atonal. She listened. The tune sounded familiar. Finally she recognized it as being *Ouija Chords*, the first single from the new Slain Jane album *Parasite Paradise*. As Greg hummed on, she rolled her brain over the song lyrics:

Don't talk to me about the afterlife.
I don't wanna know about no afterlife,
Screw your damn spooky board and your psychic wife,
I don't wanna talk to folks no longer alive.

Hey hey, Ghost, leave me alone,
You wanna contact the living? Use the telephone!
All that psychic shit is a bottomless pit.
But I'll hold a grateful séance if this song's a hit!

I'm gonna find out the truth for myself.
After death, I'm going straight down to Hell,
I got a suite reservation in a burning hotel,
And we'll party Satan deaf with our decibels!

Allie felt better once they were approaching Route 20 again. Now that the moon and stars were once more visible, the night no longer felt like a monster stalking them.

However, a mental cloud still hung over her, one made worse by her passengers' silence.

Damn, she thought, *we're so normal here. You'd never believe that we just killed two people.* Or—she corrected herself—*killed one and left the other to be eaten by his own hounds.*

That was a death sentence too, she knew. There was absolutely no chance of Jesse escaping. A snowflake in Hell had better odds of survival. No one was going to find and rescue Jesse—the McArthurs would never keep that worm there on the farm if they had regular visitors. And with all four of his limbs broken in two places apiece, as well as his being bound ankle and wrist, he'd never get free. And he was gagged, so screaming was out of the question too.

And soon those dogs are gonna get really hungry.

Allie began hoping Jesse died before they did. She doubted he would. Tommy had been really careful with making certain Jesse didn't bleed too much. Even the blood flow from the gash through his belly had begun clotting before they'd abandoned him to his fate.

She could picture the future horror in her mind. It was certain to start in complete innocence: First one dog sniffing its way across and licking the blood off of Jesse's wounded belly. (This would of course happen only after they'd eaten up all her own vomit.) The German shepherd might also stick its tongue in one or two of the spaces between the jagged suturing and slurp at its food.

Then it would return to sit in its corner again, hungry, but too well domesticated to attack a human being; and meanwhile still able to smell what it was used to eating packed away just out of reach. She visualized both dogs drinking water and trying to ignore the pangs of their hunger, then trying to escape the room rather than attack the wounded, groaning man, but being foiled by the barred windows; then finally, as a primal survival switch flicked on inside their little brains, starting to view Jesse McArthur—his belly at least—as merely an obstacle they needed to get through to reach their food. So they'd stalk across to him again and begin licking his sutures, then pulling at the edges of the hole with their teeth, just trying to ease a way inside him.

But of course, Jesse wouldn't know this. He'd fight to get away from the dogs, and in his haste, their canines would snag on the thread and . . . he'd end up ripping his own belly open. And then the dogs would start eating, first just dog food, but, seeing as it was mingled with his intestines they'd start biting accidental chunks of Jesse's guts too. And once they'd tasted that sweet flow of fresh blood on their tongues, that was it: their careful domestication, their artificial human conditioning into 'man's best friend' would suddenly snap, and they'd revert to wild animals, hungry carnivorous beasts that viewed Jesse McArthur as nothing more than prey, that viewed him the same way their lupine ancestors had viewed the rabbits and deer they'd hunted out in the wild . . . and then the real feeding would commence.

Allie shuddered and forced the awful images from her thoughts. She got a grip on her emotions. She mustn't continue thinking like this. Her impression of Jesse's inescapable fate had been so vivid just now, she'd felt like puking again. The guys certainly wouldn't appreciate her throwing up all over the inside of the pickup truck.

"So what now?" she asked as they approached the state highway. She glanced at the dashboard clock. "Are we still making Springfield tonight?"

"Nah," Tommy said. "It's way too late now. I'll call Jose tomorrow and set up another meeting for us for Monday."

"And I," Greg added, "need to get back home." He grimaced. "I've got so many text messages from Aunt Grace . . . ah, I didn't go visit her today. Didn't feel up to it—I had a really bad case of the runs." Then he grinned. "Good thing she doesn't have any baseball bats in her hospital room, right? And great thing Dave stored Manuela's where she wouldn't ever find it."

They all laughed at that. Manuela's bat was now stowed away under the front seats. And Allie understood that sink or swim, they considered her one of them now. *Of course, Chloe is gonna raise Massachusetts greatest ever stink once she finds out, but . . .*

But . . . Allie currently had a different sort of situation on her hands.

Now that tonight's horrors were fading behind her by the mile, she found that she was extremely aroused, more horny than a billy goat on Cialis. As part of Allie's anticipation and excitement at coming out on this job, a subconscious erotic charge had built up in her on their drive over to the farm. There, the craziness had drained it. However, now that erotic charge wasn't just growing again, but with the need for action past, this previously subdued, latent amorousness was forcing its insistent way to the vanguard of her mind. Her fright and triumph over the thrill of danger had converted to the desire for sex.

She wanted to fuck.

It had been three months since Allie had last had a man, and inappropriate timing or not—even if a hungry dog was biting its way into Jesse McArthur's guts while she made love—she wanted a man tonight. And she had a very willing man here in the RAM pickup with her.

So, yes, she was definitely having sex tonight.

Allie was delighted that her longstanding problem of which suitor to choose had been resolved for her No longer was she unable to make up her mind. She knew that one reason the problem had persisted was because, seeing as Dave and Tommy were a team, she'd be stuck with whichever of them she picked. She'd intuitively understood that she'd be unable to alter her choice later without sparking friction between the partners.

But now? With Dave out of the picture for the foreseeable future, she felt able to think clearly. Like a shopper examining a trader's wares, she calmly weighed each man's relative merits in her mind. She also considered her sister Chloe's advice.

Oh, Dave, Dave! Even now, Allie knew that if Dave Fontaine so much as winked seductively at her, she'd leap into bed with him.

But . . . Chloe had assured her that on average, Dave's romantic relationships never lasted longer than a month; by then he was sick of the woman and on the lookout for his next conquest. The only reason

Manuela Costa had lasted so long in his bed (three months) was because she was so fierce.

Allie again remembered how the baseball bat had arrived in the rear of the pickup truck. Frowning, she ticked a bold demerit in the 'Dave' column of her mental list. Uh uh. Dave would never change. In his own way, he was as bad as Brian Kemp.

So, in the end she chose Tommy.

Of course, once she'd made her choice, it seemed to her the inevitable conclusion to her emotional journey. Now that she'd reached her decision, she understood that it was the only one she could have made. For ages, Tommy had kept looking at her like he was utterly in love with her. Dave, on the other hand, had only looked at her like he wanted to fuck her. That latter look was fun too, but . . . the average woman wanted something permanent.

Tommy looked sideways at her and grinned. Allie instantly got wet between the legs. She now realized that her arousal also stemmed from the cumulative memory of his desire for her.

She grinned broadly as they drove back to Dover, passing through sleepy town after sleepy town.

They were right on the outskirts of Dover when she slipped her hand off the steering wheel and over onto Tommy's thigh. She did it slowly, so Greg wouldn't notice.

Tommy stiffened when Allie's hand touched him, but to her satisfaction, he didn't push it off. She slipped her hand further inward, to the heart of his maleness. She stroked him there till he got hard, then moved her hand back to the wheel.

She heard Tommy's labored breathing beside her in the darkness. She glanced at his face. His expression was fierce; he seemed almost in pain. His expression increased her own excitement.

It was as settled as tomorrow's sunrise then.

It was. They drove through Dover towards Boston. Instead of Tommy and Greg dropping Allie off at her sister's, she and Tommy dropped Greg off at home in West Roxbury. Then they drove over to Tommy's Hyde Park house.

Tommy's place was small and quite messy. Once Allie and he got down to kissing each other though, the small dwelling felt like Heaven to her.

"You know," he said as he slipped her bra off her shoulders to free her breasts, "I fell in love with you from the very first moment I saw you. Having you here tonight is a dream come true for me."

That sounded very good to Allie. Very, very good. Then he slipped his lips over her exposed nipples and she instantly forgot the night's prior madness.

And when a short while later, Tommy slid his male hardness into her, she felt complete as a woman for the first time in ages. She was ready for him, as wet and willing as an Indian virgin on her wedding night. It felt like rewinding the past, like once again making love for the very first time. The lips of her sex blossomed like a rain-blessed rose around him; they parted like petals and enclosed him possessively. He was hers, all hers.

Their lovemaking that night was pure, a delightful communion of their flesh that completed for Allie the healing process which had begun with her moving out to her sister's place in Dover.

CHAPTER 41

Anderson & Futana

While Anderson drove them back out to Dorchester Avenue, Laurie Futana drove down a tortuous mental road. She rode over a psychic highway of intense uneasiness of soul, travelled a long freeway of chaotic emotions where she couldn't even count on the pale moon of conscience for light. She dreaded reaching the end of her trail because that end might have fangs.

Her companion didn't sense her worries. She glanced over at Tom Anderson. He seemed lost in his thoughts. Even though he was driving, his expression spoke of him being miles away from her side in the squad car.

She wondered what he was thinking. Was he planning his revenge?

She shivered. Did he suspect her? Did he have any idea that it was she, not Brian, who'd sexually abused him? She who'd raped his tight virgin sweetness and filled his backside with her semen?

Now, with the damning benefit of hindsight, she wondered why she'd done it, where the momentary craziness had come from. She wondered what devil had filled her mind and blinded her with its satanic craving. Back then, she'd thought she'd felt something take her over, but had she really? Hadn't her action really been fueled by her own evil desires? She'd come to her senses only *after* her orgasm; before then she'd been in a frenzy of sexual arousal, desirous only of Tom's hairy behind.

But that, she knew, was no excuse. Her behavior on that day had been completely inexcusable. Criminal and unacceptable. It had been a nasty thing to do to Tom, not to mention suicidal. She knew what would have happened if he'd woken up to find her inside his ass:

By now I'd be a stiff, laid out cold on an autopsy table, en route to being laid to rest underground. And I wouldn't have blamed him for shooting me either.

277

She wondered what he thought of gay people now. She winced. *He probably doesn't like us very much.* Then she shrugged. *It's too late to cry over spilt semen, I guess. I just pray he never finds out. If he does, I'm leaving the US on the next plane bound for Australia.*

On that thought, Futana relaxed a little. She realized she was worrying for nothing: if Tom hadn't figured it out by now (and he clearly hadn't), he never would.

She heaved a massive sigh of relief. She was in the clear.

***

Finally they reached Dorchester Avenue. They parked half a block from the pet shop, under a burnt-out streetlamp beside the Boston Youth Sanctuary. The area was quiet; the shops all closed for the night. Like mechanical rats, every now and then a car rolled slowly past the squad car.

Anderson gestured at the dashboard clock. "Five to midnight."

"We wait then," Futana said. "Sure, there may be nothing to see, but if our visit rattled Stacy Lovejoy as much as I suspect it did, she'll either have visitors soon, or be off to see someone."

"She may already have left."

Futana grinned at him. "Trust me, she hasn't."

Anderson shrugged. "Yeah, yeah, like you say—feminine intuition." He made a strangling gesture with his hands. "Me, I just wanna find that hayseed Brian McArthur and wring his neck."

"That's murder, man," Futana teased.

"This is a murder investigation, woman," Anderson shot right back, his lack of a sense of humor dropping him right into her trap where she wanted him.

Each satisfied with the status quo, they watched the McArthur Pet shop. They waited with eyes glued to binoculars.

On the exact stroke of midnight, the front door of the pet shop opened and Stacy Lovejoy stepped out into the street. The redhead was clad in denim and sneakers. After a cursory look up and down the road, Stacy got into a car and drove off.

"Well, there goes our pigeon," Futana said. "Should I follow her?"

Anderson shook his head. "No, let's look around the premises. You already pointed out that she'll be desperate to destroy any evidence."

They left the squad car and hurried over to the building. In the storefront window an aviary of caged birds slumbered, several species with their heads tucked beneath their wings.

"I wonder . . ." Futana said and tried the front door. "Oh no, we can't be this damn lucky," she added when the door clicked open.

Anderson stood staring at the door. "Where the hell can she be in such a hurry to get to that she didn't even remember to lock up?"

"Maybe we should have followed her. She might have been going to visit the damn cryptid monster."

"Maybe. Too late to fix that now. Whatever the case, Ms. Lovejoy just helped further our investigation of her activities." Anderson gestured impatiently at the open door. "Let's step inside. If she comes back now, we'll just say we found her door open and wanted to check that she was okay. It's my guess that she either lives upstairs or round the back of the building."

"Upstairs," Futana said. "That's why she exited through the shop." She moved to step in through the open door, then paused.

"What's the matter?"

"Man, I feel weird about this all of a sudden. Remember what happened the last time on this case that we encountered an unlocked front door?"

"Laurie, let's just . . ."

Futana shrugged in mock resignation. "Alright, just don't say afterwards that I didn't warn you."

She stepped over the threshold and into the pet world. Anderson followed.

They shut the door behind them and each clicked on a flashlight.

They were surrounded by animal smells and sounds. The birds were all asleep. All of the hamsters and half of the caged snakes weren't. Drowsy puppies and kittens regarded them curiously, wondering if it was already feeding time again. The older cats were busily washing themselves, as were a few kittens too, their little colored eyes glittering in the dimness, their mechanical motions of little pink tongues over fur seeming almost like a practice session for the responsibilities of feline adulthood.

Anderson shone the flashlight along a row of aquariums. The captive pisceans gazed somnolently back, as though they were gravely pissed off at being disturbed. In a nearby fishbowl a goldfish was chasing its tail in a circle.

"Business seems to be booming," Anderson commented drily. "You wanna buy a cat?"

"Not from a witch, I don't. She'll just use the damn thing to keep tabs on me. At least that's what they say. Witches use cats as familiars. Sometimes rats and birds too."

"I thought you didn't believe in all that mumbo-jumbo crap."

"I don't. I'm just trying to spook you."

"Enough already." Beside him, several hamsters were racing noisily on their wheels. The damn things were making quite a racket. He wondered if they weren't responsible for keeping all the other pets awake. He reconsidered; maybe not. Right besides the hyperactive hamsters, a number of rabbits and guinea pigs lay on their sides snoring. Beside those, several aquariums of newts and salamanders were in the same somnolent condition. The aquarium aerators relentlessly bubbled up their water.

"Hey, hey!" Futana stepped over a little Dalmatian puppy in a basket. "Don't they have kennels for these things?"

"They'll be out back. Maybe this guy is unpopular. It's a dog-eat-dog world out there."

"Hey, Tom!"

He was studying the dog food shelves. Futana wondered what for. What was making the most impact on her now was the richness of variety of the smells in the pet shop. It wasn't something she'd ever considered before. This place was a veritable cornucopia of odors. The smell of fur and body heat; of feather-trapped sweat, of scales and discarded skins, of shed down and plumes. The pervasive subdued reptile musk. The smell of sand and sawdust mingled with that of cat litter and deodorant. Of dog and cat and fish food. The subtle yet sharp tang of ammonia from the salamander tanks. The reek of rabbit pellets and rat shit and dog poo and mouse urine . . . the cold smell of living fish, of tortoise and turtle excretions, guano and old birdseed, and of yet more deodorizers to prevent it all seeming like one was standing inside a zoo.

"To-om, over here dammit! What the hell are you looking for there? Packs of 'Chopped Housewife'?"

"Yeah, you never know with crazy folks nowadays." He noted that several large packs of Premium Grade dog food were missing, then forgot it. He'd not been here when the shelves were stocked.

"Tom, will you please pay attention to me for a second?"

He shone his flashlight her way. She was right; he'd been distracted. The pet shop had a magical ambience. It reminded him of his childhood wish for a puppy. He'd never gotten the puppy. That might be why he enjoyed lingering here. Searching the shelves for evidence was just an excuse to hang around the animals.

Futana was standing beside a parrot. The green bird was fast asleep. Anderson found the sleeping parrot fascinating. It looked like it would topple off its perch at any minute.

When she saw she'd gotten his attention, Futana shone her flashlight into the alcove behind her. "Behold the stairs to the upstairs. I'm not sure what we're doing downstairs anyways. If our redheaded suspect suddenly returns . . ."

"Well, we still got our excuse that we're trying to protect her."

They made their way upstairs.

"Nice place," Futana commented as they stepped off the top stairs.

They'd emerged onto a short hallway. The hallway light was on. On their right was a large living room, with seemingly a dining room extension. On their left, the hallway ended in an open bathroom. Between living room and bathroom were three shut doors and an open space in which stood a bookshelf.

Anderson gruffly took in their surroundings. Now that they'd left the pet shop, he was all business again. "Yeah, yeah, the lady ain't starving."

"Alright, let's do this," Futana said. "And we need to be quick about it."

"Searching her place without a warrant?" Anderson scratched his chin. "Well, I guess it's okay when she doesn't know we searched it."

Futana scowled. "Man, this is bigger than us following the letter of the damn law. Let's just get on with it?"

"Alright, alright. We do it like last time, you look in the living room and kitchen. I'll—"

"No," Futana cut him off brusquely, with more than a hint of nervousness in her voice. "*You* search the damn kitchen. I can cope with a severed head, but you never saw what was in that kitchen the last time. I spared you that horrible experience."

Anderson shrugged. "Yeah, sure, if that's how you want it. No need to get your dick and balls in a tangle over who searches where."

She rolled her eyes. "Don't be trans-sexist; just search the damn kitchen. I'll handle the other rooms."

"Yeah, yeah. Sure."

They split up. Anderson went right; Futana left.

***

Anderson shone his flashlight around the living room. There was nothing suspicious here. That much was obvious from a single glance. The room contained just furniture, a TV/DVD player on a stand and some horror movies, and a few copies of *Paranormal Monthly* & *Astral Digest* on the coffee table. The magazines could be overlooked: they already knew the suspect was a witch. The place was neat; Stacy Lovejoy clearly took pride in how her home looked.

Anderson momentarily pondered Futana's refusal to handle what he considered the easier search. He was always considerate of her in that regard, even if she didn't appreciate it. He wandered off into the dining room extension, and from there into the kitchen.

Even before seeing the bloody mess in Stacy Lovejoy's kitchen sink, Anderson knew something was wrong in there. He'd had an eerie feeling on approaching the kitchen door. The hair on the back of his neck and arms had stood up like the fur of an angry cat.

Then he spotlighted the flashlight on the sink's grisly contents.

What the . . . ?

Now, while searching for the light switch, he began smelling something strange: A raw musk that clawed his brain with its violence pheromones. An animal odor nothing like those that had made the pet shop a magical place to him. This was the sort of smell that one smelt in nightmares—indescribable and impossible to recall afterwards, but yet so potent that one woke up drenched in sweat and scared to turn off the lights for the rest of the night.

Anderson was scared to turn *on* the lights, but he had to. He didn't know what it was that he was about facing, but nonetheless, it struck him as suicidal to face whatever it was in the dark. And now, he couldn't just *smell* the creature there in the kitchen with him, he could hear it too. Hear it breathing.

It was breathing heavily, as if excited.

He found the light switch and flicked it on.

He spun around. His breath froze in his throat. His eyes gaped wide. *C'mon, God, give me a fucking break here! You don't hate me that much, do you? Stuff like this just doesn't happen in the real world!*

"What the hell?" he gasped when he found his voice.

"I see you've discovered my little secret!" the impossible creature facing him said. It grinned broadly, displaying long yellow fangs in its large red mouth. It flexed its massive hairy arms, scratched the floor tiles with its hairy clawed feet. "Too bad for you that you have! Now I'm gonna eat you, policeman!" The creature sounded like a bear that had learnt human speech. While talking, it splattered his face with its disgusting saliva.

It was now that Anderson realized that he'd not yet drawn his gun. There'd been no need to, since they'd known the house was empty.

Shit!

He went for his gun but the monster was already lunging at him, its jaws and claws spread wide with flesh-tearing intent.

"Laurie!" he yelled as he went down under its immense weight.

***

A small ornate chest of drawers stood in one corner of Stacy Lovejoy's bedroom. On top of it lay a weird-looking knife. The knife had a bone handle and a long glittering blade that curved like a snake in a hurry to get to the end of the world. There were etchings like Chinese writing on the blade. Touching the knife gave Futana a really bad feeling . . . the sort she'd felt both over at the Watt's house and at the Hourigan Farm. She removed her fingers from it with relief. For a moment it had seemed as though she'd sensed dead people screaming at her from inside the silver blade. The feeling was too creepy for words.

She composed herself again. *I'm here to search this room. I'd better get on with it before Tom gets angry again. At least, I don't have to search the kitchen.*

Seeing as she was already at the chest of drawers, she decided to begin there. She pulled the top drawer open.

"Okay, now this is just too weird."

The opened drawer was full of cellphones. It was literally packed with them. All sorts, shapes and sizes of cellphones. HTCs, iPhones, ZTEs, Blackberrys, Samsung Galaxys, LGs, Motorolas, Windows phones, Google phones, Alcatels . . . the variety seemed endless. Wherever Futana stared in the drawer lay a different type of LCD-faced plastic telecom device. Touchscreens, Qwertys, flip-ups, sliding ones. Newly-evolved models and more-extinct-than-the-dinosaurs ones.

The sight of the phones started Futana's mind ticking over. *Now just what is a pet shop owner doing with all these?* She was certain she was looking at proof of Stacy Lovejoy's involvement in long sequence of crimes. *There have to be at least sixty phones in this drawer. And I think all their owners are dead. I'd better call Tom to come see this.*

Then she heard Anderson yell her name.

In a flash she'd turned and was running towards the kitchen. Somewhere between bedroom and dining room she got her gun out.

Then, when she got to the kitchen entrance, she stood there gaping.

"What!?" she mouthed in surprised silence. "What!?"

The sole reason Futana didn't piss herself from fright was because detectives didn't piss themselves from fright. It wasn't considered cool to do. Else, she'd have voided her fear and confusion in a long soothing liquid stream down her pants' leg.

But the shock was . . .

At first glance, Anderson appeared to be covered by a large reddish-brown carpet that had come to a horrible, hungry life. He lay there while it flopped over him, trying to bite him.

Then Futana's perplexed mind resolved the 'carpet' into an animal of some kind. She made out four legs and a tail and a wolf's head. But that still wasn't right, mainly because the furry creature looked more human than animal. Or like a crazy hybrid of human and animal. Whatever. It was larger than Anderson. Its eyes were violet. Its mouth was filled with long teeth and a slobbering tongue. Its smell of beast was thick in the kitchen.

Is that a werewolf? Am I actually looking at a werewolf?

She had no time to resolve her confusion. The writhing pair on the kitchen floor suddenly shifted positions. Futana saw that Anderson was in massive trouble. The werewolf thing had clawed his suit apart. It had also clawed him open. He was bleeding profusely from the chest. It was ripping at him with its claws, each swipe further shredding his jacket.

For his part, Anderson had both hands locked around the werewolf's neck and his arms stretched out. He was keeping its slobbering jaws as far from his face as possible. Anderson didn't look scared, he just looked intense.

Hit by a sense of Déjà vu, Futana thought desperately on what to do. What was the folklore concerning werewolves? Silver bullets . . . anything silver. She looked around the kitchen. No silver in sight. What else will do it? Crosses . . . shapeshifters hate crosses and other holy relics. She quickly nixed this suggestion too. *I'm in a witch's house— there's no chance I'll find a cross anywhere nearby other than the inverted ones she's painted on her bedroom walls!*

So what to do then? Anderson was covered in sweat and blood and didn't look like he'd be able to hold out against the werewolf's attack much longer.

The werewolf apparently sensed this too. It also seemed so carried away in its bloodlust that it hadn't noticed the baffled policewoman standing behind it.

Sensing its kill in the offing, the werewolf grew so excited that it began urinating all over Anderson.

That really upset Anderson. "Oh, shit, stop pissing on me, you overgrown mutt! And, for God's sake, Laurie, don't just stand there watching like you hired this damn thing to kill me. Shoot the damn thing!"

"I-I-I . . . don't I need silver bullets?"

Anderson ducked a swipe of the werewolf's claws. The creature's claws tore open his left jacket sleeve. "Just *shoot* it. I'm telling you, Laurie, if you let this damn thing kill me—I swear to God Almighty I'll haunt you till you goddamn die!"

Futana decided to just shoot the werewolf. She stepped forward toward the struggling pair, then noticed Anderson's service pistol on the floor by the kitchen counter. She scooped up the second Glock 22 in her left hand. Then she stepped quickly over to the werewolf. She took careful aim behind it, ensuring that she'd be firing over Anderson's head. Thirty bullets in its shaggy cranium ought to do the deadly trick.

Then, a second short of pulling both triggers, she changed her mind. Suddenly as cool as arctic ice, she understood exactly what would kill the monster.

"Hey, where the fuck are you going!?" Anderson growled as she turned and headed out of the kitchen. She thought he sounded almost like a werewolf himself.

"Oh, I'll be back!" she shouted over her shoulder. "Try to stay alive for another half-minute!"

She ran for Stacy's bedroom.

Fifteen seconds later, she was back in the kitchen with Stacy's weirdly curved knife in her hand.

In the interim nothing had changed. Anderson was still on the floor and the werewolf was still snapping at his throat and pissing on him in its excitement.

Futana calmly walked up to the creature and stabbed it in the neck with the ritual knife. She stabbed it with both hands gripping the knife's hilt, and as hard as she could.

The werewolf howled in pain. Blood exploded out of its neck in a thick crimson jet. Futana dug the knife in as far as it would go. Then she began sawing away, forcing the wavy blade in even deeper still.

The werewolf howled again, really loud this time. It reared up and clawed the air in agony.

And then, just like that, it was over. The werewolf collapsed on Anderson. Then it rolled off Anderson onto its back and died.

Futana helped Anderson to his feet. They stood staring down at the dead monster.

Then, before either detective could even blink, the werewolf transformed.

They found themselves staring now at Stacy Lovejoy. She was dead. Butt-naked and dead . . . with the ritual knife stuck right through her neck and blood everywhere. Blood was still squirting from her throat.

"I figured her own stuff would kill her," Futana said. "It'd be mortally ironic if there happens to be silver in that blade." She smirked down at the dead woman. "Anyway it worked, thank God. Hey, Tom, I keep saving your ass. This is like the third time on just this case. Hey, you gonna marry me out of gratitude, or what?"

"We both saw her leave the house," Anderson protested. "How the hell did she get back inside—up here—before we did? She was expecting us, you know. That was why she left the shop door unlocked, so she could lure us in."

Futana was pondering the same. But she figured it didn't make any difference. They were safe; that was what counted. They were both splattered with blood and Tom was still bleeding and there was an ocean of blood all over the kitchen floor and . . .

"You're overlooking the real question, man. How the hell did she transform into . . . shit, no I don't . . . I *can't* believe what we just saw. I just killed the bitch and I still don't believe it."

Anderson examined himself for damage. He had several very deep scratches on him that felt as if his chest and shoulder muscles had been sliced open down to the bone. "Forget it, Laurie, this remains strictly between the two of us. We'll think up an excuse for the others."

Futana studied the kitchen sink. It contained a gnawed human arm. The arm wasn't a kid's, but it didn't look too old either. Maybe it was a teenager's.

Futana managed not to be sick.

Though looking a lot worse for wear, Anderson remained calm. Something was bothering him though: in a corner of her kitchen, Stacy Lovejoy had one of those large upright freezers. After seeing the arm in the sink, Anderson was wondering exactly what Stacy's freezer contained.

He stepped around the blood on the floor and opened it up.

He winced. "Well now, what have we got here?"

Futana took one look at the neatly bagged body parts in the pet shop owner's freezer and was sick for real. She threw up all over the severed arm in the sink.

Anderson waited patiently until she'd rinsed out her mouth. "Well, we're definitely putting the pieces of the puzzle together now," he said, gesturing at the body parts in the freezer. "I just wonder how many dead people this puzzle is."

"Tom, shut the damn fridge. I don't wanna see that shit."

"Yeah, sure." He shut the freezer, stepped back over the blood again, then squatted beside Stacy. Taking hold of the dead woman's chin, he turned her face this way and that.

"The hell you doing, man?"

"Making sure she's dead."

"And?"

"She's as dead as fried chicken. Hey, give me a knife. Something really big. A meat cleaver perhaps."

"Tom, she's a werewolf. It's vampire heads that you chop off." For a moment her attention was taken by a tattoo on the corpse's right breast—an elaborate inverted 'A.' It was an eerie, unusual etching. It made her shiver.

"I ain't chopping her head off," Anderson retorted. He felt pain from his ripped chest and winced. "Just hand me a goddamn knife."

Futana looked round the counter. As though she handled butcher services for the neighborhood, Stacy Lovejoy had an impressive selection of knives and cleavers.

"Tom, this woman was like frigging Walmart. How big a knife you want?"

"The biggest you got there."

After some consideration she handed him a meat cleaver with a blade so large, it could have come from a guillotine. "This good?"

He measured it with his eyes. "Marie Antoinette, this ain't the bloody French Revolution. Something smaller."

She searched again. "How's this one?"

"Yeah, lemme have that one."

She handed it over to him. She was surprised when he rubbed the cleaver in the blood on the floor. Then when it was messy all over, he prized open Stacy Lovejoy's right hand fingers and fit her hand around the cleaver's handle.

He nodded at the result. "Good. Now we don't need to worry about the werewolf explanation. She came at me with a butcher knife, that's all."

"How 'bout the blood on you? And your wounds?"

Anderson winced in pain, as if she'd just reminded him he was hurt. Then he smiled coldly. "Don't worry about those. The way I'm figuring this out, Laurie, no one's gonna bother about me . . . Not after they see what Ms. Lovejoy's been up to in here. Once they look in that freezer, it's gonna be Panic City."

"We'd better call the station then," Futana said. "Get the guys over here."

"No need to. We've been making so much frigging noise in here, one of the neighbors is certain to have dialed 911. Those wolf howls must have woken up the entire neighborhood. Everyone likely thinks she's being killed by her pets."

As confirmation, at that moment they heard the first sirens arriving. Reinforcements coming fast and loud.

"So what now?" Futana asked.

Anderson staggered against the kitchen counter. "Shit, it hurts me to think—the hairy bitch cracked my head real hard against the floor tiles. And she pissed on me, can you imagine that?—I'm all wet and stinking." He smelt himself and grimaced. "Help me out into the living room. We'll wait for our guys there. That way they won't accidentally think we're the perps and shoot us."

Futana helped him into the living room. There, she turned on the lights and got out her badge. Tom was right; with the amount of blood on them, they could easily be mistaken for criminals instead of victims.

"You know," Anderson said slowly when they were both seated, "In all my life I've never believed in werewolves. Believing in God's hard enough, with some of the stuff He allows sickos to get away with, but I can hack that—maybe the Head Dude was having a bad day when they were born. But this shit . . . hell no. I wanna forget what just happened. And I'm gonna do my damned best to try to."

Futana just nodded. She felt exactly the same. Then, thankfully, she found a less-insane, more earthbound topic to talk about: "Yeah, and before I forget, man: this lady is . . . well was . . . definitely connected to our Wet Bones investigation. She's got a whole bureau full of cellphones inside. I'm willing to bet my life that they belong to our skeleton crew."

Anderson nodded. "You don't say?" He was in too much pain to really care. Now that all the excitement was past, he just wanted to see a doctor and then fall into bed. Both cellphones and skeletons would still around tomorrow. Sure, Anderson wasn't dying, but he was damn sure hurting like he was dying.

And then the house was full of police officers and it was time for identifications and explanations. And then Futana took Anderson to the ER to get stitched up.

And there in the hospital they both had to convince the doctor not to write in his report that Anderson seemed to have been attacked by a large wild animal, possibly a bear or a wolf.

Because (as Futana patiently pointed out to the perplexed man), how the hell could two urban Boston police detectives possibly have been attacked by a wolf in a downtown apartment?

CHAPTER 42

Allie

Friday morning. Warm sunlight.

Allie awoke to the feeling that something was wrong.

Whatever was wrong with the day, however, wasn't wrong with *her*. She felt fine; she felt lovely and loved. Above all, she felt happy.

The feeling of something being wrong didn't leave Allie though. If anything, it intensified. It was like being asleep and dreaming that someone was watching you, but being unable to wake up to confront them.

She sat up, yawned, stretched, then looked sideways at Tommy. He was turned away from her and still fast asleep. She grinned at him and stroked his dark hair. Then her odd feeling returned and she stopped grinning.

It suddenly hit Allie what the problem was: the cottage felt unnaturally cold. The bedroom door was open and an early morning draft was blowing right through the house, as though the front door were open too.

But we locked it last night.

Allie's first thought was that they'd been burgled. (Like all girlfriends, she now thought of herself and Tommy as a single unit.) But, seeing as she wasn't certain this was actually the case, she decided to go investigate before waking Tommy up.

She was naked except for her panties. She got out of bed and pulled on a nightie. Then, still a little cold, she draped a bathrobe over that.

She picked up a switchblade knife from the dressing table, then stepped out into the hallway. She padded silently towards the living room. Her feet were stealthy on the faded beige carpeting. She made less sound than a cat. She walked with a hand on the wall. Memories filled her mind. Memories of last night's business, from the chilling to the exhilarating.

She was still shocked by what had transpired at that farmhouse. Most of all she was shocked by herself: what she'd done; what she'd discovered herself to be capable of. She considered her baptism of fire on joining the Rectifiers a positive one. It had shown her that she could rise to the occasion—even if the occasion involved a whole lot of violence.

And there'd been the addition thrill of sticking it to *Brian*. Even though a different Brian, Brian McArthur had possessed that same deep existential quality of asshole-ism.

Last night had solidified Allie's character in some way. It was the reason she only trembled from the cold now, not from fear.

At least until she reached the living room.

The first thing that caught her eyes on reaching the living room was the message scrawled in large red letters on the ash-colored wall, to the left of the front door. The red message riveted Allie's attention. It made her overlook the fact that, yes, the front door *was* open. The red message read:

Well, we warned Dave, didn't we? You two look in the box on the coffee table and keep your mouths shut. We'll be back by 9 a.m. to dispose of the evidence. Ensure you guys ain't here then. B&W.

Allie read it twice. At first it didn't make much sense. The shock of seeing it disoriented her. She stood there like one mentally-challenged, staring at the wall like she had dyslexia. It was so crazy to wake up and see stuff like this in one's house, like you'd angered a gang of ghetto fifteen-year-olds who'd then gone spray paint crazy on you, only the only color of paint they'd had available had been red.

Then her mind took in the fact that most of the crimson lettering had dripped during the writing.

It's blood! she now understood. *That's a message written in blood!*

Slowly, her eyes fell towards the foreground. The box on the coffee table. Of course it was there. The red message had merely neutralized her appreciation of its lesser presence. The box was a large brown carton that might have been used to pack one of those old-school CRT TVs, or maybe an extra-large microwave oven nowadays. It was big, that was the main thing. And its bottom was stained red. Some of that red had seeped out over the coffee table, staining the edges of an old *Playboy* magazine.

The front door was open. A frigid draft was blowing in. The breeze was out of place on this otherwise warm morning.

Allie wasn't certain where she found the courage to walk over to the brown box and open it up. She did though. Each step of that five yards seemed a mile long. During the short trip to the box, Allie's heart accelerated frantically then threatened to stall on her altogether. Whatever was in that box was going to be utterly horrible. She knew it and yet couldn't stop herself stepping up to view it.

They cut off Dave's head! she desperately imagined. *They cut off Dave's head!*

Allie flipped back the box covers and stood gaping.

No, they'd not cut off Dave's head. What they'd done to him was infinitely worse. ('They' had to be the nefarious Black and White.)

The box was packed full of meat. Raw, wet bloody meat and skin that was unmistakably human. Her eyes tracked the details of the crimson pile, seeing muscles and a motley array of organs. There were intestines in the box. In a prolapsed moment of time Allie made out a dark liver and kidneys and pale lungs and . . . The smell of the raw flesh rose to assail her senses. Allie felt like she was in an abattoir. The smell was everywhere.

They killed Dave and chopped him into pieces.

However, this wasn't just random chopping up. There was a method to this madness. Allie finally worked out what it was: there were no bones in the meat-pile. Dave's head was missing too. And everything that looked like a limb was still in one piece.

As if . . . as if . . . as if Black and White had simply cut Dave's skeleton out of him.

And from what she'd heard of the pair, Allie had the terrifying impression that they'd begun cutting Dave's skeleton out of him while he was still alive.

Allie's experience of the previous night had toughened her up a whole lot more than she'd realized. In old times she'd have fainted outright. Now, she just stood there staring at Dave Fontaine's remains with tears running down both of her cheeks.

CHAPTER 43

Petra

Petra Velli was having a nightmare. It was a really horrible nightmare. It was the worst nightmare she'd ever had.

In her bad dream, she was downstairs in her husband's basement where he kept his kidnapped persons. She was chained to a bed there.

Dave Fontaine was seated opposite her. Dave was dead. He was staring at her with a miserable expression. His eyes accused her of not eloping with him. "See what happened because you didn't love me enough?" his eyes asked. "See what your husband did to me?"

Then Dave got up from his chair and walked across to her. As he crossed the room, his flesh evaporated into gas, until finally it was just a skeleton approaching her with both bony hands outstretched and reaching for her throat to strangle her.

***

Petra woke up whimpering. She was drenched in sweat. She'd never had such a vivid nightmare before.

Thank God that was just a dream, she thought, gasping in great gulps of air. She relaxed and the overwhelming terror subsided. She breathed better and prepared to get out of bed.

Only . . . it was dark, much too dark. She could hardly see a thing. Yes, yes . . . the lights were off, but her bedroom had three wide windows. Even if it was still the middle of the night, moonlight should be streaming in now and a breeze fluttering the expensive handmade drapes she had purchased on her last trip to Croatia with the children to visit Marko's aged mother. (The old lady had so far steadfastly refused to relocate to America.)

But that wasn't the case here. This place seemed not to have any windows at all.

So Petra wasn't in her bedroom anymore. Last night, she'd gone to sleep next to Marko, but where was she now?

Startled and questioning, Petra paid more attention to her surroundings. She squinted and tried to partition the darkness into shapes. She slowly worked out that she was in a small room. The room's furniture was the bed she was sleeping on, two chairs and a table.

Where am I?

Then she knew: *I'm in Marko's crazy basement where he keeps all the kidnapped people.*

Panic set it. She'd also just realized that she was chained to the bed. The chain was attached to her left ankle. It felt extremely sturdy.

Her attention was diverted from her captivity. She wasn't alone down here. Someone was seated at the table.

"Hey, who's there?" she asked. "Who are you?"

No reply came to her. She revised her opinion. The basement shadows were tricking her. She *was* alone down here.

She waited for someone to come. She was extremely scared now. *Marko must have discovered I was screwing Dave. Oh shit.*

She didn't need to wait long. Shortly afterward, the door opened and the basement lights came on. Lonnie Black and Carrie White walked in. The pair were smiling.

"Hello, Mrs. Velli," White said.

"Let me out of here!" she immediately screamed at them. "How dare you keep me down here!"

Neither of them replied. They kept smiling at her. Then White pointed to the table.

Petra Velli looked at the chair pulled up to the table and fainted.

***

Petra revived. Her brain was instantly filled with the memory of what she'd seen in the chair.

No, it can't be, she told herself with determination. *I'm still dreaming, I just took a detour out of dreamland. I'm still asleep! All I need to do is wake up. Once I wake up properly, everything will be just like it was before I went to bed!*

She bravely opened her eyes. This time she didn't faint. She merely wished she could. Black and White had left the basement. They'd left the basement lights on.

Davey!

The thing seated at the table was Dave Fontaine. Except it was really just his stripped skeleton with his head on top of it. Petra found the sight insane: from the neck down all of the flesh on Dave's body was missing. From the neck down, he was just a linkage of wet bones. Collarbones, ribs and sternum, shoulder blades, arm and leg bones, hand and foot bones, vertebrae and pelvis, all were complete. All were wet with body fluids.

To hold it upright, the body was secured to the chair with wires.

Petra sat up. Just like in her dream, Dave was staring at her with his eyes open. His mouth was slack and his tongue poked between his lips. There was blood at both corners of his mouth. He had a vivid purple bruise on his left temple, like he'd been socked with a set of brass knucks.

Petra began weeping. *Dave! Oh, Dave baby, I should have listened to you! We should have run away together! I'm sorry, baby. I'm really sorry!*

She couldn't take it. She had no idea what Marko had planned for her. She just knew it would be very, very bad.

She stared at the grotesque horror that her husband had made of her lover. Again she waited, this time for Black and White to return.

***

"Now, Mrs. Velli," Black said when they returned to the basement, "you're very lucky that your husband loves you so much. I'm not sure *why* he still does, but then, love is one of life's greatest mysteries, isn't it?"

"Yeah, it sure is," White agreed, pointing to Dave's corpse. "Or else . . ."

"What are you going to do to me?" Petra asked. "I want to see Marko. I can explain."

The little black woman laughed, dimples forming in her dusky cheeks. "That's a good one, Mrs. Velli. You're gonna explain *what?* How you screwed around on him until you passed the crabs to him?"

The crabs? Oh, my God! Petra's eyes widened in horror. Crabs? She'd not even realized that she'd had them. Was that what that crotch itch had been? It had vanished after a while and she'd forgotten all about it.

"C'mon, girl, I mean, the boss even got the crabs on his *eyelashes*."

"They must've climbed up there while he was eating your dirty pussy."

She looked pleadingly at the scary pair, both dressed alike in black T-shirts, white pants, and black sneakers. Both with similarly short hair. Both with the same unnatural 'too focused' look in their matching dark eyes.

"Look, stop looking at us like we're gonna hurt you," Black said.

"No, we ain't gonna hurt you," White agreed. "Not unless you deserve it."

"I still want to talk to Marko. I insist. I have to talk to my husband."

"He ain't around, lady. He's taken the kids to Disneyland."

"On the phone then."

"He said not to disturb him; he wants quality time with his kids."

Her heart sank. That meant Marko wanted nothing to do with her. She was stuck her with these two psychopaths—the Caucasian and the Negress with the mismatched names—until . . . until . . .

Her shoulder sagged.

"Now, let's stop wasting time," White said impatiently. "You need to understand this clearly: we don't plan on babysitting you forever. We got lives to live."

"What she means," Black continued, with a vulpine smirk on his long pale face, "is that you're not going to be down here forever."

"I'm not?" Petra felt hope.

"No, you're not, dammit," White went on. "But see, when you leave here is entirely up to you."

"The boss has a job for you to finish. You finish quick, you leave quick. You spend three months at it? Well, that's exactly how long you'll be locked up down here."

"Yeah, so the faster the better. And then you can get right back to playing unfaithful housewife again—if you dare!"

The pair laughed at that.

"What's the job?" Petra asked, feeling some of her old boldness returning. "Does he want me to start screwing his staff?"

The pair laughed again. White shook her head. "You got a real dirty mind, Mrs. Velli," she said. "And you clearly ain't much in the brains department either. Why on earth, if your husband's so pissed off that you're screwing around, would he give you the chance to screw around on him some more?"

"You're already a slut. He's trying to cure you, not encourage you."

"Watch your mouth," Petra snapped. "Watch how you talk to me. I'm still Marko's wife!"

"Only 'cos you were once smart enough to have three kids for him," White said. "And judging from how you've been behaving since then, that may be the only sensible decision you ever made in your dumb life." She leaned up close to Petra and grinned. "And you'd better watch your mouth, before I pull out all your teeth with pliers. We've got your man's full permission to hurt you all we like."

She grabbed Petra's left ear and twisted it hard till the woman screamed. "Yeah, understand this, bitch: the only thing we aren't permitted to do is kill you."

White shoved Petra back onto the bed. "And you don't want us to disfigure you now, do you? The boss won't wanna fuck you if you ain't got a nose or no ears, or no eyes, will he? So you're gonna damn well behave yourself and we'll let you remain in one attractive piece." The rage that had flared in the black woman's eyes died. She smiled sweetly again. "Now, you just listen to what your husband wants done and comply, and we'll get along just fine, all three of us. Comprende, bitch?"

Petra nodded hastily. "Yes, yes, yes!" She looked expectantly at Black.

He smiled ruthlessly at Petra. "All the boss wants is that you help him dispose of Dave." He grinned broadly at Petra's shocked expression. "Yeah, Mrs. Velli, you're gonna eat up all of Dave Fontaine until he's all gone."

"Yeah," White confirmed, "you're gonna eat all the meat we stripped off his bones. We're cooking it for you right now, and there's enough to last you for about . . ." She looked at Black. "How long was it again, man?"

"One month at three square meals a day. At two meals a day, maybe a month and a half. If we add veggies in for roughage and occasionally throw in some eggs and cheese sandwiches, maybe two months. But not longer than that."

"Hey, but I thought . . . what about the blood sausage?"

"Not enough blood left. We used it all up painting the message on Tommy's wall."

"Yeah, I forgot. And the brain?"

"I'll cut it out of his head later with the circular saw. She can either have it in an omelet or fluffed into an ice cream sundae."

Petra Velli had been listening to their description of her punishment in stunned silence. It struck her as insane that anyone would force someone else to eat another person. But then she remembered that the interracial pair addressing her *were* insane— they'd both spent time in lunatic asylums.

"No!" she whimpered as the horror of it sank in. "No, you can't make me do that!" She stole a glance at the stripped skeleton with the head balanced on it. "I will not eat a human being! I won't eat Dave!"

"Yes you will," White countered angrily. " 'Cos if you don't . . . bitch, let me give you just a li'l taste of what's gonna happen to you."

She produced a pair of hand pruners from her pocket then looked at Black. "Finger or toe?"

"Toe," he replied easily. "Then she can cover it with a shoe. Otherwise, she's gonna look like she pissed off the Yakuza."

And next thing she knew, Petra Velli was screaming as the pair grabbed her and White methodically snipped her left pinky toe completely off her foot with the shears. The pain could only be imagined. Petra howled and howled.

Black and White watched her in emotionless silence. When she'd calmed from her agonized screams to mere weeping, White threw the severed toe onto the bed. "You've still got nine toes left, Mrs. Velli. Ten fingers too. Keeping them is entirely up to you."

She gaped in disbelief at her tormentors. She glanced down at the severed toe. This made no sense to her. She was looking at a part of her body . . . only it wasn't any more. *That's a part of my body.* She looked at her left foot: four toes and a red space (they'd snipped the digit off right at its base) that shone wetly as blood dribbled from it. The insanity of what had just happened was impossible for her brain to grasp. It was easier to understand that she'd been hurt and was in intense pain; not *why* she was hurting.

She looked back up at White. "My foot . . . my foot . . ."

Black smiled understandingly at her confusion. "Like I said, we don't want the boss having an ugly wife. Next offence you commit, we'll remove your other little toe so it'll look nice and balanced when you wear slippers. Four toes on each foot ain't gonna be that noticeable."

White leaned in close to Petra. "So are you gonna eat the damn meat or not?"

"I'll eat it," Petra whimpered, now scared to death of the little black woman.

"We can't hear your weeping ass," White said. "What'd you just say?"

"I'll eat it! I'll eat him! I'll eat Dave!"

White laughed. "Now there's a desperate housewife for you. "Aw, girl, don't cry so much. It ain't gonna all be pain." She pointed to 'Dave' and chortled. "The boss wants you to have some pleasure too.

The pain in Petra's foot was a raging agony. Still she managed to ask, "What are you talking about? What pleasure?"

Black pulled something from his pocket. Staring at it, Petra decided madness would be a welcome release now. The seemingly impossible had just happened to her: everything had just gone from 'bad' to 'worst,' without even pit-stopping at 'worse' along the race track of crazy happenings.

Black stroked the object he was holding. "The boss wants you to carry on screwing Davey while you're eating him. So we stripped the skin off his dick and rolled it over this little vibrator. That way when it's inside you, you'll feel just the same as always." He tapped a sac at the bottom of the flesh-covered tube. "See, we even left his balls intact. Just the way you playgirls like it."

"I think sex twice a day is best," White said. "What you say, man?"

"Yeah," Black agreed. "Two orgasms a day keeps sexual frustration away. That's as fine a cure for adultery as I've ever heard of." He turned the sex toy on so it hummed.

Petra stared at the vibrator that they'd covered with Dave's penis skin. She stared at the hairy scrotum dangling at its end. Then she stared down at the toe they'd cut off her body, and at her blood splashed on the bed. Once more, the room's walls began spinning.

Despite the agony in her foot, Petra fainted again.

***

"Hey, Mrs. Velli, wake up."

"Yeah, wakey, wakey, food's ready."

"I've a hunch that it's time for lunch."

She woke up. She'd been moved while she slept. She'd been seated at the table opposite 'Dave.' A heaped plate of meat was stacked in front of her. Her severed little toe had been placed at a corner of the table; just as a reminder.

"Eat, Mrs. Velli," they said nicely, their voices as oily and ingratiating as if they were serving her caviar in a five-star hotel.

"Yeah, eat it or lose your other toes. You don't want that now, do you?"

"Ho ho ho, you never know—next to go might be a big toe."

She cringed at the threat. She was terrified. They were so blasé about hurting her. It was surreal. *They have to be crazy to treat me like this. But . . . yes they are both certifiably mad, and now they have me as a focus for their insanity.*

Petra began eating. She ate Dave. She ate, then she threw it all up. It utterly revolted her; her stomach couldn't keep the ghoulish food down. It wasn't so much the taste of the meat unsettling her, as the horrible knowledge of what it was. Worst of all, 'Dave'—the head with no body—was still seated opposite her, watching her eat him.

It didn't matter that she'd vomited. Black and White helpfully loaded the puke back onto the plate for her. They scooped it up with spoons and plopped it back onto the plate as though it were gravy.

"Try to understand this, Mrs. Velli," Black explained calmly, "the boss says you gotta eat *all* of Dave. That means no puking. The only way Dave leaves your body is through your asshole."

"Yeah, mama, shitting him out is what it's all about."

Black nodded. "Now, as generous as you tend to be with your orifices, I'm assuming Dave's been in your butt already, so you shouldn't have any issues with letting him out of you that way too."

White waved the pruners in her face. "Keep the meat down, bitch. Or else, you'll lose some fingers too. And you wouldn't that want now, would you? How you gonna wear your wedding ring without fingers? Or . . . or . . . or you want us to prove to you again that we ain't joking?"

Petra shook her head violently. She got to work eating up the puked meat. This time she kept it down. Mind over matter; willing herself not to vomit. She wasn't losing any more toes. She'd accepted that her resistance was pointless; all acting stubborn would achieve would be hurt to herself. As fond as she'd been of Dave, her not eating him wasn't helping him in any way; he was well beyond her assistance now.

She didn't look at him, at what was left of him. She concentrated on eating the meat. They'd cooked Dave soft, so he was easy to chew and swallow.

She finished that serving. They loaded up her plate again. And she ate that too. She kept it down too. She was getting the hang of it now.

Just imagine that it's pork. Just imagine it's pork.

Then they left her. Down there in the basement with her dead lover.

"We'll be back later for your sex therapy," they said, waving the flesh-coated dildo at her.

And then, there was also what they said just before closing the door, speaking as if she wasn't even there with them:

"Man, you sure she ain't gonna go crazy on us?"

"You heard what the boss said: it doesn't matter if she goes nuts down here. What's important is that she keeps her pussy at home afterwards. A crazy woman ain't gonna be donating her ass all over Massachusetts, is she?"

"She might rat on us afterwards."

"Rat on us? Girl, what have you been smoking? What's she gonna tell the fuzz?: 'Oh, Officer, I've just spent the past month eating my dead boyfriend?' 'Alright, ma'am, now where's the evidence of the crime? Where's the damn body?' 'Oh shit, officer, didn't I just tell you that I ate it?' 'Oh, okay, ma'am, in that case, we'll need to do a DNA analysis of your poop.' "

They laughed.

Petra burst into tears. She stared at the skeleton man and wept and wept and wept and wept and wept and wept and wept.

Then the basement door opened again. Just a little bit. Petra's first thought was that White and Black hadn't locked it properly. The thought kindled no hope in her. An unlocked door was useless to her; she couldn't escape: the shackle on her ankle meant she wasn't going anywhere.

She was about losing interest in the opened door, when she caught sight of something moving right at the bottom of it.

She looked hard. It was a crab. A large orange crab was scuttling into the room.

301

"Just a little reminder of why you're down here," said Black's voice from outside the room.

Petra stared at the crab.

The crab looked back at her, black eyes swiveling on eyestalks. Then suddenly, it skittered across the basement to hide itself in the shadows under the bed.

She could hear it under there though. The damn crustacean was moving about, wondering how it had gotten from its nice sandy beach to this wetless place. The sounds it made, jerky and unpredictable, rattled Petra's nerves. She began gibbering in horror. Then she calmed down and just stared at the dead man opposite her and trembled.

The corpse stared back, unheeding her despair. The head on no body. A dead but still handsome face suspended in midair on a framework of meatless bones. Wet Bones, like the flesh had all evaporated away.

One of its skeleton hands rested on the table. Its stripped index finger pointed towards her, as if saying, "You ate me, baby! How dare you!"

But she couldn't stop eating him, could she? Her detached toe lay on the table beside the corpse; a clear warning of what would happen if she dared attempt a hunger strike.

And this was still only the *first* day of her imprisonment and punishment. And knowing her husband, she wasn't getting out till Dave was all eaten up.

CHAPTER 44

Greg

After breakfast, Greg browsed through his text messages.

He had three from Aunt Grace. She'd also called him six times so far this morning, two of those being WhatsApp video calls.

Why hadn't he heard the phone ring then? Oh, the phone was switched to 'Silent.'

He winced. His wallet was missing. In a sudden burst of panic he looked through the house for it. He was about phoning Jojo to ask if he'd left it at her place when he recalled using a bank card taken from it to buy gas after leaving her. So it couldn't be at Jojo's. And it wasn't out in the car because . . .

He finally realized he'd left his wallet over at the farm last night. That wasn't cool, the wallet contained his driver's license and his bank cards. He figured he'd have to talk Tommy and Allie into driving back out there before their agreed-on week.

He returned his attention to Aunt Grace's text messages.

Each was simple and precisely worded:

'Are you okay, dear? Please call me.'

'Greg, are you alright? I hope nothing's happened to you. Please answer the phone, dear, you're getting me worried.'

'Greg, what is going on with you? Don't you dare treat me like this! Call me, and stop playing silly games, you ungrateful little boy!'

He grimaced. Her first two texts expressing her concern for him would give anyone the wrong impression about her. The third

303

message was the *real* Aunt Grace. The control freak Aunt Grace. All she wanted to do was run—no, *ruin*—his life.

He grinned at the cellphone. He felt a sudden deep surge of gratitude to Jojo Kim. *Well, it's over, witch!*

***

Debbie came over after lunch.

"I wanna go get a tattoo," she declared after a frenetic bout of window sex during which she spotted two nuthatches, a flock of blue jays, a seagull, and a circling flock of little brown birds that she couldn't identify because they were so far off, but which she suspected were Carolina wrens. "There's this place called Skin Art up in Cambridge that a friend told me about. She says they're really good."

Greg nodded. "Yeah, sure. But what do you want to ink on yourself?" He suspected he already knew though: In Debbie's case, with her ornithological-erotic fixation, any inking she got done was certain to be a flying fluffy-feathered friend of some kind, maybe a bright red robin over her pubis.

However, her mention of a tattoo started Greg thinking along macabre lines. His thoughts became gloomy. His mind went back to last night, to the identical tattoos the McArthur brothers had had on their left thighs: that eerie inverted 'A'; and Allie's insistence that the tattoos meant something abstruse.

Frowning, he wondered how Jesse was getting on with the dogs and all that dog food they'd sewn into his belly. Had the dogs bitten into him yet?

For a moment he felt remorse for what they'd done last night. But then his regret left him. Those two McArthur jerks deserved everything they'd gotten. *They tried to kill us, for chrissakes!*

"Hey, baby, I'm talking to you," Debbie said. "I was saying, I wanna get a pair of blue jays inked on my shoulder blades . . . Greg? Greg? Hey—what's on your mind? Why are you frowning like that?"

He returned his attention to her. "Sorry, honey, it's nothing. I've lost my wallet, that's all. My driver's license was in it, so I can't drive you over to the tattoo place." He found his smile again when his eyes settled on her succulent breasts with their super-cute nipples.

She shrugged. "Don't worry, *I'll* drive us." She raised her hands over her head and stretched. "Hey, that reminds me—your aunt called me. She says she's been trying to get you all morning. She said to tell you to call her at the hospital."

Greg's smile soured again. He'd not even known Aunt Grace had Debbie's cell number. *All the better to keep track of me, I guess.*

"Baby, you do know that your aunt scares me, right?" Debbie asked.

"She's harmless enough," he replied. "Please pass me my phone. I'd better call her and see what she wants."

"No," Debbie replied. "I've a better idea."

"What's that?"

"Let's go visit her in the clinic."

"I just saw on Wednesday; day before yesterday."

"It doesn't matter. The only reason she could possibly be calling you so frantically is because she loves and misses you."

Greg recalled the irate tone of his aunt's third text message. "Oh, she misses me alright. Deb, you don't even know the half of it."

"Let's go," Debbie pressed. "I'd like to see her."

"Yeah, alright . . . but . . . what about your tattoo?"

"I'll get inked some other time. But for now, I really want to see your Aunt. I feel a warm connection between both of us that I want to develop."

Greg stared at her in surprise. "But you just said . . ."

"Well, she does still scare me . . . but I'm going to make an effort to like her because I love you."

"I love you too, baby." They kissed, then he asked, "Wow, aren't you the loving prospective daughter-in-law all of a sudden?"

After saying this, Greg paused for a moment. He considered what he'd just said. *Daughter-in-law? Have I actually begun thinking of Aunt Grace as my mom?*

***

Aunt Grace was delighted to see them both. Her beaming smile the moment they stepped into her private room assured Greg that all was forgiven.

"Come, come, darling. I was so, so worried when I couldn't get through to you. Sit here on the edge of the bed so I can see you better."

Greg did as she requested. He felt like a sheep cozying up to a wolf. He managed to smile back when she gripped his hand in her cold fingers.

"I'm just so lonely here without you, darling," she told him. "Detective Anderson was supposed to come visit me, but he got beaten up during an investigation and is home in bed."

"Beaten up? Whatever happened?" Debbie asked while settling herself in a chair.

"Yeah," Greg added, "what happened to him?"

Aunt Grace shrugged. "It's all very cloak-and-dagger, dear. They went to arrest someone and a fight started. The crazy woman had a knife. Anderson got the worse of it. He's had to have a lot of stitches across his chest. He's unsure if he's got a concussion or not."

Greg noted how worried she sounded about Detective Anderson. He mused on the relationship between her and the stolid cop. He wondered why they didn't just get married and out of his hair.

"Anyway," Aunt Grace continued before they could ask her any further questions, "it's so lonely here. I miss being at home with you, Greg." She winked. "And I *really* miss the smoothie club meetings."

Greg understood her wink. She missed her semen smoothies. He grinned. Oh, she had a real shock in store when she got back home. He wasn't going to tell her now; he was conscious of her weak heart. If he alarmed her, she might suffer a heart attack and die from sheer frustration. Then he'd get the blame for killing her. He wondered how Jojo was coming along with erasing the files from his aunt's laptop. He looked around the hospital room. His aunt's laptop was running a screensaver—clearly Jojo Kim's work—a GIF file of hilarious scenes from smoothie club meetings.

She's obsessed with yoghurt . . . and she's obsessed with me!

She gripped his hand tight and he smiled down at her; this frail and aging woman who although so near her grave, refused to let him be.

Well I'm free now, aren't I? And she doesn't even know it. She doesn't even suspect that she's lost all her power over me!

He remembered the disgusting price he'd paid for his freedom. He grimaced. *I had to poop on a woman to escape your clutches, auntie, but it was worth it. Ha ha ha!*

He wished he could shout it at her. He resisted the urge to laugh in her face.

But still, he felt a touch of sympathy for her. She looked weak. Pretty but pallid, like a movie vampire desperate for a youth-restoring infusion of blood after a hundred years asleep in its crypt. She seemed drained of vitality. And for the doctors to insist she remain on admission meant something was really wrong with her.

For a moment he suspected she might have cancer. He really thought this might be the case. If so, was she keeping the news from him so as not to hurt him? So long as it didn't involve the contents of his testicles, Aunt Grace was always solicitous of his feelings. She hated seeing him upset.

But no, he finally decided, *she doesn't have cancer. She's too happy to be dying. It's just a stubborn stomach bug. The doctors warning her off smoothies proves that. And it'll shortly be taken care of.*

"Why not have your smoothie club meetings here in the hospital?" Debbie suggested. "They're only once a week, aren't they? I doubt that you'd be disturbing anyone."

Aunt Grace looked mournful. "Oh, I've asked, but the doctors all say no. They say there's too much chance of people introducing germs into their sterile environment." She managed a small smile. "They explained it so nicely that I had to agree with them. We don't want to accidently infect someone."

Debbie nodded. "Any news about Dez?" she asked. "Have the cops found him yet?"

Aunt Grace shook her head sadly. "Oh, no. I find it very sad. Jenny thinks he's run off with another woman. She's totally sedated up now and their kids are all over at her mother's." Her expression turned pensive for a moment. "It's really odd, you know. Jenny says Dez went to see an old friend that night . . . Ah, what's his name again? . . . Yes, I remember: Brian McArthur. That's right. And the really worrying thing is, now no one can find Brian either. It's almost like the earth's opened up and swallowed them both."

Debbie giggled. "Or maybe . . . they both fell in love and eloped to San Francisco."

Aunt Grace giggled too. "Oh, you kids and your dirty minds. Everything is about sex with you young girls nowadays, isn't it?"

Greg grimaced. Then he quickly evened out his expression again before either his girlfriend or his aunt questioned him over why he suddenly looked so moody.

His thoughts were bitter; darker than midnight and as remorseless as a those of a medieval hangman at the moment he sent a convict swinging from the morbid gallows:

Yes, Brian McArthur deserved what he got. So he killed Dez too?

CHAPTER 45

Anderson & Futana

"Has to be here," Anderson said. "If it ain't, well . . ."

"It *is* here," Futana replied. "The place has 'Human Vermin Lodgings' stamped all over it."

The detectives were standing outside of yet another disused central Massachusetts farm.

It was three days now since the Stacy Lovejoy incident. Under his suit, Anderson was all stitched up and bandaged up. He ached really badly.

In fact, he felt like shit.

He'd been unable to get out of bed the next day. The doctors still insisted that he stay at home and rest, but Anderson's sense of justice being delayed by his inaction (as well as his intense desire to get his hands on Brian McArthur) had made rest impossible for him.

So he'd pulled himself out of bed and now here they were.

***

Back at the station, everything was bedlam. Phones were ringing off the hook. Seemingly every police agency in Massachusetts was calling every other police agency. And all at the same time.

All those recovered cellphones . . . The phone numbers, most of them long ago deactivated and resold to fresh subscribers by the phone companies, all belonged to vanished people. Ten of them belonged to folks who'd turned up as Wet Bones skeletons. (By the weekend, another six phones would have been identified as belonging to people who'd been arranged as body parts inside Stacy Lovejoy's freezer.)

A press release was imminent. The media vultures were out en masse, preparing to gorge themselves on this latest decaying morsel of info-carrion. CNN and Fox News were salivating with delight. Everything was set to blow up worldwide in Pressville, with Stacy Lovejoy being heralded as the Bay State's most prolific serial killer ever. Possibly America's most prolific even. She was being touted as being well up there with John Wayne Gacy, Jeffrey Dahmer and Ted Bundy. And fans of female serial killers would finally have a satisfactory replacement for Juana Barraza and Jane Toppan.

Anderson and Futana knew better, but didn't say anything. The advantage of all this misconception was that it enabled them to fly under the radar and continue their investigation unhindered. There would be more than enough time to fill in the accurate details of the case for everyone once they'd located their monster.

The flipside, the disadvantage of all the excitement, was that everyone in Policeland was so busy either calling the relatives of the cellphone owners or investigating some other detail to do with the case, that it had taken Anderson and Futana four whole days to dredge up several routine pieces of information.

But they'd finally gotten that info. And now here they were. At this ancient, long abandoned farm out in Hampden County, a mile south of the Brimfield State Forest, about a mile northwest of the town of Wales, and barely three miles north of the Connecticut border. The Lincourt place: Brian and Jesse McArthur's maternal grandfather's homestead.

***

They stepped cautiously up the short driveway. The Lincourt farmhouse was thirty or so yards in from the road. The whole area spoke of gross disuse; clearly no one had farmed anything here for decades.

"Pay dirt," Anderson said. "Someone's living here for sure. See how low the grass is cut? And all those ruts and tire tracks up ahead?"

"I knew it," Futana agreed. She gestured with her gun at the building they were approaching. "How do you wanna do this? You wanna split up again?"

Anderson shook his head. "So far that approach hasn't brought me much happiness. We stay together."

310

Futana smirked. "Great that you've learned your lesson. I can't keep babysitting your ass, you know."

He scowled and she realized she'd struck a sore nerve. It was an ego nerve of course. By now his ass must have stopped hurting.

For her part, she was uncertain how she felt. She had no idea what her reaction would be on seeing Brian McArthur again, face-to-face after all these years. Would she shoot him or get a hard-on? God knew the bastard deserved to die for what he was into now.

I think I'll just shoot him on sight and get it over with. Left to Tom, he'll start reading Brian his rights.

She focused again on their mission here. "Where do we check first? Main house, or . . ." she gestured once more with her gun, "the barns behind it?"

"The barns. If our beastie's here, that's where it's gonna be hiding. Remember, Steph says the thing is *big*."

"We'll be taking a chance on Brian hearing us and getting away."

"Point taken. Let's start with the farmhouse then."

***

The farmhouse showed clear signs of recent occupation, but was empty. (As seemed to be a trend in this curious case, the front door was unlocked. They just walked in and began looking around.)

"Alright, Laurie," Anderson said on descending the stairs after a quick search of the upper floor, "our boy definitely lives here."

"His brown pickup truck is parked out back," she replied. "And there's another car out there too. Black, but I can't tell the make."

"Which means he's home. And if he's not in here . . ." Anderson looked meaningly towards the back corridor.

Futana scratched the blonde hair over her forehead then frowned. "I think we'd best check out the barns now."

"Yeah."

They left the house via its back door, emerging onto a walkway that led directly past Brian's Ford truck.

"Damn," Futana whispered as they passed the mud-splattered vehicle. "Hasn't this guy ever heard of a carwash?"

Anderson pointed to the second car, a black Honda Civic. "Just be on your guard so we don't get ambushed *again*. We may have two McArthur brothers to deal with here instead of one."

They entered the first and largest barn. It was the logical one to enter. This gambrel-roofed building was the only barn still in good repair. The other two looked like shipwrecks dragged onto land and abandoned.

The first thing that struck them both on entering the old barn was the smell. Death hung in the air. It was something a detective grew sensitive to over the years: that often barely-perceptible taint of expiration, like the bloody signature at the bottom of a suicide note that lasted fifty pages, one page for each year of the departed one's miserable life. In this case, Death's signature struck one both as a component of the nasal atmosphere and also as that morbid ambience which the presence of a corpse always bestowed on even the most serene of scenes. Once attuned to it, there was something almost psychic about how one could sense that a dead human body existed on a premises; it was almost as though the dead person was still hanging around their mortal remains, stirring up the ether so they'd be found. And such might well be the case. No one wished to be an anonymous death, to be an unclaimed and unaccounted-for statistic, overlooked and unwanted at their end as though their passage through life had meant nothing at all.

Anderson and Futana sensed that trace of lingering dead persons in the Lincourt barn. It felt like a psychic load placed on their shoulders. In addition (also unmistakable to two individuals with their combined investigative experience), the barn smelt of spilled blood. Some of said spilled blood smelled fresh; some of it smelt rotten; some of it just smelt old, like it had dried over many years and their nostrils were unearthing its memory.

More immediately perceptible, more to the front of their minds, was a clear reek of decomposing flesh.

And then there was another smell, one so alien it was impossible to place. During her werewolf transformation, Stacy Lovejoy had had a clearly discernable canine odor to her. She'd stunk like a dog pound full of bitches in heat. This smell, however, was nothing like that. This smell raised the hairs on the back of both detective's necks. The smell was an unnatural one, calling to mind books and movies about arcane artifacts unearthed in ancient gothic temples. It was the smell of things buried and forgotten in the dusty cupboards of the primal race subconscious. If prehistory had an odor, Futana felt it would smell like this.

312

It was the smell of an unknown creature, the smell of an animal as yet unclassified by human science. A smell alien to them both because it had no parallel anywhere on the third planet from the sun. It wasn't a pervasive odor. It was in fact quite faint, but nonetheless it commanded their attention by its very inexplicableness.

However, the mingled odors, familiar and unusual, only distracted Anderson and Futana for a few seconds. The barn lights were on. Staring into the barn, they were met by an extremely strange and grotesque sight.

After a wordless glance at each other and nodding, they set off for it.

About three quarters of the way into the barn, something that looked like a long brown pipe lay beside a pool of water. This in itself wouldn't have attracted their attention, except that a six-foot section of the brown pipe bulged oddly.

"Are my eyes deceiving me," Anderson asked, "or does that thing have a human skeleton inside it?"

They reached the 'pipe' and the pool. Now they saw that the pipe-creature was coiled around the pool's stone rim. The entire area around the pool was covered by a thick transparent slime. The goop was several inches deep.

Both detectives recalled the supposed properties of that slime. They'd halted eight feet from the pool, at the point where the ooze began. They made no attempt to approach any closer.

"It looks like a giant snake," Futana said. "Was that all this was about then? A snake cult?"

"It ain't a snake," Anderson countered. "See how its body is all pinched up into sections by those black bands? Those are segments. Snakes don't have segments."

"What the damn hell fuck is it then?"

"Laurie, I think it's a damn worm."

"Ugh!" Futana said. She looked sick. She felt sick. She was tougher than leather, but some things were just horrible. The idea of a worm this large offended both her humanity and her femininity. Worse still, the unnatural odor in the barn was clearly coming from this worm-thing.

They put their guns away. The worm was clearly dead. Even though still smothered in slime, its body was all withered up. It was motionless and just . . . it just looked *dead*; that was all. It gave off not the faintest hint of any animating spark of life remaining in it.

Death preserved in its own terrible emission.

It had apparently shrunk after its death too. They had two evidences of this:

Firstly, on tracing the creature's length—it had to be at least forty feet long—to its head, they saw that its head was a whole lot wider than its body. Its head was at least two feet wide. In contrast to this, its dried body was an even four inches thick all around.

And secondly, the portion of the worm's body that contained the human skeleton was stretched to ripping point. Indeed, at several points its tubular form had split around the skeleton. The white bones of a human foot poked out through one such split. Even from their safe distance the detectives could see the glistening jelly that coated the bones.

"Well, case solved for sure," Futana said. "We can call headquarters and then both take a long vacation to Hawaii."

"I sure as hell hope that's Brian McArthur in there," Anderson said dryly.

"I doubt it," Futana said. "Assholes like that tend to have more spare lives than a witch's cat. It's likely some poor innocent, maybe the owner of the other car. Only, if that's the case, then where is—?"

"Shush!" Anderson said, raising a hand. "I can hear something!"

Futana kept quiet and listened. "It sounds like a dog," she said after a while. "Yes, that's a dog growling. And it's very nearby." She pointed back toward the barn entrance. "I think the sound is coming from behind that side door over there."

"Stacy Lovejoy owned a pet shop," Anderson said. "It figures. Let's go find the poor dogs."

"They must be really hungry by now," Futana said. "They may have been locked in there for quite a while."

Anderson wrinkled his nose. "I ain't too sure 'bout that *hunger* bit, Laurie. I think that's also where the stink of rotting meat's coming from."

On that statement, Futana gave him a worried and quizzical look. Then she quickly set off for the side door.

***

Behind the locked door was utter carnage. The mess was so absolute that for a moment neither detective realized what they were actually looking at.

"Oh, my God!" Futana finally yelped. "Oh, my dear, dear God!"

The room was covered with the pieces of a man. His remains were strewn everywhere. Entrails, chewed organs, half-eaten kidneys, the whole lot. There was a husk of torso in a corner, but the rest of him was everywhere else, mingled in with rags of ripped clothing. At first the corpse's head seemed to be missing altogether, but then they located it—the face was peeled almost completely off the skull, folded up over the bone like an opened trapdoor.

The smell of spoiled meat in the room was atrocious.

The floor and lower portions of the walls were covered with blood.

The two dogs in the room—large German shepherds—were equally covered with the dead man's blood, as if they'd been using their bodies as paintbrushes to color the walls.

But that wasn't the worst of it. It looked like the dogs had *eaten* the man. Eaten him alive.

"There's a whole lot less of him here than there should be to make up a complete person," Anderson commented. He then pointed to a pile of neatly arranged turds in a corner: "Someone's gonna be pissed off to have to analyze all that dog shit over there." The normally unperturbed Anderson could feel his balls shrinking up into his belly. Talking tough was his way of coping with his disgust and fear.

Futana winced. Her eyes were fixed on the two dogs. She wondered why they'd killed the man, and so violently at that. She liked animals, and dogs in particular. She was just so upset. She felt herself about to cry.

The two German shepherds crouched in a corner, growling like they were crazy, regarding the detectives with red eyes, daring them to come take their meal away from them. One had a thighbone between its jaws; the other was chewing one of the dead man's hands.

"Put them out of their misery," Futana said. She had tears in her eyes now. "Oh, my God, how could anyone do this . . . ?"

Anderson shot both dogs. He put a bullet in each canine head. He agreed it was the merciful thing to do. (This whole scenario was affecting him too, a whole lot more than he'd ever admit to anyone.) Then he walked over and retrieved the half-chewed hand from the second dog's mouth. "Yeah, all the fingerprints are still on it," he said coldly. "Forensics'll be delighted about that."

Futana kept weeping. After a while Anderson gave up on his macho posing and wrapped an arm around her shoulders to comfort her.

"I'd just love for one of these corpses to be Brian and the other Jesse," he said wistfully. "Two vehicles out there, two brothers in here—a nice clean wrap-up to this messy case. But yeah, don't say it; I already friggin' know what you're gonna say: If wishes were horses, right?"

She managed a laugh. "I wasn't about to contradict you. One of the bodies has to be Brian anyway. Where else can he be around here, except in the belly of his beasts?"

They left to go properly search the farmhouse.

***

"Well, everything's connected for sure," Futana said, holding up a knife with a wavy blade that she'd found in a living room drawer. "This one's exactly like the one Stacy Lovejoy had."

"It's most likely hers too," Anderson replied. Then frowning, he added, "Hey, Laurie, come over here a minute. I think we've just linked everything together."

Confused, Futana crossed the living room to his side. Anderson was sitting in a threadbare armchair and had just forced the lock of a large leather case. Futana took one look at the case's contents and whistled. "That damn many?"

Just like Stacy Lovejoy's dresser had been filled with cellphones, this case was filled with ID documents: wallets and purses with cards spilling out over each other like toppled dominos.

"At least now we'll be able to work out exactly how many folks these guys killed to feed their monster," Anderson said. He shut the case and moodily regarded Futana.

"It's not that worrying me," Futana said. "What bothers me is how these guys—Stacy and Brian and his brother—could get away with this crap for years with no one even suspecting them."

Anderson grunted. "It's easy, Laurie girl. All you need is an abandoned farmhouse somewhere, or a basement. If *you* ever decide to step off the straight-and-narrow, lemme know, I'll gladly give ya tips on serial killin'. I don't recall America having any tranny mass murderers—you'll be a star before you even get started."

She stared at him. Then angered by his comment, she wheeled away from him. "I don't think it's in the least bit funny, Tom. Just think of all those innocent dead people. None of them did a thing to deserve this sort of grisly fate."

"No one ever does, girl."

Still angry, she strode off into the hallway.

"Hey, where you off to?" he called after her.

"I'm going to search the kitchen," she shot back at him.

"You don't like kitchens, remember?"

She grimaced. "Just let me be. Hopefully, Brian wasn't eating his victims too. It seems to be a trend in this horrible case. Even feeding dogs . . . ugh! I mean, we've got giant worms eating people, werewolves eating people . . . even dogs eating people. . . . What is this place? A man-eating animal shelter? Shit!"

Anderson waited till she was out of sight, then he quickly reopened the case and removed one of the topmost wallets. It was just good fortune that he'd noticed it before Laurie had. It was good fortune too that it had been lying both open and face up, so he could read the name on a bank card and also recognize the face on the driving license. On seeing those, he'd quickly shut the case again so Laurie wouldn't notice the wallet too. Then he'd riled her up just so she'd leave the living room. This was one of the few times when her short emotional fuse had paid dividends.

The wallet he'd removed belonged to Grace Barbanell's nephew Greg. As far as Anderson recalled, Greg was still alive. Anderson figured the young man had quite some explaining to do.

He checked to make certain the leather folder hadn't spilled any bank cards into the case, then slipped Greg Madden's wallet into his jacket pocket.

Then, groaning in pain (the damn werewolf slashes on his chest felt like they'd all opened up again during his exertions) he walked into the kitchen to pacify Futana.

She was standing beside Brian's open fridge. To her obvious relief (and Anderson's too) this fridge had no grisly contents. Its shelves were mainly occupied by cans of beer and packs of lunch meat. The rest of the kitchen seemed equally innocent, with randomly discarded empty wine and whiskey bottles and an unwashed mess of plates in the sink.

"Hey, Laurie," Anderson said in a joking, conciliatory tone, "we better call in to headquarters, then start planning that Pacific cruise of ours. Hey, you know what? We can even ask Gracie along, once she's out of the clinic!"

She shook her head at him. "Just admit, man, you're in love with the old bag!"

"Hey, don't call her a bag! She's just fifty-nine!"

"Old bag! Old bag!"

CHAPTER 46

Greg

Until Aunt Grace was let of out hospital, Greg breathed an air of freedom the like of which he'd forgotten existed.

Her hold on him was truly finished for good. Jojo had assured him that she'd deleted every single incriminating onanism video. He saw no reason to doubt her. He'd even promised her that if it was true, he'd come fuck her again, with all the attendant mess. Jojo had loved that. She'd leapt on him and kissed him and told him he was utterly the best.

Aunt Grace, of course, had no idea of any of this.

Greg saw her again at the Carney Clinic. It was hard not to gloat. He sat beside her hospital bed and fussed over her like she was grievously ill.

"You've become very caring all of a sudden," she said. She winked. "I'm not about dying, darling. Don't get your hopes up. It'll be a while yet before you get your hands on my money."

"Oh, Aunt Gracie, I don't want you to die." It was true. He really didn't wish her dead any more. He was merely awaiting her discharge from the clinic, which, according to the doctors, would be any day now, once their final set of blood tests came back negative.

Greg wanted Aunt Grace hale and hearty when he sprang the surprise of his emancipation on her. He still feared that if he alarmed her here in the hospital, she might have a heart attack. If she died here and right now he'd definitely get the blame.

"Oh, you're just happy because your testicles are resting," she teased him. "Well, warn those nuts of yours that I'm coming back stronger than ever."

They both laughed about that. Each for different reasons.

319

***

Two days later, Aunt Grace was back home.

"O.K., darling, the honeymoon's over," she whispered to him immediately she was through the front door. "Make me a smoothie, kiddo—chocolate, strawberries, vanilla . . . load it with anything and everything, and"—she winked lasciviously—"Don't forget the nut. I want lots of nut. You've no frigging idea how much I've missed the damn things. Every time Anderson came to visit me I'd beg him to sneak one in but he'd refuse. Damn that policeman: all he knows to do is eat donuts and chase crooks." She snapped her fingers at Greg to indicate her haste. "Get to it, dear!"

"No," Greg said immediately.

"No? But why?" She looked at him oddly. Her face, so much like his mother's, but *older*. But then, contractually, she *was* his mother now. Hadn't he even already begun thinking of her that way?—viewing Debbie as her future daughter-in-law? She looked sweet and weak, her graying hair (his fashionable mother never let her gray show) neatly brushed about her long face.

Her eyes hardened and she was the old Aunt Grace he hated again. She now looked strange to him; like a distant relative one needed to recall from memory. In the time she'd been away he'd forgotten this version of her existed.

"Remember our agreement, darling," she said softly. "Remember all the nasty things I'll do to you if you don't comply with my demands."

"Forget it, auntie," Greg said airily, no longer afraid of her. "I'm not making you any more smoothies and that's that."

She laughed out loud. "You've finally grown some balls? Good, 'cos I'm going to enjoy milking them dry. Now, you listen to me, young man. You'll keep making me smoothies when I want and *how* I want them. And from now on, I want them everyday, no twice a day, or else . . ." She let the threat hang.

"Or else what, auntie?" Greg asked cockily. They'd reached the foot of the stairs.

"Or else . . ." She broke off. "Just you wait for me to get my laptop and I'll show you 'what else.' "

Grinning smugly, Greg waited while she made her way back outside to his car. She was in for a huge surprise once she found out all her blackmail files had been deleted.

***

Ten minutes later, Greg sat motionless in an armchair feeling like he'd been stabbed in the heart.

Jojo Kim had been true to her word: she'd erased the files of him masturbating that were on his aunt's laptop. However, what she'd replaced those with was a whole lot worse: Greg was currently watching himself shit all over her on her red bed. Then he watched himself fuck her while poop smeared all over the two of them like melted chocolate. There was so much shit on display, it looked like they were mud wrestling. It was revolting to watch.

"You'd never think Jojo had it in her, would you?" Aunt Grace quipped, pointing out the massive turd forcing itself out of Jojo's anus as she reached her orgasm. The turd was an unbroken brown rod. It was flecked with little red and green specks. It looked like a psychedelic dildo stuck up her butt. "Such a sweet little girl, such a nasty *big* poop."

Greg felt dead. From the way the video was recorded—as glossy as HD porn and shot from multiple angles—there must have been at least six cameras working all the time, none of which he'd noticed in her bedroom.

But the worst thing of all was that Jojo's face was completely pixelated out in each scene. Her parted, gasping lips were occasionally visible, but that was all. Whereas his own face was visible in almost every scene. With occasional close-ups even.

Greg watched and watched. '2 girls 1 cup' had nothing on he and Jojo's lovemaking. This was '2 pervs 1 bed.'

Aunt Grace was once again seated behind him and running her fingers through his hair. This time she had something of the smell of the clinic about her, a cold sterility that added a horrible ambience to the scenario. Once again, he didn't look at her. He'd not looked at her since she'd clicked on the video.

"You're quite the stud, Greg," she said. "I wonder what dear little Debbie will think when she sees this. Ha ha. Oh, but I already know what she'll think: She'll think you're a pervert who hooks up with equally-perverted women to poop on them. You wouldn't want sweet and squeaky-clean Debbie to think that about you now, would you?"

His mouth was dry. He had no reply. Oh no, Debbie definitely mustn't see this!

The scat video ended with two scenes from the previous 'kitchen' video: A thirty-second collage of Greg masturbating into the blender, followed by Detective Anderson drinking his smoothie and licking his lips.

He got it. Jojo had made her point.

"I don't get it," he groaned. "Why'd she do this to me? She promised."

"I'll tell you why: a hundred grand. She was short the money for her sisters' band's *Aunt Grace* promo video—and I offered to make up the difference. As much as she enjoyed having sex with you, there was no chance she'd say no."

"Then it was all a con?"

Aunt Grace cackled like a witch. "No, no. She really does have that pathetic poop hangup. You saw her bedroom, all the incense and the rubber sheets. I think sometimes she even eats the stuff. Anyway, it merely played into my plan for *us*. Think about it—all I need do is show anyone I want this file and you're ruined for life."

Greg didn't dispute it. If the semen smoothies videos had been poison for his career plans, this scat film was total dynamite. If this ever got out online, merely changing his name wouldn't suffice. He'd need plastic surgery.

"And for the record," Aunt Grace said with a touch of pity in her voice, "she's not faking orgasm. You really did get her off, multiple times at that."

"That's supposed to make me feel better? That I helped some nutty Asian-American hybrid bitch get her rocks off?"

"Now don't get racist, dear. You should be proud you're such a satisfying lover. Kiki says Jojo might even be falling for you."

Now he turned to stare at her. "Just stop it already! I don't wanna hear that crap!" He pointed at the video. "Jojo Kim is nuts. The bitch is nuts, and you . . . you . . . why, you're nuts too. I get it now: all this is because you're as nuts as Jojo is."

She faked a swipe at his crotch. "Only for *your* nuts, dear."

Greg sagged. He now realized something else: Right from the start of their conversation, his aunt's voice had been completely matter-of-fact. Nothing she'd so far said had conveyed an air of either malice or triumph to him. She was neither vindictive nor gloating. This bothered him greatly: it made the individual aspects of his problem seem not to sum up into a coherent whole anymore.

His facial expression now reflected his confusion. "But what exactly is all this about? I don't get it, Aunt Grace. Why in the world would you pay Jojo Kim a hundred grand to make a poop video of me? Why?"

She got up from the arm of the chair and walked around in front of him, to stand behind the stool on which her laptop rested. "Oh, Jojo did a whole lot more for me than that, dear. I owe her more than you can possibly imagine."

Greg felt tired. This just got more and more convoluted. First Aunt Grace was paying Jojo; now she was *indebted* to Jojo. By now, the poop video didn't really matter anymore. He thought he'd escaped, but he'd failed. That was it. His aunt was crazy, that was all. She'd never dare show the film to anyone; his mother would kill her if she did. That was for certain.

But the mystery remained: what was all this about?

"What the hell are you talking about?" he asked in a tired voice.

She backed away from the laptop, finally sitting on a couch. She picked up her purse, flung there when they'd first entered the living room. She opened her purse and smiled at its contents.

"Aunt Grace, answer me, will you?"

She looked over at him. "Forgive me, dear, I'm just so happy. It's hard to express myself."

"What are you talking about? What is all this about? What did Jojo Kim help you out with that you're so delighted about?"

She took a moment to compose herself. "I'm pregnant, Greg. And you're the father."

"Pregnant? . . . Father? . . . You're crazy. I never slept with you. I wouldn't . . . you're family."

She smiled serenely. "The condom you were wearing in the video." She tapped her belly. "Here's where the semen it contained ended up. IVF."

Greg goggled at her. "IVF?"

"Yes. I'm about to be a test-tube mommy. You're about to be a daddy."

He had no idea what to think now. He felt like the living room was caving in on him. He felt like his mind was caving in on itself. He felt like he was standing on a skyscraper and looking down into Hell's abyss. Total vertigo. Every feeling of despair imaginable assaulted him. It felt like he'd faint from shock. Thinking was impossible; all he could do was feel . . . feel intense horror, as though he was witnessing the end of the world.

"Everything was planned out then, beforehand?" he asked. "That's what you were really doing in the clinic, wasn't it?"

She nodded. "I've been taking fertility treatments for six months. Jojo's such a sweet kid, you know. She even offered me some of her own eggs if mine proved to be too old for fertilization—that does happen sometimes. But I didn't need them, everything worked out fine. You came, Kiki transported the come to the clinic, and now I'm pregnant with twins."

"Twins?"

She grinned. "If they're a boy and a girl, I'll call them Doug and Barbara Madden . . ."

It was her smile that did it. Greg still wasn't really thinking; his mind still found no logic in what was happening. But Aunt Grace's smile reminded him of a bully. That bully in grade school who took your candy and smugly dared you to do something about it. And then gave you a bloody nose when you did.

Oh, God, was he so going to do something about it! He'd kill this evil scheming witch who seemed to have no other human function than causing him intense misery.

He leapt up and charged at her.

Then he stopped. Reason halted his charge just in time or he had no idea what might have happened next. Aunt Grace was pointing a gun at him. A small ladylike revolver.

She gestured at him with the gun. "Sit down. I'll shoot you if I have to. I love you more than I love anyone else in this world, Greg, but I'll shoot you if you make me."

Greg believed her. She had a crazy look in her eyes. He raised his hands, stepped back, and sat down again.

"Good," she said. "Good. Just plump your ass down there." Her voice was firm, but not unsympathetic. "Listen, I know you don't believe me, but I didn't do this to hurt you. I didn't do any of it to hurt you." Still holding the gun covering him, she dabbed tears from her eyes with a Kleenex. "You've no idea how much I've wanted this baby . . . these babies." She looked at him firmly. "These kids are the one thing I've never had, and I'm having them now." Her eyes were still wet. She continued dabbing at them with the tissue.

"But why me?" Greg asked. "You're my goddamn aunt, for crying out loud. Why couldn't you just look for a sperm donor?"

"You're the only one it could be, Greg. The only one." Then she really began crying.

Greg watched her. Her gun was still pointed at him, but she was mostly concerned with wiping her eyes now. He could rush her, take the gun away from her. But then what? He couldn't kill her. She was just a lonely old woman who'd just fucked up his life. It wasn't worth it. None of this was worth it.

Aunt Grace got a firm hold of herself again. This time, when she spoke, her words carried deep conviction. She no longer sought either his understanding or sympathy: "It's done, dear, and that's that. I'm pregnant with *our* children. And I'm having them." She grinned cattily. "And don't even think of praying I have a miscarriage. If I do . . . there's enough of your come on ice for fifty more attempts." She let the implications of that sink in. "Wow, you must really like Jojo to ejaculate that much."

"Yeah, yeah." Greg figured he'd just kill himself once this discussion was over. "So what now?"

"Well, now we're right back where we were when we stepped in through the front door: you go into the kitchen, unzip your pants, get your thing out, and make mamma a nice cool drink . . . with, like I said, *everything* in it." She pointed to her laptop. "Relax, dear. I'm not going to start blackmailing you. That video is simply my insurance against you making a fuss over the paternity of my pregnancy. As long as you keep your mouth shut, it'll never see the light of day. That's a promise."

"Erase it."

"Not till our kids are in high school. Oh yes, and one more thing."

Our kids. Shit! "What's that?"

"From now on you work for me. No questions asked. I'll up your salary a bit. You can have forty-five grand a year. And a brand new car."

"I'm already working with Tommy Collins in the Rectifiers."

"Quit then."

"No."

"Do it—Okay, I'll pay you fifty grand per annum. I'll pay Tommy off too—give him five grand to let you leave. I can't imagine what he needs you for anyway."

Greg decided it really didn't matter. Nothing mattered anymore. "Yes, alright, *mother*. You haven't just got my balls in your hands now, you've got my poop on them too."

She found that immensely funny and began laughing.

Greg got up and shambled towards the kitchen. He dragged foot after foot. There was nothing else he could do.

I've gotten my aunt pregnant! he thought in horror. *I've gotten Aunt Grace pregnant!*

He turned at the kitchen door. A thought had just occurred to him. A horrible thought.

"Aunt Grace, are you still, you know . . . a virgin?" He knew she didn't currently have a man, but had she *never* had a man? His mother had subtly hinted as much, but was it true? Did such women—unfucked, hymen-still-intact old maids—still actually exist in this sexually liberated day and age?

"That's quite an impertinent question, young man."

"Impertinent? That's a funny joke. You're pregnant for me and *I'm* being impertinent?" Then his voice softened slightly. "Answer the question, please?"

She waved the revolver at him. "Technically, yes . . . I am a virgin. Why?"

"Don't even *think* of calling yourself the Virgin Grace," Greg said with feeling. "If you do, guns or not, I'll kill you. All the cops in this world won't stop me."

Leaving her to muse on that, he stepped into the kitchen.

Her voice shortly came to him in there: "Hey, and remember, darling son, leave the kitchen door open—I've already seen what you're hiding. I promise not to come in and peek!" She began laughing.

She was just rubbing in her victory. Either that or she'd forgotten she'd already ordered him to leave the kitchen door unlocked while making her drinks. It wasn't a big deal anyway. What would she want next though? Would she insist on watching him ejaculate into the blender, as part of his duties as her employee? And if she did, what would be so horrible about that? Hadn't he already gotten her pregnant? What could ever be more gross than impregnating your mother's older sister?

He could hear her laughing out there while the scat video replayed. Shit!

He got to work making her smoothie. He wished, wished, really wished now that he'd not, in the throes of perceived victory, thrown out all that come he'd frozen while she'd been in hospital. If he still had those he could just defrost some of it for her.

While dicing apples and bananas, he pondered his fall from grace. His fall from *Grace*. That was a mean joke. A simple (though very ill-advised) prank had led him to . . . and then to . . . and further on to . . . and finally to becoming both a scat-porn star and a soon-to-be-father.

Worst still, he had to work for her. She'd now be around him twenty-four hours a day.

His future was in shambles. The fantastic Rectifiers job was already finished, over before it had really begun. Even without financial inducement, Tommy Collins would never refuse Aunt Grace anything.

The soon-to-arrive babies were the last straw. Greg winced as he considered them. Aunt Grace was completely loony tunes. Once the children grew up, someone—possibly even his mother—was certain to notice how much they looked like him.

Killing himself suddenly seemed like a really good idea. No, it'd be a better idea to simply kill *her*. Then himself. No, just her. But no, he couldn't kill her—she was pregnant. One didn't shoot pregnant women. But the children were going to be incestuous, inbred . . . And what if he did marry Debbie and one day she noticed how much like him Aunt Grace's twins looked. That would completely ruin his marriage, wouldn't it? Yes, he really should just kill them both now and save on all the bother later. His mother wouldn't mind too much; she'd likely inherit all of Aunt Grace's money then. But no, killing aunts—even evil manipulative ones—was wrong . . . But so was ruining nephews' lives. Shit! Shit! SHIT!

He finished cutting the fruits and loaded them into the blender. He was anticipating a flash of inspiration to save him. None came.

On his phone, he pulled up a scene from *Asa Akira is Insatiable*. He found his video choice fitting: in her own way, Aunt Grace was also insatiable. She was committed to leeching him of his essence forever.

By the time she died (if she ever did), Greg was certain that there'd be so little left of him that the undertaker might as well bury them both together.

He'd just gotten his penis out when the front doorbell rang.

"Oh, shoot—it's Anderson!" Aunt Grace yelped from the living room. "I forgot he said he was coming over. Greg! Greg, you sweet young thing, please put your manhood back in your pants and let the detective in!"

Greg was glad for the respite. He put his penis away again, put Asa Akira away, washed his hands, and made his way to the front door.

***

"Hi, sir."

Anderson was carrying a bouquet of roses.

"Hello, son." Anderson extended his hand for a shake. Greg shook his hand. There was something unfamiliar in Anderson's gaze today. The old cop was normally taciturn, but right now he seemed pleased. He was half-smiling, which on Anderson was as bad as a frown.

Greg felt a strong vibe of intimidation. He couldn't help how he felt. His old resentment against the man returned. No, he didn't like Anderson. He doubted anyone did, except for his aunt and the man's gorgeous work partner.

Anderson stepped into the house. Greg looked behind him for his car. The cop didn't seem to have driven over. He wondered where Detective Futana was now.

He followed Anderson through the house. The man's bouquet of roses had a nice smell.

Greg decided to make the most of his temporary reprieve. He'd put the unblended smoothie in the fridge and go out, walk next door to Debbie's house. Or better still, he'd first call Tommy Collins, then head over to Tommy's with Debbie. Debbie could either drive them there or they'd just Uber a ride.

Tommy had said Dave was dead, but hadn't given any details over the phone. He'd however cancelled that Saturday's job, saying his current state of mind couldn't handle it.

He sounded really upset. I'd best go check up on him and find out exactly how Dave died. And besides, I need my driver's license back.

Greg was about turning off into the kitchen when Anderson said, "No, son, come along with me to see your aunt. I wanna discuss something with you."

Greg looked bemused. "What about?"

Anderson nodded towards the living room. "Just come on, son. Won't take too long."

Greg followed him.

"Oh, Tom, how sweet of you," Aunt Grace gushed on being presented with the roses. "Oh, they're just lovely." They kissed cheeks and hugged, then Aunt Grace smiled at Greg. "Be a darling and fetch a vase for the flowers, will you?"

Greg brought over a porcelain jar from a corner.

When the roses were in the jar and everyone was seated, Anderson handed Greg his wallet. "Hope nothing's missing. I checked, but we were in a hurry."

Greg looked at the detective with dismay on his face. "Sir . . . sir . . . where'd you get this?"

Anderson shrugged. "Where d'you think? Where'd you forget it?"

A thousand scenarios played through Greg's mind, each one uglier than the last: *Oh, we're fucked. Big bad cop here knows what we did. Me and Tommy and Allie are all going to jail forever!* The only plus side of that was no more smoothie blackmail. *But there'll be no more Debbie at the window either . . .*

"Relax, son," Anderson said gruffly, correctly reading the young man's panic. "I ain't here to arrest ya. I'm here to thank you actually, and ask you a couple of questions, that's all." Then he smiled at Aunt Grace. "And to see your aunt, who just looks extra-lovely today. "Yeah, Gracie, I dunno what they fed you in that clinic but it's done wonders for your looks. You seem so radiant."

Aunt Grace had been admiring her roses and looking pretty and listening. Now she blushed. "Oh, it's just those special vitamins." Then she looked confused and worried. "But, Tom, I don't understand—what's going on? Greg hasn't done anything wrong, has he?"

Anderson smiled his ugly smile. "On the contrary, Gracie. Greg here, and I think Tommy Collins too"—he paused to give Greg an enquiring look that was replied with a nod—"have just done the entire state of Massachusetts a great service."

"What did they do?" Aunt Grace enquired breathlessly. "Tell me, Tom. All along you've been so I-Spy about all this. I really want to know."

"Oh, I can't tell you—I wasn't there to see it happen. That's the sad part about the whole thing: I really wish I'd watched it go down. But you can ask your nephew later if you like. But if you do"—another glance at Greg—"be certain to both keep mum about it all."

"Oh, I'll keep your secrets!" Aunt Grace looked at Greg. "You'll tell me later what it was all about, dear?"

He frowned then nodded. He'd just make up some tall tale for her. She already had too much leverage over him; he wasn't about adding a murder confession to that. For all he knew Jojo Kim might have their living room wired with cameras too.

"Oh, alright then." Aunt Grace went back to staring at her roses.

"Now concerning those questions . . ."

Greg nodded at Anderson. "Yeah, go on."

"Tell me, son: who died there at the farmhouse—was it both Brian and Jesse McArthur? Now don't lie to me—I ain't here to either arrest you or take a confession. I got personal reasons for knowing, that's all."

Greg nodded. "Yes, it was both of the McArthur brothers there."

"Anyone else was there besides you and Tommy?"

Greg shook his head. "Just Tommy's girlfriend. But she didn't get involved in anything."

Anderson smiled cruelly. "Alright then. Now, forensics have already identified the dead guy in the side room with the German shepherds as Jesse. They had his fingerprints for that. But that skeleton *inside* the creature . . . how big was that goddam worm anyhow when it was alive?"

Greg noted the *past tense* Anderson used. He spread his hands three feet across. "Really, really big, sir."

"And it was a worm, not some giant snake?"

"Yes. It was a worm. I've never seen anything like that before, and I hope never to again. It kept making slime like it was a Jell-O factory."

"And that skeleton we found in it? That was Brian?"

"Yeah. He accidentally fell into the pool and it got him."

"*Accidentally?* C'mon, son, don't lie to me now."

Greg shrugged, then smiled. "Aw well, Tommy and I kinda helped him lose his balance. The guy was a real jerk, you know . . ."

Anderson grinned broadly. His grin expressed a deep satisfaction that Greg sensed had little to do with law enforcement.

"Alright then, that's all I wanted to know. Just know, Greg, that the Bay State is indebted to you three for helping us wrap up the Wet Bones case."

Aunt Grace had been following their discussion with little comprehension. Now she asked, "Wet bones? Oh, is that what this is all about? It was all over CNN this morning: that crazy redhead with the human body parts in her freezer. Is that what you're both discussing?"

"Not really," Greg quickly replied, though unsure what she was talking about. "Don't worry, auntie, I'll fill you in later."

Aunt Grace said, "Now that that's all out of the way, Tom, how about a smoothie? Greg was just about making me one of his specials."

"Well, I don't mind if I do," Anderson replied.

Aunt Grace winked at Greg. "How about it, darling? A delicious special for Tom as well."

Greg suddenly saw the bars of a jail cell crashing down in front of him. What was it with this crazy old woman? He shook his palms at his aunt, then leapt to his feet. "Hell no! I'm going out. I've got a date with Deb!"

He hurried towards the front door. Behind him, he heard them discussing his abrupt departure:

"What the hell's the matter with him? I ain't planning on arresting him."

"Ah, kids these days. No damn respect at all for their elders. Don't worry, Tom, *I'll* make you a smoothie instead. I still don't know what the kid puts in his though. I think it's some kinda Jamaican spice . . ."

"No, don't worry yourself. You just got back from the hospital. You should be resting. Besides, I'm expecting Laurie to come pick me up from here. She'll be arriving any minute now. We're both expected back at the station. The Captain wants some first-hand info from us."

"Oh, but I insist. I've missed doing this."

"Okay, but only if I give you a hand."

Greg had by now reached the front door. He opened it.

"Hi, baby!" a brightly grinning Debbie waved and stepped inside.

CHAPTER 47

Greg & Debbie

Greg stared at his girlfriend, framed there in the doorway. If anything, Debbie looked prettier than ever.

"I was just coming over to your house," he whispered urgently. "I gotta get out of here."

She pushed the door shut behind her, then placed both her hands on his chest and pushed him back towards the hallway.

"No, no," she whispered back. "My mom's cleaning; she's got everywhere turned both upside-down and inside-out. If I go back home, she's gonna make me help her, and right now I'm so not in the mood to play housemaid."

"Let's go have a drink then."

Grinning, Debbie shook her head. Then she whispered in his ear: "Later. I'm horny. I wanna bird-watch right now. Let's go!"

Then she was steering him back through the living room. His aunt and Detective Anderson were just entering the kitchen. Debbie yelled hurried greetings to them and then rushed Greg up the stairs and into his bedroom.

***

"Dammit!" Debbie gasped once she'd locked the bedroom door behind them, "I've been wanting to come fuck you all morning, but my mom insisted I help her prune the bushes in our garden."

He stared at her mournfully. Seeing her, he recalled his problems.

She's so innocent and pretty, so full of bubbles and romance. And I love her so much! How the hell could I mess up our future like I did? Oh, damn Jojo Kim!

Greg felt like killing Jojo. But he knew that he wouldn't.

Debbie loosened his pants and got his penis out. "You've no idea how much I need this thing inside me!"

She knelt and began sucking on him.

He wasn't in the mood. It took longer than usual for him to get hard. She noticed. She looked up at him with worried eyes. "Darling, are you okay?"

He smiled down at her. "I'm just having a crap day so far. My aunt's already back to her old tricks."

She smiled. "Relax, baby. Let me improve the day for you."

He relaxed, pulling his shirt off while she resumed sucking on him. This time it went much better. He was soon hard. Very hard and throbbing in anticipation of sweet release into her body. She was right, of course: sex *would* relax him.

He stepped out of his pants. Debbie kicked off her shoes and dropped her pants. She was left braless beneath her blue Kimchi Chocolate Stereo T-shirt, the front of which featured Lulu Kim seemingly eating her microphone.

Once Greg was completely naked, Debbie put a condom on him, pulled him to the window, leaned out of it, and pulled the curtains shut between them.

They began making love. "Do it deep, baby," Debbie grunted. "I want to feel you right inside my belly."

He grunted back. He relaxed and really got into it, gripping her hips firmly and thrusting hard between her sweet and tight backside. Her sex welcomed him happily.

"Ooh, there's a bird," she yelped excitedly after a while. "I'm not sure what sort it is though. It's black and has a long horrible beak."

"Maybe a crow," Greg gasped back. "They're generally black and horrible looking."

"They're also supposed to be harbingers of bad omen," Debbie said. Her voice was classroom-teacher cool, though her legs were trembling against his and she was standing up on tiptoes to get more of him inside her and as deep as possible too. Greg wondered how she managed it: pretending such calm while *he* felt he was dying from the excruciating pleasure of her juicy vagina.

"Hey, there's two more crows up there. I hope I'm not going to fall out of the window today. You're doing me disgustingly hard."

This was a warning to Greg. Nothing more could possibly go worse for him today than Debbie also toppling from the window. He relaxed the force of his thrusts a bit.

"Hey, don't slack," she instantly complained. "I was only teasing." She began slamming her buttocks forcefully back at him. Now their bodies smacked loudly together each time he went deep into her. She'd never been this forceful before. He enjoyed it. It was just, as always, so weird with the top half of their bodies separated by the curtains.

"Hey, baby, when we're done here at the window, I wanna go check out that tattoo parlor again, okay? Like I said, I can't go home yet."

He grunted an assent. Just this once, he wished she'd stop talking. He was close to coming and really desired to grab her succulent breasts and squeeze them. But of course, he couldn't do this because someone might see them from the road.

"Hey, Detective Anderson, you leaving already?" Debbie shouted down.

"Yeah! Laurie's here!"

"Okay, sir, have a nice day capturing those wicked criminals and keepin' us all safe."

"I will, girl!"

Debbie leaned forward to wave to the departing Anderson.

Then, all of a sudden, she overbalanced and was falling out of the window.

Greg reacted just in time. He caught hold of her hair and shoulders, and pulled her back to safety.

"Wow, that was close," she giggled.

"You okay up there?" Anderson called from downstairs.

"Yeah, I'm fine, sir, thanks. I just got carried away staring at those crows." She half-turned to whisper back at Greg, "Don't stop, baby, I'm almost here."

Greg carried on. All of a sudden he felt tired. That almost-fall of hers had been too damn close. And with Anderson downstairs!

Still, he thought philosophically, *the sooner she comes, the sooner she'll leave the window.*

Keeping a firm grip on her hips, he resumed thrusting away. Thankfully, he was almost here himself now. He'd spurt any moment.

Then he'd keep the semen-filled condom for Aunt Grace's next smoothie. Emission accomplished for today.

"Oh yeah, baby," Debbie groaned, "fuck me hard like that!"

Suddenly Greg heard a loud noise in his head. A noise like a blowing wind.

Simultaneously, Debbie overbalanced again. Once more, as though she'd been taking suicide lessons since the last time he'd seen her, she went out through the window. This time, however, Greg was more alert. He reached through the curtains and grabbed her breasts to steady her. He didn't care who saw him do so.

Anderson was still down there, but he was staring out towards the road. Detective Futana had just pulled into the drive in their unmarked squad car.

Greg heaved a sigh of relief as he got Debbie back inside.

"Wow, this is so exciting," Debbie gasped as she righted herself again. She gripped the windowsill to steady herself. "Okay, darling, time to finish this lovemaking off."

There and then, Greg decided that what they'd do from now on would be to lower the window sash so it was pressing on Debbie's waist. That way, even if she began spilling out of the window, her buttocks wouldn't get through the opening.

But, before he could put this new plan into effect, something inexplicable happened: As Debbie leaned forward again, Greg felt a force—it felt like a cold pair of hands—grab hold of their legs and tip them out of the bedroom window.

He fought to remain on his feet and on the floor, but it wasn't happening.

What!? He looked desperately behind him, but there was no one else in the bedroom. Yet he could feel it—a cold pair of hands like an arctic wind made flesh—lifting them both up and flinging them outside with great force.

"Oh God!" Debbie moaned. "I'm coming! I'm flying! It's incredible!"

They were both airborne for two seconds then crashed down hard in the front yard.

Greg hit the ground shoulder first. He felt a jarring moment of pain all through his body.

Then . . .

For a crazy split second, Greg felt something like an immense, freezing hand first grab, then twist his neck. He both heard a horrible '**krakkKK**' in his neck and felt a shifting of his neck bones.

Then he was lying on the ground unable to feel anything, unable even to move his hands to wipe the tears from his eyes. He couldn't even turn his head or speak. All he could do was stare at the sky and watch several crows circle like vultures.

What the hell just happened to us?

He sensed Debbie beside him, her body unmoving. He instantly began worrying about her instead of himself. Was she dead? Oh no! That would be just horrible. *Don't die, baby, I love you!* He forgot his own dilemma. He focused on Debbie. With all his mental strength he willed her to be alright.

Then, as footsteps came running over, he heard Debbie moving.

"Wow, that was intense!" she groaned beside him. "I've never come that hard before in my life!"

That said, she slowly got to her feet. He followed her with his eyes. She was dizzy and staggering.

He heard voices: "Grab her, Tom. She's about to fall over again!"

"I got her! Laurie, I don't like the way he's lying there. He's not moving."

"Call 911, man! I'll get Gracie!"

There was the sound of footsteps running off towards the house. Greg could hear Debbie moaning. He managed to turn his head slightly. Debbie was unhurt. She'd skinned her right elbow but that seemed to be all. Unconcerned that she was naked from the waist down, she was gripping Anderson tightly.

Debbie was staring down at him in fright. It was only now that the full horror of Greg's situation dawned on him. *I'm paralyzed from the neck down! That thing—whatever it was—broke my neck! I'm quadriplegic! . . . I'm . . . !*

To keep himself from freaking out, he forced his mind over the strange events that had led him to his current state. Those cold hands that had flung them both out of the window. Those wind-like hands that hadn't been there. Then those same cold hands wrapping themselves around his throat and twisting . . .

What just happened to us?

Anderson, meanwhile, was on the phone: "Is that 911? Detective Thomas Anderson calling. . . . Yeah, *the* Tom Anderson. Alright, listen up, I got a bad situation here . . . I need an ambulance pronto! Tell the driver to drive at breakneck speed. . . . Two kids fell out of a window. 190 Corey Street. It's just a second floor window, but the pair of them were joined at the hip. . . . What do I mean—joined at the hip? They were fucking—that's what I goddamn mean, woman. Just send the damn ambulance over. . . . The girl's okay. She's back on her feet, just looks stunned. I dunno, she may or may not have a concussion. . . . The boy though looks to have broken his neck. It's set at an odd angle, and there's a little bit of wet bone sticking out down near the clavicle. . . . Nah, he ain't moving at all. He's alive though: his eyes are still blinking and he's moving his lips, but he can't talk. . . ."

A sudden scream erupted from the direction of the house. Greg knew that was Aunt Grace.

"Tom, she's fainted," Detective Futana's voice came floating over.

"I can see that. Hold on to her; I'll come give you a hand with getting her back inside."

There was a pause, then Greg heard Anderson asking Debbie: "Alright, girl, do you feel okay enough to stay with Greg for a few minutes while we carry Gracie inside? The ambulance'll be here any minute now."

"Yes, I'll manage," Debbie replied. "But I need some clothes. I can't go to the hospital with him looking like this."

"You're a strong young woman," Anderson replied her. "I like that. Once we've got Gracie inside, I'll hurry back out so you can run in and get dressed."

Then Anderson was gone and it was just Greg and Debbie left in the front yard.

Fleetingly, Greg prayed that his aunt's faint would lead to a miscarriage. But he knew it wouldn't ever happen.

Lacking further distractions, his mind returned to his own miserable predicament: *I'm frigging paralyzed from the neck down!*

Then Debbie was kneeling beside him. She was staring down at him with a smile on her face. A cold, cold smile that didn't fit in at all with their current situation.

"Mmmmmmmm!" He tried, but couldn't talk. Something was stuck in his vocal cords. Over on his right he could hear the detectives moving his aunt back into the house.

"Easy, Laurie," Anderson was saying, "We don't want anything to happen to Gracie too."

"You're in love with her, man—just admit it and propose!" Futana's statement was whispered but it carried across to Greg's ears.

"Shush, woman, the kids might hear you!"

"And see, you're so lucky to have me, aren't you?"

"What the hell you talking about?"

"I'm gender-flexible, Tom. When you two say 'I do,' I can be either your best man or her chief bridesmaid, which would you prefer?"

"Don't drop her, Laurie, or I'll . . . !"

Their voices faded away through the front door. Greg was left alone with his confusion and his oddly unsympathetic-seeming girlfriend.

"Ha ha ha!" Debbie said. "How do you feel now, asshole? How's it feel to be paralyzed forever?"

Greg lay there feeling bewildered. He stared up at her beaming face. She was gloating at him.

Debbie went on: "I got my tattoo, baby. I want you to see it." She spread her thighs and leaned over him, till he could smell her vagina with its musky scent of orgasmic afterglow.

He saw her new tattoo. It was an inverted 'A' high up on her left thigh.

His mind instantly made the connection: *She's got the same tattoo as Jesse and Brian McArthur had!*

She was laughing down at him now. Gently, so no one passing by the house would hear. "Yes, stupid, I'm *also* a member of the Abyss Club. This is payback for what you, Tommy, and that stupid Allie did to Boku Ke Houzz. That hand that flung us out of the bedroom was summoned by me. It's the Graveyard Wind. It broke your neck too, exactly how I instructed it to."

Why? The silent question formed on Greg's lips.

Debbie bent lower and whispered in his ear: "I'll tell you *why!* Because it took us ten good years to bring the demon-worm in from the cold Outerness of SADE's Enlightenment zone, and you three jerks went and killed it. Now we have to start again from scratch."

Unable to speak, Greg studied her face instead.

Then, all at once, a shocking transformation came over Debbie. Gone completely was the girl he loved; in her place he was staring at a wizened hag.

The hag's eyes were as black as a starless night and colder than winter solstice. Her teeth looked like little bits of coal. She had a long nose with horrid purple moles on it. Long coarse white hairs sprouted both from the moles and from her nostrils. The hair on her head was gray with age and matted with dirt and grease. Her gray skin resembled cracked tombstone marble. A stench of mildew rained on him from her as if he'd been shoved into an ancient crypt.

Her expression was one of intense sadistic satisfaction.

The hag cackled down at him. Her breath reeked like poisoned apples. Its noisome odor had him close to retching. "Yes, you bastards killed Boku Ke Houzz. You shattered its head. For all its powers, the demon had a delicate skull. You cracked its skull open. After its last meal its brains leaked out and it died." She stroked Greg's cheek with a knobbly old hand that resembled a monstrous chicken's foot. "And you're *all* going to pay for that. All of you will pay! You're already paying, baby. You have your entire quadriplegic life ahead of you to regret your stupidity. Ha ha ha ha ha!"

Then, just as suddenly as she'd appeared, the terrible old woman was gone. Greg was staring at the normal Debbie again. Beautiful sweet Debbie who'd just informed him that she was really a nasty witch.

Simultaneously, Greg heard both Detective Anderson's returning footsteps and the arriving ambulance siren.

Debbie now began weeping a river of crocodile tears. "Oh, Greg! Oh, baby, please, please, please be okay!"

"You'd better go dress up properly," Anderson told her gently. "Then you can accompany him to the hospital."

Still weeping fake tears, Debbie ran off to the house.

Anderson bent over Greg. "Just hang in there, son. I know this looks real bad for you, but nowadays the doctors can work some real miracles. So just try to be strong. Now c'mon, son, don't cry. Aw, don't you cry!"

But Greg couldn't help it. The tears just kept pouring from his eyes.

CHAPTER 48

Allie

Allie drove slowly back towards Dover. She was returning from the Lincourt Farm. (Allie, of course, didn't know that was the farm's actual name, she still thought of it as the McArthur brothers' place).

Allie had a whole lot on her mind. Most of it was bad.

Tommy Collins had been missing for two days now. Allie had taken the Rectifier's Toyota over to her sister's place to pick up a few things, and when she'd gotten back he was nowhere to be found. The front door had been open and nothing was in disarray, but Tommy had vanished.

That was crazy enough. But then there was the equally crazy matter of Greg breaking his neck and totaling his spinal cord.

She'd since spoken to Greg; he could talk now. She'd visited him at the hospital. What he'd told her there had chilled her to the marrow: a crazy tale about a coven of witches who were mad that they'd killed that giant worm in the McArthur brothers' barn. And equally as crazy, Greg's own girlfriend being one of the witches.

Allie believed Greg. Considering the strange nature of Tommy's disappearance, it would be silly not to. How else did a grown adult man vanish, leaving no sign, no trace of himself anywhere? And no one who'd seen him since either?

But of course, she and Greg had no way to prove any of this to anyone.

***

And now, the present:

With no idea of where else to search for her boyfriend, Allie had driven back out to the Lincourt Farm on the off chance that he might be there. She didn't expect him to be there. He no reason to be there. But she couldn't just sit at home biting her nails. She'd considered going to the police but her brother-in-law had cautioned against it, because of the nature of the Rectifiers' business. Giorgio had himself been calling around all of his mob contacts without success. Allie and Tommy hadn't yet told him about Dave's death. He'd likely learn the news for himself over the underground grapevine before long.

Allie still shivered when she thought about Dave's gangland execution.

And also about the aftermath: taking Black and White's blood-scribbled advice, she and Tommy had vacated the house an hour later.

Leaving the mess in the living room exactly how they'd found it, they'd driven out and ordered breakfast at a seafront diner. They'd sat there in the diner in horrified silence, staring at the rippling blue harbor water, both unable to eat, both unable to even compose their thoughts enough to talk to one another.

They'd returned home at noon. By that time, lo and behold, the house looked normal again. The blood on the living room wall had all been cleaned off. The wall itself had been repainted back to its previous ash color.

Except for the fact that they'd both known they wouldn't ever be seeing Dave Fontaine again (and that the paint on the front living-room wall was still wet), Allie and Tommy could have written the morning's experience off as merely a bad dream.

And then Tommy himself vanished. Allie had at first wondered if maybe Mr. Velli had snatched Tommy too, but after a little consideration, she'd realized that couldn't be the case. She and Tommy had both been asleep when the 'Dave' package had been delivered. It would have been easy enough for Black and White to slit both their throats then. (Allie hadn't even *seen* Black and White yet, but Tommy's description of the loony interracial pair was upsetting and unsettling enough.)

So no, Tommy hadn't been snatched by a vengeful mob kingpin. Her brother-in-law had confirmed as much. Giorgio said word on the street was clear on that fact: Marko was as perplexed by Tommy's vanishing as anyone else. In fact, because of his close relationship with Tommy's dad Vince Collins, Marko Velli had his own people out looking for Tommy. Marko didn't want Vince thinking *he'd* ordered a hit on the kid.

So, unable to ask the police to do something, Allie felt compelled to carry out her own search. And her suspicions quickly turned to the Lincourt Farm. Maybe (hoping against hope), just maybe, Tommy had driven out there to check on the dogs . . . and gotten wounded. She remembered how abruptly and easily Dave had broken his ankle.

But even as she drove out to the old farm, she hadn't actually believed her own reasoning. If Tommy was hurt, he'd have phoned her. And he couldn't have *driven* out to the farm anyway. Not without a ride: the Rectifier's RAM pickup truck was still parked out front . . . and she'd taken their Toyota Camry over to Giorgio's.

Still, she'd headed out to the Lincourt Farm.

***

However, on arriving at the old farm, Allie had found a massive police presence there: flashing lights, patrol cars, ambulances and agitated men and women in raincoats (it was drizzling), along with seemingly a zillion feet of yellow 'Crime Scene' tape stretched across everything in sight.

She'd driven past without stopping. Nothing doing here then. Greg had already filled her in on Detective Anderson handing him back his missing wallet, so she knew that the police would be cleaning house down there. (She figured it was a good thing she was in the RAM: driving a pickup truck was much less suspicious out here in Nowhereland.)

Greg had said the witches had promised revenge on she and Tommy as well.

So the coven must have abducted Tommy. Which left just herself, Allie.

She'd now arrived in the town of Auburn. She parked outside a café. She sat in the pickup for a few minutes, just thinking; trying to come up with a plan of action.

After a while she flipped open the glove compartment. She nodded grimly at the gun there. The gun was her sister's—a small Ruger 9mm; Giorgio wanted Chloe armed whenever he wasn't home. Allie hadn't yet told her sister she'd borrowed her pistol. Sure, she'd return it. She'd return it once she got a licensed weapon of her own.

But for the moment . . .

Since Tommy's vanishing, Allie had suspected someone was stalking her. She'd not seen anyone, of course, but she kept getting a niggling feeling at the back of her neck like someone was watching her, just waiting for the right moment to snatch her away into a horrible overwhelming darkness from which she'd never return. It was a terrifying feeling, one that almost turned her heart to water.

True, her worries might just be her imagination overworking, but once bitten by a snake, even the most innocent piece of rope got the complete suspicion treatment. After what had happened to Greg, Allie wasn't taking any chances. She didn't want to wind up like he had—unable to move his arms and legs, trapped in a wheelchair for the rest of his life. At least his aunt was rich. Greg definitely wouldn't lack for anything, but that was an utterly shitty fate for anyone to suffer.

And for what reason? Because some crazies are angry that I killed their demon worm? How was I supposed to know that its skull was so fragile?

The rain had stopped. Allie slipped the gun into her handbag. Then she entered the café and bought a coffee.

While drinking her coffee, she thought grimly. She was very frightened, but at the same time determined not to go under. Her courage surprised her. She had no idea what the Abyss Club—that was the name Greg's girlfriend had called them—were going to try with her, but she wasn't about lying down for them to have their Satanist way.

No, I'll give them the fight of their lives.

And she was determined to find Tommy and get him back too.

A man and woman sat down at the next table. She looked over at them. They smiled at her and nodded. She smiled back. They seemed normal enough; an everyday couple having lunch.

But that's the problem, isn't it? Greg's evil girlfriend Debbie is the ultimate girlfriend-next-door. So I'm in danger from everyday folk . . . shit!

From what Greg had told her, the Abyss Club's members had a single guaranteed identifying mark—that upside-down 'A' tattoo both the McArthur siblings had shared. But the tattoo was usually hidden beneath clothes. Out of sight of the innocent and unwary. Still, it was something to watch out for.

She regarded the dining couple again. *What will I find if I pull your pants down, guys? Witchy signs on your behinds?*

It was a question with no answer. Neither there nor here.

She left her coffee unfinished. She left the café.

Once back in the truck, she watched the café for a moment. She wanted to be certain the 'nice' couple weren't following her. If they got up and came after her . . . She fingered the Ruger pistol—it was cold, just like that strange invisible hand Greg had described. She shivered as if that same spectral hand was touching her.

I'm going crazy, she thought. *I'm losing it!* She was determined not to crack up though. *That'll be playing right into their hands. And they're not getting me, no matter what!*

The café couple never even glanced her way.

She drove off. It began raining again, heavily now. She flicked on the wipers.

Approaching Dover, she began feeling better. She missed Tommy though. *If I could just be certain that he's okay, I'd be okay too.*

But deep in her heart she knew that wasn't the case. She didn't want to accept that she'd likely never see Tommy Collins again. Or that if she did, she'd likely wish he was dead instead.

This knowledge filled Allie with intense emotional pain. *Oh, I'd do anything to bring Tommy back to me.*

Her pain turned to anger. Her anger became determination. Determination became strength.

Allie sneered. She had a gun now. She wasn't anybody's prey. She wasn't playing sheep to their wolf. No, she wasn't lying meekly down and dying like some lamb on the chopping block. If they wanted her dead, they'd have to really work at it.

Greg had no idea what was coming. Neither did Tommy. But I do, and I'm ready!

Lightning split the sky ahead of her. A distant thunderclap followed. Allie drove through the rain, resolved to dare the encroaching darkness.

CHAPTER 49

Kimchi Chocolate Stereo & the Cow

How the cow, a prime piebald Holstein heifer, got up on the roof of Boston Chinatown's 16-story Quincy Tower took some explaining.

It was Manuela Costa's idea. Manuela, Dave Fontaine's singer ex, was assisting Jojo Kim with filming the video for *Reversed Sunset Cowgirls*, Kimchi Chocolate Stereo's next single.

"Since the song is about cowgirls, we can use a cow in it," she'd suggested.

"The song's about *fucking*," Kiki Kim enlightened her. "Reverse cowgirl's my favorite sex position."

The gorgeous Manuela took a drag on her cigarette. Her black face crinkled up in puzzlement. "Then why the 'Sunset' in the title, baby?"

" 'Cos the biatch loves fucking in the evening," Jojo explained. "She almost makes moo noises too."

"I still think it's a good idea," Manuela insisted.

"Hey, aren't cowgirls supposed to ride *horses?*" Lulu Kim asked, deadpan as ever. "Just sayin', ya know. We'll be filming up on a roof. I don't wanna get pitched off some crazy animal's back."

"Use a *cow*. It makes the point better. Besides, I think horses get vertigo. Beef is too dumb to be scared of heights."

"Oh."

The cow . . .

Reversed Sunset Cowgirls wasn't supposed to be the band's next single. That was meant to be *Aunt Grace*. But, since Greg's tragic accident, Aunt Grace had been in no condition whatsoever to star in her own rock video. And Jojo and the band really wanted her in it.

(Jojo considered it a miracle that Grace Barbanell hadn't suffered a miscarriage from the sheer shock of what had happened to her nephew. At the moment Aunt Grace was sedated around the clock.

345

For her part, Jojo really sympathized with Greg. He was a good kid. He'd been wonderful in bed too: so full of shit!)

So, until Aunt Grace felt better, the band decided to release another track off the new *Psychic Diva Apocalypse* CD as their single instead. One of the other single/video contenders was V.O.I.D (Vagina of Infinite Depth). This song was vetoed by Kiki, who believed Slasher had written it about her, though she loved the chorus: *She's such a deep lady, such a sweet lady. She sucks me inside her, like a vacuum cleaner.*

Long story short, they'd finally settled on *Reversed Sunset Cowgirls.*

And then Manuela suggested they rent a cow. She and the band had been up on the Quincy Tower's roof, accessing the location's suitability for filming .

"A cow? Up here on the Boston skyline?" Jojo protested. "No way. It'll look tacky as fuck."

"It'll look iconic, baby," Manuela insisted, gesturing around with her cigarette at the spread of Chinatown roofs. Directly north of them was the sprawling expanse of the Tufts Medical Center. Nearer by (right next to them but not immediately noticeable from this high up) was Chinatown's Wang YMCA. The Quincy Tower itself was mainly a residence for senior citizens. It was currently emptying for renovation, but a few of the hardier, more crotchety old tenants were yet to move to alternate dwellings.

Manuela had gone on: "Remember that dinosaur LP with the flying pig on the cover?—I don't remember the name of the band now, but my dad was really into them—well this will be on the same level as that."

Everyone finally agreed and a cow was ordered.

It was airlifted in by helicopter. Once on the roof, the cow was tethered to the door of the roof hut, given enough hay and food pellets to keep it happy, and forgotten by everyone.

Once the band had all their instruments set up and all the cameras, screens, and lights were in position, it was time to fetch the cow. The idea was to have Lulu Kim ride it while lip-synching the chorus: "Bump and grind, shake my hot behind, in rewind as the sun goes down!"

Manuela went to fetch the cow, which was lying by the roof hut chewing the cud.

"Ouch," she yelped a moment later. "It bit me!"

She showed everyone the bite. The cow hadn't drawn any blood but its blunt teeth had indented deeply in her palm.

"It damn hurts," she said. "Hey, someone, give me a hand?"

"Forget it," Jojo and her sisters replied, with Kiki (always the outspoken one of the trio) adding, "That thing is *your* idea, Manuela, *you* friggin' deal with it."

Manuela made another attempt to rouse the cow. This time everyone saw the sudden flare of anger in its bovine eyes as it snapped at her. She skittered back on her six-inch heels and glared back at it.

"That animal sure don't like you, baby," Kiki's boyfriend Slasher said. Laughing, he walked away to tune his guitars.

"Hey, hurry up over there!" Jojo called. "We need to make the most of the daylight! I want natural lighting in the animal shots!"

"It won't budge, baby! The damn thing hates me!"

"It likely thinks you look like the guy who butchered its mama for McDonalds."

"Try singing to it," Kiki suggested. "Animals like music." To make her point, she hit a few notes on her bass.

Manuela tried singing to the cow. This was worse. The moment the animal heard her sultry contralto voice, it went all tense. It began getting up. Problem was, it was clearly getting up to charge at Manuela and maybe butt her over the edge of the roof.

She stopped singing and the beast settled down to chew the cud again.

Finally, Lulu's boyfriend, the band's drummer Zombie Joe, agreed to herd the cow. Maybe the pot in Zombie's joint reminded the cow of sweet green pasture, or maybe it got the animal high, but whatever the cause, or the case, the cow got up and meekly followed Zombie Joe over to where the band was set up.

Everyone noted, however, that as it passed Manuela it tensed up again, and seemed to be making its mind up whether to charge her or not.

"Damn racist cow!" Manuela griped. "How come it's only the black woman you not like, huh? You from goddamn Mississippi or what?"

The cow relaxed and went quietly to where the drums were set up. It refused to leave Zombie Joe's side, however, so they set up a green screen to block it out.

"You know, darling," Jojo told Manuela, "I think you should just stay as far away from that animal as possible. I've never seen a cow look at anyone like that before. Not even in Disney movies."

Manuela sat in her provided director's chair and began analyzing the shadows behind the band.

"Hey, Jojo, we need to shift Zombie Joe a little. The sun's getting into his face."

"Don't bother. He looks dead anyway. I'll put a filter on him, space him out. He'll look better than Alice Cooper."

"Yeah, okay."

The video shoot began. A HD-cam-fitted drone circled overhead, recording a 360-degree aerial view of the scene.

The band mimed to the track several times to Jojo's satisfaction, then it was time to do the choruses with the cow. The screen was removed and the cow brought forward. The animal didn't seem too traumatized by the loudness of KCS's music.

Lulu Kim got up on the cow's back. She'd now changed from rock chick attire into pink cowgirl threads complete with pink ten-gallon hat. She was handed a microphone and began singing:

"Hey, hey, honey, I know this sounds funny,
But the sun is going down, so stop making that money,
And come back home already.
You know what I need you for, knock knock on my lower door.
I'm gonna ride you like a horse, rock and roll you some more."

At this point Jojo, Kiki, and band keyboardist Doll Face, all dressed in squaw attire and carrying bows and arrows, did a choreographed Indian war dance across the foreground, while singing background vocals:

"Bump and grind in rewind as the sun waves goodbye to another day . . .
Bump and grind, shake my hot behind, in rewind as the sun goes down!"

Manuela had helped the band with background vocals on the record. She was supposed to be in this part of the video, but seeing as the cow disliked her, it had been agreed that Jojo would substitute for her.

It was a good recording. Everyone could feel the solid metal vibe in the air. Dancing across the stage, Jojo felt it too. She was delighted. They were making a hit for sure, maybe even rock and roll history. This video was going to be watched to death on YouTube and elsewhere.

Even the cow seemed to get into it. One would almost think it was dancing to the music.

But then the damn thing started looking at Manuela Costa again.

And, focused as they were on recording Lulu and the cow, no one except Zombie Joe noticed that Manuela was making some weird gestures with her hands. Zombie Joe was also the only person to notice Manuela's eyes flare up suddenly like there was fire burning in them. Zombie shrugged and slammed his toms extra-hard.

And only Manuela saw the responding flare of red fire in the cow's dull bovine eyes.

Everyone, however, saw what happened next.

First, the previously placid farm animal reared up like a horse. It did this slowly, almost majestically, so that Lulu Kim slid unharmed off its back, though she wound up landing in a cow pat. (At this point Jojo, Kiki, and Doll Face were on the far left of the soundstage, preparing to dance back across.)

Then the cow lowered itself to all fours again. Then, before anyone could intervene, the animal charged. It headed straight for Manuela. Accelerating at speed, the cow crashed between two video cameras, knocking one over.

"Damn," Zombie Joe murmured to himself, "Manuela is so fucking dead right now."

But she wasn't.

Just before it would have crashed into Manuela Costa, the cow made an abrupt right turn. Then it made a prodigious leap over the concrete and steel parapet that fenced in the rooftop. Then the cow was airborne.

All present watched in surprise. For a second, the cow seemed to hang in space, sixteen floors above Washington Street. Then, mooing in fright, it fell out of sight.

"Sure, I've heard of the cow jumping over the moon," Kiki said as it vanished, "But this is just absurd."

***

Down on Washington Street, Allie's car was stopped at the Oak Street intersection, at a traffic light that had abruptly turned red on her.

Allie had left home in a rush after a phone caller told her that Tommy Collins had been found.

The man on the phone had said Tommy had been beaten up in a fight; he was alive but unconscious. He was on admission at the Tufts Medical Center on Washington Street, right beside the Wang YMCA.

Now Allie was right here, separated from her lover by merely an adamant streetlight. In just a few seconds, the light would turn green again and all her worries would be over.

Allie was still thanking her lucky stars that Tommy was okay when the falling cow crashed into her car. The cow flattened the car. As the animal had landed with pinpoint accuracy on the driver's seat area of the Nissan' roof, it flattened Allie as well. She was compressed as completely (and as viciously) as if the vehicle had been shoved into a compactor with her still inside it.

She was reduced to a mess of wet bones and quivering shredded flesh.

Allie was dead long before the ambulances arrived, her passing announced by the wide pool of blood seeping from the driver's side door.

***

Up on the roof, everyone stared horrified at the carnage down below.

Lulu Kim, once more her deadpan self, pulled out her phone and began filming the scene down in the street.

"I-I-I th-th-think they're dead!" Kiki Kim yelped. "The cow just killed someone."

"Yeah," Lulu agreed. "Yeah, it really looks that way."

"I told you the damn thing was crazy," Manuela said with an exaggerated shiver. She strode away from the roof edge to sit on an air-conditioning unit.

"Hey, guys," Kiki was saying, "the cow's still alive! Hey, it's getting down off the car!"

There was a chorus of astonished murmurs at the cow that had just fallen sixteen floors and was now standing unharmed in the middle of Washington Street.

"Man, I ain't never seen anything like this before," Zombie Joe said. Then he turned to stare fearfully at Manuela. *What was that shit she just did?* He decided to keep quiet about what he'd seen. He might mention it just to Lulu later, but most likely he wouldn't.

"Hey, Jojo, we did get the right permits to have the cow up here, right?" Kiki asked. " 'Cos the cops are gonna be here soon. Our fucking cow has killed someone."

"Shut up, sis, we can all see that our cow's murdered someone."

Lulu chimed in: "Animals can't commit murder, biatch. It's beasticide."

"Don't you call me 'biatch,' biatch sister. And beasticide? What high school did you go to, anyway?"

"Yeah, Lulu, are you viewing life through your marijuana cloud again?"

"Shut up, baby sister. Go eat Slasher's wiener."

"Hey, Mikey, did you bring the permits?"

"I forgot to apply. Did we need any?"

"Oh, you asshole! I told you to get authorization to fly that damn cow in."

"Calm down, Jojo baby. Lots of cows travel through Boston everyday."

"Yes they do, Mikey, but . . . but no one puts them on top of high rise buildings. And they don't fall off and . . . shit!"

"Look, screw that, Jojo. The cops can't bust us for this; we didn't push it off the roof. It went mad and jumped down on its own. We all saw it happen."

"Guys, how's Manuela doing? The cow almost hit her."

"She's okay. She's having a smoke over there."

"Man, that cow is possessed. Did you see how much it hated Manuela? She's lucky she survived."

"Maybe it has mad cow disease."

"Zombie, Zombie, put out that fucking roach! And that goes for the rest of you guys too! Anyone gets busted by the cops, you're on your own."

***

Away from the huddle, Manuela was sending a WhatsApp message to a friend.

Mission accomplished, she wrote. *Allie Jackson is no more. The bitch is dead. No one messes with the Abyss Club and gets away with it.*

She sent the message, put her phone away and lit a fresh cigarette.

Manuela thought about Tommy Collins. Her lovely face reflected her distraught feelings (which the others all misinterpreted as being relief over her narrow escape from death). It was a sad mess, all this. Something she'd have wished on a hated enemy, not on a close friend like Tommy. (Even the girl she'd just killed, Allie, had been a nice person. Manuela clearly recalled meeting Allie at the concert and being very impressed by the young woman's class. She'd been happy for Tommy, whom she felt deserved a good girlfriend.)

But the Abyss Club leadership had decreed it, and their word was law.

The Abyss Club currently had Tommy Collins doped and unconscious at a secret club facility in Medfield. At the next witches sabbat he'd be sacrificed to the Goat.

After a while, Manuela got out her phone again. This time she dialed Dave Fontaine's number. She frowned. His number was still out of service. That had been the case for almost a week now. She wondered what had happened to him. Tommy would likely know, but at the moment, Tommy wasn't in any condition to talk to anyone.

Manuela was very bothered by her inability to get a hold of Dave Fontaine. She still wanted to get back together with him, to give their relationship another chance to grow. She'd promised herself that this time, she'd do her utmost best to control her temper. No more tantrums. No more baseball bats.

But, she'd also conceded to herself, she didn't know how long her resolution would last. It was impossible for a woman to endlessly look the other way, when the man she loved was so unfaithful.

***

Meanwhile, Jojo Kim was thinking hard. Yes, this was a disaster, but there was also the old show business saying 'there's no such thing as bad publicity' to consider. The trick was to manipulate the press, to convert this seeming negative into a glowing positive, and then milk the opportunity for all it was worth.

Milking, huh? She smirked. How ironic that it was a *cow* that had presented her sisters with this opportunity. And in such a bizarre fashion too.

This was the kind of disaster that careers were built on.

I couldn't have planned it better myself.

Despite how loud the band was, this 'murder cow' video was certain to get heavily requested and shown/watched everywhere. She visualized KCS doing repeat interviews on MTV's TRL show.

Great, just great.

But to really capitalize on the presented opportunity, they needed a little more film footage. So . . .

She tapped Mikey on the shoulder. Once she had the cameraman's attention, she indicated that he follow her. They both left the confused huddle at the roof's edge and walked back over to the abandoned soundstage.

There, Jojo picked up a small video camera. She intended recording a few overhead takes of the cow. Lulu was doing the same, but Lulu was only recording on her phone, so she could upload the video on Instagram; the video bitrate was certain to be shitty.

"Hey, Mikey," Jojo whispered, "activate the drone for some aerial footage of the accident. Try to capture as clear a view of the blood and carnage as you can. And try to film whoever gets cut out of the wreckage."

"We'll get the pants sued off us for this. The relatives of whoever's dead down there are gonna be mad at us."

"We'll put a psychedelic filter on the footage. No one'll be certain of what they're seeing, other than that it's the same cow as in the stage shots. We'll let the rumor mill spread the word. Hurry, man, we need to be done with it before the police arrive."

They got to work recording Allie's death for youth entertainment.

After a while, Manuela, cigarette dangling from her purple lips, walked over to give them a hand.

***

A large crowd was gathered below now, with everyone acting bewildered. It was the novelty of the cow causing the confusion.

An ambulance from the Tufts Medical Center was trying to reach the crushed car, but the backwash of stopped vehicles was making it impossible to drive through to the scene.

In the end, the frustrated paramedics parked their ambulance by the roadside and resorted to carrying a gurney at a run through the stalled traffic.

They had no idea that it was already much too late for the woman in the destroyed vehicle.

***

While zooming in on the accident scene below, Jojo hid her smile. She already knew what was going to happen:

The crazy scandal of this—how many rock bands had actually killed someone while making a video—was going to catapult Kimchi Chocolate Stereo to rock infamy and international superstardom.

The End.

ABOUT THE AUTHOR

Wol-vriey is Nigerian, and quite tall.

He believes there actually are things that go bump in the night.

He writes horror fiction—for adults only, please. And also some surrealist stuff.

Wol-vriey blogs at: *http://oddityfarm.wordpress.com*

WOL-VRIEY
BIZARRO AND TRANSGRESSIVE FICTION

BOSTON POSH (BUD MALONE #1)

In 2028 AD, the USA is a nation ravaged by hungry dragons and dinosaurs. In Boston, Massachusetts, private eye Bud Malone is hired to rescue a kidnapped heiress. But nothing is as it seems.

Malone works to unravel a tangled web involving Boston Chinatown, a 200-year-old woman with a 9-year-old body, white robots, a human-liver-eating psychopath, a golem, a porcelain dragon, and a snake goddess with a crush on him. There's also a woman obsessed with chicken sex. Then Malone meets Posh Lane, a gorgeous call girl who's desperate to quit her pimp.

Romantic sparks ignite between Posh and Malone, but Posh's past suddenly catches up with her in a BIG way. To save Posh, Malone agrees to run a quest for Earth's new rulers, the Forks. But, Malone has no idea that agreeing to the Fork's odd request will send him on the weirdest trip he's ever been on in his life.

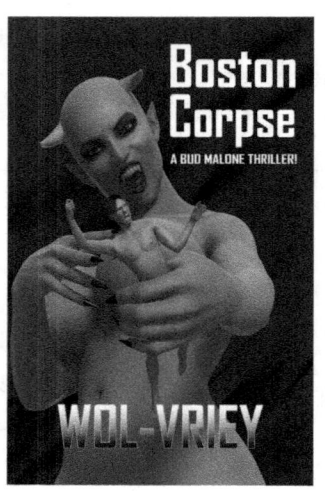

BOSTON CORPSE (BUD MALONE #2)

MAGIC CAN BE MURDER! - Drag queen Lucy Tang is back in Boston, and is hell-bent on settling her vindetta against casino owner Sookie Ling. And suddenly, Bud Malone, PI, has the case of his life to resolve.

When Boston's robot police force are baffled by a mind transfer case, they come to Malone for help. The one person who can likely help Malone out here is the witch Soledad Bathory. But Soledad seems to know a lot more than she's telling him. It's a case not made easier when Malone meets Soledad's beautiful cousin, Josephine 'Slave' Bailey. Slave has her own plans for Malone, most of which involve teaching him BDSM and making him her new Master.

Oh, and Rick Rogers owes Sookie Ling a whole lot of money, a gambling debt that's going to be literally Hell to pay!

BOSTON CORPSE - Not your average detective novel!

Burning Bulb
PUBLISHING

WOL-VRIEY
BIZARRO AND TRANSGRESSIVE FICTION

BOSTON LUST (BUD MALONE #3)

"Bless it, Father, for she has sinned."

Seven murdered gay women, all their bodies completely drained of blood. All also with large parts of their bodies dissolved away like acid has been pumped into their veins.

Bud Malone has to find the female vampire preying on Boston's lesbian population.

Then Malone meets the beautiful Trudi Carmen and the case gets even more tangled. Trudi needs Malone's help in recovering a ring that's gone missing. But how in the world is one little black ring related to either the dead women or their killer?

Resolving this case will lead Malone deep into Lucy Tang's legacy—The Abstracta. And then to the city of Genesis.

Boston Lust—Just when you thought Bean Town was safe to visit again.

HELL DANCER

Six people find themselves trapped in Detention, a nightmare realm where the demonic Schoolmaster is hell-bent on reforming them . . . until they die.

Porn superstar Venus Deluxe came to Springfield, MA to party, and next found her life hanging by a thread. One wrong answer will mean her death.

Suspended BPD detective Tanya Rockford was trying to stop one kind of violence, but found a terrifying another. With her and her companion's lives hanging in the balance, it's going to take all of her courage and resourcefulness to escape this hell she's stumbled into.

Porn stud Chad Cannon has made a career from his ten-inch penis. Here in Detention, however, it's his brains that matter. He'll soon be hoping all the pot he's smoked over the years hasn't completely messed up his memory.

The three students, Sherri, Jordan, and Mike? They were all just in the wrong place at the right time. Will anyone survive Detention? The evil Schoolmaster doesn't plan on letting that happen . . .

Burning Bulb
PUBLISHING

WOL-VRIEY
BIZARRO AND TRANSGRESSIVE FICTION

VAGINA MUNDI

Rachel Risk is a professional thief with super-strong hair that can stretch like tentacles to manipulate objects. Ashley Status has both a digitally augmented brain, and 'muscle-purses' in her arms and legs in which she stores inflatable objects—cars, guns, rocket launchers, etc.

When Raye is framed as the fall girl in a jewel robbery, the pair flee Chicago's vengeful robot gangsters and take refuge in the Hotel Bizarre, where the gorgeous 'vagina singer,' Femina, is performing for a week.

But the Hotel Bizarre is even stranger than its name suggests, and very soon Raye and Ash are involved in an deadly adventure, a struggle for survival the likes of which they'd never imagined possible—with loads of deviant sex, drugs, music, and violence at every turn. And just what is the old woman in the skin desert really doing with all those cats glued to her walls?

VAGINA MUNDI—a Bizarro Hymn in praise of WOMAN!

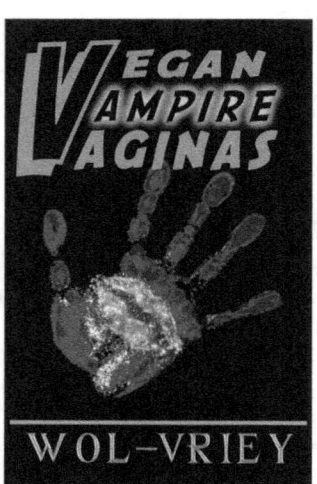

VEGAN VAMPIRE VAGINAS

The biggest bank heist in US history. And Tom Palmer can't remember pulling it off. And no, this isn't your standard case of amnesia. After a one-night-stand gone horribly wrong, Boston salesman Tom Palmer wakes up with a vagina implanted in his left hand. Then his day gets worse.

Tom is transported across space-time to a nightmare version of Boston, one where the Bizarro virus has transformed half the population into cannibals. Worst of all, Tom discovers that in this new Boston, he's the infamous gangster Pussypalm, wanted for robbing the Federal Reserve Bank of Boston a year ago. He also learns that the vagina in his hand is prophetic, i.e. it talks . . . after sex.

With 130 people left dead during his bank heist and six billion dollars missing, Tom knows he's living on borrowed time. It is in his best interests not to remember anything. Because once he does . . .

Burning Bulb
PUBLISHING

WOL-VRIEY
BIZARRO AND TRANSGRESSIVE FICTION

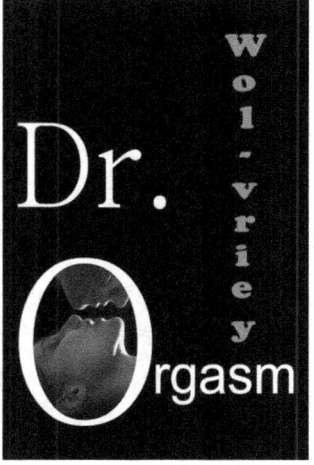

Dr. Orgasm

Courtney Taylor is young, intelligent, beautiful, and successful. She also has a boyfriend who loves her deeply. The problem is, no matter what Courtney does, she can't climax during sex.

When Florence Rigid's communist forces destroy the city of Metaphor, Courtney and her friends Teresa, Highball, Miki, and Heather are cast into the midst of a quest to find the only person able to save the land of Innuendo—Dr. Carol Orgasm, wanted by the communists for developing the O-Pill, a wonder drug that grants women sexual ecstasy on demand.

The communists will do anything to get their hands on the O-Pill and prevent its reaching the millions of Innuendo's women. But Courtney desperately wants that pill too. And so it's now a race between Courtney and the communists to find Dr. Orgasm first.

And Courtney has no choice but to win this race. She must win it: For her own orgasm . . . and for the freedom of female sexuality everywhere.

PUSSY TRANSMISSION

Pussy Transmission were the most decadent Pop Art ensemble of the 90's. Led by the beautiful painter Isis Lynch, the trio revolutionized the art world. Then suddenly, without explanation, Pussy Transmission vanished into historical obscurity. Now, twenty years later, three women come to Lynch Place. Lily and Nina are journalists desperate to interview Isis Lynch. Raven, on the other hand, wants to find her boyfriend, who's gone missing inside Isis's house. Raven's worried—she's heard that Pussy Transmission broke up because Isis began dabbling in black magic . . . with devastating results. All three women will shortly wish they'd never left home. Particularly once the rats in Lynch Place start warning them that they're going to die . . . and Raven meets Betty Butcher, the bouncy supernatural psycho who's intent on chopping her into bits. Pussy Transmission, Baby! Just because . . .

Burning Bulb
PUBLISHING

WOL-VRIEY
BIZARRO AND TRANSGRESSIVE FICTION

VEGAN ZOMBIE APOCALYPSE

In the post-apocalypse worlderness, zombies rule the earth. They're allergic to meat, and brains literally make them explode. Zombie now eat blood potatoes, parasitic tubers grown in the flesh of h mancows corralled in maximum security farms. Two fugitives me in the ancient ruins of Texas. The first is Soil 15-f, a womanco who's escaped her farm a week before she's due to be killed and he blood potato crop harvested. The second fugitive is Able Kan former head necros food technician, now sentenced to death f heresy. But Soil is no ordinary humancow.

Unknown to herself, she's the vegan zombie agricultural revolution and the zombies desperately want her back. And the necros equall desperately want Able Kane dead. He's fled with a forbidden disco ery which will reshape the world for the worse if used. And Able just hardheaded/misguided enough to use it.

MELANIE NEMESIS CATCHPOLE

In Springfield, Massachusetts, Melanie Catchpole is hired to fet back a magic teddy bear worth millions of dollars from a warehou across town. Problem is, the warehouse is down in Springfield's C Zone-that totally weird sector of the city where Bizarro fell to Earth The 'O' is a fairytale land, a place where dreams and nightmares lit rally live and breathe.

Worse still, the gingers—mutant cannibals—prowl the O. The ginge have already eaten everyone else Melanie's employers sent to get ba the magic teddy bear.

Accompanied by the handsome but ruthless Doug Fisher (who s finds sexy but doesn't dare entrust her heart to), Melanie enters th O-Zone. Melanie and Doug are instantly caught up in an adventu they'd never have believed credible even if written as fiction . . . ar Melanie's used to experiencing the very weird as the norm.

And now, additionally, there's a mystery to unravel: What does th dark, freezing-cold being called The Fixer want with Mary, th barkeep's daughter?

Burning Bulb
PUBLISHING

WOL-VRIEY
BIZARRO AND TRANSGRESSIVE FICTION

BIG TROUBLE IN LITTLE ASS

From Bizarro master storyteller Wol-vriey comes a truly weird western tale that will leave you awe-struck and on the edge of your seat...

In the town named Little Ass, tight-assed prostitute Rosa overhears a gunslinger's plans to assassinate rancher Edison Bennett. Once the badass Bennett learns of the plot, he ensures there'll be hell to pay for any attempt on his life!

Yes, it's going to take all of gunslinger Jude's shooting prowess, his eclectic collection of strange firearms, a trusty horse that requires an owners' manual, and the help of the lovely and invigorating Nell (who's EXTREMELY odd when the going gets weird), to survive the Bizarro hell that Edison Bennett unleashes in order to hold onto the land that he'd stolen from Madam Zizi.

BIZARRO 101 (A BASIC PRIMER)

Welcome to the strange place:

A collection of 37 flash fiction stories designed to introduce one to the Bizarro/New Weird Genre.

Weird, dreamy, nightmarish, absurd, sad, surreal, humorous . . . this collection of tales is all this and more.

***

"This primer is the very essence of any and all styles and types of Bizarro writing. Wol-vriey collects, distills, and bottles up these 37 tiny stories for your sensory enjoyment. This is an absolute must-read for anyone new to the genre, because it demonstrates the scope of what Bizarro is, and what it can be."
                    –Teresa Pollack, Bizarro commentator and blogger

Burning Bulb
PUBLISHING

WOL-VRIEY
BIZARRO AND TRANSGRESSIVE FICTION

GIRLS ARE NOT SMILING

Welcome To The Road Trip From Hell

Pagan is demon-possessed.

Lori is suicidal.

Britt is just terminally pissed off.

Meet three young Boston women on the run from the law, each with problems that will fuse into more than the sum of their individual parts, becoming a holocaust of sex and violence and terror, a literal rain of blood and horror and gore and evil.

And if that wasn't already bad enough, Pagan's pet demon is slowly transforming her into something both unspeakable and unholy. Truly, these girls aren't smiling.

BLUE NIGHTMARES

Consummate EVIL is coming. It is relentless and unavoidable. It is Blue.

Jessica Schreiber is seeing things. Very horrible things. Since arriving in Raynham for what should have been a relaxing vacation, she's been seeing *The Big Blue.*

Jessica is smelling things too—dead and rotting things that she can't see. She is sure those dead and rotting things are dead people. Lots of dead people.

Jessica's worst nightmares will soon become her reality. Her reality will soon become a terrifying nightmare.

The tentacled residents of the House of Death have a lot that they wish to show Jessica Schreiber. They have a lot that they wish to tell her. But will she survive long enough to learn their lessons?

Burning Bulb
PUBLISHING

WOL-VRIEY
BIZARRO AND TRANSGRESSIVE FICTION

BRAINCHEW

It was supposed to be a simple jewel heist, but it went badly wrong. Chuck got shot and died.

Lance hid his friend's corpse in the Pleasant Street Cemetery. But that was a big mistake—there was something undead, something extremely hungry . . . something eXXXtremely horrible, buried in the Pleasant Street Cemetery.

And Lance had just woken it up.

They called the monster Brainchew because it ate brains. Human brains. And it preferred those brains fresh from the heads . . . of the living.

And now it was awake again, Brainchew planned on feeding big-time tonight. Oh hell yes, it did.

BRAINCHEW 2: OUT OF THEIR HEADS

After Tiff Hooper recognizes Josh Penham, the man who abducted her and kept her in his basement and abused her, she brings her three friends to Raynham for a night of well-deserved revenge on him.

Only things don't go according to plan.

It is never a good idea to leave a corpse in Raynham's Pleasant Street Cemetery. You run the very real risk of awakening what lies underground there. And that thing—Brainchew—is more horrible and more evil than anything the average mind conceives of even in its worst nightmares.

Brainchew is back! And this time the monster is extra-hungry. But there are plenty of delicious human brains about tonight, and Brainchew intends to eat them all before dawn.

Burning Bulb
PUBLISHING

WOL-VRIEY
BIZARRO AND TRANSGRESSIVE FICTION

DARIA: AN EROTIC NIGHTMARE

Even the best laid women can go wrong.

Daria Simpson is HUNGRY. She's HUNGRY for sex and bloodshed and death.

Shelly Parker just wanted to have a threesome with her boyfriend Craig and her best friend Erica. Everything was shaping up nicely for their weekend of sexual fun and games, until they stopped at the creepy Crossway Diner and met Daria.

From the moment they met Daria, EVERYTHING went wrong for them; and it went wrong in the most horrific and terrifying of ways!

Daria: Paranormal service has been resumed.

WET BONES

Greg is about learning the hard way that you don't mess with Aunt Grace.

Nine completely fleshless skeletons recovered in the Massachusetts woods. Two detectives on the trail of a horrible, hungry monster.

Broken-hearted Allie Jackson has a date with a creature from Hell.

Things are about to get well out of hand for everyone, and in horrifying, terrifying ways they don't expect.

Burning Bulb
PUBLISHING

www.ingramcontent.com/pod-product-compliance
Lightning Source LLC
Chambersburg PA
CBHW070404260626
47161CB00001B/275